THE OPIUM ROA

Also available by Shaun Clarke:

THE OPIUM ROAD

SHAUN CLARKE

POCKET BOOKS

LONDON · SYDNEY · NEW YORK · TOKYO · SINGAPORE · TORONTO

First published in Great Britain by Simon & Schuster, 1998
Published simultaneously in paperback by Pocket Books, 1998
An imprint of Simon & Schuster Ltd
A Viacom Company

Simon & Schuster UK Ltd
Africa House
64–78 Kingsway
London
WC2B 6AH

Simon & Schuster of Australia
Sydney

A CIP catalogue record for this book is available from the British Library.

Paperback ISBN 0-671-01591-5

1 3 5 7 9 10 8 6 4 2

Typeset by Palimpsest Book Productions Limted,
Polmont, Stirlingshire
Printed and bound in Great Britain by
Cox and Wyman Ltd, Reading, Berkshire

For Ken and Arlene Brown

CHAPTER ONE

The convoy of canvas-topped trucks was moving slowly through the eerie dawn mist, along the so-called 'Road of Life' that linked the Osh region of Kyrgyzstan, formerly a Soviet Socialist Republic, with the rugged, snow-capped Pamir mountains. Here, on the lower slopes of the mountains, the land was free of snow, but a bitter wind was blowing across the road to numb those huddled up in the rear of the trucks. These were mostly half-starved women and children, with a few elderly men thrown in, all of them Ismaili Muslims from Tajikistan – the families of the younger men either driving the trucks or sitting beside the drivers and keeping their eyes peeled for any sign of Russian border guards.

The sun was slowly rising in the east, casting its pale light on the flower-strewn pastures and wooded ravines of the lowlands, on the streams that poured down from the mountains into the inner basins, and on the source of the streams: the glittering, ice-capped peaks wreathed in dense, dark, oppressive clouds. In the rear of the heavily rolling, battered old trucks, the faces of the women and children, now striped erratically with bands of darkness and light, were gaunt with deprivation and dread, their eyes large and too bright. Most glanced frequently out of the backs of the trucks, fearful of what they might see out there, but there was only the empty road unwinding behind them in the slowly brightening light.

The younger men in the drivers' cabins were also watchful. Aware that this so-called 'Road of Life' could also be a road of death, the men beside the drivers were alert every second, holding Kalashnikov sub-machine guns on their laps. They had sold everything they owned to buy these weapons and now they were desperate, hoping that this dangerous journey across the mountains would lead them to plenty.

That hope died on the instant.

The first mortar shell exploded with a shocking roar about ten metres in front of the leading truck, filling the air with erupting soil and billowing smoke. It had been aimed there deliberately to avoid damaging the leading truck and instead force it to stop. When the driver, too shocked to yet realise what was happening, his ears ringing from the explosion and also filled with the terrified wailing of the women and children in the rear, kept his foot on the accelerator, heading straight for that spewing soil and boiling smoke, a second shell fell in virtually the same place, creating another deafening explosion and hammering the truck with its whiplash. This time the driver swerved automatically, violently, and the truck careened to the side of the road and juddered to a halt by the coniferous trees that covered the lower slopes of the mountain. The trucks behind also screeched to a halt – and then all hell broke loose.

When the Tajiks in the trucks heard the roaring of machine guns, firing from the upper slopes, they realised that they were not being attacked by border guards but by the brigands who lived in the mountains and controlled the drugs trade. Knowing this, the women in the rear of the trucks wailed even more, thus increasing the terror of the howling children, as the Tajiks with the Kalashnikovs jumped out of the trucks to defend the column.

The first man out – the guard from the leading truck – had barely touched the ground when a hail of machine-gun bullets made the soil spit around his feet and then, finding him, turned him into a wildly convulsing, screaming mess. Slammed into the side of the truck by the impact of the bullets, he dropped his weapon, shuddered violently and slid to the ground, smearing the bonnet and tyres with his blood. The driver, who had jumped down from the other side, was caught in another hail of bullets and also died in convulsions.

The women, children and older men remained in the trucks, huddled together for protection, while the younger men jumped out, either to die instantly or to fire their own weapons blindly in the general direction of the roaring machine guns. They fell one after the other, cut down by the hail of bullets. Some were only wounded and lay there writhing and moaning.

The fight was short and brutal, a virtual massacre, and within minutes most of the younger men had been killed or wounded. The few remaining, seeing the hopelessness of their situation, threw down their weapons and raised their hands above their heads, accepting the inevitable.

Some of the women, seeing their dead or wounded men, hearing that abrupt, eerie silence, scrambled frantically out of the trucks and rushed to where the men lay. They fell to their knees and sobbed over the fallen men, some covering the dead with their own bodies, others holding the wounded in their arms whilst weeping profusely.

Eventually, after a minute that seemed like an hour, as the sun grew in strength and cut through the thinning mist, bringing with it a warmth that would soon be fierce heat, men appeared on the hills above, stepping out from behind tree trunks, rising up from behind boulders, to advance at a careful pace down the hill, all carrying weapons at the ready and clearly ready to use them. At the sight of them, some of the women wailed in despair and others, scarcely knowing what they were doing, tried to make their escape by running back along the road, dragging their children with them or urging their adolescent daughters to run on ahead of them. Those women and the daughters were cut off by the brigands who hurried down the slopes ahead of them and blocked off the road. Either grim-faced or laughing, the brigands forced the women and children back to the column of stalled trucks, to where the dead and wounded lay with dreadful wounds in pools of blood, and hammered at them with the butts of their rifles if they tried to resist.

By now, the rest of the brigands had surrounded the stalled column and some were, with brutal efficiency, herding the Tajiks outside the trucks into a single, panic-stricken group. Others went to the open rear of the trucks and, using a mixture of Russian and Kyrgyz, ordered those inside to come out. Most did, many sobbing or muttering prayers; others, half-demented with fear, scrambled frantically deeper into the trucks and had to be forcibly dragged out by the brigands. Soon, all the trucks had been emptied.

Only when the captured Tajiks were gathered together in a single, protoplasmic, calamitous mass did another man appear on the hill above the road.

He rose slowly, though fearlessly, from behind a rock outcropping to cast his calm gaze upon the scene below. Dressed, like the other brigands, in a jacket of goatskin, with a fur-lined cap on his head and leather boots, he was just under six feet tall, as solid as a rock, and had unusually handsome, ascetic features. These were marred only by the scar of an old knife wound that ran down his left cheek and the small, round scar of an old bullet wound in the other cheek. These wounds made him look brutal. His eyes were as cold and blue as Siberian ice, but they were bright with intelligence.

After glancing in both directions along the road below, satisfying himself that all was in order, he advanced at a leisurely pace down the hill and eventually stopped in front of the group of captured Tajiks. His only weapon was the Glock 9mm semi-automatic handgun holstered on his right hip.

He eyed the group of wailing women, sobbing children and dazed or praying old men with remote objectivity, as if they barely existed, then turned his attention to the three younger men who had survived the massacre and been separated from the rest of the group. Walking up to them, he ordered them in Russian to drop to their knees. When they looked uncomprehending, he repeated the order in Kyrgyz and immediately they did as they were told. He then removed his Glock handgun from its holster, applied pressure to the trigger to disengage the safety mechanism, then placed the barrel of the weapon against the sweating forehead of the young man nearest to him.

'Where is the opium?' he asked, his voice as soft as a light breeze over a wasteland and every bit as desolate.

Instantly, the young man burst forth with an impassioned monologue, insisting that he and his friends were not carrying opium but had merely been making their way from Osh to Fergana in the hope of a better life. Eventually, when he had exhausted himself, he fell into silence, whilst still looking up with wide, pleading eyes.

'Where is the opium?' his interrogator repeated, now cocking the striker of the handgun.

The young man glanced desperately left and right, first looking at his comrades, then at the group of women, children and praying old men. He raised his eyes again to his interrogator, the barrel of the handgun still pressing against his forehead, and said, speaking Turkic, 'I swear to you, we are not carrying opium. We—'

The handgun roared, blowing the young man's brains out, and as he convulsed and fell backwards onto the hard road, there were hysterical shrieks and sobs from the group nearby.

Ignoring them, the handsome, scarred brigand took a single step sideways and placed the barrel of his handgun against the forehead of the second young man kneeling before him.

'Where is the opium?' he asked, still speaking calmly, quietly, with no feeling. 'Please answer the question.'

Glancing desperately left and right, as his dead friend had done, clearly not wishing to betray the others, the young man eventually looked up with large, brown, glistening eyes and repeated his dead friend's words by insisting that the group was not carrying opium.

The handgun roared again and the young man's head exploded. As he jerked sideways and fell to the ground, the lamentations of the women and children nearby climbed to a dreadful, heartbreaking crescendo. Ignoring them again, the man with the handsome, scarred features took another step sideways until he was standing over the last of the young men. He placed the barrel of the handgun against the young man's temple and repeated his question.

'Where is the opium?'

This young man, who looked contemptuous of his interrogator, merely glanced at the wailing women and children. Then, clearly concerned for their welfare even more than for himself, he returned his clear gaze to the handsome, scarred man and said, his voice steady, 'In the tyres and above the diesel tanks.'

Smiling, though keeping the barrel of his handgun pressed against the young man's forehead, the leader of the brigands nodded at those nearest to him, indicating the stalled trucks lined up behind them. Instantly, some of the men hurried to the trucks and, removing knives from sheaths belted by their holsters, either proceeded to slash the tyres or to look for the secret compartments located above the diesel tanks. Whooping with glee, they removed a great many packages from the four trucks and, when they had laid them out on the ground, between the dead, bloody bodies, ascertained that each truck had been carrying approximately forty kilograms of opium. It was a princely catch.

'Don't do this,' the young man said, kneeling on the ground and looking upwards above the barrel of the handgun still resting against his forehead.

'I beg your pardon?' the handsome, scarred man responded, continuing to speak in that eerily soft, disengaged tone of voice.

The young man, whose gaze was fearless, turned his head slightly, not removing it from the gun barrel, and nodded as best he could towards the huddled group of his people. 'My wife is over there,' he said. 'She's no older than I am. My two children are there, one four years old, one five, and my ageing mother and father and grandparents.' He turned his head back to stare up at his executioner, but he was more proud than fearful. 'I have given you what you want, so you have no reason to do this. If you insist on doing it, then please do it out of sight. Give me that much, at least.'

The handsome, scarred man smiled, but he did not remove the barrel of the pistol from the young man's forehead.

'I admire your courage,' he said. 'I also respect your concern for them. But what you did cannot be permitted nor forgiven because it might encourage others to do the same. You knew what you were doing, the chance you were taking, and now you must pay the price. You've behaved like a man – you *are* a man – so die like a man.'

'What's your name?' the young man asked, as if he needed that final contact with a real person before his life ended: perhaps to damn him to hell.

'Dmitry,' the handsome, scarred man replied. 'Dmitry Petrov.'

Then he fired the handgun.

The young man's head exploded. He fell back onto the road. Some women screamed as if stabbed – obviously the young man's wife and mother – then other women and the children added to the heart-rending bedlam.

The handsome, scarred man ignored them. This was life and he was living it. He simply nodded to his men, letting them know what they must do, and they responded by herding the stunned and grieving Tajiks into a column of tormented human beings that could be easily contained.

He led them away from the dead and dying, from the brightening light of the Opium Road, and marched them away from the growing heat, up into the hills, on a murderous, draining hike, until they were in the mountains, sun-scorched and merciless, but still climbing towards the ice-covered peaks. He ignored their cries and lamentations, pretending not to be aware of them, and eventually, having passed from the increasing heat of the lower grounds, they advanced into the deepening cold of the upper slopes where the snow fell gently.

The snowflakes kept falling, growing thicker as the cold increased, and soon they were lost in a white landscape which gave pity to none. Prodded on by rifle barrels, slapped and hammered by fists, they kept climbing, covered in snow, frozen by ice, whipped by wind, until they reached the absolute, pure whiteness of the vale of the lost.

They were doomed to that white hell.

CHAPTER TWO

He felt like the walking dead. As he walked to the CO's office, past the open-plan cubbyholes of the secretaries, clerks and various administrators of this hastily modernised, more bureaucratic Special Air Services headquarters, albeit still in Hereford, England (not yet in Brussels, thank God), Captain Neil Scott felt drained by his recent problems. Aware that everyone knew about them, he silently prayed that he was not in for a chaplin's lecture or, even worse, a so-called 'debriefing' about his personal life. To his relief, the only two men in the office were the CO himself, Lieutenant Colonel Richard T. Lyons, and Major Dwight Reynolds, a senior officer with the SAS Intelligence Corps or, as Scott translated it in his head, a Green Slime Head Shed from the Kremlin. Both men were seated behind the CO's desk, with Lyons in his customary position in the middle, Reynolds in a chair placed at one end of the desk. On the wall behind both men was a large, black-framed display board covered in a white cloth. Scott was wearing his beige beret with its winged dagger badge and he snapped a sharp salute and then stood at ease.

'You wanted to see me, boss?' he said to the CO.

Lyons nodded, indicating that Scott should take the chair

facing the desk. He waited until Scott was seated, then said, 'So how are things with you, Captain?'

'I'm fine, boss. I'm okay.'

'Are you sure?'

'Yes, I'm sure.'

Lyons stared thoughtfully at him, his grey gaze steady. 'I gather you're still working well,' he said.

'I try to,' Scott replied, feeling uncomfortable, again thinking that this was what he had feared: an attempt to find out how the recent tragedy had affected him. In fact, it had devastated him and he was still haunted by it, but he had used his work to block it from his thoughts and in that much he hadn't failed.

'Sleeping nights?' Lyons asked.

'About as well as can be expected. I've no need of a psychiatrist and I haven't resorted to sleeping pills, so you've no need to worry, boss.'

Lyons smiled slightly at that. He was a handsome man in his mid-fifties with a healthy thatch of grey hair and unlined skin flushed with fresh air and sunshine. Though serving his three-year stint as Commanding Officer of 22 SAS, he tried to get out of the office as much as possible and work side by side with his men. The men – and Scott personally – respected him for it.

'I gather your work with the CRW Wing is keeping you busy,' he now said, referring to the Counter Revolutionary Warfare Wing of the SAS intelligence centre, known as the Kremlin.

Scott shrugged. 'We're all busy enough, but it hardly makes up for the lack of any real work to do. I'd like a real task to tackle instead of training men for jobs that are unlikely to come up. So would the others.'

This was true enough. Scott had first transferred to the SAS in 1982, when he was twenty-one years old, just in time to take part in the Falklands War. Fighting in South Georgia, about thirteen hundred kilometres east of the Falklands, and all the way to Port Stanley in East Falkland, had been one of the great experiences of his life. The second had come eight years later, when he was twenty-nine and had been privileged to take part in covert operations in the Gulf War, engaging in dangerous hit-and-run raids in Pink Panther dune buggies behind enemy lines. Between those two major events, however, there had been precious little to do and, since returning from Iraq, even less of interest. Applying for and receiving a commission, he had been caught in the trap of the old SAS ruling that forbade an officer to spend more than three years at a time with the regiment, so he had passed most of the past decade repeatedly transferring between his original unit, the Queen's Guards, and the SAS, constantly hoping that a truly challenging opportunity would arise. Unfortunately, nothing had. Instead, the SAS, with no real wars to fight, had been used ever more frequently as an uneasy combination of civil guard and special training group, neither of which gave the men, or Scott, much satisfaction. Indeed, the lack of real challenge in the force, combined with his personal tragedy of a few months back, had led him to seriously consider resigning his commission and leaving the army altogether. He had not yet broached this thought to his commanding officer and he did not do so now.

Lieutenant Colonel Lyons sighed. 'Yes,' he agreed, 'it's certainly a problem, particularly for our more experienced men, such as yourself. It's also a problem for the regiment as a whole in that it's left us exposed to those who would attempt to cut our budget or even have us disbanded altogether as a supposed irrelevancy in the modern world. What men like you need – and, quite frankly, what the regiment needs as a propaganda exercise – is something out of the ordinary . . . and at last we think we might have it.'

The tension that had been building eased out of Scott and was replaced by a trickle of hope and curiosity. Nevertheless, he couldn't imagine for one second what the CO could possibly have that would be of real interest to him, other than yet another home-based social or criminal problem. Only last year, for instance, 22 Squadron had been assigned the humiliating task of testing the security of a new prison by actually *breaking in* and taking a warden captive. They had, of course, succeeded, but few of the men involved had wanted the job, which they viewed as unsavoury, and the resultant public furore over what was deemed to be an irresponsible use of the regiment had done little to enhance its reputation. Small wonder that there were those in authority who were loudly proclaiming that the SAS had no place in the modern world and should be disbanded for good. Given this dire situation, Scott could seriously not imagine a new operation worth doing. He was, however, despite himself, filled with hope at the very possibility.

'What is it?' he asked.

When he noted the CO's hesitation, he felt uneasy again.

'Opium,' Lyons said after a long pause.

Scott was shocked to the very roots of his being, feeling almost insulted, even betrayed, returned on the instant to all the pain he had suffered over the past few months and was still trying to combat. Flustered, he straightened up in his chair; then, not knowing what else to say, he simply repeated the dreaded word as a question: 'Opium?'

'You heard me,' Lyons said.

'You're considering me, of all people, for a job relating to . . . *opium*?'

Lyons was embarrassed, but he also seemed determined. 'Who better?' he said bluntly. 'You have a personal interest. Also, you now have more reason than most for the distraction of something truly challenging. It may not be nice, but it makes sense and that's why I picked you.'

'I don't think . . .'

'I *know* what you think,' Lyons interjected hastily. 'You think you'll be too close to comfort for this—'

'I will be.'

'—but you'll also be angry,' Lyons interjected, 'and I think that'll work on your favour. If this sounds like I'm using your misfortune – well, yes, I am, but I don't have a choice. Under the circumstances, surprising though it may seem, you're the best man for the job.'

'It sounds like a sleazy job,' Scott retorted boldly, too far into his pain to give a damn what Lyons or anyone else thought. 'It sounds like another police operation of the kind we've been called to do before only because we'd nothing better to do. I don't want to deal with kids like my son and you've no right to ask me to. I don't want to work in the streets of Britain, acting like a rogue cop. This isn't right, boss.'

Reynolds, the intelligence officer, flabby from lack of exercise, almost bald, round-cheeked, was about to make an angry retort, but Lyons, who encouraged blunt speaking in his men, shut him up with a curt wave of his hand, while saying to Scott, 'You won't be in the streets of Britain and you won't be dealing with teenage junkies or the scumbags who sell to them. This job is overseas and it's considerably more elevated than some we've had to do in the past few years. We're talking about a major operation in a foreign country. It's a job in a million.'

'It's opium,' Scott responded immediately, 'and I don't want to be reminded on a daily basis – not while trying to do a job – of exactly what it was that killed my son and the kind of bastards who killed him.'

There, it was out. They could all relax now. Scott could sit there and recall the sheer horror of what had happened, what had broken his heart and then broken up his marriage, while these two men, one of whom he respected, pretended to offer him a way to ease his pain by utilising his rage. As soon as he thought this, however, he felt a stab of guilty shame, knowing that Lyons wasn't like that, and that the offer, which was certainly in the long-term interests of the regiment, had also been made with particular regard to his own concerns. Yes, he *did* have a particular interest, one based on his rage, and he was being offered something that would not only take him away from Britain altogether, away from everything that reminded him of what had occurred, but would also help him to vent that rage and perhaps, in an indirect way, avenge what had been done. For this reason, no matter how much pain the very word 'opium' give him, he could not turn down this offer.

'Where are we talking about?' he asked.

Rising from his chair, Major Reynolds rolled up the white cover concealing the black-framed board to reveal a large map of an area of central Asia hemmed in by Afghanistan. Reynolds tapped that particular area with his forefinger.

'Kyrgyzstan,' he said, letting his finger remain on that word on the map. 'Formerly part of the Soviet Union, it's become one of the world's key transit points for the drugs now flooding the streets of Britain. This drug threat is now so large that the British government has determined to stop it at its source.' He moved his finger down the map to Afghanistan. 'Opium is moving along the Old Silk Road from Afghanistan into Tajikistan,' he continued, sliding his finger upwards again, 'and northwards to Osh, the trade centre of Kyrgyzstan, at an estimated rate of a hundred kilos a day.' He tapped 'Osh' repeatedly with his finger. 'Channelled from Osh through Russia into Europe, it's turned into the heroin injected by the growing number of junkies all over the British Isles.' Realising what he had said, he turned away from the map, glanced nervously at Lieutenant Colonel Lyons, then faced Scott's steady gaze and said, 'Sorry. That was an unfortunate slip of the tongue.'

'A junkie is a junkie,' Scott replied, refusing to let his voice reveal his pain. 'There's no other term for it. Who's in charge of the drug trade?'

'A rather extraordinary Russian mafia chief called Dmitry Petrov.'

'Why extraordinary?'

'Most of his past is shrouded in mystery and he first came to our attention, virtually out of nowhere, only in 1992, when he turned up in Russia as a former professional wrestler who had close ties with local criminals and worked as a security agent for some of the city's most successful businessmen.

Obviously a man of considerable skill and persuasiveness, he became President Boris Yeltsin's personal bodyguard, close friend and confidant in 1993, when the so-called Russian reforms were actually turning the country into a hotbed of corruption. Petrov was in the thick of all that, using his high position to do whatever the hell he wanted to do, most of which was brazenly criminal and, reportedly, conducted with ruthless, brutal efficiency.'

'You mean violence.'

'Correct.' Reynolds nodded affirmatively, then continued. 'Naturally he made enemies and soon became an embarrassment to the administration. Though charged eventually with mafia-related activities, including drug-running and organised prostitution in Moscow, his friendship with Yeltsin saved him from execution. Instead, he was sent as a counter-intelligence officer to Kyrgyzstan, charged with stemming the flow of opium along the so-called Road of Life that links Osh with the Pamir mountains. Instead, he ruthlessly exploited his position, using bribery, blackmail, intimidation and murder, to turn himself into the biggest Russian crime baron of them all.'

'So in order to stop Russian drugs flooding this country, we have to neutralise Petrov.'

'Correct,' Major Reynolds said, noisily pulling up his chair and sitting down again. 'So, are you interested?' he asked.

'Yes,' Scott said.

Reynolds nodded. 'Good.' He nodded again, this time at Lieutenant Colonel Lyons.

'Petrov hides out in the Pamir mountains,' Lyons said, picking up the story, 'With his gang of murderous brigands, he controls the flow of opium along the Road of Life, so-called because the 200,000 people in the mountains, suffering economically from the collapse of the Soviet Union, now survive by two means only. The first is humanitarian aid supplied by the Aga Khan; the second is the money they earn from drug-trafficking. Indeed, so dependent are they upon the latter that if the road were closed completely, which Kyrgyz officials are recommending, those people would probably starve to death.'

'If we neutralise Petrov,' Scott said, 'that's likely to happen anyway.'

'We want to neutralise Petrov,' Lyons replied, 'not to stop the drug trafficking entirely. Likewise, though Kyrgyz officials want to close the road merely to save themselves from the difficult task of policing it, the Russian government, while publicly denouncing the drugs trade, secretly wants it to continue, albeit locally only, to prevent the people in that area from starving and being driven to violent insurrection as a consequence. However, they, too, need to put a stop to Petrov, who's becoming an embarrassment to them all over again.'

'Because of his raids along the Road of Life,' Scott said.

'Correct. Petrov controls that road by terrorizing the peasants trying to smuggle the drug from Tajikistan to Osh. Invariably, when he does so, he attacks the peasants with mortars, machine guns and light weapons, cold-bloodedly kills all the younger men and the old, then abducts the women and children, taking them to one or another of the many camps he has hidden high in the mountains. Those unfortunate people are never seen again. It's widely believed that the women are used as whores and slave labour for Petrov's men while the boys, separated from their parents, are brought up to become fanatically loyal, absolutely ruthless brigands, living and dying solely for Petrov.'

'This Petrov sounds like quite a guy,' Scott said sardonically.

'A monster,' Lyons replied. 'However, the Russian government, while being embarrassed by Petrov's brazen activities in the Pamir mountains, are even more concerned by the fact that he transports his own opium in heavily armed columns along the same road and fights his way through any Russian border guards who make the mistake of trying to stop him. In the early days, he had captured border guards decapitated and their heads stuck up on raised poles as a warning to others. These days, the border guards are less keen to go up against him – not only because of his known ferocity, but also because they, too, are paid starvation wages and increasingly open to corruption. So, when not slaughtering his way from the Pamir mountains to Osh, Petrov is bribing his way there. Either way, he succeeds in getting the opium into Osh, and there selling it to the men who ship it through Russia and then on to Europe.'

'So how did the Brits get involved in this?' Scott asked.

'Politics,' Reynolds said bluntly. 'As well as being embarrassed by its own media's increasingly hysterical stories about Petrov, the Russian government is under pressure from the EU countries, notably Britain, to do something about the situation. The new Russian administration has therefore agreed to our request for an operation designed to neutralise Petrov.'

'Neat,' Scott responded. 'If we fail, they lose nothing. If we succeed, they can deny responsibility in the matter. Am I right?'

'Yes, you are. Whatever happens, they'll insist that they knew nothing about the British operation. In this way they hope to solve their own problem without causing violent insurrection in Kyrgyzstan amongst the people who can no longer traffic in opium.'

'All well and good,' Scott said, 'but what's our own interest in the matter?'

'The growing drug problem in the streets of Britain,' Lieutenant Colonel Lyons said. 'Our sole interest in this operation, therefore, is to keep the traffic in opium contained in Kyrgyzstan by stopping its onward flow to Russia and thence into Europe. That flow is controlled by one man and one man only – and that man is Petrov. Neutralise him and the local trade will continue, but on a much lesser scale, and the opium will stop filtering down to us to cause social devastation in the form of heroin.'

This was Scott's personal interest and now he knew exactly why they had called him in. Reminded of the growing problem of drugs in the streets of Great Britain, the same streets that his son had walked, crawled and eventually died in, he felt his suppressed revulsion for the drug dealers boiling up to motivate him and give him courage. What these two men were proposing was an almost suicidal mission that could only succeed with highly motivated volunteers. They were asking him to lead it – they would not make it an order – and recalling the past few months, his rage and grief, his despair, he realised that they were giving him the chance to get away from home, from everything that reminded him of it, and, at the same time, to cure himself by helping to alleviate the problem. In this knowledge, he saw the light of hope in the distance, at the end of his personal dark tunnel.

'What's the game plan?' Scott asked.

CHAPTER THREE

The game plan was to resort to the old, tried and trusted SAS strategy of using four-man teams – in this case, two teams, totalling eight men. This decision was given to, and taken by, Scott who firmly believed that the four-man team, first devised by David Stirling during World War Two, remained the most efficient and effective size for raids behind enemy lines or, as in this case, for combat in unknown territory against an ever-shifting, unpredictable enemy.

Having decided this, Scott then had to choose the men he needed. Fully aware of the fact that this operation was as close to suicidal as one could possibly get short of becoming a Kamikaze pilot, he decided to look for men of particular daring and exceptional motivation.

He did not have to look hard for the man he most wanted to take along: his friend, Sergeant William 'Paddy' Devlin. Like Scott, Paddy had distinguished himself both in the Falklands Campaign and the Gulf War. In fact, as a corporal he had shared a Pink Panther Land Rover with Scott when the Mobility Group of 22 SAS had made its many daring hit-and-run raids behind enemy lines in the deserts of Iraq. Paddy had also been the man with whom Scott had undertaken his greatest ordeal and most acclaimed achievement: an epic trek from the western desert of Iraq to the Syrian border, pursued all the way by Iraqi troops. That trek had begun when Scott's two four-man teams, each sharing a Pink Panther, had been cut off behind enemy lines, lost both Pink Panthers in subsequent fire fights, and had no choice but to head on foot for the Syrian border. Of the eight men who began that epic hike, two were killed in fire fights, one died of hypothermia, three were captured by the Iraqis, and only two eventually made it across the border: Scott and Paddy. This was a singular achievement, but it took many days, during which they were scorched by the blazing sun, frozen by the desert night, almost drowned in flash floods, nearly driven mad with thirst, and practically starved to death, gradually weakening to the point where, when they finally reached the Syrian border, they could hardly walk. In fact, Scott had almost given in, but Paddy, refusing to do so, had virtually dragged him the last mile or so until they stumbled into the first allied border patrol and knew they were safe at last. That epic trek had made Scott and Paddy heroes within the regiment, particularly admired and envied by troopers who had not yet fought in a war, and it had also forged an unbreakable bond between them.

Since then, though increasingly frustrated by the lack of a real challenge, Scott had gone on to become an Operations Planning Officer in the Kremlin's CRW Intelligence Wing and Paddy had become one of the most popular drill instructors in the regiment, even though he was personally responsible for supervising the dreaded 'sickeners' of the increasingly demanding Selection and Continuation Training courses. This, Scott knew, was because Paddy, born and bred in Belfast, was the kind of NCO who would invite a troublesome trooper outside to settle a matter with fisticuffs rather than report him or put him on a charge. Ergo, though the troopers naturally revered him as a legendary Gulf War hero, they also respected him because he was willing to deal with them on their own level. So Paddy, Scott knew, would be invaluable on this operation as his second-in-command and

Team 2's patrol commander. The PC of Team 1 would be Scott himself.

'Of course, it's purely voluntary,' Scott now said to Paddy as they sat facing each other over pints of bitter at a table in the Paludrine Club, the noisy bar of the SAS base at Stirling Lines, Hereford, named after the anti-Malaria drug administered to all SAS troopers posted overseas. He had detailed the mission to Paddy and his friend, who had a low boredom threshold, was clearly excited. 'I mean, if you'd prefer to remain here as a DI, by all means . . .'

'Go fuck yourself,' Paddy replied, seeing Scott's sly grin and grinning back as he raised his pint of bitter to his lips. 'I'm in and you know it. This is the first real job we've had since Iraq and I'm not going to miss it.'

'What will Molly say?' Scott asked him.

Paddy raised his eyebrows in a mock questioning manner. He lived with his wife Molly and their two teenage boys in a house in Redhill, located within driving distance of the base in Hereford. Molly, born in Liverpool of an Irish father and English mother, was a good-humoured, loving wife with a sharp tongue. She and Paddy fought a lot, made up a lot, and were as thick as two thieves. However, like most SAS wives, Molly worried about Paddy when he was overseas and was happier when he was working in Stirling Lines. If she knew that Paddy was volunteering for such a dangerous mission, she would most likely blow her stack.

'I won't tell her I'm volunteering,' Paddy said, grinning to expose healthy, slightly crooked front teeth under a broken nose, bright green eyes and a thick thatch of unruly red hair. 'I'll say it's an overseas training mission and I was chosen because I'm a good DI. That should sound pretty normal. I mean, we'll only be gone a few weeks, right?'

'We might not come back,' Scott said bluntly.

'I might be run over by a bus, choke on a fish bone, or get cancer,' Paddy replied in a droll manner. 'So I'm in and you only need six more men. But why such a small number for such an important operation?'

'I still think it's the best way to operate. Less than four men to a team would restrict what we could carry with regard to firepower and supplies. It'd also leave us unable to defend ourselves properly if one of our number was killed or wounded.'

'A true optimist,' Paddy said.

'On the other hand,' Scott continued, ignoring the friendly jibe, 'more than four men would make for teams that would be less cohesive and harder to conceal from the enemy. Also, as you surely know from your own experience, there are sound psychological reasons for having precisely four men to each team.'

'Yeah, right,' Paddy said. 'The bonding instinct that few women can understand.'

'Right,' Scott said, thinking of how his own former wife, Vicki, even before their personal tragedy and final break-up, had never understood that particular male instinct and had, indeed, often viewed it with grave suspicion. 'Soldiers divide into pairs instinctively,' he continued, 'when it comes to tackling most tasks.'

'We're all closet homosexuals,' Paddy said with a broad, wicked grin. 'Hot-bedding and so on,' he added, having fun with the phrase used by the SAS to describe the sharing of one or two sleeping bags between the members of a four-man patrol. 'We just can't admit it.'

'Homosexual, hell!' Scott responded, though he too was grinning. 'Each man can more easily look after his partner while sharing the less exciting daily duties.'

'Right,' Paddy said, clearly not thrilled by the prospect of that particular part of the forthcoming mission. 'Brewing up, cooking meals, erecting shelters, camouflaging watch positions, cleaning up before moving on and so forth ... the whole bloody works.'

'Exactly,' Scott said, amused by his friend's look of loathing. 'So the four-man team still holds good in my book and that's how we'll do it. Eight men. Two teams.'

'Any ideas, so far, about who to take along?'

'Only that they have to be the *crème de la crème* and that they go out there fully aware of the risks. No cowboys. No percentage players. What we want are men who'll be healthily stimulated by the risk without being reckless or suicidal. Men of rare common sense as well as courage. Also men with exceptional crossover skills, no matter which of the four Sabre squadron troops they come from.'

While each one of 22 SAS Regiment's four Sabre, or fighting, squadrons was made up of four troops, each having its own specialist role (the Boat Troop for amphibious warfare; the Mobility Troop for operations in Land Rovers and other vehicles; the Air Troop for freefall parachuting; and the Mountain Troop for mountaineering and winter warfare operations), the troopers within each troop were cross-trained in at least one other patrol specialisation and a second troop skill.

'What we can't do without,' Scott continued, 'are a linguist, a medic, a demolitions specialist and a signals expert. If we can find troopers in those fields who have crossover skills in a particularly apt secondary skill – say, a demolition man with a crossover skill in signals – that would be perfect.'

'Why that particular example?' Paddy asked.

'We may have to destroy enemy communications,' Scott explained, 'and a demolitions man with crossover skills in signals would know exactly what communications to destroy and how to go about it. Likewise, if we can find, say, a linguist with crossover skills as a medic, we could use him not only for our own medical requirements, but to win the hearts and minds of locals, who're bound to be suspicious, by talking to them in their own language *and* by giving them the medical attention they couldn't normally afford in an impoverished country. That would place them more securely on our side.'

'Very wise,' Paddy said, though his comment was imbued with a certain amount of cynical amusement. 'So what about the remaining four?'

'A man from the Mobility Troop would be useful if we have to repair or, just as likely, steal and maintain local vehicles. A member from the Boat Troop, since we'll probably have to either ford local rivers or travel down them in DIY or stolen craft. Naturally, again, it would be best if their crossover skills were in signals or demolitions, in the event that someone is seriously wounded or killed early in the proceedings.'

This blunt statement of a chilling possibility did not deter Paddy.

'And the final two?' he asked pragmatically.

'As we'll be operating in mountainous territory, it'd be best if they came from the Mountain Troop, though, again, I think their specialist crossover skills should be in demolitions, signals, medicine or languages.'

'So how do we find these supermen?' Paddy asked sardonically.

Grinning, Scott said, 'The CO has just put out a memorandum asking for volunteers for a top-secret, highly dangerous mission. I don't expect the words "highly dangerous" to put off too many of *our* men, but a few irate wives might helpfully reduce the number of applicants. Once we've received the applications, we'll start the weeding process by hauling the applicants' asses over the Brecon Beacons on the very worse Sickener we can devise. I'm talking a real Sickener here, something diabolically awful, one guaranteed to whittle down the numbers of even the best, leaving only the top bastards.'

'You're a diabolical bastard,' Paddy said.

'Better believe it,' Scott responded. 'Anyway, once we have what we believe to be the *crème de la crème*, we'll go through their records to ascertain which of them best suit our requirements with regard to their specialist and crossover skills. That should eliminate another lot and leave us with a manageable number to be individually interviewed with regard to their psychological profiles and motivation. We'll conduct those interviews personally and the six finally chosen by us will be submitted to the CO for final approval. I don't doubt that he'll approve anyone we select, so that submission is just a formality.'

Smiling with pleasure and nodding his agreement, Paddy

had another sip of his bitter, wiped his lips with the back of his left hand, then glanced around the noisy, almost smoke-free bar. Though some of the SAS troopers still smoked, they were in the minority these days; the seasoned troopers could never forget that younger men were queuing up to join the regiment and that their personal physical fitness would be matched against those of the newcomers. This, more than political correctness, had greatly reduced the number of smokers in the regiment. Sighing, having once been a joyful smoker and now trying to wean himself off, Paddy turned back to Scott.

'So what happens when we have our two teams?' he asked. 'Do we then have a rehearsal?'

'No,' Scott said. 'There's no real point to that. We can't embark on this mission with any specific plan because we haven't a clue what's going to happen. We don't know exactly where the enemy is; we don't know if he will, or will not, be aware of our presence in the area; and we don't know what to expect when we finally reach the point of engagement. We're dealing with a shifting enemy, one who operates on impulse, changing his strategy from day to day, and we're going to have to do the same, so a game plan would be useless. However, what we *do* know is the nature of the terrain – hot, desert lowlands leading up to snow-and-ice-covered mountains – so we'll concentrate on retraining the men for living and fighting in those environments . . . What say you, Paddy?'

'I say it sounds great, boss.'

'Good,' Scott said, finishing off his pint, licking his wet lips, and feeling better, more liberated, every second. 'So let's get up and go.'

'Go where?' Paddy asked, still holding his pint and looking bewildered.

'To the CO's office,' Scott replied, determined to escape from his grief and pain by losing himself in hard work. 'I'll lay you any odds that right now a pile of applications has already landed on his desk. So let's go and study them.'

Grinning, Paddy finished off his pint, then pushed his chair back and eagerly followed Scott out of the bar. As they walked side by side to the CO'S office, Scott saw the lights of the Sports and Social, the barracks, coming on one after the other, in rapid succession, to illuminate the deepening darkness of early evening. He glanced beyond the barracks, to the black hills of Hereford, and imagined them as the icy peaks of the Pamir mountains where, if he did not find his release in death, he might find resurrection through vengeance.

He would risk all for that.

CHAPTER FOUR

As he walked the short distance from his office, located near the Lubyanka, the former KGB headquarters, to the Up and Down nightclub, located in a Foreign Ministry building, Dmitry Petrov was aware of the bright lights all around him and realised once more just how much Moscow had changed since the collapse of the Soviet Union. When he had first arrived in Moscow, almost a decade ago, it had been like a graveyard with ill-lit streets, monolithic, oppressive architecture and ragged, grim-faced citizens queuing up endlessly for rationed food. Now the nocturnal, snow-covered streets were illuminated by the bright lights of new shops and restaurants, while the only queues were formed by the well-heeled, the so-called New Russians, defying the falling snow and freezing cold to get into packed theatres and nightclubs. The once-silent streets were now a riot of gridlocked, noisily hooting, imported cars, punk-rock music blaring out of vehicle radios and speakers fixed to public walls, and the raucous laughter of drunken or drugged citizens, most of whom were wearing expensive Western clothing.

The New Russians, Dmitry thought with contempt as he glanced about him to be dazzled by streetlights, garish neon-lit signs and the rainswept beams of the headlamps of passing vehicles. The entrepreneurs and robber barons of the building boom and the crime wave. I'm no longer a rarity in this city. I have at last become commonplace.

This, of course, was not quite true and Dmitry knew it by the deference with which he was treated when he reached the Up and Down nightclub. While the facade of the club was unusually discreet for these heady times, blending subtly into the monolithic architecture of the Foreign Ministry building, the number of BMWs and Mercedes parked outside were an indication of the kind of wealth required to get in. Recognised by the Amazonian women guarding the marble, glass and gold-mirrored lobby, all wearing fashionable, figure-hugging combat fatigues and high-heeled boots, Dmitry was allowed to enter without paying a fee or being checked with a metal detector. Stepping into a deafening cacophony of pounding rock music, drunken laughter, girlish shrieks and bawled obscenities, he pushed his way through the tightly packed revellers, past artfully illuminated, multicoloured, metallically tinkling fountains, to make his way to the upper floor. There, in a packed, smoke-filled room illuminated by dazzling strobe lights that flickered over the artificially tanned and sinuously gyrating bodies of professional strippers, performing for an audience composed of well-dressed young men and their glamorous girlfriends, he found Boris Surgeyevich waiting for him.

As obese as Orson Welles, though with a face less genial, his mad brown eyes reddened by the brandy he was greedily swilling, Boris was seated between two young women, a blonde and a brunette, both wearing skintight, low-cut sweaters, tightly belted miniskirts, stiletto-heeled shoes and far too much make-up, including false eyelashes and moistened lips. Obviously prostitutes who performed as a team, they were tightly sandwiching the gross Boris while stroking and squeezing him with practised, artful fingers. In a normal world, as Dmitry knew, no attractive woman would have looked twice at Boris, but here he was King. He was a well-known member of the *Mafiya*, the Russian underworld, and that meant he was wealthy. Wealth makes foul men attractive.

'Dmitry!' Boris bawled in Russian, raising his right hand in greeting and offering a lascivious grin in a flushed, sweaty face. 'You made it down from the mountains again!'

'Just for you,' Dmitry said, also speaking in Russian.

Bellowing with laughter, Boris waved for Dmitry to be seated. Dmitry took the chair facing the grotesque threesome, then, ignoring the welcoming smiles of the two whores, he glanced about him, taking in the strippers gyrating sensuously on the stage and their audience of wealthy, mostly young people who bawled obscene remarks, clapped repeatedly, raised clenched fists, all washed in the multicoloured strobe lights which formed dazzling kaleidoscopes about them.

'A good place, yes?' Boris said, not bothering to introduce the two whores; instead swigging brandy and wiping his fat lips with the back of his free hand.

'More Las Vegas than Moscow,' Dmitry said, reaching out for the bottle of brandy on the table to fill up the empty glass before him.

'Western decadence,' Boris said. 'Everything we always dreamed of. Which is why we can't get enough of it and, indeed, now put even the West to shame. Have you seen the crazy menu, my friend?'

'No,' Dmitry replied.

Boris grinned and rolled his eyes, making his two whores giggle and wriggle. He slugged more brandy and then wiped his lips with the back of his large hand. 'For fifteen thousand dollars,' he said, 'you can turn off all the lights in the club. For twenty thousand you can fire one of the waitresses. As some of these waitresses would starve if they lost their job, that's the favourite option.'

'A twenty thousand dollar option,' Dmitry said. 'Do they actually want it in US dollars or will rubles suffice?'

Boris roared with laughter, slapping his thigh with his ham fist. The blonde whore shrieked and withdrew her fingers from his crotch, which she had been gently, expertly massaging while casting secret, seductive glances and fleeting smiles in Dmitry's direction. Though Dmitry's features were badly scarred, he was still handsome enough to attract the ladies. He accepted this fact without vanity. He had gone way beyond that.

'A good one!' Boris managed to say while gasping for the breath lost through laughter. 'You always *were* a cynical bastard, Dmitry. That's why you're a rich man.'

'I'm rich because I'm an entrepreneur like you,' Dmitry replied. What he really meant was that they were both part of the rapidly growing criminal element, the *Mafiya* and *biznessmeni*, who were now virtually running the country. 'So how are things in Moscow these days?'

Shrugging, Boris looped his right arm over the bare shoulders of the blonde hooker to distractedly fondle her breast with his thick, scarred fingers. 'Not much different from when you were last here, though the murder rate goes up every day – gangster killings, robbery and so forth. According to *Izvestia*, our murder rate's now three times greater than in the United States. I hope you're well armed, my friend.'

'I am,' Dmitry said.

The guards down in the entrance lobby were highly selective in who they checked with their metal detectors – usually only strangers – and Dmitry knew that many of the older, harder men in this thriving club – men like the bloated, possibly psychopathic Boris – were carrying handguns and would use them at the slightest provocation. Dmitry himself never went anywhere without his lightweight Glock 19 semi-automatic handgun holstered at his waist, slightly to the rear where it could not be seen; and like the other *Mafiya*, he wouldn't hesitate to use it if the need arose. The criminals of Moscow were a violent, ruthless breed and the city was dangerous.

'They also tell me,' Boris continued while still squeezing the blonde's breast and sliding his other hand along the brunette's smooth, bare thigh, 'there's been an alarming rise in suicides and accidents on the road or at work! Caused by *this*, of course,' he added, grinning as he removed his hand from the brunette's knee to pick up his glass of brandy, shaking it to and fro.

'Russians drink vodka,' Dmitry said, reminding Boris that he was not a real Russian, but a brandy-swilling, yoghurt-eating Georgian from Tbilisi, renowned for its financial and political scandals. Boris was, of course, proud to be from Georgia. It had, after all, given Mother Russia some of its most spectacularly perverse citizens, including Joseph Vissarionovich Dzhugashvili, better known as Stalin, and Lavrenty Beria, the dreaded head of the Soviet secret police.

'Correction,' Boris said, not offended. 'Russians drink *anything*. Russian alcoholism has returned, worse than ever. In fact, most politicians are turning a blind eye to the drugs trade, which they reckon is a less damaging social problem than alcoholism. Which isn't harming our business – far from it! Indeed, the drug trade is thriving . . . So what have you brought me?'

Dmitry silently nodded, indicating the two hookers sand-wiching his hefty, sweating friend. Realising what was meant by that nod, Boris fished into his left-hand pocket, withdrew a fat roll of notes, peeled some off and divided them between the two women, telling them to go to the powder room and take their time about it. Delighted by the generosity of the handout, they hurried away, wriggling and giggling as they wended their way between the other crowded tables, erratically illuminated by the flashing strobe lights. Boris observed them with a smirk of self-satisfaction, then he turned back to Dmitry, raising his eyebrows enquiringly.

'Fifteen hundred kilos of the finest Afghanistan heroin,' Dmitry said.

Boris gave a soft whistle. 'That's a lot,' he said.

'We're having a good run,' Dmitry told him. 'Right now, it's being shifted along the Old Silk Road, from Afghanistan into Tajikistan and northwards to Osh, at a rate of about a hundred kilos a day. I control the road from Tajikistan to

Osh and the Kyrgyz police turn a blind eye, in return for a cut – a *very small* cut.'

Boris grinned, revealing rotting teeth. They were the teeth he'd had throughout the old regime and he could now afford to have them fixed, but, although he terrified most people, he was frightened of dentists. 'Very good,' he said. 'And clearly you had no trouble in bringing it in.'

'No trouble,' Dmitry said, recalling the ease with which he had passed through Sheremetyevo airport where he had been recognised by the Customs officials and treated with all the deference due to President Yeltsin's former bodyguard and confidant. Though Dmitry had been sent to Kyrgyzstan as a punishment for his criminal activities, this fact had not been made known to the public; ergo, he was still viewed widely as the president's close friend and as a man of considerable influence in the higher echelons of government. Instantly recognisable because of his former notoriety with the Moscow newspapers, he still received great respect wherever he went and was awarded all the benefits of a diplomat, including the most valuable benefit of all: diplomatic immunity. He could therefore bring his heroin into Russia without fear of being searched.

'Where is it?' Boris asked.

'In a room in my hotel,' Dmitry told him. 'Protected by one of my men. You can pick it up anytime.'

'What about tomorrow evening before dinner? Say, seven o'clock.'

'That's fine by me.'

Dmitry had another sip of brandy, lit a cigarette, inhaled deeply and squinted through the exhaled smoke at the young women stripping on the stage: smooth-skinned, big-breasted, long-legged, and exquisitely shaped in G-strings with halters. Before the collapse of the Soviet Union, they would not have been allowed to do this. Now they came from far and wide to make a living which, though not the most dignified, was better than whoring or starvation. Prostitution was, of course, now well spread throughout Moscow and tightly controlled by the likes of Boris, whose supply of young women, just like his drugs, mostly came from Dmitry.

'What's happening with the distribution?' he asked, since Boris did not pay him for the heroin but gave him a large percentage of the revenue accrued from its sale in foreign countries.

'We're still expanding,' Boris said, 'and presently negoti-ating with the US Mafia for the right to move our product into South Florida. We're also using the heroin as currency to buy our way into prostitution, money laundering and general racketeering in the same area – it's wide open to just about anything, right now. So don't worry, comrade . . .' He used the word 'comrade' to mock the old, strict regime. 'We're making money hand over fist and the pile grows bigger each day.'

'Any problems here in Moscow?'

'What problems could we possibly have,' Boris asked rhetorically with a big, salacious grin, 'when the President and his First Deputy Premier are preoccupied with the task of bringing the new oligarchy to heel? You think they're worried about the *Mafiya*? No, comrade, they're not. They're only worried by the fact that the businessmen and bankers, the fabulously rich, the new oligarchy, now control as much as half of the country's gross domestic product as well as the most powerful media outlets – television, radio and the press. In short, the new oligarchy controls the economy and, if they're not soon reined in, they'll almost certainly be running the whole country by the Millennium. So while the government frantically battles with the new oligarchy, they don't have much time for the *Mafiya* and we can do virtually anything we want. There are no problems here.'

Dmitry knew what Boris was talking about because his own rise to power, before his untimely expulsion to the wilds of Kyrgyzstan, had come through his connections with the shadowy *biznessmeni* in the final, convulsive years of the 1980s. Though they strenuously denied it, most of the new millionaires had received their start-up money from the Com-munist Party, the KGB or the other giants of the old system.

For that very reason, they had done particularly well during the privatisation of the Russian economy in the early years of liberalisation. Their biggest break, however, came in 1995 when Yeltsin's nearly bankrupt government offered shares in some of the country's biggest concerns, such as oil and other mineral resources. The business oligarchy therefore gained control of one enterprise after another, at huge discounts to their real value.

In fact, Dmitry, then Yeltsin's confidant, had personally recommended that plan to the President in return for huge fees from the very *biznessmeni* whose names he was putting forward. When Yeltsin realised, too late, that the *biznessmeni*, through those sales, had virtually gained control of the country's economy – and also learned through an informer of Dmitry's part in the affair – he banished Dmitry to Kyrgyzstan and began his ongoing battle to wrest control of the country's economy back from the new oligarchy. Unfortunately for him, the same former Communist Party members and former KGB agents who had financed the new oligarchy now worked hand-in-glove with them and, as an increasingly powerful *Mafiya*, protected the likes of Boris and Dmitry while they went about their illegal activities. Therefore, Dmitry's supposed banishment from the corridors of power had caused him no pain and had, indeed, made him wealthier than he had been before. He had much to be grateful for.

'On the other hand,' Boris said, no longer smiling as he slumped deeper into his chair, lit up a fat cigar and blew a stream of smoke across the table, 'you could soon have trouble in Kyrgyzstan.'

At first, because of the pounding rock music that filled the packed room, Dmitry thought that he wasn't hearing correctly.

'In Kyrgyzstan?' he asked.

Boris nodded. 'Correct.'

'What kind of trouble?' Dmitry asked. 'No one gives a damn about Kyrgyzstan. It's too far away, too impoverished, to concern anyone here.'

'Not anymore,' Boris said. He puffed another cloud of cigar smoke, studied the strippers on the stage through squinting, piggish eyes, then turned back to Dmitry. 'Whether you like it or not, your activities in the Pamir mountains have been reported in the Moscow press and caused great embarrassment to the government.'

'I didn't encourage it,' Dmitry said.

'That's irrelevant,' Boris responded. 'It's now widely known that the drugs coming into Russia from Osh are ending up in the streets of Great Britain. The British authorities don't like it.'

'Fuck them,' Dmitry said with quiet defiance, feeling no fear at all.

'The British government,' Boris continued, ignoring Dmitry's show of defiance, 'has put pressure on the Russians to put an end to drug-running in that area.'

'If Russia stops the drugs trade,' Dmitry said, 'it'll bring Kyrgyzstan to its knees and turn most of the country against it. Russia can't afford that.'

'No,' Boris said. 'But the Russian government can certainly afford to get rid of you and then limit the flow of drugs to local traffic only, controlled by the locals themselves. In doing that, they would please the British by keeping the drugs off their streets whilst also allowing the Kyrgyz to continue making a living. Indeed, they would make a better living with you gone than they do with you there, since you bleed the poor, pig-ignorant *muzhiks* dry. Anyway, word on the grapevine has it that the government is planning to get rid of you, once and for all – and, if I may say so, almost certainly in a terminal manner.'

Dmitry was neither amused nor frightened. 'If they want rid of me,' he said, 'why don't they just pick me up while I'm here in Moscow?'

'Because they can't be seen to be disposing of one of their former best friends and confidants. More importantly, they can't be seen to be interfering in Kyrgyzstan. The populace depends too heavily on the drugs trade for its economic survival.'

'So how *do* they propose getting rid of me?' Dmitry asked,

speaking with academic detachment, as if discussing someone else.

'By letting the British do it for them,' Boris told him.

'The British? In Kyrgyzstan?'

'SAS,' Boris said. 'Special Air Services. They'll be inserted into Kyrgyzstan with Russian help – through Moscow, of course – to hunt you down and, in their vernacular, neutralise you.'

'Kill me.'

'You're so bright, Dmitry.'

'And whether they succeed or fail, they'll be reported as British and my old friends can claim innocence in the matter, thus appeasing the citizens of Kyrgyzstan.'

'You're not merely bright, you're a genius!' Boris exclaimed, raising his glass in tribute and then, scarcely concerned for the threat to Dmitry, glancing sideways across the smoke-filled, strobe-streaked nightclub with its teeming mass of New Russian *Mafiya* and *biznessmeni*, prostitutes and pimps, strippers, mobile-phone addicts, alcoholics and AIDS carriers, to see his blonde and his brunette, already paid and soon to earn it, wending their way back, still wriggling and giggling, across the packed room. He returned his gaze to Dmitry.

'Here they come,' he said. 'Two bird-brains game for anything. We're going back to my place for the evening, so why don't you join us? Since your head is on a plate, you can take your pick – the blonde or the brunette. But we must all share the same bed.'

'No, thanks,' Dmitry said.

The two girls returned to the table, arm-in-arm, giggling hysterically, clearly having inhaled something potent in the so-called powder room, and resumed their places on both sides of Boris, one stretching her arm around his neck to lay her hand on his chest, the other placing her hand on his thick thigh to give it a squeeze. When Dmitry stood up to take his leave, they both pouted with histrionic disappointment as Boris studied him thoughtfully.

'You're so strange,' Boris said. 'I've never quite worked

you out. You deal in drugs and run prostitutes and kill without blinking ... and yet you're so puritancial about certain matters. I offer you one of these heavenly creatures and you say "No" and prepare to take flight. Is it them?' He indicated each woman with a nod of his head. 'Or the fact that you'd have to share them with me? Come on, Dmitry. *Tell me!*'

'I enjoy the pleasures of women,' Dmitry said, 'but only one at a time – and only when alone with that one.'

'You *are* a puritan,' Boris responded, grinning lasciviously as he placed a hand over his own crotch and pretended to masturbate himself – a crude act that only made the two whores giggle again.

'Only about certain things,' Dmitry said. 'I'll see you at my hotel tomorrow evening.'

'It's a date,' Boris said.

Leaving the packed, smoke-filled room, glad to get away from the noise, the relentlessly pounding rock music, Dmitry went down the stairs to the ground floor, smiled automatically at the stone-faced women guarding the lobby, then walked out into the freezing, snow-filled night. As he made his way back to his hotel, walking because he enjoyed it, wanting to see what was happening – the new filth and squalor, the whores and the drunks and drug addicts, the neon-lit, fantastic new decadence arising out of the ashes of the puritanical old Soviet Union – he thought about what Boris had said and realised it was serious.

If they're using the SAS, he thought, they must be determined. The British revere the SAS. They think those bastards are heroes. They think they're supermen who can do just about anything and so they only use them for the most important tasks. That means *I'm* important. I'm important to *them*. It means that they want me to disappear and they'll go all out to ensure that I do. I've been challenged at last.

That thought came out of the blue, like a bolt of lighting, and it had its effect.

Dmitry knew just what he needed and he still could not

believe it. What he needed was a form of suicide that did not seem like weakness. What he needed was a challenge so pure, so absolute, that its only consequence could be death or resurrection. He had already been sentenced to death – he certainly knew that much because Boris had told him so – and the realisation merely made him smile. He was a marked man and that made him separate from other men. It made him feel like the newly born.

Come and get me, Dmitry said in his thoughts, speaking to that unknown man charged with finding him. Come and find me and then see what you can do when we're standing there face to face. Come and find your own destiny.

By midnight, Dmitry was drunk, having killed most of a bottle of vodka, but as he slept all alone in his hotel room, his contentment was deep.

The following day, feeling suicidally excited, he flew back to Kyrgyzstan.

CHAPTER FIVE

The response to the CO's memorandum was overwhelming, with applications from over eighty percent of the regiment – an indication of the sheer extent of the frustration of these men who had been rigorously trained to do the kind of work that rarely came along these days. Faced with such a daunting number, Scott was forced to reduce it by eliminating all applicants with no previous battle experience, those over forty years of age, those with the reputation of being percentage players (men who took unnecessary chances) and those who had complicated family commitments, such as ageing relatives or dependent children. This meant that a lot of applicants who might otherwise have been excellent were dropped even before they had a chance to prove themselves, but it did at least reduce the pile of application forms to fifty – a manageable number when it came to organising the Sickener designed to weed out even more and leave only the cream of the crop.

'So here we have them,' Scott said to Paddy Devlin when, in the CO's outer office, they had gone through the application forms together and systematically used the slightest excuse to eliminate enough applicants to bring the remaining number down to fifty. 'A nice round figure – five and oh – which now has to be narrowed down to six. What's your game plan, Paddy?'

'To put 'em through hell and select from those who survive.'

'Christian charity was always beyond you, Paddy, but that sounds right to me. Where do we start?'

'Dead easy,' Paddy said with a confident grin. 'We just *test* 'em, right?'

'If you say so.'

'Right!'

The test that Scott had designed for the fifty hopefuls was not unlike the two Sickeners used to stretch a man to his absolute limits during the Test Week of the Selection and Continuation Training programme for new recruits to the regiment – except that this one was more brutal and merciless. First the applicants, under Paddy's remorseless gaze, with Scott always quietly by his side, were put through a gruelling week of tests covering patrol tactics, combat survival, close-quarter battle, demolitions, signals, language and medicine. While most of the applicants were trained in all of those skills, some were better at certain of them than others and the elimination process, taking into account the crossover skills required for this particular mission, soon led to an elimination of men who could not believe their bad luck when told they had been rejected.

With the numbers already reduced on paper, as it were, the remaining men were placed in competition with one another on the firing range, displaying their skill with the wide variety of weapons that would be required for this particular campaign. In fact, this meant most of the weapons favoured by the regiment since the 1970s – the SA-80 assault rifle, the Heckler & Koch MP5 sub-machine gun and the ever-reliable L7A2 GPMG (General Purpose Machine Gun) – but it also included the relatively new Barrett Light .50 rifle (the so-called 'sniper's supergun') and the exceptionally powerful FN Herstal Five-seveN pistol which had replaced the old and nostalgically remembered Browning 9mm High Power handgun.

Paddy ensured that the tests on the outdoor firing range were made even more difficult by deliberately waiting for bad weather; as this was the winter, he didn't have to wait long. Thus, the men were not only given unusually high strike points to attain – scores that could only be gained by truly expert marksmen – but were compelled to aim at the targets through the murk of heavy, windswept rain while lying belly down on ground that soon became a sea of mud. When test-firing from this position had eliminated some more men, the rest were made to fire at pop-up targets while advancing at the half-crouch as fast as they could in the increasingly thick, slippery mud. Some slipped and fell while others simply missed targets obscured by the pissing rain. These men, also, were struck off the list. A few simply said 'Fuck it!' and angrily stomped off the firing range. Others, though sticking it through to the bitter end, were rigorously pruned from the list only because the points they had scored, while certainly high by normal marksman standards, were below the exceptionally demanding pass score set by Scott and Paddy. By the end of the third hellish day on the firing range, the original fifty men had been reduced to forty.

'You men,' Paddy said to those still in the running, 'have made it through to the next stage, but don't let this knowledge go to your heads. The next part of the selection process is an assault on the Killing House and you'll be judged not only on whether or not you survive but on how many points you score if you *do* survive. This assault will be more complicated than any you've done so far and only the sharpest and quickest of you will make it through. So go back to the spider, put on your CRW assault kit, arm yourselves with fully loaded MP5s, handguns and flash-bangs, then make your way to the Killing House. You've got ten minutes to get there.'

'I'll get there,' Trooper Randolph 'Rudi' Blackwood said defiantly as he stood up with the others to leave the briefing hall. A veteran of the Gulf War, he was small, lean and tough, with the scarred and battered features of a born fighter. 'I'll get there and I'll go through the Killing House like a bandsaw through butter.'

'Your confidence has been noted,' Scott observed. 'Let's hope it's backed up in action.'

'It will be,' Blackwood said, grinning and receiving grins from his mates as he sauntered cockily out of the briefing hall.

The Killing House was the Close Quarter Battle (CQB) building located on the SAS base. Used for rigorous training in Counter Revolutionary Warfare (CRW) tactics, with a special emphasis on hostage-rescue drills, the building had two rooms containing 'terrorists' and 'hostages' in the form of pop-up cardboard dummies. The rooms were connected by a camera system that gave a 'real-time' coverage of events occurring in one room to a 'wraparound' life-sized screen in the other, and vice versa. Thus, the assault team could fire at the images of the 'terrorists' projected onto the bullet-absorbent walls and the 'terrorists' could do the same with their screen. The success or failure of the assault could be judged after the event by the placement of the bullets in the cardboard targets.

For this particular exercise, Paddy had decided to make life even more difficult for the applicants by tasking them with a hostage-rescue assault that had to take place in total darkness. In their attempt to rescue the 'hostages', the men would be forced to display their skill in rapid magazine changes, shooting on the move and from unconventional positions, rapid target acquisition, exact shot placement and accuracy in the 'head shots' favoured in real life hostage-rescue situations. In teams of four, they had to enter the dark building and, using a combination of 'flash-bang' stun grenades, sub-machine guns and handguns, fight their way past the cardboard 'terrorists' without accidentally shooting a 'hostage' or being shot themselves. A man was deemed to be shot if he fired upon and missed a pop-up dummy terrorist.

For even the most experienced SAS trooper, the Killing House could be a daunting experience, more demanding and nerve-racking than the real thing. The fear of missing a terrorist or, even worse, of firing before a dummy target had been properly identified, thus accidentally killing a hostage, could fill even the strongest of men with unbearable tension. Thus, when Paddy Devlin's applicants made their assault on the Killing House, moving through it in total darkness, further blinded by their own flash-bangs and often deafened by their own gunfire, some were quickly disoriented and fired at the wrong targets while others fired too slowly when the dummy terrorists popped up, thus qualifying as having been shot. In either case, these men were deemed to have failed and were struck off the list.

Trooper Rudi Blackwood was not one of them. When he emerged from the Killing House and removed the CRW mask from his scarred, battered face, he was sporting the grin of someone who knew that he'd succeeded.

'Fucking Ace!' he said excitedly to Scott and Paddy as he brushed past them, heading back to the briefing room. 'Call me anytime, gentlemen.'

'He looks promising,' Paddy said.

Not all were so lucky. Another eight men failed in the Killing House, leaving thirty-two still in the running.

'You men,' Paddy told the remaining applicants at the next briefing, 'probably think you're the ant's pants, but you've still got a long way to go. In fact, you're just about to embark on the worst Sickener ever devised – devised specifically to break the best of the best – so don't get too confident. Now go back to the spider, put your outdoors kit together, and prepare yourselves for a long time in the Brecon Beacons.'

''Scuse me, boss,' Corporal Dave 'Killer' Parker said, 'but isn't it snowing right now in the Brecon Beacons?'

'That's right,' Scott replied. 'Why do you ask? Does snow give you a problem?'

'Only that when it snows on the Brecon Beacons men tend to get killed. SAS troopers have died up there, usually frozen to death.'

'Does *that* give you a problem?'

'I'm merely making an observation,' Parker replied, his wintry grey gaze as steady as his voice. A veteran of both the Falklands Campaign and the Gulf War, he was widely viewed as a quietly spoken, unshakeable killing machine. 'If it doesn't bother you, I'm game to try it. You just get me up there, boss.'

Realising that he had already selected Parker in his head, Scott let his gaze roam over the other men. 'Does anyone else have a problem with the Brecon Beacons at this time of the year? If so, now's the time to back out. Hands up if you want that.'

In fact, three men raised their hands, obviously deciding that the Brecon Beacons at this time of the year was sheer insanity. That left twenty-nine applicants.

In preparation for the Beacons, those men were put through three days of hell. From four in the morning to ten at night, they alternated between more weapons training in the freezing cold of the open firing range at Stirling Lines and brutal routemarches over the hills of the surrounding Hereford countryside. Each successive hike was longer and tougher than the one before it, culminating in a final, merciless slog up an ever-steeper gradient that brutally tortured lungs and muscles. These forced marches, or 'tabs', through rain, sleet, hail and snow, were rendered even more difficult when the formerly empty rucksacks were loaded with bricks, the load being increased every day as the routes were made progressively longer. Even with the minimum load, which was eleven kilos, the weight, combined with the difficult terrain and vile weather, was enough to make more candidates drop out.

However, when he saw that not as many as he had expected were giving up, Paddy kept adding more bricks to the rucksacks until the total weight was a back-breaking, physically draining twenty-five kilograms.

To make matters worse, the routemarches also took place at night, invariably after the men had endured a long, demanding day of the same thing. A dangerously high degree of stress was then deliberately introduced by forcing the men to hike in a given direction but to an RV not shown on their maps. This meant that they didn't know how long the hike would take and, therefore, could not keep their spirits up by counting off the number of miles still to go. Also, as Paddy had grimly promised, only when the candidate had reached the first RV was he given the direction (but not the location) of the next one . . . and so on until the whole hike was completed. He would not know, until the very end, just when his ordeal would be over.

This lack of knowledge about just how much longer he would have to march could be psychologically devastating to the individual hiking solo, particularly with regard to navigating in pitch darkness, and it led to more men dropping out, either exhausted, in a state of complete despair, or just plain bloody angry.

'Fuck you!' bawled Corporal Phil 'Philco' Weatherby, who had, with Scott and Paddy, fought through the whole of the Falklands Campaign. 'Fuck you, Paddy! This isn't even remotely fair play and I've had enough, you fucking arseholing bastard!'

'Take him down,' was Paddy's only response – and the corporal, formerly one of his best friends, was dropped as a candidate.

'You're one hell of a friend,' Corporal 'Mad Mike' Nicholson observed cynically, having completed the latest hike and still not out of breath. Another veteran of both wars, he was just under the maximum age for this mission and as hard as they come. 'If I had friends like you, Sarge, I'd start believing that God didn't exist.'

'You don't believe in God anyway,' Paddy replied. 'Though by the time I'm through with you, you just might believe in the devil.'

'I'm looking at him,' Mad Mike said.

By the end of the three days, Paddy was piling on the pressure, with the distances of the cross-country marches increased and the time to complete them decreased proportionately. More men dropped out, but not enough to make Scott and Paddy happy.

'I think it's time for the Long Drag,' the latter said to the former as they watched more weary, mud-splattered men stumbling into the base after yet another dreadful hike. 'What do you think, boss?'

'I think you're right,' Scott said. 'There's still too many for the final selection. It's an indication of just how frustrated these men are that they'll put up with this shit. Christ, they're tough and as determined as they can be, but we still need only six. So, yes, let's go for a Long Drag and make it something exceptional.'

'It's a fuckin' beaut',' Paddy said proudly.

And it was indeed. In the early hours of the selected morning, the candidates, now greatly reduced in number, wearily picked up their M16 assault rifles and brick-filled rucksacks to be run to the four-ton trucks that were waiting for them in the early morning darkness of Hereford. As they had been instructed to carefully study their Ordnance Survey maps of the Elan Valley, in the Cambrian Mountains of Mid-Wales, the traditional SAS testing ground, none of them were too surprised when the Bedfords dropped them off at that very location. Gazing about them, at the dauntingly steep hills and craggy, towering ridges, presently wreathed in a hellish mixture of rain, snow and mist, they all shared a stomach-churning intimation of what they were in for.

'The Long Drag,' Paddy told his assembled candidates with an air of deep satisfaction. Scott stood by his side, amused on the one hand, on the other sympathising with the men, knowing what they were in for. 'This is a twenty-four hour hike,' Paddy continued, then paused briefly to take in the shock and disbelief on their faces. 'By that, I mean that you have *no more* than twenty-four hours to complete it, though you're unlikely to do it in much less. Even worse is that again you won't be told where or when the hike will end until you actually *reach* the end – and you can only do that by making your way to the first RV shown on your map. The map will *not* show the second RV, so you'll have to make that first stretch without knowing just how long the second stretch is going to be. This, as you already know, is a form of psychological torture, only this time much worse because the route's a lot longer and much more difficult. So some of you, even though you survived the last hikes, won't be able to bear this one. If you can't – or if you fail, for any reason, to reach an RV – you'll be dropped from the list.'

'So what happens if we get injured?' Trooper Sydney 'Syd' Loomis asked, his twisted upper lip turning his grin into a Rottweiler's snarl.

'A physical injury is no excuse,' Paddy told him. 'You get injured? Tough shit! You get lost in a snowstorm and freeze in the mountains? That's tough shit as well.'

'Thanks a million,' Loomis said, tightening the straps on his brick-filled rucksack and grinning as if about to bite someone. A veteran of the Gulf War and undercover work in Belfast, Northern Ireland, he wasn't about to be put down. 'Well, I'm tough shit as well, Sarge.'

'You'd better be,' Paddy said. 'Your task is to make it the whole length of the Long Drag and, in this particular instance, it's going to be the longest drag you've ever experienced. So are there any more questions?' There were not. 'Okay, move out.'

They marched into the swirling, blinding snow, one after the other, at thirty-minute intervals. As they soon found out, the hike to the first RV took them up ever steeper, higher hills. Indeed, in some places the gradients were so steep, the men felt that they were climbing a sheer cliff face. In other places, the route had been deliberately chosen to force them over dangerously loose gravel that rolled beneath their boots and frequently made them slide backwards, losing precious time. Even worse, when dawn broke, the mist, rain and snow badly reduced visibility and turned them numb with cold, to the degree where some of them simply could not go on and had to be rescued, thus failing the test.

Paddy had picked the right weather. The wind howled constantly, hammering brutally at the candidates, often threatening to throw them off balance and send them tumbling downhill to a point where, as happened in so many cases, they simply hadn't the strength to pick themselves up and start climbing again. To make this even more nightmarish, the DS, under instructions from Scott and Paddy, frequently jumped out from their hiding places in rock formations to bawl abuse at those lagging behind, thus further undermining their confidence. Those who lost their nerve at that point or, as happened occasionally, lost their tempers and either vocally or physically abused the DS, were sent back down the mountain to join the other crap-hats, or failures, and be dropped from the list.

The remainder were allowed to rest up for the night – though even this was turned into a night in hell, since the spot sadistically chosen for the laying-up positions (LUPs) was located on the summit of an exposed, windswept hill. Frozen and wet, with badly swollen feet and shoulders rubbed raw from carrying the brick-filled rucksacks, the candidates spent the night in appalling weather, eating cold, high-calorie rations and bedding down in sleeping bags, only protected from the howling wind and sweeping snow by their noisily snapping ponchos. Because of this they didn't really sleep much at all and eventually, in dawn's dead light, clambered back to their feet, even more tired than they'd been the night before.

'Feeling up to it, are you?' Paddy asked of Trooper Arnold 'Arnie' Basham when he and Scott had pulled up to the LUPs in their jeep, having had a good night's sleep in a large, well-equipped tent on the lower, less windy slopes. 'I mean, you look blue with cold and pretty tired.'

'Man, I'm that right enough,' Basham replied, wiping the clean white snow from his handsome, black face, then yawning and stretching his great bulk. 'I mean, my parents didn't get this weather in Barbados, so my blood's a bit thin, like.'

'Do you want to go back down?' Scott asked him. 'I think you might need to.'

'Don't try fucking me, boss,' Basham replied, his big soft brown eyes brightening with the good-humoured defiance that had helped him survive the deserts of Iraq during the Gulf War. 'If I go down there before I complete the Long Drag, it'll be in a pine box. No way am I giving up.'

'Your thin black blood,' Paddy said, 'might not be able to take the cold higher up. I mean, it's *really* cold up there.'

'Fuck you, Sarge, I won't stop till I drop.'

'Be my guest,' Paddy said.

Again, the hike commenced in foul weather, taking them up a series of increasingly steeper, higher hills, down the other side and then on to the dangerous rapids of a flooded, rock-strewn river that flowed along the base of another soaring, snow-covered hill. Too frightened to attempt the crossing (doubtless filled with the exaggerated fears of the exhausted) one man turned back. Another, after managing to make it halfway across, slipped on a rock, plunged into the freezing river, and was swept away, bounced brutally from one rock to the next, until he had disappeared. He, too, when eventually he was found, was dropped from the list.

Reaching the other side and the penultimate RV, the remaining men found Scott and Paddy waiting for them. The latter was trying not to grin as Scott informed the almost terminally exhausted survivors that the final RV was only a mile away and that if they managed to make it that far, waiting trucks would take them back to the base.

When Scott had passed on this information, he saw corporals Killer Parker and Mad Mike Nicholson exchanging veiled glances and knowing smiles. Realising that the two men, both battle-hardened and astute, knew what was going to happen but were keeping quiet about it, Scott decided that they were perfect and that the forthcoming interviews with them would be mere formalities.

All of the men made the mile hike to the last RV, preceded by Scott and Paddy in the jeep. However, as Scott and Paddy had deliberately planned it (and as Parker and Nicholson had clearly guessed) when the soaked, frozen, seriously exhausted troopers stumbled into the RV they found only Scott and Paddy waiting for them. There were no trucks in sight.

'We changed our minds,' Paddy informed the shocked men. 'Instead of getting a lift, you now have to hike the final ten miles to the base, holding your rifles at the ready. Undoubtedly this will give you a great deal of pain – across your back, in your shoulders and particularly in your arms – but if you're found by a DS patrol with your rifle lowered you'll be struck off the list. Likewise if you drop your rifle or fail to make it the whole way back. Now move out, you dumb bastards.'

Trooper Tom Bradbury released a hoarse cry of outrage and threw himself bodily at Paddy, determined to strangle him. Pulled off and pacified by some of his comrades, he was ordered by Scott to clamber up into the rear of the jeep, to be driven back to the base. He did so gratefully, though clearly humiliated, dropping his rifle onto the seat beside him, shrugging off his brick-filled rucksack, then holding his head in his hands, taking deep, anguished breaths.

'Anyone want to go with him?' Scott asked. When the remaining men shook their heads in denial, he said, 'Okay, move out.'

Not all made it back. A few simply couldn't go on and collapsed to the snow to rest against the frozen treetrunks, gasping for breath, until they were picked up by a DS patrol and returned to the base in a jeep. Another dropped his rifle from numbed fingers and was too disorientated to know what he had done until ten minutes later; finally realising his mistake, he turned back to find his weapon and became hopelessly lost in the snowswept forest until found, a good three hours later, by a DS search party. A third, almost blinded by the swirling snow, turning blue with cold, too exhausted to walk properly, tripped on a fallen log, broke his ankle and rolled down into a gully where, a few hours later, he was found, almost frozen to death, by another DS patrol. Heroic though his efforts had seemed to him, he too was failed.

There were now less than twenty men left and before the final test, they were allowed a good night's sleep in the spider, or barracks. In fact, even this was another form of torture. Exhausted to the point where they were feverish and disorientated, many of them could not sleep properly and simply tossed and turned all night, drifting in and out of consciousness, to awaken at first light feeling even worse. Nevertheless, before the dawn had broken completely, they were ordered to have a good breakfast in the canteen, then gather together, wearing full kit, at the Bedford trucks parked outside the motor pool. This, they were informed by Scott, would be their final test.

The trucks took them to the snow-covered, freezing fields of Llanfihangel, Wales. There, to their dismay, particularly given the terrible weather, they were tasked with completing a murderously long 'Fan Dance': a 'cross-graining' of the peaks of Pen-y-fan, the highest mountain in the Brecon Beacons. What this meant, in effect, is that they had to climb to a designated trig point (a vantage point suitable for map reading) in the snow-and-ice-covered mountains, then make their way for a distance of forty miles from one summit, or trig point, to another by hiking up and down the sheer hills, instead of taking the easy route around them. Even worse, they would have to do this in the blinding hail and snow.

'You leave at thirty-minute intervals,' Scott told them just before they commenced the hike, 'so you'll each be on your own out there. No help at all. Not a soul to talk to. Just you, the darkness, sleet and snow, and that murderous tab. The best of luck. You'll sure need it.'

'The man wished us luck at last,' Trooper Pete Welsh said, grinning crookedly out of a lean, pock-marked face while wiping the snow from his dishevelled blonde hair. Though looking younger than his thirty-one years, he had fought in the Gulf War. 'We should thank God for small mercies.'

'Thank God you got this far,' Paddy retorted. 'Now get your arse up that mountain.'

'I'll get my arse up that mountain so fast you won't see me for dust.'

'I live in hope,' Paddy said, already deciding that Welsh was a man for him. 'Now get the fuck out of here.'

This final test took the remaining men on a cruelly demanding, dreadfully lonely, forty-mile hike up and down the sheer slopes of the soaring Pen-y-fan, from one trig point to another, following a course diabolically designed by Paddy to guarantee maximum discomfort. In no time at all, they found themselves crossing icy rivers, peat bogs, pools of stagnant water and fields of dense fern and overgrown grass. Some of them simply couldn't deal with it – not after what they had already been through – and either collapsed where they were, to be picked up by the DS patrols, or to make their way alone back down the mountain, some cursing, some sobbing. As for those who conquered the lower slopes and kept climbing, instead of finding release from their trials they were faced with loose gravel paths and ridges so sheer, some practically vertical, that they had to pull themselves up by their fingers. They were, of course, doing this in blinding fog, freezing wind, driving rain and swirling snow while carrying a rucksack weighted that morning by Paddy to an energy-draining thirty kilograms of bricks. Knowing that before this the heaviest load had been twenty-five kilograms, some good men were psychologically devastated and then physically broken. Giving in at last – and even worse, at the last moment – they either sat in the snow and forlornly waited to be rescued or made their own way back down the treacherous mountain to live with their failure.

Nevertheless, while this final test lost a lot of men, slightly over a dozen made it across the many trig points to the highest, bleakest summit of Pen-y-fan where, shivering with cold, ravenous, in a state of almost total exhaustion, they slipped in and out of consciousness – throughout what had to be, Scott realised, as he observed them through his binoculars from the lower, safer slopes, one of the longest, most uncomfortable nights of their lives.

At first light, however, they came back down the mountain, emerging from the dawn mist, covered in mud-smeared snow and ice, their eyes red from lack of sleep, their faces haggard.

When the last of them was standing in front of Scott, he did a head count of nine.

Nine men out of fifty.

Those nine men had to be really exceptional, but Scott still only needed six. Though all of them equally deserved this mission, three would have to be dropped.

'I don't think I can do this,' Scott said when he and Paddy were facing each other across a table in the briefing room in Stirling Lines, where the interviews for the final six places were about to take place. 'It's just too bloody cruel.'

'Who dares wins,' Paddy replied.

They called in the first man.

CHAPTER SIX

The first man to enter the room was Corporal Dave Parker. He didn't exactly come to attention when he stopped in front of the desk behind which Scott and Paddy where sitting in hard wooden chairs, but simply spread his legs and clasped his hands behind his back to stare steadily at them with his wintry grey gaze. He had gained his notoriety first with the Boat Troop in the Falklands Campaign, then in the Mobility Troop in the Gulf War. In both of those wars, he had taken part in some hair-raising operations and pulled off some spectacular stunts. He was now a member of the Directing Staff, helping to run the Selection and Continuation Training courses here at Stirling Lines, but clearly not thrilled by the work. When Scott deliberately stared hard at him, Parker held his gaze.

'At ease, Corporal,' Scott said eventually.

'I am at ease, boss.'

Scott smiled. Paddy did not. 'Let me start,' Scott said, 'by reminding you that while we still can't tell you just what this mission is, we can assure you that it's exceptionally dangerous. Do you still wish to volunteer?'

'Yes, boss.'

'Why?'

'I'm bored shitless.'

'You don't enjoy your work as a DS?'

'It's not exactly what I joined the regiment for.'

'It's a real war you're after, is it?' Paddy asked.

'You've hit the nail on the head, Sarge.'

'What we don't want on this mission,' Paddy said without the trace of a smile, 'are percentage players or cowboys. Maybe that's what you are.'

'It's not what I am and you know it,' Parker replied evenly, his voice as steady as his wintry grey gaze. 'I've fought two wars with this regiment and I'm good and we all know it, but I'm certainly no percentage player or cowboy. I'm not out for personal glory and I always work closely with my team.'

Hiding his smile, Scott glanced down at his notes, then looked up again. 'I note that your marriage broke up last year.'

'That's correct, boss.'

'Any problem with that?'

'No problem at all. We were unhappily married for twenty years; now the kids have grown up we decided to give each other a break. We still see each other now and then and life hasn't changed much. I take it you can gather from my records that my work's as good as always.'

'We'll make that judgement,' Paddy said. 'Not you.'

'I'm sure you will,' Parker said.

Paddy stared steadily at him, then offered a slight grin and nodded at Scott. The latter glanced again at his notes and then raised his eyes to that grey, unrevealing gaze.

'You speak Spanish and Russian.'

'Yes, boss. I had to learn Spanish for CT work with the GEO,' he said, meaning counter-terrorist work with Spain's *Grupo Especial de Operaciones*. 'I learnt Russian at the regimental School of Languages here in Hereford and perfected it in Moscow when we went in there, undercover, in 1998, to check out the Russian crime scene.'

'That's helpful,' Paddy said. 'So what's your specialist crossover skill?'

'Signals. I was trained to Regimental Signaller standard by the Royal Corps of Signals unit.'

'How up to date are you?' Scott asked him.

'I can use all of the very latest SATCOM systems.'

'Good,' Scott said. 'That could be useful.' He glanced at Paddy, who just nodded his approval, then he turned back to Parker. 'Okay, corporal, that's all we need to know for now. Please send in Corporal Nicholson.'

Parker nodded and left, leaving the office door open, and Mad Mike Nicholson entered a few seconds later to stand at ease in front of the desk. Just under forty years of age, the maximum permitted for this particular mission, he was, like Parker, a veteran of the Falklands Campaign and the Gulf War. As a member of the Mountain Troop, he had taken part in the near disastrous but heroic climb up the Fortuna Glacier in South Georgia, but survived that appalling ordeal to fight throughout the rest of the campaign, all the way to Port Stanley in East Falkland. Transferred to the Mobility Group, he had taken part in many of the daring Pink Panther Land Rover hit-and-run raids alongside Scott and Paddy. Thus, they knew him well and were already convinced that they wanted him in on this mission. Nevertheless, they still required this brief interview.

'Not much point in asking you too many questions,' Scott said, 'as we've previously worked together, Corporal.'

'We sure have, boss.'

'Still specialising in demolitions, I see.'

'That's right, boss, though I haven't really blown anything up since we knocked out those communications towers in that desert in Iraq.'

'You blow up things during the training courses.'

'It's not the same thing, boss.'

'Which is why you want to come on this mission.'

'Naturally. Why else?'

'This mission is exceptionally dangerous,' Paddy said.

Nicholson raised his eyebrows, looking cynical. 'So the Falklands Campaign and the Gulf War weren't dangerous?'

'You enjoy danger a bit too much for my liking,' Paddy retorted. 'That's why you're nicknamed Mad Mike.'

'You can't hold that against me,' Nicholson replied, 'unless you hold it against every other trooper applying for this mission. Men only transfer to the SAS if they like danger and anyone who says anything else is talking bullshit.'

'I take that as fair comment,' Scott said, glancing sideways at Paddy. 'And your specialist crossover skill,' he added, 'is still listed as medicine.'

'Right, boss.'

'With special training, I note, at the US Army's special forces medical course, first at Fort Sam Houston, Texas, then at Fort Bragg, North Carolina.'

'You've got your facts right, boss.'

'You must be good,' Paddy said.

'You could do worse,' Mad Mike responded.

'It says here,' Scott said, 'that you're living with your second wife in Hereford and have four grown-up children, all of whom are now living away from home.'

'What's the point, boss?'

'You'll be leaving your wife alone if you go on this mission – and as it's an exceptionally dangerous mission, you may not be coming back. How do you feel about that?'

'It won't make me lose sleep at nights,' Mad Mike replied, 'if that's what you mean.'

'That's what I mean. So don't you care about your wife in this regard?'

'That's a bullshit question, boss. I'm a professional soldier, I've fought in two major wars, and my wife, being a professional soldier's wife, knows just what to expect. As for me not coming back, well, she's learned to live with that expectation and, besides, if I actually *don't* come back, she won't be alone. The children are all married, and they're all deeply fond of her. She'll be well looked after, boss.'

'Fine,' Scott said. 'Any questions about the mission?'

'Would you answer if I asked?'

'I don't believe so.'

'Then I've no questions, boss.'

'Good. Send in Corporal Weatherby.'

'Okay, boss, will do.'

Mad Mike left and Corporal Weatherby entered to take up his position in front of the desk. Weatherby had done well in the Killing House and on the sickeners. Also, his track record regarding the Gulf War was excellent. He made the mistake, however, of using the interview as a platform for asking a lot of questions about the mission. When Scott avoided answering the questions, Weatherby became visibly annoyed and that was enough to make him an issue of doubt. Dismissed, he was followed by another corporal, William 'Bill' Wilson, who would have been perfect had it not been for the fact that he had an ailing mother in a nursing home in Reigate and it was possible she would die during his absence. For that reason – and that reason alone – Scott and Paddy decided against him, though he would not be told this until the lucky six had been selected.

The unlucky Weatherby was followed by Trooper Randolph 'Rudi' Blackwood, a 32-year-old Mobility Troop veteran of the Gulf War. Hailing orginally from Merseyside, he was small, lean and tough, with the scarred, battered features of someone who had fought a lot in the past. A broadly grinning bantamcock, good-natured but hot-tempered, he had made good his boast by coming in third of all the men tested in the Killing House, beaten only by Parker and Nicholson, who had almost legendary status regarding those particular skills. Blackwood was a demolitions specialist with crossover skills in signals. He was also a single man.

'So why did you never marry?' Paddy asked when halfway through the interview.

'That's not your concern,' Blackwood replied.

'Are you being impertinent?'

'You're being impertinent by asking that question, Sarge. Are you suggesting I'm a poofter, or what?'

'A poofter?' Paddy retorted sarcastically. 'What's a poofter? Do you mean a homosexual? If so, you're using politically incorrect terminology that could be offensive.'

'A homosexual couldn't survive in this regiment even *if* he managed to get into it, which is highly unlikely. What's the next question, boss?'

'The next question,' Scott said, 'is the one we've just asked. We're trying to build a psychological profile here, so please answer the question.'

'I don't know why I'm not married yet. Maybe because my mum and dad fought cats and dogs and set me a bad example. I left home as soon as I could and I still don't like home life. I like life in the barracks, in the spider, and I don't want any kids to look after. That's all there is to it.'

'So why do you want to go on this mission?'

'Because we haven't had a proper mission in years and I joined this regiment to do exciting work. We rarely get that kind of work these days, so I want this job.'

'Do you want to know what it is?'

'I don't give a shit what it is. I just want to get into it.'

'Okay, Trooper, that's all we need to know,' Scott said. 'Send in Trooper Loomis.'

'Will do,' Blackwood said.

Trooper Sydney 'Syd' Loomis had been born to English parents in Glasgow, Scotland, but had grown up in Newcastle-on-Tyne and worked as a trucker before joining the Army. Eventually transferring to the SAS, he had served with the Air Troop during the Gulf War, then went undercover in Belfast, Northern Ireland, just before the peace initiative led to most of the army being sent home. A specialist in signals, he had employed state-of-the-art audio and laser surveillance systems for his undercover work for the then still highly active 14th Intelligence Group. His specialist crossover skill was medicine and, like Mad Mike Nicholson, he had studied the subject at Fort Sam Houston, Texas and Fort Bragg, North Carolina.

'That's thought by many to be the most intensive course

of its kind,' Scott remarked during a brief discussion about Loomis's medical skills.

'It sure seemed like it,' Loomis replied, looking weary at the very recollection of his intensive US special forces training.

'You must be good.'

'You can take that as read, boss.'

'What else are you good at?' Paddy asked, 'apart from getting into fist-fights when drunk?'

Loomis offered his snarling grin, then shrugged as if the question was a redundancy. 'You name it, I can do it,' he said. 'I've been in the Air Troop, the Mobility Troop, the Mountain Troop and the Boat troop, so there's not much I can't actually do. I'm neither the best nor the worst at any skill, but I'm pretty damned good at all of them. That makes me a damned good all-rounder and I'll bet you need that.'

'Have you any idea what kind of mission this is?' Scott asked him.

'No, boss, I haven't.'

'Do you care?'

'No, boss. I don't care if it's on land, sea or air; if where we're going is hot or cold; if we're going away for months or only days. I just want to get up and go – to get the fuck out of Hereford.'

'You're married,' Paddy said.

'That's pretty normal,' Loomis responded cockily.

'You don't have any children,' Scott said.

'We've only been married four months.'

'That's exactly the point, Trooper. You've only been married four months. Would you take a chance on leaving and not coming back, what with your wife being so young and all?'

'She knew what she was getting into when she married me and she'll have no complaints. You don't marry an SAS trooper and then complain when he pisses off on a job.'

'You might miss her when you're away,' Paddy said. 'You might turn all lovesick and droopy, which means you'd be useless.'

'I'm not the lovesick kind, Sarge,' Loomis replied, grinning savagely. 'I married for sex and I'll miss that, but we *all* miss that, don't we? What about you, Sarge?'

'I ask the questions, you answer.'

'I'll put a hold on my tongue, Sarge.'

'You don't have to,' Scott said. 'This interview is hereby concluded. Send in Trooper Blake.'

'Am I in or out?' Loomis asked.

'You'll know that within the hour,' Paddy said. 'Now send in Trooper Blake.'

'Right, Sarge. Thanks, boss.'

Blake was another good man who had fought his one war – the Gulf War – and had suffered the Peace Time Blues ever since. Fed up, like most of his mates, with being used for trivial local tasks or as a DS for new recruits, he instantly made it clear that he would take any kind of mission that was out of the ordinary. He gave bright answers to all the questions, seemed as reliable as he could be, and might have been chosen had it not been for the fact that he was close to the maximum age and the two interviewed after him, though no better than him in other respects, were that much younger and less tied up with family concerns.

The first of the final two was Trooper Arnie Basham, a massively proportioned, dazzlingly handsome, ebullient black man born in Kennington, London of mixed parentage, his father a local taxi driver, his mother a British citizen originally from Barbados. Enlisting in the regular army in 1990, when he was twenty, he turned out to be a natural soldier with an awful lot of energy to burn up. Easily bored, he transferred to 42 Commando Marines, proved himself in the Gulf War and then, after the war, transferred again, this time to the SAS.

'So why the SAS?' Scott asked him.

Basham raised his big hands in the air and rolled his beautiful brown eyes. 'Where else?' he exclaimed. 'I mean, nothing was happening, right? The Gulf War was over, the Red Berets were practically made redundant, and the SAS seemed the logical place to go for a man with ambitions. So I went for the SAS.'

'And ended up going to the Hereford School of Languages.'

Basham rolled his eyes again and shook his head forlornly. 'Yes, boss, I sure did.'

'A genius at languages, I gather,' Scott said. 'Spanish and German and Russian, according to this report.'

'That's a sweet report, boss.'

'So why do you want to go on this mission, since you don't even know what it is, let alone where you're going?'

''Cause I'm being pressured into becoming a teacher at the School of Languages and that isn't what I became a soldier for. I'm no desk man, boss. That Gulf War – I still haven't forgotten it. That's what I joined up for. So I need a new war, boss – or at least a good fight.'

'What are you?' Paddy asked. 'Some kind of cowboy?'

'I've never seen a cowboy movie in my life, so I hardly know what the word means. No, Sarge, I'm just a nat'ral-born soldier who's happier outdoors than in a classroom. Now that's not much to ask for and it certainly doesn't make me a cowboy or any other kind of wild percentage player. I just want something challenging in my life and I won't get that at language school.'

'According to this report,' Scott said, 'your specialist crossover skill is medicine.'

'Yes, boss.'

'You've kept that up?'

'It must say so in the report, boss – and those reports never lie, so we're told.'

'You're not always told the truth,' Scott said, grinning, 'but personal reports are usually accurate. Do you have any kind of family commitments that we don't know about?'

'My parents are both healthy and they're mad about my kids, so my family are well looked after when I'm not at home. I can travel. Believe me.'

'I believe you,' Scott said. 'Do you have any questions about the mission?'

'The only question I'd ask you won't answer yet, so I won't bother asking.'

'Present the question anyway,' Paddy said.

'Can I go?' Basham asked.

'We can't answer that question,' Scott said, 'though we think it's a fair one. You'll know one way or the other within the hour, now send in Trooper Welsh.'

'No problem,' Basham said.

Trooper Pete Welsh was the last to be interviewed and he entered the room with the look of a young man who would be glad to get the interview over and done with. Grinning nervously, crookedly, out of a lean, pock-marked face, tugging at the tufts of blond hair sticking out from under his beige, badged beret, he looked considerably younger than his thirty-one years – indeed, almost like a gangly adolescent. That appearance, Scott knew, was deceptive, since Welsh, a member of the Mobility Troop, had been with him and Paddy in Iraq. A Signaller with a specialist crossover skill in demolitions, he had proved his worth in Iraq not only by taking part in the extremely dangerous Pink Panther hit-and-run raids, but also by going behind enemy lines to blow up Saddam Hussein's communications towers and to locate and 'paint' Iraqi HAS with laser designators, before calling in the fighter-bombers to destroy them. He was, then, an essentially unsophisticated young man from Stoke-on-Trent, who just happened to be a top-notch soldier. Men like him, while never the leading lights of a Sabre squadron, could be the mortar between the bricks; therefore, they were always invaluable.

'You've gotten as far as this interview,' Scott informed him, 'because you did very well in all the tests and proved that you have what it takes for this particular mission.'

Welsh nodded his understanding, but said nothing.

'So now,' Paddy said, 'having proved that you're fit to go, we'd like to know exactly *why* you want to go.'

Welsh shrugged. 'Why not, Sarge?'

'You want to die young, is that it?'

'It's that dangerous, is it?'

'Yes,' Paddy said, then sat back, folded his arms across his chest and waited for a response. There was none.

'Excuse me,' Paddy said after a lengthy silence, 'but do you have anything to say about that?'

'Sorry, Sarge, about what?'

'About the fact that this mission is extremely dangerous.'

Welsh scratched at his pale, pimpled cheek and furrowed his brow, clearly not sure how to respond. 'Well . . .'

'Yes?' Scott prompted him.

Welsh shrugged, at a loss. 'No, boss, I've nothing to say. I mean, what did I join the regiment for if it wasn't for a bit of adventure? Danger doesn't come into it. I mean, what we did in Iraq – I mean, all of us, you two included – that was dangerous, wasn't it? But you don't really think about that, do you? I mean, why join the SAS if you do? That just doesn't make sense to me.'

Paddy, normally more demanding than Scott, nodded his agreement. He was impressed by this young man.

'So what's your personal situation?' Scott asked.

'Personal?'

Welsh could give the impression of being dim, but this, too, Scott knew, was deceptive.

'Yes,' Paddy said, 'personal. Do you have any major commitments or problems in your personal life?'

Welsh gave the matter his lengthy, silent consideration, then shook his head. 'No, Sarge.'

'Still not married, I note,' Scott said.

Welsh shook his head, meaning, 'No.'

'Anyone in mind?'

Welsh shook his head again.

'You don't have a girlfriend?'

Welsh shrugged. 'A bit of fluff here and there,' he managed, 'but nothing too serious.'

'Parents?' Paddy asked.

'What about them?' Welsh responded.

Paddy sighed with exasperation. 'What's their situation? Or, to be more precise, what's your situation with regard to them. Do you have any commitments?'

'Sorry, Sarge, what's that mean?'

This time, even Paddy could hardly conceal his grin, but he managed to keep his face straight when he said, 'Do they need looking after? What would their situation be if you didn't come back?'

'Same as always,' Welsh informed him. 'They still live together in Stoke-on-Trent and that's not going to change, no matter what becomes of me.'

'They're in good health?' Scott asked.

'They're only in their mid-fifties,' Welsh replied, 'and they're both fit as fiddles, so there's no problem there. They can look after themselves.'

'Thank you,' Paddy said, caught between his impatience and his amusement. 'That's all we wanted to know.'

'Oh, good,' Welsh said, nodding, again distractedly scratching his chin and looking like a rather dim schoolboy who had never fought a war nor killed in battle although, in fact, he had done both. 'So am I going or not?'

Scott and Paddy glanced at each other, trying to read each other's mind, then both of them broke out in a grin, realising that they had made up their minds about which six to take.

Turning back to the solemn-faced, expectant Trooper Welsh, Scott said, 'We haven't decided yet, but you'll be notified within the hour. We'll pin the list of names up on the notice board in the spider, with further instructions for those who've been chosen. You're now relieved, Trooper Welsh.'

'I sure am,' Welsh said, then he turned away and hurried out of the room.

When Welsh had closed the door behind him, Scott and Paddy separately wrote out their six personal choices and then exchanged lists.

They had both picked the same six men.

'So be it,' Scott said.

CHAPTER SEVEN

The dark cloak of death fell from the sky, over Dmitry, and made him cry out in his sleep. Awakened by his own fearful screaming, he jerked upright on his bed, dripping cold sweat, his heart racing dangerously, then felt the soothing warmth of the woman beside him as she moved closer. She was naked and hot, soft as only a woman could be, and when he looked down he saw her large brown eyes looking up, filled with grave concern. She was used to his many nightmares, which doubtless made him more human to her and, like most slaves, she was grateful for her slavery, which at least gave her life. Now she displayed her gratitude, reaching out to him, placing her small hand on his breast, over his racing heart, then sliding her outspread fingers down his chest, along his belly, to take hold of him and bring him back to life. She did it because she was still alive and that meant everything to her.

Dmitry smiled and groaned softly then rolled over to fall upon her, stretching out along her silk-smooth, burning body as she opened her legs to him. He entered her with ease, closing his eyes, concentrating, making the most of this brief moment of sensual pleasure before the real world rushed back. It came soon enough, when he had spent himself, convulsing, and he groaned and rolled off the gasping girl to stare up at the ceiling. The wind howled outside. The branches of trees were creaking and snapping. The only warm place in the whole world was in this bed, but he couldn't stay here forever. Life was harsh in the mountains.

'Breakfast,' he said, speaking Russian, and the Tajik girl slipped instantly out of bed, shivering from the shock of the sudden cold, to tighten a thick, white dressing gown about her body. Dmitry lowered his sleepy gaze and turned his head to follow her movements. Still held in the thrall of his nightmare, he needed distraction. She was the kind of girl he liked, slim, firm-breasted, with long legs and dark skin, her black hair tumbling around her large brown eyes with their silky eyelashes. He watched her hurrying across the floor, leaping lightly from one Turkish carpet to the other, avoiding the cold wooden boards of the floor, until she reached the *pechka*, the wood-fired stove, which she expertly topped up until it was blazing brightly. She shivered again, though this time with pleasure, as the heat warmed her body.

'Breakfast!' Dmitry repeated, now deliberately barking to make her think he was impatient, which in fact he was not. 'And warm the water for washing.'

'Yes!' Lalya exclaimed, also speaking Russian, obediently placing a big pot of cold water on top of the burning stove. 'There,' she added with a slight trace of defiance, then she turned away to prepare their breakfast, not saying another word.

Sighing, Dmitry sat upright on the bed, rubbing the sleep from his eyes and glancing about him. The house, if such it could be called, was made of logs cut from the trees of the surrounding forest. Similar to the houses in the *kyshtaks* – the Kyrgyz villages scattered throughout the forested hills around the Fergana Valley – it consisted of one very big room, in which he and the woman of his choice slept and ate, with an additional side room used as a toilet and bathroom. It was different, however, in that its walls, normally bare in the *kyshtaks*, were decorated with framed reproductions of famous Russian paintings, notably the supremely realistic works of the 'Wanderer', Ilya Repin, and the Symbolist works of Pavek Kuznetsov. Dmitry was drawn to the works of the latter because of their ethereal, dreamlike nature. When he studied Kuznetsov's work, which he did now, from his bed, he saw an eerily still and silent, timeless world of the kind he often saw, disturbingly, in his dreams.

'Krasee'vee!' he whispered with real reverence. For indeed, they were beautiful, if hauntingly so.

While the paintings on the walls were reproductions, Dmitry owned the originals of many of them, but kept them in his safe-deposit vault in a Moscow bank. They had been there, along with many of his other most valuable possessions, since his banishment to this hell-hole in the mountains of Kyrgyzstan. Much as he loved them and missed them, he could not bring them here because this camp (now almost as large as a *kyshtak*), though well hidden and rigorously guarded, could still be attacked by rival gangs who would, if they managed to take it over, set it to the torch. Dmitry couldn't bear the thought of that happening to his collection of old masters, most of which had been purchased illegally from well-placed *biznessmeni* in Moscow with the money gained from his ruthless profiteering.

Seeing that Lalya had entered the bathroom with the tub of steaming water, he rolled out of bed and slipped into a thick, warm dressing gown. He neither spoke to, nor smiled at, the girl as they brushed past each other in the bathroom doorway, she leaving, he entering, and he closed the door resolutely behind him to ensure his privacy. He had a mild paranoia about privacy in certain matters, a hangover from his childhood in a crowded log cabin in the bleak hills of Chechnya, and he could only attend to his ablutions when completely alone.

I cannot be completely sane, he thought, but who is these days?

When he had washed and shaved, he put on thermal underwear, a black, rolled-necked pullover, olive-green army pants and rubber-soled, lace-up leather boots, then left the bathroom and sat down to breakfast, facing Lalya over the large wood table. She was his slave, but he treated her like a human being and that made her a better slave.

While eating his breakfast of honeyed yoghurt, thickly buttered black bread and strong, sugared black tea in silence, Dmitry studied the girl opposite and found himself again wondering, as he had done so often, at the extraordinary resilience of human beings. Lalya had been one of those travelling the Road of Life when Dmitry and his men had made their last raid, ruthlessly killing the younger men and the elderly, then taking the women, young girls and children prisoner. As usual, they had brought them back here, to this camp hidden high in the mountains. The children had been separated from their parents, to be educated in the ways of the brigands, and the women and young girls had been, depending upon their age and appearance, either allocated domestic duties – cooks, housekeepers, general labourers – or been given to those men who needed women. They were not *exactly* turned into whores – they were more like common-law wives – but they certainly had no choice in the matter and, to make it worse for them, their Islamic principles regarding sexual matters were completely ignored. In short, they were slaves.

'Is the breakfast to your liking?' Lalya asked, while staring solemnly, penetratingly at him out of her big, *kakah'o*-brown eyes.

'The breakfast is the same as always,' he replied, 'so liking it or not is irrelevant.'

'I only want to please you—'

'That's advisable,' he interjected.

'—but you never let me see what you think.'

'If you displease me, you'll know about it soon enough and that's all you need to understand.'

The cruelty was deliberate. As the leader of more than a hundred brigands, Dmitry could pick any woman he wanted, changing her for another when the mood struck him. He had automatically chosen Lalya as the most attractive girl captured in the last raid on the Road of Life and, casting out the girl previously sharing his bed, moved Lalya in. He had also chosen her, perversely, because her mother and father had been killed during the raid and, even more so, because one of the young Tajiks personally executed by him had been her older brother. That execution had been witnessed by Lalya, who had howled like the damned and then gone into a state of shock for days. To make matters worse, though her younger brother, Taji, being only thirteen years old, had been spared, he was now being 'educated' by the brigands to become one of their gang. His education included vicious punishments for the slightest infraction – whippings, beatings, food deprivation and exposure to cold – and invariably these punishments were carried out in full view of the other prisoners as a warning to them not to displease their new masters. Thus, Lalya, with the rest of her family dead, was compelled to witness the torturing of her only surviving – and younger – beloved brother. She shed tears every time.

Which is exactly why Dmitry, in his perversity, had forced her to share his bed.

Since adolescence, after a traumatic childhood, he had been fascinated by the limits of human endurance, the strength of the will to live even when life seemed meaningless, the ability to transcend complete despair at the slightest flicker of hope. Dmitry had seen this in his own benighted childhood, in his reading of Russian history, in his more violent criminal activities; but he had seen it most of all (and certainly most ironically) in the reactions of the prisoners he had taken on the Road of Life. Since coming to this alien region and, in personal morality, going beyond the pale, he had been amazed at how much his prisoners, his victims, would endure simply in order to ... *live*. Since life, for Dmitry, appeared to be no great gift, he felt compelled to constantly push his victims to their limits and was continually surprised at just how vague those limits could be. Though in shock at the deaths of loved ones, deprived of their personal freedom, denied their former religious principles, humiliated beyond belief, they would desperately cling to life, or the mere hope of life, and do anything for it.

In this, Lalya was typical. Her parents had been killed in a raid led by Dmitry, her eldest brother had been cold-bloodedly executed by Dmitry even as she looked on, her only surviving relative, her youngest brother, was virtually a slave in Dmitry's camp, daily abused by Dmitry's men and, on top of all this, she was forced to share Dmitry's bed, to be his whore, despite her deeply felt Islamic principles. She should have hated him vehemently, only giving in to him when kicking and screaming in protest, but instead she had passively come to his bed and now seemed to need it as much as he did. Dmitry knew why this was so. It was because even involuntary sex was better than starvation; because slavery was better than death. No matter how much she might secretly despise him, Lalya wanted to live. Being alive was the bottom line.

'You always seem so cold and distant,' she said, staring solemnly at him, her dark eyes glittering with an emotion he could not comprehend and, therefore, did not trust. 'I had hoped that in time you might come to respect me, but you still treat me like dirt.'

'I treat you as the thing you are – as my slave – but at least I don't beat you. You live a decent life with me. You eat well and work only a little for it; even less than most housewives would do. You should ask no more than this.'

'I only ask to be shown more warmth.'

'How could you possibly receive it after what I've done to you and your family? You must despise me, even though you share my bed, so don't pretend otherwise.'

'I do not despise you. I accept you for what you are. You live a hard life here in the mountains and did what you had to do.'

'You're a liar, my sweet Lalya. You despise me and pretend not to only because you're frightened of being cast out or, perhaps, executed. Like most people, men and women alike, you'll do anything, dissemble in any way, to live. Let us not pretend otherwise.'

Yet he knew in his heart that not all men and women were like that. He could not forget how Lalya's brother had chosen to die rather than betray his friends. He could not forget it because he could scarcely believe it and, in truth, felt shamed by it. Therefore, he kept Lalya as his mistress not only because she was attractive, but because he was fascinated by her will to live and by how far she would let herself be degraded in order to have that life.

Maybe some night she'll try to cut my throat when I'm sleeping, he thought. If she does, I'll respect her more.

'Here,' he said, reverting to Russian, which Lalya spoke as well. 'Take these dishes away and bring me a glass of brandy, then go about your business, doing what housewives do. Don't annoy me by forgetting your place. Don't annoy me at all.'

'Can I ask you one favour?' she responded while rising from the table and gathering the dishes together.

'What?'

'About my brother . . .'

'No,' he cut her short. 'I'll do no favours for him. Count your blessings that he's not in his grave and leave it at that.'

'I just want . . .'

'No! Whatever it is, no! Now fetch me a brandy.'

'Yes,' she said softly, lowering her head and padding away on bare feet, carrying the dishes on a tray to the sink at the far side of the room. He watched her moving about there. She had natural grace and beauty. Had he not captured her, she would have become a Tajik wife and mother: fattened by childbirth and aged prematurely by hard work. In truth, she was lucky to be with him. He should get an award.

Pushing his chair back, he stood up and crossed the room to remove his *telogreika*, a thickly-quilted jacket, from the coathanger by the front door. He was putting the jacket on when Lalya returned with his large glass of brandy. After zipping up the jacket and putting on his furred cap with ear-protectors, he took the glass from her, swallowed the brandy in one gulp, felt it warming his belly, then opened the door and stepped out into the shocking, bitter cold of the morning.

Lalya closed the door behind him as he marched across the clearing between encircling log huts, blinking against the falling snow, but still dazzled by his sudden exposure to the glittering whiteness of the snow-covered hills around his well-hidden encampment. Below the soaring, glittering ice peaks of the mountains, the woodlands were spread out in all directions over the normally flower-strewn slopes, though the flowers were now covered in snow. Draped in that pristine white mantle, they looked beautiful and eerily empty, though Dmitry knew from personal experience that they were filled with wildlife, including brown bear, grey wolf, wild pig, lynx, snow leopards, deer, goats and the ubiquitous mountain sheep known as the *arkhar*. They had once also been teeming with other violent brigands, but these were now under Dmitry's control. Apart from the generally impotent activities of the border guards, he practically owned this whole area.

The camp itself was a carefully designed collection of log cabins and large huts, many with corrugated-iron roofs. The buildings were located strategically to form a great rectangle guarded on all sides by watchtowers containing machine-gun crews and spotters with high-power military binoculars and infrared thermal imagers for night viewing. Dmitry's men lived with their captured women (no legal wives were permitted) in the log cabins; the corrugated-iron constructions either housed armaments and supplies or were used as workshops for the processing of the opium gathered locally rather than being brought in, along the legendary Old Silk Road, from Afghanistan. The camp also had its own motor pool with massive snow ploughs, jeeps and four-ton trucks for the transportation of men and opium.

As Dmitry walked around the camp, greeting his lieutenants and troops, all of whom looked bulky, almost Neanderthal, in their quilted jackets, greatcoats and furred caps with ear-protectors, covered in the falling snow, he thought with little joy of how much his world had changed in recent years. The Soviet Union had been a major opium producer for decades, but in the late 1980s the authorities had virtually eradicated the trade by destroying the poppy fields and consficating the remaining drugs. Since then, however, with the end of Communist rule, cooperation between the Central Asian republics had virtually ceased, while the law enforcement agencies had all but collapsed, leaving the field wide open to local clans and criminal groups. The republics, including Kyrgyzstan and Tajikistan, had become major poppy-growing regions, producing their own opium, and numerous *Mafiya*-style gangs had been fighting each other for control of the supply routes through the mountains between Afghanistan and Osh. Originally operating in ethnic groups dating back hundreds of years, they had evolved, with the collapse of the Soviet Union, into criminal gangs filled with former KGB men who had expert knowledge of undercover and underworld operations. Those men were as ruthless as mobsters as they had been as KGB agents, torturers and killers – and Dmitry was one of them.

Now, recalling how his gross friend, Boris Surgeyevich, had not been offended when he had mocked him for not being a proper Russian – for being, in fact, a Georgian from Tbilisi – Dmitry smiled cynically. Boris had not taken offence because he knew that Dmitry, too, was a Georgian, though born and bred in Chechnya, where most of the hard-core *Mafiya* came from. This explained why Dmitry knew the face of his enemies and why he had been able to gradually take control of most of those in the mountains and, eventually, of the greater part of the mountainous territory through which the main supply route for the opium ran. There were still other gangs on the loose out there, but Dmitry, though he could never relax his vigilance, generally reigned supreme.

As usual, the camp was busy. Trucks and snow ploughs were moving constantly, noisily in and out of the camp, through the wide gates guarded by high watchtowers. Smoke was belching darkly from the chimneys of the workshops where the raw opium, in gum form, was being processed. First it was beaten into a homogeneous mass, then moulded into cakes, balls or blocks that could be wrapped in plastic and stored for months until it hardened. It was then cooked in boiling water until it dissolved and its impurities floated to the surface. After being passed through a fine sieve until its impurities were removed, it was brought to the boil again as pure, liquid opium and left to simmer until it had turned into a thick brown paste. This paste was pressed into trays, or moulds, and dried in the sun until it had the consistency of a clay that would harden until it matured. In this state it was ready for transportation to the dealer or addict. The people in the workshops, mostly teenage boys and women, sweating even in the fierce cold, were prisoners being used as slave labour to process the opium.

Dmitry made his rounds of the camp every morning, ritualistically checking that his defences were in order, that the opium processing was being done properly, and that all the other aspects of running such a large, illicit establishment – administration, domestic chores, sanitary arrangements and so forth – were running smoothly.

However, he had another, less pleasant duty to perform on a daily basis, which was passing judgement upon, and punishing, those guilty of infractions, be they his own men or prisoners. The sins of his own men invariably took the form of drunkenness, falling asleep on guard duty, petty theft or unwarranted violence against the female prisoners; but this morning, when he entered the log cabin known mockingly as 'the Kremlin', he was asked by his most trusted lieutenant, Misha Tolkachov, to pass judgement on two female prisoners who had been stealing moulds of mature opium and secretly selling them to one of Dmitry's truck drivers. The driver, in his turn, was selling the opium off to corrupt Kyrgyz border guards.

Entering the Kremlin, Dmitry found the terrified truck driver already standing in front of his desk, between the two visibly trembling women. Standing by the desk and gazing steadily at them, with his right hand resting lightly on the handgun holstered at his hip, was Misha Tolkachov. Misha was a young man with a finely featured pale face, pale grey, long-lashed eyes, and a body so slim that even in his heavy *shinyel*, or greatcoat, he seemed unnaturally fragile and wan. He was, however, as ruthless as Dmitry when it came to punishing sinners.

When Dmitry had taken his chair behind the desk, Misha repeated the offences of the three guilty parties and Dmitry, after listening patiently to what he already knew, then gave the three offenders the opportunity to defend themselves. This was a charade, as no excuse in the world would be acceptable to him, but he nevertheless went through the motions and listened just as patiently while the guard blubbered on about the dreadful cost of medical treatment for his sick wife which was why, as he explained, he had let himself be seduced by the two women into purchasing the opium from them. The driver's unacceptable excuse was followed by the entreaties of the two women who, one after the other, burst into tears, insisted that they had been desperate to smuggle money out of the camp to support their struggling families in Osh (almost certainly true, though this failed to move Dmitry) and then tearfully begged him to forgive them, or at least not punish them too severely for their dreadful 'mistake'.

Dmitry remained unmoved. With no show of emotion, he condemned the man to death. He then told the women that they would be moved out of the camp that afternoon, without the opportunity to say goodbye to their children, and sold to local slavers who used women as whores in the dreadful brothels located in primitive mountain retreats just across the border in Afghanistan. Those brothels, highly secret and certainly not known to the authorities, were used by soldiers, brigands, and a wide variety of often violent degenerates and drug addicts, many of whom had AIDS. No woman condemned to one of those brothels had ever come out again.

Though sobbing hysterically, the two unfortunate women were ushered out of the hut by armed guards to be taken away and tied up in the back of a truck in the motor pool, prior to transportation out of the camp later that afternoon, when almost surely they would be blue with cold and possibly half crazed with fear and despair. Nor was any time wasted on the unfortunate driver who was, without preamble, stripped to the waist and then marched, barefooted, through the howling wind and whipping snow, to one of the half dozen poles raised in the centre of the camp, placed deliberately in full view of all. He was tied to the pole and left there, freezing and shivering, looking fearful, while Misha went to fetch some armed soldiers and turn on the music selected by Dmitry for this particular event.

Dmitry knew all about the Nazi extermination camps and was intrigued by the rituals they had employed to add a dreadful irony to deeds that were already beyond imagining. Dmitry did, of course, love music and used it on these occasions not only to draw spectators to the execution, but to add an almost unbearable poignancy to the event whilst, at the same time, letting the onlookers know in what contempt he held the sinner about to die. In this instance, he had chosen his beloved Tchaikovsky's Sixth Symphony, the exquisite *Pathétique*. As the convicted man shivered and sobbed, covered in snow, numb with cold, and the poetic-looking Misha returned with three armed brigands, the grandiloquent, heart-rending despair of the symphony filled the air, emanating from speakers placed on the roof of a building nearby. The man's sobbing and the music wove into an eerie threnody as Misha lined the members of his firing squad up mere yards from their victim. The clearing was filled with onlookers, all called out by the music (which, they knew, represented a command, not a request) and they stood there, also shivering with cold, as Dmitry nodded at Misha. The latter raised his right hand in the air and then brought it down sharply.

The three riflemen fired at once. The man tied to the pole convulsed like a puppet on a string and then slumped in a bloody mess against his ropes. Instantly, Dmitry stepped forward, put the barrel of his pistol to the dead man's head and ritualistically delivered the *coup de grâce*. When this deed was done, another brigand cut the ropes, letting the man fall to the snow-covered ground. His body would be left there until last light as an example to everyone.

Turning away from the place of execution, Dmitry glanced across the camp and saw Lalya standing in the doorway of his house. Smiling, he nodded at Misha, indicating that his trusted lieutenant should fall in beside him. The two men walked side by side across the clearing, heading for the administration building where Dmitry had his HQ.

'We have a problem,' Dmitry said. 'According to a friend in Moscow, the British SAS have been ordered to seek us out and destroy us.'

'The *British*?' Misha queried.

'Yes. Don't ask me why – the reasons are irrelevant – but I've been marked for death, this camp's been marked for extermination, and the SAS have been given the task.'

'I know of the SAS,' Misha said, his dreamy pale grey gaze taking in the money-producing activities going on all around them. 'If it's them, it's serious.'

'Quite.' They had now reached Dmitry's HQ and he stopped at the steps of the large log-walled building and glanced over Misha's shoulder to see the black smoke spewing out of the chimneys of the workhouses where his own opium, the opium not from Afghanistan, was being processed. 'Almost certainly they'll be inserted by air somewhere in this vicinity, so I want you to send out special watch patrols, covering the whole of the Fergana Valley. When those British bastards drop out of the sky, I want to be informed.'

'You will be,' Misha said. 'Anything else?'

'Just make sure that those two women, when they're being driven out of here, are in the back of an open-topped truck where everyone can see them. That should be warning enough to the others not to try the same thing.'

'That makes sense,' Misha said, looking like a sensitive poet, but not remotely concerned for the dreadful fate awaiting the two unfortunate women. 'And I'll organise those watch patrols immediately,' he added.

'You do that,' Dmitry said.

Misha nodded and walked away. Dmitry stood on for a moment, whipped by the howling, freezing wind, soaked by the falling snow, recollecting the nightmare that had made him cry out so desperately that morning – that dark cloak of death falling over him like some great, carnivorous bird. Then he thought of the men who would, like that same great bird of doom, fall magically from the sky to seek him out. They would be led by one man – a man who had to be determined, perhaps even suicidal – and Dmitry tried to imagine what that man looked like and wondered what motivated him.

Determined or suicidal? Dmitry wondered. Either way, he's a man after my own heart and I'm looking forward to meeting him.

Startled by this thought, wondering what it implied (perhaps the first hint of the insanity that he had long expected would destroy him) Dmitry glanced across the clearing and saw Lalya, his slave and whore. She was still standing in the doorway of his ice-encased log house, her face turned in his direction, her features not distinguishable from this distance but no doubt accusing. He shivered, though not with the bitter cold, then turned away and entered his HQ to make plans for the future. This amused him because the future, as he knew from past experience, could not be predicted.

Come and find me, he thought.

CHAPTER EIGHT

'Kyrgyzstan,' Scott said, opening the briefing in a room in the Kremlin by uncovering his large map and indicating the location with a wooden pointer. 'Formerly the Kirgiz Soviet Socialist Republic. Mountainous territory dominated by the massive Tien Shan range, thrusting eastward into China, and by the Pamir range, lying to the south and spreading westward over most of Kyrgyzstan. These mountain ranges frame the Fergana Valley, which is where we'll insert.'

'So now we know where we are,' Mad Mike Nicholson said laconically. Like the other five men, he was seated in front of the raised dais in a folding steel-framed chair, wearing his standard-issue olive-greens (OGs) and his beige beret with winged-dagger badge. Paddy Devlin was seated beside Scott at the table on the raised dais. It was evening and the overhead lights were on, casting a harsh white glare down from the ceiling.

'The valley is continental and dry,' Scott continued, ignoring Nicholson's comment because this meeting, rather than being a formal briefing, was what the SAS referred to as a Chinese Parliament – an informal discussion about the plan of action in which everyone was free to say what he liked. 'The Pamir mountains, which is where we'll be heading ultimately, climb to snow and ice. There are five towns around the edge of the valley, all coal-mining towns except for Osh, a silk-processing centre. Russian and Ukrainian villages are scattered in the north, together with communities of Dungans, or Hui – Chinese Muslims. Old Uzbek settlements, known as *qishlaqs*, are widely scattered around the south and Kyrgyz *kyshtaks* – villages built during the Soviet period – plus collective and state farms, are scattered all over the area. Less than half of the population is urban. The remainder live in the foothill valleys where cotton and other crops, including the opium-producing poppy seed, are grown on irrigated land.'

'We can all get high,' Rudi Blackwood intoned, 'if life becomes too boring.'

'You try to get high on that opium,' Paddy Devlin said from his chair beside Scott, 'and I'll bring you down so low you'll be scraping sheep shit from your nostrils. So don't even consider it.'

'I take every word back, Sarge.'

'Sheep are raised on the steppe and alpine pastures,' Scott went on, ignoring the sideways glances and grins directed at the mischievous Blackwood. 'Besides the Kyrgyz, who live mainly in the mountains, there are Uzbeks in the foothill valleys and Russians and Ukrainians in the towns. We'll be staying well clear of the towns, but we may have to deal with Kyrgyz border patrols and their Russian taskmasters.'

'So what language do they use?' Parker, a specialist in languages, asked promptly, though still speaking in his quiet, oddly chilling manner.

'Russian and Kyrgyz,' Scott informed him.

'That's a member of the Turkic languages,' Arnie Basham pointed out, he also being a specialist in languages and proud of the fact. 'A subfamily of the Altaic languages.'

'I'm befuddled already,' Trooper Syd Loomis said, shaking his head from side to side in bemusement and tugging at his twisted upper lip. 'It might as well be bleedin' Swahili.'

'A lot of the locals speak both languages,' Scott informed

him, 'and almost certainly the few people we might meet will converse in Russian.'

'What's the local transportation system?' Pete Welsh asked, being a member of the Mobility Group and interested in what kind of vehicles he might have to beg, borrow or steal and then maintain.

'Lots of commerical traffic – heavy duty trucks, delivery vans, private cars and so forth – flowing mainly along the highway out of Osh, which we'll probably have to cross in order to reach the base of the Pamir mountains. In the mountains themselves, a network of highways is gradually replacing the winding paths formerly used by horse-riding or camel-riding traders and by men on foot.'

'So no shortage of mechanical transport if required,' Welsh said with a crooked, hesitant grin as he ruffled his untidy blond hair with ever-restless fingers.

'No problem at all.' Scott turned back to the blackboard and touched his pointer against the area marked as the Fergana Valley. 'As stated, we insert here in a nocturnal HALO drop, then make our way covertly across the irrigated fields to the so-called Road of Life that links Osh to the Pamir mountains. Once beyond the road, which we'll cross under cover of darkness, we'll make our way up into the mountains and, once above the snow line, commence to seek out and neutralise our target.'

'I love the sound of "neutralise",' Mad Mike said. 'It sounds so inoffensive.'

'Sounds as sweet as a Mars bar,' Trooper Syd Loomis added, his twisted upper lip turning his broad smile into a snarl. 'So who's our target and how do we find him?'

'A Russian *mafiya* drug baron named Dmitry Petrov, formerly a friend and bodyguard to President Yeltsin, but banished to Kyrgyzstan as a punishment for extensive criminal activities in Moscow. He can, however, fly in and out of Russia on short visits and he uses those trips to keep in touch with old *Mafiya* friends and take care of his finances in that country. Our concern is not with his criminal activities in Russia, but with his control of the opium-traffic routes through the Pamir mountains. According to our intelligence, his gang of brigands conducts bloody raids against local traders transporting opium along the Road of Life, which runs from Osh to Tajikistan, and then melts back into the Pamir mountains, hiding out in a camp located high above the snow line and, no doubt, heavily guarded. Thus, we have no sure way of finding him. We can only insert in the Fergana Valley, then make our way to the base of the Pamirs and, once there, try to pick up local intelligence about his whereabouts. Once we do, we'll seek him out wherever he's hiding.'

'Why not save ourselves a hike by parachuting directly into the mountains?'

'The mountains are too dangerous, filled with rocky out-croppings and gulleys, and so forth. They're made even more dangerous by the thick snow and ice on the upper slopes. Also, we want to insert well out of sight of Petrov's watch patrols and the Fergana Valley is some distance from the base of the mountains – a good twenty kilos. We're also using a HALO descent as a means of insertion to further minimise the risk of being observed.'

With a High Altitude, Low Opening parachute descent, the trooper exited the aircraft at a high altitude – usually 10,000 metres – but only opened his 'chute when he reached an altitude as low as 760 metres. It certainly minimised the risk of being seen but it was extremely dangerous.

'How many men does this Petrov have?' Killer Parker asked quietly.

'The only figure we have is over a hundred.'

'Over a *hundred*?' Mad Mike asked rhetorically while raising his thick black eyebrows in a questioning manner.

'That's right,' Scott said.

'To the best of our knowledge,' Paddy Devlin interjected from where he was sitting beside Scott, 'Petrov's men live in a log-cabin camp the size of a small village and hidden somewhere above the snow line of the mountain. It's not our intention to have an all out fire-fight with those men. What we would prefer to do, given the choice, is penetrate the camp, preferably under cover of darkness, and quietly take Petrov out, either as a prisoner or as a dead man. Have you any objections?'

'None at all,' Mad Mike replied.

'So how do we get to Kyrgyzstan?' Arnie Basham asked, his big brown eyes flashing brightly in his black face, his perfect white teeth gleaming. 'I mean, not many of our aircraft could fly that far direct – and we're talking about Russian territory to boot.'

'With the help of the Russians,' Scott informed him. 'This operation is being secretly backed by the Russians – they simply can't be seen to be involved – and so we'll fly out to Moscow as regular tourists on Aeroflot and be met at the other end by an officer of the Russian air force. That gentleman will take us through the airport as VIPs, bypassing customs. We'll then be driven in a truck to a Russian air force base located just outside the city. From there, after a good night's sleep and our usual pre-operational checks, we'll be flown to the drop zone. That final flight will take six-and-a-half hours.'

'That gets us in,' Mad Mike said. 'But how do we get out again?'

'If we fail to neutralise Petrov,' Paddy Devlin said bluntly, 'he'll certainly neutralise us – every man jack of us – and your question will become redundant. If, on the other hand, we succeed in our task, we'll contact the same Russian air force base, using our SATCOM system, and ask to be lifted out. We'll be returned to England the same way we left it, but in reverse order.'

'Weather?' Trooper Syd Loomis asked.

'We're actually flying out at the best time of the year,' Scott said, 'when it's neither too hot nor too cold. However, even in April we'll be faced with uncomfortable extremes in weather. The Fergana Valley, where we insert, will be hot during the day and bitterly cold at night. The upper slopes of the Pamir mountains will be freezing, with high winds and a lot of snow-storms; perhaps even the white-out blizzard they call the *myatel*. Because of this, we'll have to take along two different sets of clothing: normal DPMs for the Fergana Valley and Chairman Mao suits for the mountains.'

He meant by this that when in the Fergana Valley they would wear standard-issue British Army clothing of disruptive pattern material – DPMs – while in the mountains they would change to British Army quilted, insulated suits – Chairman Mao suits – specially designed for troops operating in extremely cold conditions.

'Communications?' Trooper Pete Welsh asked, knowing that as a Signaller he would be placed in charge of his team's communications.

'PRC 319 radio systems for communication between the two teams when they're far apart. Landmaster III hand-held transceivers for communication between individuals. We'll also have Precise Lightweight GPS – global positioning systems – to give us read-outs of our exact locations and help us move accurately through unfamiliar territory. No SARBE radio beacons because we won't require communication with support aircraft; but we will take along a SATCOM system to enable us to contact the Russian air force when it's time to be lifted out.'

'Weapons?' Killer Parker asked; this always had been, and remained, his major preoccupation.

'The ones you were asked to fire during the tests to get onto this mission: the SA-80 assault rifle, the MP5 sub-machine gun, the Barrett Light .50 rifle, the ever-reliable GPMG and the Five-seveN pistol. Also, a couple of M72 rocket launchers with HEAT warheads, which could be useful for taking out enemy strongholds or when attacking that mountain retreat. M79 and M203 grenade launchers, and a good supply of Claymore mines.'

'Explosives?' Trooper Rudi Blackwood asked, being a specialist in demolitions and always keen to blow up something or other.

'We may have to blow mountain bridges behind us or place

explosives in the enemy camp once we find it, so we'll want whatever's required for those two tasks.'

'C3 and C4 plastic explosives,' Rudi said enthusiastically. 'TNT slab explosive. Semtex. M118 demolition charges. Electrical initiators and timing fuses.'

'I'm sure you're right,' Scott said.

'What about scran?' Syd Loomis asked, meaning food. Loomis was a man who thought a lot about his belly.

'Proper rations to begin with, enough to last fourteen days, gradually reducing to survival kit. Then, if we're still alive but empty-handed, we forage off the land.'

'Fun and games,' Arnie Basham said laconically. 'There's plenty of sheep in them thar hills, so we should have no problems.'

'You skin it, I'll eat it,' Syd said. 'Just make sure it's not moving.'

'Any questions?' Paddy Devlin said to discourage an outbreak of bullshit.

'Yeah,' Killer Parker responded. 'When do we move out?'

'Tomorrow night,' Scott told him. 'You'll spend most of the day preparing for the trip – collecting, checking and packing weapons, and so forth – then move out of here at six in the evening, wearing civilian clothing. You'll be transported in hired vans to the Household Cavalry Barracks in Albany Street, Regents Park, and spend the night there. The following morning the same vans will take you to Heathrow Airport for the flight to Moscow. You'll travel as ordinary civilians. Your kit and armaments will be flown separately in a C-130 Hercules transport to the Russian air force base outside Moscow, where you'll pick it up when you get there. The rest you know. Are there any more questions?'

The six men in the chairs glanced at one another, then all shook their heads from side to side.

'Good,' Scott said. 'Dismissed.'

CHAPTER NINE

Dmitry performed the execution personally in broad daylight while Lalya was looking on from the porch of his log house. He did it quite deliberately, in cold rage and calculation, by marching up to the thirteen-year-old boy where he was kneeling in the middle of the clearing, being beaten methodically by some of Dmitry's brigands, grabbing his hair and jerking his head back. He placed the barrel of his handgun to the boy's temple and blew his brains out.

As Dmitry released the dead boy to let him flop face down into the snow, which already was being stained with spurting blood, Lalya let out a wail of grief lacerating in its intensity and jumped down off the porch to run to her brother's prostrate body.

Dmitry saw her coming, rushing and stumbling through the deep snow, wearing only her white dressing gown, not concerned for her modesty, covering her ears with her hands as if to blot out the sound of that single shot – as if to blot out reality – and still screaming like an animal being slaughtered. He turned to block her path, to keep her away from her brother's body, and nodded at the pale-faced, pale-eyed Misha, who instantly stepped forward to grab her and stop her advance. She struggled violently in his arms, sobbing and screaming abuse at once, but Misha held her firmly, almost squeezing the breath out of her, while looking to Dmitry for further instructions.

'Don't let her escape,' Dmitry said coldly. 'Don't let her near him.' Ignoring Lalya's wails of grief, which did not sound remotely human, he glanced down at the dead boy, then said to the four men standing around him, the ones who had been beating him so methodically and brutally, 'Take him away and bury him. *Now!*'

Impelled into action by the whiplash of his voice, the men each took one of the boy's extremities and carried him away from where he had fallen, to the waste ground beyond the motor pool, which was used as a burial ground. A lot of bodies were buried out there, all in unmarked, snow-covered graves.

'*Nyet!*' Lalya screamed.

Turning away from that bloody patch of snow, Dmitry observed Lalya with detached curiosity and a rage so cold he hardly knew he was experiencing it. He did know, however, that he was intrigued by her resilience, by what seemed to be her acceptance of all the horrors he had inflicted upon her (the deaths of her parents and older brother, his deliberate brutalising and humiliation of the boy he had just shot) and by what seemed to be her willingness to surrender to him, to forgive him for his past transgressions, no matter how normally unforgivable. He had been pushing her to the limit to ascertain just how much more she could take.

Still fascinated by the limits of human endurance, by how far people will sink in order to stay alive, he had felt that he was starting to love her even as he despised her. This in itself was a shock – the very idea that he could love someone – and perhaps it had frightened him enough to make him want to kill off the feeling before it could take hold and soften him to a dangerous degree.

There was that – he could not deny it – but there was also his cynicism; his refusal to believe that she could forgive him for what he had done. They made love on a bed of nails, he pressing her down upon it, inflicting pain and waiting for her to cry out, which so far she had not done. Not, at least, until he had committed the ultimate outrage by killing the only surviving member of her family.

Now, in Misha's arms, she was struggling violently and howling like the damned, her dark cheeks streaked with tears. He needed to know if she would accept even this once her grief had subsided.

'Let's take her back to the house,' he said to Misha, 'and lock her up in the bathroom until she calms down.'

'*No!*' Lalya screamed again, struggling even more frantically to escape from Misha's strong arm-lock and looking with dazed, disbelieving eyes to where the four men who had been beating her brother were now carrying his dead body to the graveyard and just about to disappear around the back of the motor pool. 'I have to see him! Let me pay my last respects – at least that! *Don't do this to me, you bastard!*' She was staring at Dmitry with eyes enlarged by grief and rage while struggling even more frantically to break loose from Misha's steely grasp.

'Perhaps . . .' Misha said hesitatingly, about to soften for once and recommend this one act of mercy.

'No!' Dmitry snapped, determined to push Lalya as far as she would go and ascertain her breaking point. 'He's Kyrgyz trash and will be buried like trash,' he added deliberately, loudly. 'Now let's get her inside.'

When Lalya released another inhuman wail of grief, kicking and flailing like a wild thing, Dmitry stepped forward to take hold of her free arm and twist it up behind her back. Together, as she wailed and wriggled, still trying to break free, he and Misha forced her back to the house, sometimes pushing her, sometimes practically dragging her, both finding it difficult to keep hold of her, so violently was she struggling. Eventually, however, they managed to get her as far as the porch, where she pressed her bare feet, already turning blue from the cold, against the bottom steps and attempted to push herself backwards, away from the house, to prevent them from forcing her up.

'No!' she screamed. '*No!*'

Dmitry was still holding his pistol in his left hand and he brought the barrel down hard on each of Lalya's shins, one after the other, making her cry out in pain as her feet came involuntarily off the steps. Then he and Misha half-dragged, half-pushed her up into the house.

'The bathroom!' Dmitry bawled when they were inside. Lalya still struggled frantically between them, sobbing helplessly and letting out demented, almost deafening howls of grief.

'No!' she screamed again, struggling even more frantically to break free. 'You bastards! You filth!'

Dmitry holstered his handgun, then slapped her face and grabbed her by the hair, to tug it brutally and repeatedly, forcing her forward as Misha, still holding her in an arm-lock, pushed and dragged her across the room. She was still howling like an animal when they threw her bodily into the bathroom, making her crash face-first into the far wall. There, after turning around to face them, her eyes wet and wild, she slipped in a quivering, sobbing heap to the bare boards of the floor.

Resolute, Dmitry slammed the door closed, then turned the key in the lock.

'Bastards!' Lalya screamed. 'Filth!'

She sobbed loudly again as Dmitry placed the key in the pocket of his quilted jacket and turned away to walk back across the room, followed by Misha.

'Come on,' he said. 'Let's get the hell out of here. I can't stand the noise.'

When they left the house, Dmitry closed and locked the front door, then he and Misha walked side-by-side across the clearing, passing the place where Lalya's brother had died. Fresh snow, Dmitry noted, was already covering up the blood-reddened patch, thus proving the impermanence of all things on earth.

We're all manure for the future, he thought. A mere mountain of bones.

Misha glanced sideways at the same piece of ground, his poet's features revealing nothing, then he rubbed the falling snow from his eyes and said, 'Why did you do that?'

'The boy was a nuisance,' Dmitry replied, determined to show no remorse, 'who didn't take well to his training and showed little improvement with repeated punishments. We can't keep useless people in this place and he was clearly useless.'

'He was all right,' Misha said, his pale grey gaze moving constantly left and right, up and down, instinctively checking that everything was normal: the men working in the motor pool, the guards behind the machine guns in the watchtowers, the snow ploughs and trucks moving noisily in and out of the camp, the smoke billowing up from the chimneys of the workshops, indicating that opium production was progressing. He even cast his pale gaze to the mountains soaring above the trees, always on the lookout for enemy brigands who might try to attack them. 'He was only punished so much because you asked the men to be especially tough on him. It really wasn't his fault. So why did you do it?'

Dmitry raised both his hands in the air as if to say, 'Why not?'

'That's hardly an answer,' Misha said, understanding the gesture. 'Was it to punish the woman?'

Dmitry smiled. 'You're very bold, Misha. You're also perceptive. Yes, I suppose it *was* a kind of punishment – though certainly it was also something else.' He hesitated, wondering how he could explain to his intelligent friend what he could barely comprehend himself. 'I was punishing her, I suppose, because she kept nagging me about the boy, begging me to make his life easier, even asking me to take him away from the men and put him into my house as another servant. I told her many times to stop doing it, told her it annoyed me, but she just wouldn't give up on it and finally, when she started in again, I decided to get rid of the problem by getting rid of her brother.'

'That solves one problem by creating another,' Misha said. 'Surely, if she hated you before, she's now going to hate you even more.'

'I agree,' Dmitry said. 'And maybe that's the something else I was talking about. I despise human weakness, the need to live at any cost, and because of this I'm compelled to either punish the weak – to make them reap what they sow from their very weaknesses – or to obliterate them entirely from my sight. On the other hand, I admire the strong. They may be evil, but they have dignity and don't live on bended knees. So, admiring the strong and despising the weak, I push people to their absolute limits in order to know what they are. My men here are strong and ruthless – yes, even you, Misha – you, who have the mind of a poet and the soul of a killer. Every single one of them, including you, only gained my respect and trust when he had proved that no deed was too foul for him if it brought him some benefit. That's why this camp is composed of masters and slaves. The whole world is the same, in truth.'

'And the woman?' Misha asked, being of a philosophical nature, always questing for Truth.

They had reached Dmitry's administrative building, which included the office he used as his headquarters. After mounting the steps to the porch, they entered the building. There were two offices inside: one for Dmitry's clerks, all female prisoners; the other for Dmitry alone. He led Misha into the latter and took his chair behind the desk. Misha took the chair facing him.

'The woman?' Dmitry shrugged. 'She's a special case,' he said. 'As a woman, she attracts me; as a human being, she intrigues me.'

'That's a dangerous combination,' Misha observed.

Dmitry smiled. 'Yes – and so how can I resist her? I know that she hates me even as she shares my bed and this makes the sex all the more exciting for me – my thrill comes from this conquest. But is it a true conquest? Has she really surrendered her will to me? I doubt it – I think she's stronger than that – and that's what I have to find out.'

'If she were truly weak,' said Misha, 'you wouldn't find her attractive.'

'Exactly, my friend. So I had to push her to the absolute limit and see how she responded.'

'You'll find out when you let her out of that toilet. She might cut your throat.'

'If she doesn't try, I'll probably be disappointed.'

'And if she does?'

'Alas, self-preservation will force me to kill her, but at least I'll know that I wasn't attracted to a woman not worthy of me.'

'You're egotistical and perverse,' Misha said. 'A man who will always kill the thing he loves. You live right on the edge.'

'To live anywhere else is to die of boredom, the worst torture of all. Anyway ...' Dmitry raised and lowered his hands in a languid gesture, signifying defeat. 'Who knows what moves the mind and heart of man? What about the watch patrols?'

'They're in place all around the Fergana Valley, but have seen nothing yet.'

Dmitry felt disappointed and frustrated at this news. He was a child who wanted to smash all his toys, but they were locked in another room. He had to wait for someone to come along and unlock the door. In this case, that person would drop out of the sky, but clearly in his own good time.

'So what happens when they arrive?' Misha asked. 'The drop zone will almost certainly be too far away for us to close in on them before they move on.'

'Let them move on,' Dmitry said. 'Their destination is no mystery. They're coming to seek us out and that means they have to cross the Fergana Valley and then climb these mountains. They're coming here secretly, but with the help of our own countrymen, and that means that their DZ could be protected by Russian troops. For that reason, we can't afford the risk of engaging in a major fire-fight when they land on the ground. Instead, we'll simply observe them, ascertain their strength, and then deal with them as we see fit. So when they parachute into the valley, just let me know and we'll play it by ear from there, on a day-by-day basis. It's a game I look forward to.'

Now it was Misha's turn to smile, which in normal circumstances he rarely did. 'As I said, you're egotistical and perverse. But even that doesn't explain why you actually seemed thrilled to know that you've been condemned to death by your own peers – the present Russian government – and that your executioners are already on their way here.'

'To be condemned is not to die,' Dmitry said, 'and I like a good fight.'

'This fight could be your last.'

'Every fight can be your last, so why is this one so different?'

'It's different because it's the SAS and they're being helped by our own government. That means it's serious.'

'The more serious it is, the greater the challenge – and I find that exciting.'

'Is that all it is?'

'What more could there be, Misha?'

'I feel that you're *pleased* that these men are coming and that your pleasure, like so much of you, is perverse.'

'Are you suggesting that I'm suicidal?' Dmitry asked, not smiling at all.

Misha merely rolled his eyes and pushed his chair back to stand up. 'I'm not sure what I mean. Regarding you, I'm *never* sure what I mean. Perhaps that's what real friendship is.'

'Yes, perhaps,' Dmitry said. 'Anyway, let me know as soon as your watch patrols see anything.'

'I will,' Misha said. 'In the meantime, keep your eye on your woman.'

Dmitry smiled again. 'Yes.'

When Misha left the office, Dmitry slumped into his chair,

his hands clasped behind his head, and thought of his philo-sophical friend's comments with no great deal of pleasure. In fact, Misha's comments had only confirmed for him that his urge to see the face of the man who was coming to find him – the leader of the SAS force – was at bottom the urge to be taken to the very edge of the unknown and look into the abyss.

In truth, he *was* weary of life, having lived too much too quickly, being older than his age, if only through harsh experience, and now he knew that he had the need to push himself to the limit – just as much as he needed to do it to others – because nothing less than total involve-ment with life, therefore with death, could make him feel truly alive. He believed in God Almighty and in the devil and was torn between the two, feeling that he had been rejected by the former and so yearning for acceptance by the latter.

A true Russian! he thought.

Confused and restless, he inhaled some of his own opium, waited until it had fired his brain, then tried, with no great deal of success, to concentrate on the papers on his desk: facts and figures about the opium trade, his personal profits and losses, plus intelligence on old friends and enemies, both in Russia and here in Kyrgyzstan. The opium, however, while illuminating his mind, sent his thoughts scattering like starlight through the cosmos, defying time and space, yet always returning to the image of Lalya, with her distraught, tearful, infinitely haunting eyes.

He was obsessed with those eyes, their dark brown, opaque depths, at once concealing and seductive, drawing him in against the white of the pillowcase even as he was convinced that her hatred, though carefully suppressed, was ultimately murderous. He had wanted to break her spirit, to have her confirm his contempt for virtue. Now, at last, he might have broken her, driven her over the very edge, cast her down into the abyss. If he had failed, if she returned to his bed, he would despise her and kill her.

Ironically, doing that might kill him and maybe that was what he really wanted.

Tormented by his teeming thoughts, Dmitry inhaled some more opium, let himself slip into a trance, the blessed peace of that other, more incandescent reality, and emerged to the failing light of the early evening when the mountains, as glimpsed through his office window, glinted eerily, reflecting pale moonlight.

The mountains, without the benefits of opium, looked as inviting as hell.

Leaving his office, he made his way back across the clearing – deliberately avoiding the spot where Lalya's brother had died – and entered his log house, at once fearful and excited, his senses heightened by the opium and his every impulse geared to what he would find when he opened the bathroom door.

Lalya was still seated on the floor, still wearing her dressing gown, her chin resting on her raised knees, her hands clasping her shins. When she looked up, her brown eyes, which had been wild and wet with grief, were dry and perfectly calm.

'I hate you,' she said.

'You always did,' he replied. 'The question is, what are you going to do about it?'

'What can I do?' she said.

Despising her, Dmitry turned away and said, 'Kill yourself, you Islamic whore.'

He really wanted her to do it because her death would solve his problem. Believing that she just might, thus confirming his disdain for life, justifying his contempt for weakness, he left the house again, giving her all the freedom she needed, and went to the bar beside the motor pool to have some drinks with his men. He was still drinking hours later, close to midnight, when the fire broke out.

Between the opium and the vodka he was slow to react when one of his guards rushed into the bar to inform him that his log house was on fire. Trying to grasp the import of this, Dmitry glanced left and right, scanning the faces around him, all flushed with drink or drugs, and only when the guard had repeated his message and, more effectively, when the sirens placed around the camp started wailing their alarm call, did he realise that what he had heard was correct. It sobered him up on the instant.

'*My* house?'

'Yes, boss, your house!'

He rushed out into the freezing, snow-swept night to see the flames illuminating the darkness around the forested foothills of the mountains. His house was, indeed, on fire, with flames visible through the front windows, but men and women, all prisoners, were already forming a chain to pass buckets of water from the water-tower to the men frantically dousing the burning building.

Rushing up to those men, thinking only of his paintings – his reproductions – not to mention his beloved books, Dmitry saw that the fire was not too fierce and that it could be contained. Glancing left and right, he saw no sign of Lalya and wondered, with a fear that surprised him, if she was still inside. When he asked the nearby men about her, if they had seen her, they all shook their heads and their boss, Pavel Pushkin, one of Dmitry's most trusted men, said, 'We don't know if she's inside or not, but we haven't seen her.'

'How bad is the fire?'

'It's under control, boss, but the inside – please expect it – will be a mess.'

Still shaken by the fear he had unexpectedly felt for Lalya, Dmitry could do little other than to wait until the fire had been extinguished, which it was, eventually. Even then, he remained outside while Pushkin's men entered the building to put out the last of the flames and ensure that it was safe to enter. Emerging, coughing smoke from his lungs, the pink-faced, obese Puskin shook his head from side to side and said, 'She isn't there, boss.'

'And the rest?'

'The inside of the house is a mess, as I said it would be, but the house can certainly be renovated with no great deal of trouble. Most of the contents, unfortunately, are gone for good.'

'The paintings and books?'

Pushkin shook his head again, looking histrionically bereaved, though he hadn't read a book in years and had certainly never looked at a painting. 'Sorry, boss. They're all ruined.'

'That bitch,' Dmitry said.

Yet entering the ruined house, he felt an odd exultation, a feeling of vindication, knowing that Lalya had set the house on fire. When he saw the burnt books and scorched, virtually melted paintings, he understood exactly why she had done so.

She struck at what was most precious to me, he thought. She wanted me to know how much she despised me and she certainly achieved that.

The pain of his loss was grievous – the loss of the paintings and books – but his exultation sprang from the knowledge that Lalya had defied him, taken her revenge, accepted almost certain death (as had her older brother) rather than be degraded and tormented any more. She had shown him that she had her limits, her pride, and he respected her for it.

Respect? No, it was more than that. He had been attracted to her beauty and loved her courage while, at the same time, despising what he had erroneously imagined was her surrender to him. In fact, she had not surrendered to him – she had fooled him – and he loved her for that.

She was the kind of woman he could have loved, but now – as she had proved with this act – she hated him totally. She had run away, humiliating him in front of his men, and so, in order to survive himself, he would have to find her and kill her. This was, in Dmitry's view, the punishment that God had planned for him.

Either Lalya, he thought, or that SAS man who is coming to find me. Let it be one or the other.

'Find that bitch,' he said to Pushkin. 'She can't be very far. If she's not still in the camp, find her and bring her back. And if you find her outside the camp, I want to know how she got out. Do you understand?'

'Yes, boss.'

But before Pushkin even had the chance to turn away, Misha materialised out of the snow-driven darkness, his pale face narrowed to a thin wedge by the upturned collars of his *shinyel*. 'I've just had word from one of my watch patrols,' he said. 'They saw what they thought were parachutes – they reckon over a dozen: men and equipment – descending in darkness over the Fergana Valley.'

'That's the SAS,' Dmitry said, feeling an enormous sense of relief and, perhaps even more than that, great expectation.

'I would assume so,' Misha said. 'So what do we do?'

'We track them with our watch patrols,' Dmitry said, 'until the time is ripe. Then, like the black-widow spider, we draw them in and devour them.'

'And your woman?' Pushkin asked, looking nervous to have even raised the subject. 'Do we still go out and find her?'

'I wouldn't bother searching the camp,' Misha said, 'because my men have already done so.' He looked directly, fearlessly, at Dmitry. 'I don't know how she managed to do it, but she's certainly gone.'

Dmitry turned to stare outside the camp, beyond the chimneys still pouring black smoke into the ink-black sky, producing opium and wealth and ever-expanding human corruption, to the moonlit snow covering the dense woodlands on the lower slopes of the mountain. Lalya was somewhere out there, a frail figure, poorly clothed, desperately trying to make her escape with nowhere to go. In defying him, she had accepted suicide and that was why she was out there. She would probably freeze to death before she starved and then the snow would cover her up.

'Forget her,' Dmitry said, torn between his grief and his exultation. 'We have no time to waste on Kyrgyz trash.' Then, when his exultation turned unexpectedly to pain, he turned to his friend Misha, his poetic, pale-eyed killer, and said, 'We'll have our fun and games with the SAS. Let's see what they can do.'

The SAS were descending into the Fergana Valley and this thought gave him comfort.

CHAPTER TEN

Scott was plummeting down like a stone but he had no sense of movement, place or time. The HALO descent was an experience like no other, almost like a dream, making him feel bodiless in a featureless void only illuminated by the stars that filled the darkness as silvery streaks of light. Those lights were moving constantly, shooting upwards as he descended, disappearing abruptly into the black canopy above to be replaced just as quickly by others. He was falling through the clouds, seeing the stars through the clouds, but the only thing that told him that this was so was the sight of those stars, appearing, disappearing, reappearing and shooting upwards in silvery, magically glowing streaks.

The stars, of course, were not really shooting upwards; it was he who was moving, falling out of the dark sky, through darker clouds, into a bottomless black pit. Falling in a dead silence.

It had not been so at the start, when he first leapt out of the aircraft, an old Bombay transport, purchased cheaply by the Russians, that had shuddered, creaked and roared for six-and-a-half hours until it arrived at the DZ in the Fergana Valley. The noise in the transport had become even louder when the Russian air force despatcher opened the hatch and the wind rushed through the belly of the aircraft like some ravenous, roaring beast. Standing at the hatch, tightly holding the handgrip, Scott had looked down on that vast expanse of darkness out of which the beast roared and imagined that he was staring into hell. Between him and the ground there was nothing but over 10,000 metres of thin air, pitch black except for the deeper blackness of a heaving sea of dense cloud.

He had seen his seven men out – first Sergeant Paddy Devlin, then his two corporals, Parker and Nicholson, then the four troopers, Blackwood, Loomis, Basham and Welsh – patting each on the shoulder as he stood there, poised like a man over the abyss, the wind roaring and hammering at him, that great dark void below him, before launching himself bodily into the howling maelstrom. They had plummeted to earth, one after the other, and then he had hurled himself out, holding his breath, his eyes closed, to drop like a stone.

It was like falling through the eye of a hurricane – beating wind and awesome noise. Then, abruptly, there was silence and he opened his eyes again.

He had to let himself fall for over 9,000 metres without the benefit of his parachute.

Now he was in free fall, disassociated from his own body, ears hurting, limbs useless, deprived of sense of direction, set free from the aircraft's slipstream and catching only erratic glimpses of the stars – their light distended and distorted, forming streaks of rising white light. He fell through cloud after cloud, between visibility and the lack of it, gasping for breath as time stood still and reality dissolved, counting off the seconds – which told him how far he had fallen – and thinking of his wife and son with a pain that consumed him entirely.

I'll come back, he thought. I'll return and make amends. I'll annihilate the bastard who caused this grief and then I'll look to the future. If I fail, the future won't matter because it won't be there waiting for me. I want this drug-peddling filth.

He fell through eternity.

Gradually, however, he saw circular blobs of white far

below in the expanding darkness, drifting languidly this way and that, descending towards other, motionless white blobs even farther down. Those white blobs – other parachutes: some on the ground, some still descending – were expanding at ever-increasing speed, which meant that he was approaching the ground. Having counted off the seconds and calculated the distance, he knew that he'd dropped approximately 9,000 metres and now had little over 750 metres between him and the ground.

He jerked at the ripcord.

He heard the parachute being released, making a soft snapping sound, and glanced up to see it billowing out like a white spume, directly above his head. At first he was jerked upwards like a puppet on a string, but violently, dangerously, then he was swung sideways, left to right, more languidly, as the parachute opened completely to slow his descent.

Packs of weapons, explosives and supplies, all tied to parachutes, had been tipped out directly over the DZ before the first of the men jumped out. Now, as the parachute above him billowed out to its full expanse and the violent jerking of the harness straps ceased, he returned to the vertical landing position. Glancing directly below him, he saw the white flowers of those other parachutes below the still-descending parachutes of the rest of the men. With his rate of descent greatly reduced, he could hear the rushing of the wind all around him and saw the parachutes on the ground growing bigger – or seeming to do so – as he dropped towards them.

Suddenly, the ground was rushing up at him, distant hills soared high from nowhere, and then he heard the wind again, felt his body, the strong pull of gravity. He saw the men who had jumped out before him falling to earth beneath their collapsing, manically flapping parachutes and rolling away from them. Holding himself upright, heels together, he gripped the rigging lines, preparing to swing himself clear of anything potentially harmful, such as power cables or the branches of trees. In the event, he hit only the ground, though he did so with a painful jolt. He let his knees bend, relaxed his body as he fell sideways, then rolled over and was dragged a good distance by his still open 'chute. Rolling over again, this time onto his belly, he managed to control the rigging lines and collapse the parachute's wildly tugging, snapping canopy. Though breathless and bruised, he punched the release box, unravelling his harness, then climbed to his feet.

Glancing about him, he saw the other seven men, spread out over a great distance, either disentangling themselves from their 'chute harnesses or already free and pulling the 'chutes together to bury them. They had landed on a broad, moonlit plain, mainly flower-strewn, subalpine pasture, but with stretches of sand and gravel in between, where it blended into the desert a few miles away. There were mountain ranges to the west and the north. Those in the north, Scott knew, belonged to the massive Tien Shan system, thrusting eastwards all the way to China; those in the west were the Pamirs, rising up to icy peaks, their lower slopes, now hidden in darkness, located just beyond the road that cut through the Alay Pass to join Osh to the Pamir region of Tajikistan. That was the road his patrol would have to cross if it managed to get that far.

Still gazing about him, appreciating the moonlight on the flat plain, he saw that there were woodlands on the lower slopes of the nearby hills and west of the valley. He would have to take the men through those woods to the west in order to reach the road beyond them ... and those woods could be dangerous.

Turning around slowly until he had come full circle and surveyed the land in every direction, he was pleased to see no sign of movement. They were all alone out here.

Most of the troopers, he noted, had already buried their parachutes and were now spreading out to collect the widely scattered packs of equipment, weapons and supplies. Using his own spade, which was attached to the belt of his DPM tunic, along with his commando dagger and holstered Five-seveN pistol, he dug a hole in the ground at his feet, buried his parachute, then hurried across the plain to help the other men bring in the equipment. Knowing just what to do, they worked together quickly, in total silence, releasing the supply packs from the 'chutes, burying the latter, then carrying the former from where they lay to a single pile located near the centre of the DZ. Only when all of the packs had been gathered together did they break them open and distribute their contents amongst themselves.

Every man ended up with a bergen rucksack packed tightly with food, water, personal medical kit, clothing, toiletries and spare ammunition. They were all given a personal weapon (either an SA-80 assault rifle or the MP5 sub-machine gun); a Landmaster III hand-held transceiver; and a variety of hand grenades – but each also had something heavier to carry. One of the two PRC 319 radio systems was in the care of Pete Welsh. The dismantled parts of the GPMG were divided between big Arnie Basham and Syd Loomis, with the former also placed in charge of the patrol medical kit and the latter humping the other PRC 319. The Barrett Light .50 rifle (known as the 'supergun' because of its exceptional accuracy and awesome firing power) was given, appropriately enough, to Killer Parker, the best marksman in 22 SAS. A wide variety of explosives, demolition charges, electrical initiators and timing fuses was divided equally between Rudi Blackwood and Mad Mike Nicholson. Paddy Devlin, being patrol second-in-command (2IC), was placed in charge of the MIL/UST-1 SATCOM communications system. Scott, the patrol commander (PC), got off lightest of all, having only his personal weapons and bergen rucksack to hump, leaving his hands free to handle his maps, binoculars, passive night vision goggles (PNGs), hand-held thermal imager and prismatic compass while on the move.

Indeed, even as the rest of the men were still sorting out their weapons and kit, Scott was kneeling on the ground beside Paddy Devlin, shining a thin spotlight on the local map spread out between them.

'We're approximately here,' Scott said, tapping the area of

the DZ, marked with a red X, with his index finger, 'and we have to get to here.' He indicated the road running from Osh to the Pamirs, then glanced west across the relatively flat, open plain, which looked eerie in moonlight. 'Not much cover there,' he continued, 'so I say we head north to those low hills between us and the Tien Shan range. They're covered in woodlands and they'll give us good protection. So we hike to the hills, getting there before first light, then catch some shuteye and head west at last light. We should reach the road before dawn the following day and can cross it under cover of darkness. What say you, Paddy?'

'Sounds fine to me, boss.'

'Right, let's move out. Diamond formation until we reach the woodlands. No talking unless absolutely necessary. We communicate with hand signals.'

Paddy nodded, not saying another word, then he stood up and used hand signals to indicate to the men what they should do. Selected as the lead scout and briefed as to where they were going, Parker moved out on point, well ahead of the patrol. Being the PC, Scott headed up the rest of the patrol, though keeping a good distance behind Parker. Pete Welsh and Syd Loomis, in charge of the two all-important PRC 319 radio systems, fell in behind Scott. The other men fell in behind Welsh and Loomis with Paddy Devlin, the 2IC, bringing up the rear as 'Tailend Charlie'.

Following Killer Parker, the men moved out in single file, in a long, irregularly spaced line, then gradually spread themselves out until, though still marching in the same order, they were forming the rough diamond shape favoured for crossing open ground at night, combining, as it did, the best features of both file and single file formations. It also allowed for optimum firepower to be focused on the front.

Out on point as lead scout, it was Killer Parker's job to cover a firing arc directly in front of the patrol and keep his eyes peeled for enemy movements. The men between him and Tailend Charlie had to cover firing arcs to the left and right respectively; while Tailend Charlie, in this case Paddy

Devlin, had the exhausting task of covering an arc of fire to the rear. He did this by regularly swinging around in the opposite direction to that in which the patrol was moving, always holding his MP5 at the ready. While exhausting and, for a lesser man, nerve-wracking, this ensured that the patrol had no blind spots.

They hiked throughout most of the night and the early morning. Apart from the constant moaning of the wind they heard other sounds: soft scurrying around their feet, the magnified snap of breaking twigs, the noisy crunching of trampled gravel – and this made them strain all the more nervously to make out something threatening.

Still far ahead, out on point, Killer Parker would frequently raise and lower his right hand, the fist clenched, to indicate that he had heard or seen something not familiar. He would always follow this gesture by dropping to his belly and the rest of the men did the same until, at another hand signal from Parker, they could stand up again. What Parker was seeing and hearing was the sudden movement of small animals in the darkness – rodents, yellow gophers or hares – making their way through the tall grass, which would rustle and sway as they passed on.

Halfway through the night – or, rather, the early morning – they saw lights flickering in the darkness directly in front of them, though still a good distance away. Again using a hand signal, Killer Parker indicated to Scott that he should go to the ground with the patrol while he, Parker, went on ahead to check the significance of the lights. Scott indicated his agreement, then, as Parker raced away into the darkness, he signalled to the rest of his men that they were to drop belly-down to the ground. This they did, melting into the tall grass, not moving, not making a sound.

As he lay there with his men, though they were well spread out behind him, still in diamond formation, Scott was torn between the tension he felt at that moment – wondering what lay ahead – and sudden, distracting, recollections of his son and the pain that his slow, dreadful dying had caused. It had been acute, devastating the whole family, but Scott's own pain had been tempered with his rage against those who had caused the death. Now, as he scanned the night, seeing those lights flickering in the distance, wondering what they were and if they represented danger, he found his gaze rising helplessly to the mountains beyond, etched in black under a canopy of stars, bathed in the light of a full moon. There was snow on the lower slopes and the summits gleamed with ice, but they were not the mountains he was heading for.

Turning his head, he looked west, beyond the forests, to the Pamirs, and saw the very same thing: glinting ice-peaks and unblemished, virgin snow. Somewhere up there, in that white hell, was the man who traded in the drugs that now flooded the streets of Britain and had, albeit indirectly, led to the death of Scott's son. Now he wanted to find that man, to look into the eyes of his son's killer, and then, having done so, to obliterate him. He wanted to find that man and he would, because nothing else mattered.

Sighing, realising that he was letting his personal concerns distract him from his work, he looked to the north again and saw Killer Parker emerging like a ghost from the moonlit darkness. Parker used a hand signal to indicate that he wanted to communicate by Landmaster transceiver. Scott indicated that Parker could do so, then he unclipped his own transceiver from his belt and switched it on and listened.

'No sweat,' Parker said. His voice was flat and unemotional. 'It's just an oil refinery. The flickering lights are the flames from the chimneys of the refining plants and the lights from windows. A lot of dust is blowing over those windows, covering them up and then exposing them again, so the lights seem to be flickering.'

'A big refinery?' Scott asked.

'No,' Parker said. 'Pretty average, I'd say. Not particularly important. I could see men in there working, but the place isn't guarded at all, so we just have to go round it.'

'Lead the way,' Scott said. 'Over and out.'

He turned the transceiver off and indicated to his men that

they should get to their feet again. When they had done so, he signalled to Parker to lead the way, which he did, guiding them towards the lights until they could see the refinery in detail, its chimney stacks belching flame and filthy smoke, its buildings brightly lit behind high, mesh-wire fences, its wide gates unguarded. Parker led them in a westerly direction around the refinery, a good distance away from it so that they were hidden in darkness, then turned north and headed once more for the forested hills.

They hiked for another couple of hours, still in diamond formation, repeatedly falling to the ground when Parker indicated that they should do so, climbing back to their feet when given the all clear, then marching on. As the forested hills took on a clear shape, delineated by the star-drenched sky, the patrol passed irrigated cotton fields and the darkened houses of the families that worked them. They also came to a *qishlaq* – an old Uzbek settlement – but few lights were showing and they were able to move around it without arousing those sleeping in their darkened houses.

Eventually, just before first light, they came to the edge of the woodlands. At a signal from Parker, they all fell to the ground again, then Parker loped on ahead and soon disappeared into the deep darkness between the first line of trees. He was going to check if anyone was in there before they moved on.

Lying on his belly, Scott heard the eerie moaning of the wind as well as a host of other soft, irregular, unfamiliar sounds, indicating that the tall grass in which he lay was teeming with wildlife.

No snakes, at least, he thought. No venomous spiders. If there's danger, it's going to be in the woods – the brown bear or grey wolf.

This time it was a long wait. Parker was doing his job thoroughly, covering a broad swathe of the woods, but eventually he materialised again and, after signalling to Scott for permission, communicated by means of his transceiver.

'There's not a sign of a human being in there,' he said,

'so I recommend it for LUPs.' By which he meant laying-up positions. 'Also, there's a river located about two hundred metres in from the tree line, running north-west, ideal for a night stay.'

'The Naryn River,' Scott informed him. 'It runs down from the mountains into the valley and continues north-westward as a tributary to the Syrdarya River. This particular stretch of it *should* be uninhabited and I assume, from what you say, that it is.'

'Confirmed,' Parker said.

'Lead us to it,' Scott said. 'Over and out.'

Even as he switched his transceiver off, he saw Parker rising up from the tall grass and turning away to lope towards the forest. Scott clipped his transceiver to his webbed belt, then stood up and silently signalled to the others to follow him. He followed Parker into the forest and on for a short distance – Parker's estimated two hundred metres – and arrived eventually at a semi-circular clearing, obviously formed by water erosion, beside the muddy bank of the river. Here the river was not wide, perhaps fifteen metres, and its flow was slow enough to make it perfect for bathing and other domestic business.

Pleased, Scott turned around to face the men advancing cautiously, now in single file, through the densely packed, leafy trees. He used a hand signal to give them the all clear and they visibly relaxed. Turning back to face Killer Parker's flat grey gaze, he said, 'Good one, Corporal.'

'It'll do,' Parker said.

Scott checked his wristwatch. First light would come soon. His men were now entering the clearing, and it was clear from the strained expressions on their faces that they needed a good rest. Having brought up the rear as Tailend Charlie, Paddy Devlin was the last in and he walked straight to Scott and said, 'Christ, that was a hell of a hike. Is this where we lay up?'

'Yes,' Scott said. 'Get it organised.'

In fact, Paddy had only to draw up a list of which two men would be on guard at any given time as the others did everything required without being asked. Their LUPs consisted of shallow scrapes dug out of the earth with their small spades – a job that took them mere minutes. Most of them were satisfied with unrolling their sleeping bags and laying them out in the LUPs, but some – those willing to work for their luxuries or simply convinced that it might rain – constructed temporary shelters by digging their shallow scrapes between two closely aligned trees, tying a cord from one tree trunk to the other, then looping their poncho over the cord to make a simple tent, secured with a quick-release knot.

Once the LUPs had been created, they had something to eat and drink, though since they were unable to use their portable hexamine stoves for hot food, since the flames would have revealed their positions to anyone passing through the forest, they had to settle for cold, high-calorie rations washed down with water from their water bottles.

Thirst quenched and hunger satisfied, they attended to their ablutions, taking advantage of the river. Then each man carefully sprinkled local foliage over his tent or the sleeping bag in his shallow scrape, crawled into his LUP, fully dressed, and tried to sleep as best he could.

Most of the men, being confident in themselves, fell asleep before first light.

Only three of them saw the sun rising.

Corporals Mad Mike Nicholson and Killer Parker had fallen for the first two-hour watch by drawing straws, which in fact were twigs held in Scott's hand. So they had to go out on point, north and south, and patrol an invisible perimeter from those positions, covering all directions, their weapons at the ready, until they were relieved by the next two men, Syd Loomis and Pete Welsh.

Scott, on the other hand, although he, too, would eventually be called for guard duty – since all men were equal on an SAS patrol – simply could not sleep and lay on his uncovered LUP, first gazing at the rising sun, then twisting sideways to look west to the distant Pamirs. He saw the soaring fields of snow, the icy peaks glittering in dawn light, and then thought of his quarry, the drug baron he had to find, and wondered what kind of man could survive in that white hell.

How could *anyone* survive up there? he wondered. It just doesn't seem possible.

Yet that's where he was going.

Scott closed his eyes, not believing it.

CHAPTER ELEVEN

Lalya survived. She had made her escape from Dmitry's camp by setting his house on fire at exactly the right time. For days, even before Dmitry's brutal execution of her brother, she had been planning to escape and checking the times that a certain open-topped truck driver took his daily load of rubbish away each evening to the dump located in a quarry about half a mile down the road from the camp. Though the camp had no walls, the buildings formed a great rectangle, with only narrow spaces between them, and there were watchtowers on all sides, manned by machine-gun crews who would not hesitate to shoot a prisoner seen outside the perimeter. Also, though a few had tried, no one had ever managed to escape because the camp was too high in the snow-covered, freezing mountains and getting down would have been next to impossible without proper protective clothing and transport. For this very reason, the prisoners' heavy quilted jackets, the *telogreikas*, were taken from them every night to ensure that they could not survive the cold should they decide to be stupid. Last but not least was the dreadful fear instilled in them by the knowledge of what Dmitry would do to them if he caught them outside the camp and brought them back alive. He had once had an escapee skinned alive in full view of the other prisoners and no one who had witnessed it had ever forgotten it.

Lalya didn't care. Loathing Dmitry from the very depths of her being, pretending to acquiesce to his demands only in order to buy herself time, she had decided to humiliate him by burning his house down, including his precious paintings and books, and she didn't care if she died in the attempt. She had, in fact, decided that death was preferable to the horror of surrendering to such a monster, the murderer of her whole family, the scarred but still handsome beast who brutalised her every day, and eventually she had worked out how to do it.

The truck left the motor pool at exactly the same time every evening, just before the sun went down, its open top piled high with all kinds of rubbish. The motor pool was on the same side of the camp as Dmitry's house and located only a few hundred metres away. Lalya's plan was twofold: by setting fire to Dmitry's house, she would create a major distraction for his men, including the guards in the watchtowers. She would, however, also destroy the things he most loved: his paintings and books. He would know exactly why she had done it and that thought gave her pleasure. She would have her revenge, even if she died in the process.

Lalya doused the rear of the house with gasoline a few minutes before the truck was due to leave the motor pool. She made a crude torch by tying gasoline-soaked rags around the heavy wooden base of a table lamp, then set fire to it and threw the blazing brand across the room while standing by the front door. When the rear of the house burst into flames, she made her escape through the unlocked front door, ran along the darkened porch before the flames could be seen, jumped off the far end of porch, then hurried through the darkness, in the shade of the other buildings, avoiding the moonlight, to reach the back of the motor pool a minute or so before the rubbish truck moved off.

Taking a deep breath and trying not to retch from the stench, she climbed up into the open top of the truck and wriggled her way into the mess of open tins, empty bottles, plastic bags filled with used toilet paper, and rotting food left over from that day. The driver, who was already in the truck, revving the engine to warm it up, neither saw her nor heard her. He drove out of the motor pool just before the flames from Dmitry's burning house were seen by the guards in the watchtower. He drove between two watchtowers and turned left along the mountain road as the watchtower sirens wailed the fire alarm. As this was clearly not his business, he kept driving until he reached the rubbish dump, which took only five minutes. When he slowed down again to turn into the dump, Lalya slithered back out of the rubbish and dropped off the rear of the truck, landing on her feet in the snow. She bolted back down the road, still unseen by the driver, then turned off into the trees covering the hills that soared high above her. She was not going downhill – she was going uphill, towards the summit of the mountain – and that wouldn't make sense to those pursuing her.

It made sense to Lalya. She was wearing only the clothes she normally wore around Dmitry's house – a thin cotton dress, a woollen pullover and fur-lined leather slippers – with only a *shinyel*, a greatcoat, stolen from Dmitry's coathanger as additional clothing. Knowing that this would not be enough to prevent her from freezing to death if she attempted to go back down the mountain – even assuming that Dmitry's men would not catch her, which would be a far worse fate – she had accepted that she would die and was determined that she would do so alone, unmolested by the brutes who would be sent by Dmitry to pursue her.

She had nothing more to live for anyway. That monster, Dmitry, had murdered every member of her family and now she had no one in the whole world. Now life could only consist of slavery and whoring, first for Dmitry, then, if he tired of her, perhaps for one or more of his brutes. The thought of even one more minute in the bed of the man who had killed her entire family was revolting; the thought of being passed on at a later stage to his men was unendurable. So she would rather die, at least ending her life with dignity, as well as with the knowledge that her complete disappearance would drive Dmitry wild with frustration. She would die by taking herself as high into the mountains as she could manage, where those bastards would never think to look and where they would never find her.

Lalya started climbing. While making her way up through the woodlands on the lower slopes above the road, she was able to move with relative ease, even though the snow was falling and lay thick and clean on the ground. However, the higher she went, the more steep became the slopes and soon she could only advance by using her bare hands to grab at branches and pull herself upwards. Her hands started freezing, along with her feet. To make matters worse, when she grabbed hold of the overhead branches to pull herself up, they shook violently and snow fell off to rain upon her, completely soaking her hair and clothing, then freezing upon her.

She was breathing harshly by now, her muscles aching from the effort, but she kept going until the forest thinned out and eventually gave way to the bare face of the mountain, which rose before her in immense, irregular swathes of snow-covered granite and stone, climbing majestically, one piled upon the other, to a series of jagged, ice-encased peaks wreathed in stormy, fast-moving clouds. Deprived of the protection of the trees, the mountain slopes were swept constantly by fierce, howling winds that blew the snow from east to west in swirling, hissing streams of whiteness.

Already shivering with cold, her hands and feet numb, Lalya had to advance into that blizzard, the snow sweeping across her, the wind hammering at her. Finally, almost blinded, unable to feel her face, but very aware of sharp pains in her feet and hands, she fell onto her hands and knees and kept going that way.

I'm an animal, she thought. That's all I am now . . . That's what the bastard reduced me to.

Her hatred gave her strength and she crawled forward on

hands and knees, determined to put as much distance as possible between herself and the camp, to die – like an animal – all alone, her whereabouts unknown to her tormentors. She kept going, shivering and sobbing, biting her numbed lower lip, trying to bring feeling back to it. She saw her hands turning blue in the pure white snow and winced each time bolts of pain shot through them. Her feet were hurting as well. She scratched her knees on sharp rocks. Though moving forward like an animal, she was still a human being and sometimes managed to stand up again to stagger forward a few more yards before, being hammered by the howling wind, she was knocked back down onto her hands and knees. Determined, she kept crawling forward, given strength by her hatred and contempt for Dmitry Pavlov.

The wind howled and the snow blew hissing across her, soaking her, blinding her. It was dark in the mountains, but the white slopes were moonlit, and she saw enough to avoid deep fissures and ravines. Yet even in her growing weakness, in her hatred, the night filled her with fear. She was fearful of animals – the mountain bear or the snow leopard – and dreaded the thought of dying that way instead of freezing to death. Nevertheless, she kept advancing, now mostly on hands and knees, until the strength drained out of her completely and she fell onto her belly.

Oh, you bastard, she thought, thinking of Dmitry Petrov and letting her hatred energise her just enough to haul herself forward by her numbed fingers to some final resting place. At least I fooled you, you bastard. I cheated you and you didn't expect that. In that, anyway, I defeated you.

Yet she sobbed into the snow, lying face down, when she thought of her father and mother, her two brothers, as they had been when alive. They had been a good family, a loving family, and now they were all gone.

Dmitry Petrov had murdered them.

She dug her numbed fingers into the snow, curled them over some sharp rocks, then pulled at the same time as she pushed with her feet, though they, too, were numb. She moved forward inch by inch, now less than an animal, a reptile, wriggling this way and that, gasping for breath, sobbing, hearing only the howling of the wind and the swirling snow's sibilance. She kept crawling forward and upward until she came to what she assumed was a dead end – a sheer, towering cliff face. She had gone as far as she could go.

Then, as she blinked her weeping, stinging eyes, she saw something even blacker than the darkness at the base of the cliff face, directly ahead of her.

It was the mouth of a large cave.

Now barely conscious, numb in body and spirit, she blinked repeatedly and kept staring at that large black hole in the solid rock. She tried to see into the darkness, wondering what might be in there, thinking of hungry predators and of what they could do to her. The fear shook her leaf and bough, making her want to turn back, but not having the strength to do that, she remained where she was.

Eventually, though she was hardly aware that she was doing so, she started crawling again, moving forward inch by painful inch, until she was at the mouth of the cave and could see farther inside it.

There was no sign of movement, and she could not hear a sound.

Lalya took a deep breath. She held it in for a long time. She felt her heart racing – beating with life – as she tried to choke back her fear. Finally, when she had let her breath out again, she inched into the dark cave.

The howling wind stopped hammering at her and the snow ceased to fall when she had crawled into the shelter of the cave. Nothing moved. It was dark in most areas, but rays of pale moonlight fell obliquely on the floor and on one wall. There were no animals – not even a gopher – but she saw the debris of temporary human habitation and that gave her hope.

Glancing back over her shoulder, she heard the wind howling outside and saw the snow swirling furiously about the face of the cave. Looking straight ahead again, she saw piles of unopened food tins, a battered saucepan, a tin kettle, rusty animal traps, coiled ropes, the cold ashes of what had once been a fire and, to her joyous disbelief, a can of paraffin and many boxes of matches.

A Kyrgyz trapper had obviously once stayed here for at least a couple of days while hunting for mountain bears or snow leopards. He must have left the cave intending to come back, but in fact he had not come back.

Though already half asleep from the effects of severe cold, which would soon become hypothermia and then, if not checked, death by freezing, Lalya crawled forward, impelled helplessly by the instinct to live. Then, with a great deal of effort, she pulled and pushed herself into an upright position, resting her back against the cold, hard, curving wall of the cave. Painful though it was – and it was very painful indeed – she repeatedly beat her frozen hands together until some feeling returned. When she could use her hands, she removed dried sticks from the pile gathered in by the unknown trapper who had been here before her and heaped them on top of the cold ashes in the centre of the floor. Gradually gaining strength from hope, she managed to unscrew the lid of the paraffin can and pour some over the sticks. She broke half-a-dozen matches trying to light them, but finally succeeded in her task and touched the burning match to one of the soaked sticks, jerking her hand away as it burst into flames. Those flames caught, going from one paraffin-soaked stick to another, and soon a small fire was burning healthily.

Aware that she should not warm her frozen limbs too quickly, Lalya sat well away from the fire and only gradually inched in towards it. As she did so, she saw that the hunter had made himself a primitive bed of straw and that two blankets were still spread across it. Hardly believing her good luck, wondering why the trapper had not returned, Lalya manoeuvred the bed of straw and blankets closer to the fire. She placed more sticks on the fire, then, after checking that there were no insects or small animals on the bed of straw, she crawled under the blankets. No longer concerned with mountain bears or snow leopards, imagining that she no longer cared if she lived or died, she closed her weary eyes and slept, oblivious to the wind howling outside, warm at last in her dark cave.

CHAPTER TWELVE

The two men on guard duty at the time, Troopers Arnie Basham and Rudi Blackwood, woke the rest of the men at first light. The night had passed uneventfully and the men were well rested, but now they had a lot to do before they moved on in the early afternoon. The first thing was to attend to their ablutions, heading in different directions into the forest to have their toilet in private, carefully burying their excrement and paper, then covering the mound of freshly upturned soil with local vegetation to leave no trace of their presence there. They all bathed in the river and also used it for the washing of socks and underwear, which were hung over the branches of trees to dry.

'That's one hell of a wang you've got on you,' Syd Loomis said to the big black trooper, Arnie Basham, as they were both stepping naked out of the river, 'but what can you do with it?'

'Well, man, I tell you,' Arnie answered with a dazzling, ivory-white smile, 'I can wrap it around my neck, sling it from there down my spine to my arse, bring it back up through my legs to my mouth and have a good suck on it. That way I get my own impeccable sperm back and am perpetually, superbly rejuvenated. What have *you* got to offer?'

'The only thing I'd want to offer after hearing that,' Syd replied with his oddly twisted, vicious grin, 'is a ton of my vomit.'

'We get that every time you open your mouth. Think of something original, man.'

'You hear that?' Syd said to Rudi Blackwood. 'The big Sambo, who hails from Barbados, has got a weird sense of humour.'

'I don't hail from Barbados,' Arnie replied patiently. 'I was born and bred in Kennington, south London, and that makes me as British as you. You're from Glasgow, right? That probably means you're filled with Protestant rectitude, which is why you're not married.'

'I get enough,' Syd boasted, though it wasn't quite true. 'Single men get more sex than married men, 'cause marriage kills off the urge. That's why your wang is so big – being married, you have to pull it a lot instead of putting it in where it belongs.'

'Ho, ho,' Arnie said. 'There speaks a man of true wit. But you should ask Trooper Blackwood about that. He's only been married four months. Dying off, is it, Rudi?'

'I've no complaints,' Blackwood said. 'I get it at least once a month. Before we got married, it once every two months, so now I feel like a real man at last. So what about you, Pete?'

They all stared at Pete Welsh, who just scratched his long, pale, pimply face and looked typically vague.

'What's that?'

'How much of the old in-and-out do you get being single and thirty-one?'

Welsh shrugged. 'Enough.'

'So what's enough?' Loomis asked, grinning sadistically. 'How many bints have you had since you first started getting it up? Come on, Welsh, give us the truth now.'

Welsh shrugged again, his smile shy, his gaze deceptively dim. 'Couldn't really say, guys. Never kept count, don't you know. Just took 'em for granted and let 'em come and go without tottin' the score up. I mean, I can't count very well above a hundred, so you know, I can't tell you.'

Arnie Basham laughed heartily at that one and shook his head from side to side in disbelief. 'Oh, man!' he exclaimed. 'The quiet ones are always the worst and Welsh is a quiet one. One up for you, brother!'

'Just drop all that bullshit,' Corporal Killer Parker said, already washed and dressed and sitting a few metres away in the shade of a coniferous tree, 'and get your fucking clothes back on. You've all got work to do.'

'Yes, boss!' the four troopers shouted out in unison, making a joke of it. Though rendered uneasy, as always, by Killer Parker's stony grey gaze, they were quick to obey him.

Hoping that their HALO descent into the valley had not been observed, but aware that it might have been, Scott again insisted that they could not cook a hot breakfast with their hexamine stoves in case the smoke from the fires gave away their position, so they had to content themselves with cold high-calorie rations washed down with water. There was a lot of grumbling about this, but it wasn't remotely serious and was, in fact, pure bullshit designed for their mutual entertainment.

'These wads might be full of calories,' Syd Loomis said, referring to their sandwiches of white bread and beef paste, 'but they sure as hell taste like pig shite.'

'He speaks from personal experience,' big Arnie responded, 'being one of those Glaswegians who'd rather eat shite than spend his money.'

'Admit it,' Syd retorted. 'You wouldn't know the difference between shite and shinola and you probably salt-and-pepper your shoe polish. The next time you come down from the trees for a banana, stick it up your black arse.'

'My arse may be black and your arse may be white, but the shite that comes out of them's the same. Same colour. Same stench.'

'I'm trying to eat!' Pete Welsh complained.

'So am I,' Rudi Blackwood added. 'They always start these kind of conversations when my stomach is rumbling.'

'Your stomach's rumbling,' Syd told him, 'because it can't stand the shite in these wads. You'll throw up in a minute.'

'In your face,' Blackwood warned him.

'We'd never notice,' Arnie said.

'Shut up and eat, you men,' Mad Mike Nicholson said as he wiped his lips with the back of his right hand and crumpled his sandwich paper with the other, having completed his meal. 'If I hear any more complaints about the food, I'll run you whining bastards ragged and make you eat your own puke!'

'Yes, boss!' the four troopers chanted in unison. They weren't as intimidated by Mad Mike as they were by Killer Parker, but they knew that he would make good his threat – or would, at least, run them ragged if they got on his nerves. So they concentrated on eating their sandwiches and drinking their water, this time in silence.

When breakfast was finished, they meticulously rechecked and cleaned their weapons, giving particular attention to the oiling of moveable parts. This task took up most of the morning and helped pass the time.

'I've cleaned this fucker so many times,' Mad Mike said, gazing at his disassembled SA-80 assault rifle, 'I'm dreaming about it. I could do this job in my sleep.'

'That's the idea,' Killer Parker replied without the slightest trace of humour, his grey gaze focused flatly, unblinkingly, on his supergun – the Barrett Light .50 rifle. 'It could jam at an inconvenient time, in the dead of night; then you'd have to disassemble it and put it back together in the darkness. If you can't do it in your sleep, or blindfolded, you could find yourself in deep shit.'

'I was only joking,' Mad Mike said.

'You shouldn't joke about your weapons.'

'Jesus, Killer, don't you ever give it a rest? Lighten up, for Christ's sake!'

'I lighten up when I'm at home with my wife and kids –

not on a mission. Lighten up here and you could lose your life, and I'm not ready for that yet.'

'You think this mission's that dangerous?'

'It's damned near suicidal. We're going up against a man who practically owns those fucking mountains and knows them like the back of his hand. We don't know those mountains. We don't know where he hides out. We only know that he's above the snow line and that's a cold place to be. If we get up there without being seen, it'll be a fucking miracle. It's a hard one, believe me.'

'Thanks for the encouragement,' Mad Mike said.

'My pleasure,' Parker responded.

Finally, each man dismantled his personal LUP, rolled up his blanket and poncho and strapped them to his bergen rucksack, then filled in the shallow scrape and carefully covered it with local foliage until the forest floor looked just as it had been before their arrival. They then gathered around Scott and Paddy Devlin to receive further instructions.

'We hike west,' Scott said, 'and should arrive at the road linking Osh to Fergana shortly after last light. Diamond formation all the way, the same order as yesterday. No talking. Communication by hand signals. Okay, let's move out.'

Instantly, Killer Parker moved out ahead to take up his position on point as lead scout, Scott and the others fell in well behind him, and Paddy Devlin took up the rear as Tailend Charlie. Once in line, they spread out to form a loose diamond formation that enabled them to move with relative ease through the gloomy forest without recourse to the trodden tracks that they occasionally came across, indicating that the forest was, indeed, crisscrossed by the local populace. This knowledge made them even more watchful.

It had been bitterly cold throughout the night, but now that the sun was up they could feel the heat rising, brought in on the hot, moisture-consuming winds from the deserts beyond. Once more, while they were scanning the forest in all directions, they were also compelled to listen to many unfamiliar sounds and keep their eyes peeled for the wild animals which occasionally appeared.

Approximately an hour into the hike, a wild pig burst out of the undergrowth in the middle of their formation, bellowing fearfully, causing the men nearest to it, Loomis and Welsh, to swing around with their weapons raised in the firing position. The pig raced from north to south, smashing noisily through the foliage, then disappeared into the undergrowth to the left of the formation. Relieved, having thought they were being ambushed, the men continued the hike.

As he advanced behind Killer Parker, keeping a good distance from him, watching him move repeatedly between striations of sunlight and unlit forest gloom, Scott realised that the most difficult aspect of these hikes was the imposition of total silence and the feeling of isolation caused by the great distance each man had to keep between himself and the others. The bullshit bandied between the men when they rested up was therefore a necessary antidote to the silence, the hours of feeling cut off from your comrades, always tensed for a sound or a sign of movement that could indicate an approaching enemy or, worse, for the sudden roaring of weapons that denoted an ambush.

The lack of communication with the other members of a patrol forced the individual into himself, into his own thoughts, and those thoughts – about family, friends or lovers – could prove to be a dangerous distraction. Even Scott, while he continued to cover an arc of fire to the left and right, scanning the forest intently for unfamiliar signs of movement distinct from the frequent movements caused by scurrying animals, kept slipping helplessly into reminiscences of home. The death of his son, the destruction of his marriage, and the pain he felt when these thoughts came upon him, combined with a consuming rage, gave him momentary blanks with regard to what was going on around him. When he caught himself doing this, he silently cursed and forced himself to concentrate once more on the job at hand.

Luckily, he was doing just this when Parker, still up ahead, used a hand signal to indicate that the men should all go to ground where they could not be seen.

Scott scurried behind some undergrowth and went down on one knee with his MP5 sub-machine gun raised in the firing position. Glancing about him, he saw that the other men had done the same – although they had done it so well that even he could not see them. Satisfied, he looked to the front and found that Parker, too, had disappeared.

Tensing, Scott strained to see beyond where Parker had to be hidden and eventually, after what seemed like a long time – but was, in fact, mere minutes – he heard a soft thrashing sound from up ahead, followed by the almost imperceptible shifting of the foliage. Gradually, two men appeared. They were wearing Kyrgyz peasant clothing and leading a donkey heavily burdened with bales of what appeared to be sugar beets. They did not carry weapons. Clearly, they knew the forest well, as they were not travelling along a track but wending their way between the trees, scarcely looking where they were going, while talking in normal tones to one another. This indicated to Scott that they were ordinary workers from a nearby *kolkoz*, a collective farm, or *sovkhoz*, a state farm, and that they were merely taking their wares from one location to another as a matter of routine. Relieved, Scott remained motionless, waiting for them to pass on. Gradually they moved by him, almost close enough to touch, not seeing him or anyone else. When they were out of sight and out of earshot, Scot stood up and signalled that the others should do the same. They rose from behind low bushes and stepped out from behind trees, silent, almost spectral, then fell back into the diamond formation and marched on behind Parker.

The sun crossed the cloud-strewn sky, its light illuminating the gloom, and the hike continued without incident until the sun started sinking. Just as the light was dimming, with the globe of the sun becoming a crescent as it fell to the west behind the peaks of the Pamirs, now much closer and more imposing, Syd Loomis, out on the southern tip of the formation, abruptly stopped marching.

Instantly, the other men halted as well.

Glancing in Loomis's direction, Scott was shocked to see that an enormous brown bear had emerged silently from the undergrowth and was standing directly in Loomis's path, gazing steadily at him.

Loomis did not move. He stared back at the brown bear. Man and beast stared silently at each other while Killer Parker, still out on point, thus positioned well behind the bear in a line of fire oblique to it, raised his Barrett Light .50 rifle and took aim, preparing to fire. Scott, also some distance away from the bear, slightly behind and to the side, therefore out of the huge beast's line of vision, raised his right hand and waved it slowly left and right, indicating that Parker should not fire unless the bear made a sudden move towards Loomis. The latter remained frozen, no longer looking at the bear, which might have antagonised it, but keeping his gaze lowered, focused on its steadily breathing, heaving chest. The bear, still studying Loomis, let out a soft growl, raised and lowered its huge paws, then turned away and lumbered back into the undergrowth.

The men watched it disappearing, no one moving a muscle. Only when they could no longer hear it did they heave a collective sigh of relief and advance again to the west.

Realising that if they had been forced to fire on the bear, the silence would have been broken and their presence in the forest made known to anyone in the vicinity, Scott felt a great deal of admiration for Syd Loomis's courage in not moving when faced with the bear. Yet even as he thought this, he realised that he was walking faster, wanting more urgently to get out of the darkening forest. In fact, he was gaining ground on Parker, which was a dangerous thing to do, so he silently admonished himself for his own cowardice and slowed down again.

Loomis showed more guts than you have, he thought, and he's only a trooper. Get a grip on yourself.

Slowing down, returning to his original, more measured pace, he continued advancing behind Parker, now less visible in deepening gloom, and looked up beyond the canopy of the trees to see the great snow-covered slopes of the mountains, the ice glittering in the moonlight on the peaks. The forest was now darkening quickly, which would make it more dangerous, and Scott was glad to see how close the mountains were, indicating that the road was just ahead.

This turned out to be true. They had only hiked for another fifteen minutes, advancing through a darkness relieved only by the moonlight, through a lesser density of trees, when Parker, still up ahead, stopped marching and dropped to one knee. He remained that way for some time, his head moving left and right, then he raised his right hand and waved them forward.

After signalling to the men spread out behind him that they should follow him at the half-crouch, Scott dropped into that position, then made his way slowly, carefully up to Parker. Kneeling beside Parker, he leaned forward slightly and peered out between the trees to see the road they would have to cross. It was a two-lane highway, curving dramatically at this point, dominated at the far side by the steep, forested lower slopes of the Pamir range. The trees ended about five hundred metres uphill, gradually becoming more sparse, then fading away altogether, giving way to barren slopes of rock and gravel and, even higher, the snow.

Getting up there, Scott realised, would be a formidable hike. Right now, however, their task was to get across the road and into the trees without being seen.

'Not much traffic, at least,' Parker said softly, breaking the silence at last. 'Nothing's passed since I got here. Of course that's only been a couple of minutes, so we can't bank on anything.'

The rest of the men had moved up to form a long line along the edge of the road, some to the left of Scott and Parker, others to the right, all positioned well back and hidden by wild foliage and tree trunks. As Scott was scanning the road in both directions, Paddy Devlin came up beside him and followed his shifting gaze.

'That road's a hundred metres wide,' Paddy said.

'That's right,' Scott said.

'It doesn't seem to be used much,' Parker said, 'so we shouldn't have any problems.'

Yet even as he spoke, they all heard the labouring of a vehicle's engine from around the bend to the north. Looking in that direction, they saw a battered old truck coming around the bend, its headlights illuminating the moonlit darkness. It wheezed and rattled its way past them, eventually disappearing around the bend to the south, leaving silence behind it.

'So there's traffic,' Paddy said.

'Not much,' Parker insisted.

Scott glanced left and right again. 'We can't afford to be seen,' he said. 'Not until we're well into the mountains. Armed border guards are known to patrol these roads and we can't let *them* see us. So I say we place a man on watch at each of those bends, at a point where they'll be able to see all the way around the bend while still being visible to us. They tell us when the road's clear and we cross it one man at a time, with the others giving cover just in case. When we're all across, the two men on watch will then cross as well, assuming the road's clear. Agreed?'

'Agreed,' Paddy said.

'Parker,' Scott said, 'you take the southern bend.' He turned to Mad Mike and said, 'You take the northern bend, Nicholson. We'll be able to see both of you, but you won't be able to see each other, so communicate with the Landmaster hand-held systems. You give the all clear, then you wait until each man is across before checking the road again. When the last of us has reached the other side, you two light out as well, once you've checked with each other. Okay, get going.'

Nodding silently at him, Killer Parker and Mad Mike turned in opposite directions and loped off through the trees, following the line of the road but keeping well out of sight. Even before they had reached their respective positions, in both cases where the road curved, a second vehicle came around the southern bend – a truck filled with men wearing army-style tunics and soft black caps, all of them holding their rifles upright.

'Kyrgyz border patrol guards,' Paddy Devlin noted. 'How right you were, boss.'

Scott smiled. He watched the truck disappearing around the northern bend, then saw Nicholson waving from his chosen position behind the trees, indicating his presence and telling Scott to switch on his Landmaster III hand-held transceiver.

'You go over first, Paddy,' Scott said to Sergeant Devlin. 'Then I want the two radios to be taken across. We can give covering fire from both sides – if necessary. First you, Welsh; then you, Loomis.'

'Right, boss,' Pete Welsh said.

Syd Loomis just nodded.

'You'll follow Loomis,' Scott said to Arnie Basham, 'followed by Blackwood. I go last.' Switching on his transceiver, he announced himself to Parker and Nicholson, then said, 'We're all set to go.'

'All clear,' Parker said from the southern bend.

'All clear,' Nicholson said from the northern bend.

Paddy Devlin jumped up and started across the road, running at the half-crouch and automatically weaving left to right as he would have done if under enemy gunfire. The rest of the men gave him cover, some of them aiming their guns north, the rest south. Paddy reached the opposite side without incident, turned back to wave at them, then melted into the darkness under the trees. Though invisible, he would now be covering the road with his SA-80 assault rifle.

'We're ready for the next man,' Scott said to Parker and Nicholson in turn, receiving the all clear from both men.

Instantly, Pete Welsh jumped up and lumbered off across the road, bent low under the weight of his bergen rucksack and PRC 319 radio system. He made it as well, but when Scott announced that the next man was ready, Parker told him that a vehicle was approaching.

Syd Loomis was all set to go, bent, as Welsh had been, under the weight of his radio system, but he froze when he saw Scott's hand signal and followed his southwesterly gaze. A black Volga sedan came around the southern bend, its headlights on full beam, sweeping the trees on one side of the road, then it passed by and disappeared around the northern bend. Mad Mike gave the all clear, Killer Parker did the same, and at an instruction from Scott, Loomis lumbered across the road and disappeared into the darkness at the far side.

'Are you all set, Basham?' Scott said to the big trooper.

'I sure am,' Basham said. 'No problem with me, boss. I'm so black I'll be invisible on that there road, so just set me loose.'

Smiling, Scott checked with Killer Parker and Mad Mike, received the okay from both men, then instructed Basham to start running. Basham was highly visible in the moonlight, but he made it across in no time and then it was Blackwood's turn. He, too, made it across and that left only Scott.

'I'm ready to run,' he said to Parker and Nicholson in turn, using his hand set.

'All clear,' Parker said.

'All clear this end,' Nicholson said.

Scott checked the road anyway. Seeing and hearing nothing, he took a deep breath, then jumped up and advanced at the half-crouch, automatically weaving left and right to avoid being hit by an imaginary sniper. The road was only a hundred yards wide but crossing it seemed to take forever. The silence amplified the sound of his heavy breathing; his heart was beating too quickly. He reached the far side without incident, saw the others hidden in the trees, their weapons aimed along the road in both directions, prepared to give covering fire. Reaching them, he turned back to face the road whilst dropping to one knee beside Paddy Devlin.

'Good run,' Paddy said.

Still using his hand set, Scott called Parker and Nicholson in turn, informing them that he had just crossed the road and that now it was their turn. When they acknowledged him, he turned the hand set off and clipped it back to his webbed belt. He then raised his MP5 to his shoulder and aimed it at the north bend in the road, preparing to give covering fire if necessary, as the others were doing.

In the event, nothing happened. Parker and Nicholson made it across without incident and rejoined the patrol a few minutes later. Falling into single file without being told – since the diamond formation would not be appropriate here – the men began the arduous, dangerous climb up the mountain, weaving their way silently through the trees in the still, moonlit darkness.

CHAPTER THIRTEEN

Dmitry didn't know exactly where they where, but he had a pretty good idea. Two of the watch patrols he had sent out to the Fergana Valley had caught a glimpse of a lot of parachutes descending by night at low level, less than a thousand metres above the ground, suggesting the use of the highly dangerous HALO method of insertion practised by the SAS. Reportedly, there had been a lot of parachutes, certainly well over a dozen, but Dmitry knew that some of those would have been dropping supplies, not men, and that the number of actual SAS men would therefore be smaller. The exact number had not been confirmed as the parachutes had fallen to earth behind the tree line, which had placed them out of sight of the watch patrols. Despatched to that area, with orders not to engage with the enemy, but merely to ascertain their strength and report back to Dmitry, the watch patrols had found no trace of the SAS, nor of the parachutes or supply packs that would have descended with them. To all intents and purposes, the SAS had vanished off the face of the earth and might never have been.

'They're clever,' Dmitry said to Misha as they faced each other across the table in the former's house, already patched up after the fire started by Lalya, though most of the paintings, scorched or melted by the flames, had been removed from the walls and there was hardly a book left in the place. Thank God, the paintings had only been reproductions and could be replaced; the books, alas, were gone forever and he would have to bring new ones in from Russia. As for Lalya, he thought often about her, with admiration and finely suppressed pain. He had not sent a search party out to find her and now assumed she was dead. This knowledge pained him even more, which was something he tried, without success, to deny to himself. Right now, however, he was more concerned with the SAS and looking forward to an ultimate engagement with them. Clearly, they were a formidable enemy and that was the challenge. 'Yes,' he emphasised, 'very clever. They cleared up their DZ so thoroughly that we don't know exactly where they landed. Then they must have headed into the forest and stuck to it all the way to the mountains. That way, they could have made it unseen.'

'They're known to be resourceful,' Misha said, 'and clearly they are. If they did as you suggest, they could be in the mountains by now. They'll still be low down, not too far above the highway, but they could have reached that far at least.'

'I agree.' Dmitry had a swallow of his Georgian brandy, let it burn down inside him, warming his innards, then wiped his lips with the back of his hand. 'What we need to know is where they would have crossed the road and we won't find that out unless they were seen.'

'So far no one's reported seeing them,' Misha said, while toying distractedly with the glass of vodka in his right hand. 'However, I believe I know roughly where they would have crossed.'

'Oh?' Dmitry raised his fine eyebrows enquiringly. 'Where?'

'We know roughly where they descended,' Misha said, his pale grey eyes focused elsewhere, his sensitive features disguising his true nature. 'Though leaving that DZ under cover of darkness, they would have had to continue their journey in daylight to have landmarks for navigation in unfamiliar territory.' Smiling gently, he gazed down at the map spread out on the table before him. 'My bet, therefore,' he continued, thoughtfully tracing a line on the map with his vodka glass, 'is that they would have headed for the nearest sheltered area, which is the forest running from east to west about a thousand metres north of the DZ. In fact, that forest runs west all the way to the highway separating the Fergana Valley from these mountains. But it's a narrow strip of forest in the sense that, although it runs thousands of kilometres from east to west, it only runs for about seven kilometres from north to south.'

'So?'

Misha looked up again, his smile slight but boyishly sweet. 'My bet is that they made use of the forest to travel in broad daylight from the DZ to the Osh–Fergana highway. To cross the highway unseen, they would have emerged from the forest somewhere along the stretch of forest running parallel to the road – in other words, that seven-kilometre stretch running north to south. Once across, somewhere along that relatively short stretch, they would have begun their ascent of the mountain, using the forested lower hills for cover. So assuming they've crossed the road, they'll be in an area we can easily surround and search.'

'Misha, my friend, you're a genius,' Dmitry said, raising his glass to him in a mock salute.

'And, of course,' Misha continued, 'once they climb above the tree line and emerge to the mountain proper, they'll be more exposed.'

'They'll also be more careful,' Dmitry said, 'and they're supposed to be good at that.'

'They may be good, Dmitry, but they don't know these mountains and we do. Also, the higher they climb, the colder it becomes. Snow and ice; white-out blizzards; we could just sit back and watch what that does to them before moving in on them. Attack only when they've already lost some men to the elements and are seriously demoralised.'

'You make it sound so easy,' Dmitry said, 'but from what

I've heard about the SAS, they're not men easily demoralised. They're specially trained to work in extreme environments, including mountains and Arctic weather – so they may not be defeated by these mountains.'

Misha shrugged. 'Perhaps not defeated, but certainly placed at a severe disadvantage. Once they leave the shelter of the forests on the lower slopes, we can follow them all the way, wait until they're at their weakest and then either attack them or pick them off one by one. It's your choice.'

'I want to engage them,' Dmitry said. 'I want to see their faces. Most of all, I want the man who's leading them . . . and I want him alive.'

'Why? What's this new madness, Dmitry? They're foreigners, not local, and we can learn nothing from them, so let's just despatch them all at once and go back to our business.'

Dmitry studied his friend with detached curiosity. Misha looked like a poet, studied philosophy, invariably spoke softly and was capable of wading through seas of blood without batting an eyelash. A Byelorussian, formerly from Minsk, he had been born of peasant parents and grew up to be an uncommonly bright but rebellious student, good at his work but always in some kind of trouble, including theft and bloody fist-fights. Nevertheless, his academic record got him into Minsk's Lenin University where, though proving to be academically brilliant, he was eventually thrown out because of his many inexplicable, frightening outbursts of violence. Forced by his father into joining the Russian army (which the old man thought would impose some discipline on him), he was posted to Chechnya where, in 1995, he took part in a massacre committed by Russian troops high on drugs. Most of those drugs had been supplied to the troops by Misha who had by then made contact with local drug barons and become an expert dealer for them, mainly supplying and addicting his fellow troopers. Shortly after the massacre, however, when it became clear that the authorities were going to make an example of some of the troops involved in the bloodletting, with Misha's name at the top of their list, he deserted and turned up in Moscow, where he became one of the new *Mafiya* and proved himself quietly efficient at drug-trafficking and cold-blooded murder. When introduced to Dmitry by Boris Surgeyevich, he informed the former that he had to get out of Russia before the authorities, still pursuing him because of the Chechnya massacre, finally caught up with him. Dmitry, then already taking control of the drug trade in Kyrgyzstan, invited Misha to join him and they had been firm friends ever since. Misha was a killer as to the manner born and he rarely had sleepless nights.

'These men are good,' Dmitry said, snapping out of his brief reverie and returning to the subject at hand. 'They have a legendary reputation. We may have all the advantages, but they won't make it easy for us and I want to give them a chance to prove themselves. I want to see exactly how good they are before I destroy them.'

'That seems like an excuse for something else,' Misha said, 'and it doesn't sound healthy. You're turning this into a game, Dmitry, but it's a dangerous game. If we don't terminate these men when we can, we could pay the price for our procrastination. So let's despatch them as soon as we have the chance and not play any games ... What are you *really* after here?'

Dmitry scarcely knew himself and thought hard before replying. 'It's just a feeling,' he said, 'and I'm not sure what it means, but I'm weary of my life here, of the daily routine of our drug business, and the thought of these men trying to track me down excites me more than it frightens me. The SAS are truly amongst the best fighting men in the world and those sent to find me in this godforsaken place must surely be the best of the best. That, I think, is the challenge for me. That's why I'm excited. I want to see just how good they are, how much they can endure, just how far they can go before I tire of them and obliterate what's left of them. A game? Yes, it's a dangerous game, but at least it won't be boring.'

'You've experienced too much too quickly,' Misha said, 'and now you're jaded beyond all reasonable measure. You need excitement, true enough, but now the only way you seem to be able to find it is with a life-or-death gamble. This is a suicidal impulse, my friend, and it could lead to just that: an early death, if not by your own hand, then certainly invited by you. Is that what you're disguising?'

'I don't know,' Dmitry said, meaning it, confused by his own thoughts. He was, however, aware of the fact that since Lalya's escape from this camp, and almost certain death in the mountains, he had felt more despondent than ever before; more defeated by ennui, convinced that he could only break free from it by playing this dangerous game with the men sent to kill him. Lalya had not caused his growing indifference to life – it had been there since childhood – but she had deepened it by running away to almost certain death, thus proving him wrong about her, letting him know that she would rather die than live on his terms. She had proved that some people had more dignity than he could possibly imagine. More saliently, she had thrown his love back in his face and made him feel the kind of pain that he had sworn he would never expose himself to again. It was the pain of rejection, which he had experienced in childhood, and it had returned like a plague to torment him and make him yearn even more for death. That Lalya had managed to do this to him now filled him with wonder. 'I only know,' he continued uncertainly, 'that I don't want this over with too quickly; that the game must be played out. These men have come to offer me a challenge and I cannot refuse it.'

'And the leader?' Misha asked. 'Why do you insist on taking him alive? Will he be put to the torture?'

'No,' Dmitry said. 'It isn't that at all. Quite the opposite, in fact. I think this man is the kind I could respect, a true soldier, and so he must die with dignity, like a soldier, quickly and cleanly. So, no, I don't want him taken alive just to torture him. I want to see his face, to know what he's like, to know why he's taken on a mission that is, on the face of it, suicidal.'

'You want to know if he's like you,' Misha said bluntly, striking straight to the heart of the matter. 'You believe that the only kind of man who'd accept such a mission is one whose reasons for coming here are even greater than his reasons for living.'

'Yes,' Dmitry confessed. 'That's what I believe.'

'But you're wrong, Dmitry.' Misha was being quietly ruthless, as was his nature. 'Not all of the men who volunteered could possibly be like that. They volunteered because it's what they signed up for: for truly challenging missions. In that way, therefore, they are certainly like you, but that doesn't necessarily make them suicidal. They know it's dangerous, but they also believe they can win and that's the sole challenge for them. Given this, why should their leader be so different?'

'Because he is,' Dmitry said. 'I can feel it in my bones and I've sensed it in my dreams.' In fact, Dmitry had vivid dreams, far too many nightmares, and they all told him something about the real world, which was why he believed in them. He had dreamt of the nameless man who was coming to find him, seeing him as a faceless avenger, wrapped in darkness and blinding light. He believed the dream would come true. 'This man, their leader, has a clearer picture than the others of just how dangerous his mission is, how nearly hopeless his task – yes, almost suicidal – and yet he's still taken it on and I want to know why. He has his own reasons, Misha, and they're more important than his life; and I, who have little regard for life, want to know what those reasons are. I must test this man to the absolute limit and then take him alive. I must know exactly why he came here . . . Yes, I must know before I give him what it is he possibly wants above all else.'

'Death,' Misha ventured.

'Correct,' Dmitry said. 'I think this man is in some ways my brother.'

Misha shook his head sadly from side to side, smiling sardonically. 'The brother you never had, my poor Dmitry. The lost other half you keep yearning for.'

'Maybe so,' Dmitry said, recalling his nightmarish childhood with a vividness that lacerated his soul and instantly demolished his brief moment of joy. Recovering, he continued,

'Anyway, for whatever reasons, good or bad, I must play this game and look into the face of the man who has come here to kill me.'

He finished off his brandy, put the glass back on the table and glanced around the log house, gloomily lit by oil lamps and rendered even more spartan by the lack of the paintings and books. Reminded of how Lalya had taken her revenge, he smiled painfully, forced to admire her even as he grieved for her and wanted her back. He had not yet moved another woman into the house and this fact constantly surprised him. He must have loved Lalya more than he had realised or had been willing to admit to himself. This was something to think about.

Misha sighed sadly, despairingly, then finished off his glass of vodka and lit a cigarette. Exhaling a thin stream of smoke, he said, 'All right, Dmitry. We'll play your dangerous game. So what's the first step?'

'First we find them,' Dmitry said, 'then we track them and watch how they operate, then start picking them off one by one until that one man is left.'

'If we're to do it,' Misha said, 'we have to do it immediately – before they move out of the forest. Then, their movements will become more unpredictable. At least now we know roughly where they are and we can cover that seven-kilometre length of tree line until they emerge. Once they come out, we can track them unseen from a safe distance and decide in our own good time when to make the first strike. After that, they'll know we're on their tail and things won't be so easy.'

'I agree.'

'Good. So when do we move out?'

'Tonight,' Dmitry said.

CHAPTER FOURTEEN

The patrol did not get very far up the mountain that first night because, after advancing for only thirty minutes, Scott realised that the darkness between the trees was making the hike too difficult, with the men unable to see either the many tangled roots and potholes underfoot or the spiky branches that whipped their faces as they passed by. Calling a halt to the advance when they had reached a relatively level piece of ground that was still encircled by the trees, which made for good protection, Scott told the men to make camp. As before, they could not make use of their hexamine stoves, had to content themselves with cold rations, and could only basha down in shallow scrapes or LUPs covered with ponchos draped from rope strung from one tree to another.

This time, they did not do this all at once. For certain operational purposes, the patrol had been divided into two teams. Team 1 was led by Scott and included Parker, Arnie Basham and Syd Loomis. Team 2 was led by Paddy Devlin with Mad Mike Nicholson, Rudi Blackwood and Pete Welsh. This meant that Team 1 had the disassembled parts of the GPMG, carried jointly between Basham and Loomis, while each team had a PRC 319 radio system, carried respectively by Loomis and Welsh. It also meant that the four men of

Team 1 could set up their bashas, eat and drink, attend to their ablutions, then sleep while Team 2 kept guard for the first four hours, each man placed at one of the cardinal points of the compass within communication distance of the others. When their four hours was up, they were replaced by the members of Team 2 and the situation was reversed. Every man therefore got four hours sleep which, if not exactly heaven, was enough to keep him from feeling drowsy when they moved out the next day.

They did so at first light, still wending their way through the coniferous trees, but the forest gradually thinned out and then the trees disappeared altogether, leaving only the grey rock and loose gravel of the spartan lower slopes of the mountain proper. Here the gradients were reasonably shallow and there were quite a few tracks – formerly used by traders travelling on horses or camels, now trampled flat by the feet of local goatherders – as well as a lot of babbling brooks and streams of icy water that came down the mountainside from the melting ice of the distant summits, soaring above the broad, glittering plateaus of snow. There was no snow here and though the morning was bitterly cold, the rising sun brought the hot wind with it, making them sweat. They were in no way helped by the fact that they often had to make their way gingerly over sloping swathes of loose gravel, which rolled beneath their boots, threatening to make them slide backwards, and areas of sloping, smooth granite that allowed them no foothold.

Nevertheless, they kept going, advancing uphill in single file, in a long, well-spaced line, with Killer Parker out on point as usual and Paddy Devlin back in his position as Tailend Charlie. They were dangerously exposed here, sometimes forced to advance between irregular, high walls of wind-smoothed granite, behind which enemy snipers could be lurking, or on narrow tracks that either crossed broad, open areas or ran along the rim of a deep fissure or ravine.

Glancing back over his shoulder, Scott saw the great plain of the Fergana Valley spread out far below, shimmering in the glazed heat of the morning. Looking to the front again, he was faced with the soaring slopes of the mountains, colourless at this point, with walls of granite and swathes of gravel, but rising to glistening plateaus of snow and ice-covered peaks, now shrouded in white clouds. It was freezing cold up there, but where Scott's party were advancing it was burning hot, and when Scott glanced left and right, at the shadowed gorges and ravines, he saw black-bearded vultures staring at him from where they were perched on the rocks. There were other creatures there as well – mountain goat and deer – and they, too, watched the advancing men with curiosity before bolting away.

Even as the heat increased, the slopes became steeper and soon the men, as well as sweating profusely, were panting with exertion. Eventually, when they reached a sheltered location – a gravel clearing surrounded by a rocky enclosure just off the beaten track – Scott told them to rest up. Two of them, Syd Loomis and Rudi Blackwood, were placed on watch, one above the patrol, the other well below it, both in positions giving a clear view in all directions over the mountainside, but since this was daylight they were allowed to smoke while on duty. The rest of the men were allowed to light their hexamine stoves to cook warm food and have a brew-up for the first time since they had arrived. They would have a two-hour break. Loomis and Blackwood would be relieved by two others halfway through that rest period, enabling them, also, to eat, drink and rest up.

When they had finished their own meals and repacked their bergens, Scott and Paddy sat side by side, the latter smoking a filtered cigarette. They both gazed about them, at the mountainside, wondering where the enemy was.

'How the hell are we going to find him up here,' Paddy asked, 'when we don't have a clue where he is?'

'I *do* have a clue,' Scott replied. He withdrew his map

from a pocket in his DPM tunic and spread it out over his own and Paddy's legs. 'I don't know *exactly* where Petrov's camp is hidden,' he said, 'but I have a rough idea of the general area.' He tapped the map with his index finger. 'According to intelligence gleaned from the Russians who helped us behind the scenes, Petrov uses trucks and snow ploughs to transport his men and supplies up and down the mountainside. Petrov's camp is known to be located high above the snow line, where swathes of freezing ice and frequent *myatel*s – white-out blizzards – make access extremely difficult and have discouraged the Kyrgyz border police – mostly corrupt and inept in any case – from trying to find him. The only road that's capable of carrying heavy-duty vehicles and also travels above the snow line to near the summit is this one . . .' He traced the road with his finger. 'It swings off the Osh–Fergana highway near the Alay Pass – here – and then snakes in this western-southerly loop up the face of the mountain – like so – terminating a couple of hundred metres from the highest peak – here.' Removing his finger from the map, he scanned the mountainside, then pointed to where he could see the road snaking up the mountain to disappear into the snow high above. 'That road was built years ago by the Osh authorities to give them access to a meteorological station that was, in the end, never built – so the road no longer serves any purpose. I reckon that Petrov's camp would have to be located somewhere just off that road, most likely just below its termination point a few hundred metres below the summit.'

'So we stay away from the road,' Paddy said perceptively, 'while always keeping it in sight and following it up the mountainside until we locate Petrov's camp.'

'Exactly. We can watch for any traffic on it and, failing that, send recce patrols out to eyeball the road itself for vehicle tracks or any human debris that might indicate the direction we need to go in.'

'We can do it,' Paddy said, his gaze following the distant

road to where it disappeared into the great swathes of glistening snow high above, 'but it won't be easy up there. If we even make it that far – and we might not – it's going to be hell when we get there.'

'We survived the Fortuna Glacier,' Scott said, referring to their ordeal in South Georgia during the early days of the Falklands War, 'so we can survive up there.'

Paddy nodded, agreeing, but he felt obliged to add cautiously, 'We might have been observed when we inserted. They could be watching us right now.'

'That's right,' Scott said.

'And if they are?'

Scott shrugged. 'What can I say? We can only pray that they aren't. On the other hand, if they are, we're likely to be forced into a fire-fight which, if we win it, killing Petrov in the process, will save us from having to climb the mountain. Always look on the bright side.'

Paddy grinned as he pushed one side of the map off his legs and clambered back to his feet, holding his assault rifle in his right hand. 'I like an optimistic PC,' he said. 'Now it's time to move on, boss.'

'Right,' Scott said.

For a while, as they climbed higher, the heat became more fierce, but mercifully, as the sun moved across the sky, slowly sinking, the warm air started cooling. As the light dimmed slightly, still bright but not so dazzling, bringing everything into sharper perspective, birds flew across the sky or settled upon the larger rocks: rock partridges, desert bullfinches, red starlings and, always, the black-bearded vultures. Mountain goats were silhouetted in the distance like ink-blackened cardboard cutouts. Marching on, the eight men heard the squawking of those birds, the distant bleating of the goats, the frantic padding of unseen gophers, and the muffled cacophony of other, unfamiliar creatures calling to each other. They were in a strange world, an alien world, and it made them uneasy.

'I hate those big black vultures,' Syd Loomis said when

they had stopped for a late afternoon rest and were having a smoke. 'They're filthy bastards and they can smell death a mile off, so they just sit there waiting.'

'They're God's creatures like you and me,' Arnie Basham informed him, 'and they have their own purpose.'

'The black man's speaking up for those filthy black vultures,' Rudi Blackwood retorted. 'One black defending another, as always.'

'What purpose?' Loomis asked.

'They keep the mountain clean,' Arnie explained, 'by feeding off the dead and leaving only the cleanly picked bones. That's their purpose in life, man.'

'Am I hearing right or what?' Rudi Blackwood asked rhetorically, looking around him in mock disbelief. 'What is this shite I'm being asked to swallow? Please pass me a rubbish bag!'

'It's just bullshit,' Pete Welsh said, rubbing his long, pale, pimply face, his grin shy, his gaze slipping sideways.

'Damned right, it's just bullshit.' Blackwood nodded emphatically. 'Like everything else that pours out of his big black mouth – pure bullshit and bile.'

'No harm in vultures,' Arnie persisted. 'They'll only bother you when you're dead. But up there, where the snow is, there are leopards and they're the ones to watch out for.'

'Leopards?' Blackwood said, looking uneasy.

'Don't listen to him,' Loomis said. 'It's just more of his bullshit. You get leopards in hot countries, in the fuckin' jungle, not in mountains.'

'Snow leopards,' Arnie said. His grin was wide and ivory-white. 'They live in the snow and they don't get much to eat, so they'll go for any damned thing that moves. So you watch out for them, man, when you get up there – and forget the damned vultures.'

'Bullshit!' Loomis exclaimed.

'He's telling the truth,' Pete Welsh said. 'I read our report on this place and it said there are snow leopards in the mountains. He's not bullshitting this time.'

'Fucking hell,' Blackwood said, looking even more uneasy. 'I don't like bastard leopards.'

'They're all bastards, that's for sure,' Arnie said. 'Leopards never get married.'

'Ha, ha,' Loomis said. 'Behold the black boy's rapier wit.'

'I'd rather go up against a man with a weapon,' Blackwood said, glancing uneasily up the mountain, 'than come face to face with a fucking leopard. I mean, leopards *eat* people!'

'Just stare it down,' Pete Welsh said, 'like Syd did with that brown bear.'

'That's right,' Loomis said. 'They won't go for you unless you make a fast move, in which case you're done for.'

'You didn't move when you were faced with that bear,' big Arnie said, 'because you were frozen with fear, so don't say it was tactics.'

'I fucking knew what I was doing,' Loomis said, 'and don't you imply otherwise.'

'You were frozen stiff with fear.'

'I was staring it down,' Loomis insisted.

'A leopard can pick a man up in its jaws,' Blackwood said, distracted by his fearful thoughts and again glancing uneasily up the mountain, 'and carry him into its cave to feed off him for months. I don't like leopards, I tell you.'

'If that happens to you,' Loomis said, 'just fart in his face as he's carrying you away in his jaws and your stench will make him keel over. He won't want to know, pal.'

'Shut up, the lot of you,' Killer Parker said as he scrambled back to his feet, staring stonily at each of them in turn. He and Mad Mike Nicholson, who was standing beside him, were preparing to move on again. 'Take up your positions in file formation and then keep your dumb traps shut.'

'Yes, boss!' they all chorused.

The climb continued. By now the sun was sinking, creating a great jigsaw of blue shadow and crimson light on the western face of the mountain – higher up, on the snow and ice – but down here, where the men were marching, that same sun still had dominion, though its light was gradually, inexorably dimming. Nevertheless, visibility was still good, so as he marched ahead of his men, though still well behind Killer Parker, Scott kept his eyes on that distant road, hoping in vain to see some traffic passing along it. Clearly, however, since nothing had passed in all the hours he and the others had been marching, the Green Slime in the Kremlin in Hereford had been correct when telling him that the road was now only used by Dmitry Petrov and his murderous brigands.

Studying that road where it ran uphill from the Alay Pass, then following it with his gaze to where it disappeared into that white hell near the summit, Scott thought of Dmitry Petrov and wondered what he was like. Already he felt a great contempt for Petrov – a contempt based on the revulsion he now felt for all drug dealers – but as he gazed upon those awesome ice-capped mountains, at the curtains of snow being blown across the slopes, their high, jagged peaks shrouded eerily in clouds, he realised that he was not going to be dealing with some petty, urban, English hoodlum. That kind had sold drugs to his son, first addicting him, then killing him, but this drug baron, who had addicted and killed even more, many by his own hands, would be a different kind of man altogether, shaped not by sleazy back alleys and dimly lit, claustrophobic, drug-ruined rooms, but by the dreadful hardships and challenges imposed by this alien landscape.

While in no way about to offer respect to Dmitry Petrov, Scott accepted that he would not be commonplace and almost certainly would be highly unpredictable. This would make him a formidable enemy, but Scott didn't mind that. His sole thought was to make amends for the death of Johnny, his only son, and as Dmitry Petrov was responsible for the drugs presently flooding Great Britain, therefore indirectly responsible for Johnny's death, Scott wanted to personally face him with his crimes and then execute him. In short, he did not want Petrov killed until they had spoken.

Removing his hand-held transceiver from his belt, Scott contacted Killer Parker and asked him what he could see up ahead.

'Nothing,' Parker said. 'At least nothing moving. Just slopes that are even steeper than the ones we've climbed and, above them, the snow. But it's dark on the upper slopes, boss, and it'll soon be dark here. We can't climb these mountains in the darkness, so I suggest we basha down for the night.'

'I agree,' Scott said. 'What's it like where you are?'

'Flat ground on either side of the track, both sides hemmed in by rocky outcroppings. It's a natural clearing that should do us for the night.'

'Okay. You stay there and we'll join you. Over and out.'

Clipping the transceiver back to his webbed belt, he turned to the side and used a hand signal to indicate that the others should follow him, then he made his way up the steep, gravelly path to where Killer Parker was lowering his heavy bergen to the ground. Scott glanced about him and saw that Parker had picked a good spot, with level ground on both sides of the track within a semi-circle of rocky outcroppings, some about ten feet high. A gradient of stone and gravel rose a good distance beyond the rocks, then fell away again, out of sight, before rising to a series of ridges that climbed, one on top of the other, to the immense mountain face. The sun was still above the mountain peaks, but about to sink behind them. There was nothing moving out there.

'You found a good spot,' Scott said to Parker.

'There isn't a good spot up here, boss,' Parker replied in his flat, laconic manner. 'Any rock that offers shelter to us can do the same for the enemy.'

'Pragmatic as always,' Scott said, grinning. 'Well, let's take our chances.' He turned to face the other men as they entered the clearing one by one. When they were all gathered around him, he said, 'This is where we basha up for the night, but no hexamine stoves and no ciggies. Even the end of a fag can be seen in the dark, so the smokers will just have to suffer.' He waited for the melodramatic moans and groans to fade away, then said, 'Make up your bashas, have a quick bite to eat – cold food only – then we'll draw matchsticks for who takes the first watch. Two men on each watch, one above and one below, positioned to let you see in every direction. Two hours on, two hours off throughout the night, moving on at first light. Okay, get to it.'

Still moaning and groaning melodramatically, though clearly relieved to be laying up for the night, the men went to work. Unable to dig shallow scrapes for their bashas and with no trees to which they could tie the ropes for covered LUPs, they could only roll their ponchos out on the gravel-covered earth and lay their sleeping bags on top of them. Then, hungry, they settled down to eat their cold rations, which consisted of paste-filled wads, or sandwiches, followed by chocolate and high-calorie biscuits. Some of them cleaned their teeth with the aid of water from their water bottles; other simply used chewing gum, the last being favoured by the smokers who could not have a drag.

'What's the bet I draw the first fucking watch?' Syd Loomis said to big Arnie. 'I always do. That draw's fixed.'

'You hardly ever draw first watch,' big Arnie replied. 'You just *imagine* you do. No, the one who'll draw the first watch is Rudi. That's guaranteed 'cause he's frightened of snow leopards and I can hear them growling out there.'

'Where?' Rudi Blackwood asked, his head jerking nervously left and right.

'Up there,' big Arnie said, raising his eyes to the snow-covered slopes high above, now fading into last light. 'They're up there in the snow, but they can smell a human being for miles and they'll come down in the dark. Sniff, sniff, gobble, gobble.'

'Fuck you,' Rudi said, though he still looked uneasy.

'You can't fuck a fuck-up,' Pete Welsh said with his shy grin and evasive, sideways gaze. 'And big Arnie, he's fucked up.'

'Maybe so,' big Arnie said. 'And then again, maybe not. Either way, I can tell you guys – and Pete here will confirm it – that snow leopards exist, they're out yonder in those mountains, and the first man who goes up there on watch will be the first man they smell. I is sayin' my prayers right this minute, Momma, that I's not the first one. God helps those who have faith.'

'God helps the undeserving,' Syd Loomis told him, 'and you're one of the breed. I'll get the first fucking watch – I always do – so fuck you *and* your leopard.'

'I'll fuck all of you,' Mad Mike Nicholson said as he came up to them, his right hand extended and upside down, with four matches stuck between his fingers, two of them broken, though you couldn't see which ones. 'The two who get the broken matches are on first watch,' he said. 'So stand up and take your pick.'

The four troopers stood up and stared sombrely at the matchsticks protruding from Mad Mike's gnarled fingers.

'That's only four matches,' big Arnie observed, 'and there's eight of us here.'

'The PC and the three non-coms have things to discuss,' Mad Mike said with his slow-burning, dangerous grin, 'and that means the troopers have to go first. Look on the bright side, you crap-hats. You go first and you'll lay up when you're really tired and that means you'll sleep soundly. As for us poor bastards, it's too early for bed, so we're in for a restless night. Now pick a match, you dickheads.'

The four troopers each took a match. Big Arnie and Pete Welsh grinned, but Syd Loomis shook his head in disgust and Rudi Blackwood groaned audibly.

'I knew it,' Syd Loomis said. 'I always get the first fucking watch.'

'Me, too,' Blackwood said.

'You go downhill,' Mad Mike said to Syd Loomis, then he turned to the despairing Rudi Blackwood. 'And you go uphill. Now piss off, the pair of you.'

'Why do *I* have to go uphill?' Blackwood asked.

'Because you're scared of fucking leopards,' Mad Mike said, his grin almost savage. 'Now get the hell up there.'

'Yes, boss,' Blackwood said. He picked up his MP5 and forlornly started towards the narrow track, which was darkening but still bright enough to let him see the immense face of the mountain with its glistening snowscapes. Grinning, Syd Loomis fetched his assault rifle and started walking downhill.

'Sniff, sniff, gobble, gobble,' big Arnie called out jovially to Rudi Blackwood as the latter made his way up the steep track in the darkening light of sunset.

Then the first shot rang out.

CHAPTER FIFTEEN

Dmitry decided to move out early when he saw the snow storm coming in. It was not a *myatel*, but it was certainly a heavy storm, with a fierce wind blowing the snow across the camp to dramatically reduce visibility and increase the depth of snow on the road outside. Determined to get down the mountainside before the situation worsened, he told Misha to arrange for thirty men to be ready to move out within the hour. Forty-five minutes later he stepped down the porch of his log house, his AK-47 Kalashnikov rifle slung over his shoulder, to find three troop-trucks filled with fighting men, ten to each truck, parked in the clearing. The men were wearing *telogreikas*, knee-high, black-leather boots, and furred caps with ear muffs. They were armed with a wide variety of assault rifles and sub-machine guns. Misha was seated next to the driver of the lead truck and Dmitry clambered up into that truck to take the seat beside him.

'A snow plough has gone on ahead to clear the way for us,' Misha informed him.

'Good. Let's get going.'

'*Vperyod!*' Misha snapped at the driver. 'Move!'

The truck roared into life and moved out of the camp, passing between two high watchtowers and turning left to go down the mountainside. Outside the camp, the blizzard was worse and the road was thick with snow, but a yellow snowplough was directly ahead, clearing the way for the trucks. The drivers remained in first gear, moving carefully in a well-spaced single line behind the snowploughs, keeping to the left of the road, near to a craggy cliff-face, because the right side fell away to a dizzying drop into a deep, snow-whitened ravine.

Glancing out of the driver's cabin, Dmitry saw the rise and fall of the mountains, towering peaks and great gorges, covered in an umbrella of heavy cloud under which, defying the fearsome elements, partridges and starlings were winging south. Those birds, he realised, would have a good view of the SAS men. The thought made him smile.

Glancing ahead again, he observed the snowplough, like an immense yellow insect, scooping the hardened snow up off the ground and tipping it over the right side of the road where it cascaded down in streams of glittering whiteness to the valley below. Letting his gaze roam up the cliff-face, which seemed to scrape the cloudy sky, he saw clouds of snow swirling across its face like a fluttering white veil. Returning his gaze to the valley below, which was encircled by more towering rocky ridges, all snow-covered and whipped by fierce, howling wind, he thought of Lalya trying to make her escape and wondered how far she had managed to get before she froze to death. She would be down there somewhere, encased in ice, covered in snow, and the thought of her lonely, lingering death filled him with guilt.

This surprised him. He had never felt guilt before. He had never felt love either and wasn't sure that he could recognise it, but he sensed that he had loved Lalya and, being frightened by the feeling, which he viewed as weakness, tried to kill it off by making her hate even more than she did. In this, he saw the darkness in the human heart that had always perplexed him.

'Foul weather,' Misha said. 'It won't help the SAS.'

'They won't be suffering from it yet,' Dmitry replied.

'They'll still be too far down, below the snow line, so right now they'll be all right.'

'Just how good are they?' Misha asked. 'Are they as special as reported?'

'From what I've heard – yes. They're possibly the best-trained soldiers in the world and their achievements, never mind their reputation, are truly formidable.'

'Then we'd better be careful, Dmitry.'

'I didn't know you were frightened of danger, Misha. Not you of all people.'

'I'm not frightened of danger and you know it. I want to get the job done and return to our real work. I don't like the idea of stringing it out because you want to see how far these men can go. From what you say, they might go farther than we imagine and cause us serious damage.'

'Damage limitation is an exercise I have always avoided.'

'Not true,' Misha said. 'You've always been in control, calculating, pragmatic, but now you have this peculiar obsession and it could cloud your judgement.'

'My judgement is never clouded,' Dmitry said, feeling a small, unexpected flash of anger towards this man he admired, 'and in this case it won't be. I simply want to present us with a challenge that could do us all good ... you and me ... our men, also. By finding out just how far the SAS can go, we can test our own limits. I think that's valuable, don't you?'

'I think it's disingenuous,' Misha replied, 'but I'll go as far as you take me.'

'I knew you would,' Dmitry said.

He was distracted when the driver slowed his truck down and then braked to a halt. Looking ahead, he saw that the man had done so because the snowplough up ahead had stopped.

In fact, they had come to one of their own watch patrols, men who had been ordered to check the road and, if necessary, put paid to anyone foolish enough to drive this far up the mountain. This happened only rarely and usually by accident, when a driver took the wrong turning – but when it did, that unfortunate person was usually stopped by the armed patrol, routinely executed, then pushed, still in his vehicle, over the cliff at the right-hand side of the road. In the past two years, four vehicles and their drivers had suffered that fate and now lay at the bottom of the gorge, drivers and vehicles mangled together, well covered in snow.

Dmitry and Misha always checked the watch patrols when they came down the mountain. Now, determined to do the same, they climbed down from the truck and advanced along the road, their weapons still slung across their shoulders, until they had passed the stalled snowplough and reached the watch patrol – four warmly wrapped, well-armed men in a makeshift encampment hidden from the road by a high rocky outcropping and on the edge of that terrible drop into the snow-covered gorge. Bulky in their *shinyels*, or greatcoats, they were huddled around an open fire piled high with burning sticks, warming their hands and smoking, but one of them, the patrol commander, jumped to his feet when Dmitry and Misha entered the clearing.

'Boss!' he exclaimed in surprise, looking nervous as he glanced from Dmitry to Misha, not sure whom he should address himself to first.

'How are things?' Misha asked.

The man shrugged, making loose snow fall from his shoulders. He was red-eyed and unshaven. 'Normal,' he said. 'Nothing happening. No traffic has passed by since we've been here. I think the weather ...'

'Quite,' Misha said, abruptly cutting the man off and surveying the small encampment area with his pale blue, unblinking gaze, taking in the four snow-covered sleeping bags, the tinned food piled up in a shallow well beside the fire, and the 5.56mm Steyr AUG automatic assault rifles lying on the slushy ground. Blinking in agitation when he saw the haphazard manner in which the men had scattered their weapons about them, he leaned over to pick one of them up and closely examine it. As he did so, a flush came to his pale cheeks and his eyes brightened dangerously.

'This weapon has iced over,' he said, raising his gaze to stare angrily at the trembling man. 'If you had to use it, you wouldn't be able to do so until it thawed it out. These weapons are supposed to be maintained every day, not treated like shit.'

'I'm sorry, boss,' the man stuttered, now trembling even more and raising his hands pleadingly in the air, 'but we've been here so long, we're so cold and tired, we simply forgot. I assure you . . .'

'You dumb bastard,' Misha said, cutting him off again. 'You irresponsible filth!'

'No, boss, I . . .'

But before the unfortunate man could even finish his sentence, Misha, in a sudden outburst of fury that startled all who saw it, swung the butt of the weapon up and smashed it brutally into the man's face, sending him bowling backwards to the snow with his broken nose streaming blood. He cried out in agony, clasping his hands to his bloody nose, then struggled to an upright position and stared up with wide, frightened eyes as Misha took a step forward, leaned over him, repeated the word 'Filth!', then smashed his face again with the butt of the rifle, knocking him back into the snow, spitting out broken teeth. He cried out in pain again, his lips and nose both bloody, as Misha threw the weapon to the ground in a gesture of contempt and withdrew his Glock 17 handgun from its holster.

'No, boss!' the man bawled, spitting another bloody tooth out, as Misha, visibly trembling with rage, aimed at him with the handgun. 'God Almighty, boss, don't!'

But the handgun roared, once, twice, a third time, and the man convulsed from the impact of the bullets slamming into his chest. He kicked his legs and one hand waved reflexively, then he was still. Misha holstered his handgun, then turned to the other three shocked men.

'Take this piece of shit,' he said, pointing to the dead man, 'and throw him over the edge of the ravine. *Do it now, you dumb bastards!*'

Galvanised into action by the deadly softness of Misha's command – a snake's venomous hissing – the other three men jumped to their feet and, in a state of fear and confusion, picked their dead comrade up, manhandled him to the edge of the gorge, and threw him over to let him fall a couple of hundred feet to the ground below. Then, visibly trembling, wondering what would become of them, they turned back to face Misha, whose pale grey eyes were blazing. He pointed to one of them.

'You!' he snapped. 'Go to the first truck on the road and tell the first man you see to come over here.'

'Yes, boss!' the man exclaimed, automatically picking up his ice-covered weapon, then hurrying away to the trucks.

Misha raised his right hand and repeatedly jabbed his index finger at the other two men as he talked to them.

'You pieces of lazy shit,' he said. 'If this ever happens again, if I ever come here and find your weapons in this condition, I'll do to you what I've just done to your friend. Tell this to the other two when they get here and don't ever forget it.'

'Yes, boss!' the two men chanted in unison.

Misha turned away from them and said to Dmitry, 'Let's get out of here, my friend. I can't stand the stench of this filth.'

Smiling slightly in admiration, Dmitry nodded assent, then he fell in beside Misha and they both walked back to the trucks. As they went in one direction, the third man from the watch team was returning with a man picked out of the first truck, the latter looking despondent as this particular watch patrol was not what he had been expecting and it was, indeed, the worst, most uncomfortable job that a man could be given. Misha stopped them both in their tracks.

'*Svolochi!*' he hissed at the man from the original watch team. 'Bastard!' He then turned to the unhappy man pulled out of the truck and said, 'You're in charge of these three turds. Make sure they don't repeat their mistakes or you, too, will find yourself in trouble.'

'Yes, boss!' the man snapped and hurried away with the other man, terrified by Misha's wrath.

Dmitry and Misha clambered back up into the first truck and ordered the driver to move off. As soon as he had turned on the ignition, the driver of the snowplough, forewarned by the roaring engine of the truck, moved off again, laboriously clearing a path through the snow for the column and leading them down the winding mountain road, through the still dense and swirling snowfall. By now, Misha had calmed down.

'Very good,' Dmitry said with quiet, good-humoured mockery. 'Very impressive. I don't think they'll forget that particular lesson.'

'They'd better not,' Misha said, though he, too, was smiling.

'Were you as angry as you seemed?' Dmitry asked.

'Not really,' Misha confessed. 'But such carelessness offends me. If any of the other gangs working in these mountains had come across that watch patrol, our men wouldn't have been able to defend themselves because their weapons were frozen.'

'So,' Dmitry said, 'they'd have been killed. You'd have lost no sleep over them.'

'That's not the point, Dmitry. The point is that our enemies would have had a propaganda victory and, even worse, anyone else coming up that road, even if by accident, would have ended up in our camp. It's a matter of common sense, as well as of discipline, and I believe in both.'

'Well, they certainly won't do it again, my friend.'

'No, they won't,' Misha retorted. 'So that bastard who went over the gorge has made amends for his sins.'

Dmitry smiled but said no more, having nothing more to say, and instead contented himself with observing the snowplough as it growled and rattled its way down the winding road until they emerged from the blizzard and eventually came to a point below the snow line. Once there, the driver of the snowplough slowed to a crawl, then pulled over to the side of the road to let the convoy of trucks through. The three trucks passed the snowplough one by one, then the first truck accelerated and continued down the road, now free of snow, at a more normal speed.

Glancing down over the lower slopes of the mountains, where the blizzard did not rage and the hills were all grey stone, gravel and sun-dried soil, Dmitry saw the Osh–Fergana road dividing the mountain from the vast valley beyond. North of the valley, about twenty kilometres distant, was the strip of forest mentioned by Misha, only seven kilometres north to south, but running all the way back to the eastern horizon, away from the mountain.

'That's it?' he confirmed with Misha just in case he was wrong.

'Yes, that's it, Dmitry. Those SAS men can't be too far from here. By now, they'll have emerged from the forest and crossed to this side of the road. They'll be somewhere lower down the mountainside, still not too far above the road and certainly in line with that north-south stretch of forest.'

'Good,' Dmitry said. 'We shouldn't have too much trouble finding them.'

'We won't,' Misha said.

In fact, they had even less trouble than expected. The convoy of trucks was still winding its way down the mountain road, now curving towards the Osh–Fergana road and the forest north of the valley, when a call came in over the radio system from one of the watch patrols that had seen the SAS men inserting by parachute. The PC of that watch team had called in to say that a body of men had been glimpsed emerging from the forested area on the lower slopes of the mountain opposite the forest in the valley, about halfway along it. The PC gave an approximate grid reading of where he thought the men would be right now.

'Perfect!' Dmitry exclaimed softly when Misha, who had taken the call, relayed the information to him. He glanced out of the window and saw that the sun was starting to sink above the mountains. 'Let's get there as quickly as possible,' he added, 'before darkness falls.'

'We'll make it,' Misha said.

The column kept on the move until Misha, with a map spread over his lap, checked the grid marks given by the watch patrol and eventually said, 'Somewhere here. Stop the truck.'

The driver braked to a halt.

Looking through the closed window, upon which the frost was melting in the higher temperature of the lower slopes, Dmitry saw the Osh–Fergana road far below and, just across it, the middle of the narrow stretch of forest out of which the SAS would have emerged. So they would be somewhere below, between here and the forested area this side of the road. It was an area of deep fissures, ravines and high, bizarrely shaped rocky outcroppings.

'They won't have gone north,' Dmitry said. 'They'll have learnt our approximate location from their friends in Moscow, so my guess is that they'll either have hiked straight up from the road or moved off in a south-westerly direction to take them towards our camp. That's not a large area for us to search, so I suggest that we spread out in a north-easterly direction as we make our way downhill. Two men in each team, each team with a hand-held transceiver. When spotted, they're not to be engaged. Instead, those who see them will remain under cover while the rest of us make our way to that location. Any questions?'

'No,' Misha said.

'Good. Let's get it organised.'

They clambered down from the trucks and split up to call the other men out and give them instructions. When the men were all on the ground, they were split into teams and sent out to cover the designated area. Dmitry and Misha remained together, not needing to be in charge, since the rest of the men would require no guidance until contact with the SAS had been made. When they saw the last of their men advancing down the mountainside, spreading out and disappearing behind the high rocky outcroppings, they headed off together in another direction, though one taking them into the general area to be covered.

As he hiked beside Misha, both of them holding their Kalashnikov rifles at the ready, he studied the landscape with a keen eye and thought it looked like the dark side of the moon: an awesomely desolate, cratered terrain, all rock and gravel, a little parched earth here and there, with nothing visibly moving. This was his world now – the domain of the damned – and he was convinced that if hell existed, he was already in it. He had little to lose, really, and perhaps the Englishman was the same: that man who had accepted a suicidal mission for some unknown reason.

This was, of course, crazy – what else could it be? – but Dmitry was certain that he and that stranger had been destined to meet. The heart of darkness was in these mountains and Dmitry's heart beat in that darkness, its rhythm governed by what he had lived through and thus ever erratic. Dmitry knew God's creation, that charnel-house of blood and pain, the boundless cruelty of life on earth, and in this he saw his only possible future: retribution and death. This Englishman was his dark brother, the one who had come to claim him, his great black bird of vengeance; and insane as it seemed, Dmitry was convinced that their destinies were interwoven. They would meet to look into one another's eyes and see what fate had in store for them. One way or the other, they would put an end to it. Dmitry wanted the end to come.

Haunted by his nightmares, pursued by the bloody deeds of his history, he marched beside Misha, another offspring of the damned, until the sun had almost set above the mountains, though its light still fell dimly about them. He was beginning to think that the night would defeat them when another watch team called in. They had found the SAS encampment and the details were passed on. It was only a mile away.

Consumed with an excitement that he had not felt in years, Dmitry made his way alongside the silent, pale-eyed Misha to the site called in by his watch team. Wending their way carefully, always watchful, around bizarrely shaped rock formations, along the edges of ravines, under soaring cliff faces, always high above the road that the SAS men had crossed, seeing the valley beyond as a great jigsaw of shadow and light, though the light was ever darkening, they came eventually to the summit of a rocky ridge where they found most of the other men already gathered, forming a large semi-circle along the rim of the ridge, gazing downhill with their weapons at the ready. Dmitry and Misha dropped to the half-crouch and advanced to the rim. Then they looked down and saw the men they had come to find.

They were a smaller group than he had expected – only eight men. Dmitry was heartened. If it had been a larger number, a show of strength, he would have despised them, but now he could believe all he had heard about them, these warriors trained like no others. They had come in small numbers because they had confidence and he admired them for that. Their encampment was in a semi-circle of rocky outcroppings, on level ground of stone and gravel, beside a track that curved uphill towards the rim of this ridge. As their sleeping bags were spread out on the ground, they were obviously preparing to bed down for the night, though two of them were breaking away from the others and picking up their weapons.

'Those two are preparing for guard duty,' Misha said. 'The rest are about to rest up.'

'Yes, Misha, I see that.'

'If we attack, we do it now,' Misha said, 'before those guards are in place.'

'One moment,' Dmitry said.

He knew that he was being foolish, that he could have wiped them all out there and then, but he had not come here for something so simple and he wanted one of them – at least that single individual – to live a little bit longer. He had to see that man's face.

'I want the leader,' he said, raising his binoculars to his

eyes and surveying them in the dimming light of the setting sun. He separated them by their insignia: four privates, two corporals, one sergeant and ... the patrol commander, a captain.

That was his man.

Dmitry studied him with fascination, seeing an ordinary man, neither handsome nor ugly, certainly not brutal and, indeed, almost certainly decent. He did not look like a soldier. His features were too refined. He had the look of a decent man who had lived a decent life and wanted no more than what a benevolent God would bestow upon him. Clearly, that man was civilised, perhaps even kind: the sort who would live by a moral code. That could be his weakness, his attraction as both victim and judge, and Dmitry, when he lowered the binoculars, was convinced that he had found what he had come here for.

I'm going crazy, he thought. I've never seen that man before. I've seen someone in my dreams – my dark avenger – but he was always faceless in darkness and striations of light. Yet I'm convinced, despite common sense, that this man is the one. He has come here for reasons that almost certainly he doesn't understand himself and this means something to me. We are one and the same.

'What the hell are we waiting for?' Misha asked. 'Those men are going on guard.'

'Let me fire the first shot,' Dmitry replied. 'We kill one and spread confusion amongst the others, then the real game begins.'

'You're mad,' Misha said.

'That's why we're friends,' Dmitry told him. 'Would you be with me if you wanted a normal life? No, my friend, you would not. So let me fire the first shot, make the first kill, then we move back and track them.'

'Wipe them all out now,' Misha insisted. 'Otherwise this madness will destroy us.'

'God's domain is a madhouse,' Dmitry told him, 'and you and I have always lived with that knowledge. You want certainty, Misha? Is that it? Are you growing old before your time?'

Misha shook his head, perplexed, disbelieving, but irresistibly drawn to the challenge. 'All right,' he said. 'Let's prove we're not too old. Pick your target, my friend.'

'I will,' Dmitry said.

He unslung his rifle, pressed the butt against his shoulder and looked down through his infrared, night-vision sight. He saw the men in the level clearing, a group about to break apart, with one man marching downhill and another advancing up the path that led eventually to the rim of the ridge.

Dmitry fixed his sight on the captain, the cross-hairs clear on his temple, a perfect shot, but then he smiled and moved the barrel sideways and fired his first shot.

The silence was broken.

CHAPTER SIXTEEN

'Blackwood's down!' Mad Mike Nicholson bawled as they scattered to pick up their weapons and run for cover.

Shocked by the reverberating sound of that single rifle shot, Scott spun around to see Blackwood lying on his back on the sloping path that led up to the high ridge, his left leg twitching convulsively, his right hand rising and falling like a limp rag. He had been hit in the stomach.

Oh, fuck! Scott thought, instantly wracked by guilt because, out of mistaken consideration for his weary men, he had let them rest up before arranging to guard the camp. You dumb bastard! he admonished himself.

'That ridge above the track!' Paddy Devlin bawled, reaching down to the ground for his MP5 sub-machine gun and firing it even as he sprang back to the upright position.

Like the others, Scott dropped to the ground, snatched up his MP5 as he rolled over his sleeping bag, then took up his firing position when behind a high rock, though he didn't yet start firing. By now, the rest of his men were already firing like crazy, aiming uphill, at the rim of the darkening ridge, though they could see nothing up there and, bizarrely, only that one shot had so far been fired. Glancing up the sloping path, Scott saw that Blackwood was still alive, still moving, sobbing distantly, but when he looked beyond him, at the curved edge of the ridge, he saw and heard nothing.

'A sniper,' Killer Parker said from where he was crouching beside Scott, his SA-80 assault rifle resting on the rock behind which he was hiding. The Barrett Light .50 rifle was still strapped to his backpack.

'A lone sniper,' Scott emphasised.

'Right, boss. That's why there's no more gunfire. But that bastard's still up there.'

As if to prove him right, another single shot rang out. Blackwood spasmed as if charged with a bolt of electricity and then let out a dreadful scream. He had been shot through the knee and the smashed bone was glinting dully in dying light, sticking out through his shredded, blood-soaked trousers.

'Oh, Christ!' he cried. 'Jesus!'

He was not helped. Instead, another single shot came from the ridge and Blackwood spasmed violently and screamed again in agony. This time he had been shot through the other knee, which was now a mess of blood and splintered bone. This time he said nothing at all; he just kept screaming in agony.

Mad Mike Nicholson instinctively jumped up to go to Blackwood's aid, but Killer Parker jerked him back down and said, 'Don't fucking move. You can't do a damned thing for him.'

Another shot rang out. This time it was Blackwood's shoulder. A second shot smashed his other shoulder and his screaming was dreadful.

'That bastard's playing with him!' big Arnie bawled. 'He's *torturing* that poor fucker to death. We've gotta *do* something, boss!'

But before anyone could do anything about Blackwood, the whole length of the ridge suddenly exploded with gunfire, a fusillade of sustained fire, rifles and sub-machine guns combined, filling the air with their roaring. Bullets thudded into the sleeping bags and ricocheted noisily off the rocks, sending splinters flying and creating spitting, swirling clouds of dust.

That gunfire had been aimed at the clearing, not at the SAS men.

'Shite!' Paddy Devlin cried out. 'There's more than one man up there!'

'Damned right,' Killer Parker said. 'There's a whole fucking gang of 'em.'

'They're either blind,' Scott said, 'or they're deliberately not aiming at us. They're just keeping us pinned down.'

'Fucking weird,' Mad Mike said.

Another fusillade of gunfire came from the ridge, this time deliberately aimed to tear Blackwood to shreds and put him out of his misery. His body convulsed repeatedly from the impact of the bullets, was punched this way and that, and only when the gunfire tapered off was he still for all time.

'Keep me covered!' Scott bawled, then he jumped up and ran forward at the half-crouch, weaving left and right, skirting around Blackwood's prostrate, bloody, smashed body to race up the narrow, winding track. He was about halfway up, spasmodically protected by the rocky formations to his left, forming a broken wall between him and the ridge above, when he heard someone coming up behind him. Glancing back over his shoulder, he saw Killer Parker, also weaving and advancing at the half-crouch.

'I've got to see who's up there,' Parker said.

'I'll bet you have,' Scott replied.

As Parker caught up with him, there was another sustained fusillade of fire from the curved rim of the ridge. This one was clearly aimed to deliberately miss Scott and Parker. Instead, it was designed to tear up the track ahead and keep them pinned to the irregular wall of stone.

The firing ended abruptly.

Scott and Parker listened for some time, waiting for the firing to commence again. When it did not, the former used a hand signal to indicate to the SAS men below that they were to stop their own firing. When the firing ceased, the silence was complete except for the constantly moaning wind.

In that eerie semi-silence Scott was further shocked to hear a man's voice calling out in English from the ridge above him. 'Come and find me, Englishman! Do your duty! I look forward to meeting you!' This was followed by the sound of mocking laughter, then the silence returned.

'Shit,' Parker whispered, 'did we just hear right? Was that guy speaking English?'

'Yes, he was,' Scott replied.

'That fucker was teasing us,' Parker said.

'Uh-huh,' Scott said.

Slightly stunned, wondering just what kind of game was being played on him, he glanced down the track and saw the unfortunate Rudi Blackwood, now motionless and clearly dead, in a pool of brightening moonlight. Enraged and guilty all over again, Scott used a hand signal to tell the men below that they were to make their way up the darkening track, one by one. They obeyed the silent order, advancing carefully up the track, each having to step around the dead Blackwood before inching in to the protective wall of high rocks. In the event, no more shots were fired and all the men were soon gathered around Scott, waiting for further instructions.

Using his left hand, he indicated that they were to follow him up the narrow track in their normal single file marching order, though this time he personally took the lead position, with Corporal Parker behind him. He went up slowly and as quietly as possible, virtually inching forward from one rock formation to another and silently cursing at the noise made by the gravel sliding underfoot. Reaching level ground, he dropped even lower and glanced left and right to take in the rocky field that ran from the edge of the ridge to an area of bizarrely shaped rock formations. There was no one in sight.

Nevertheless, aware that those rock formations would make ideal cover for an ambush party (the ground directly in front was clear and too flat to allow for human concealment), he signalled for the men to spread out and advance upon them, covering the whole of the flat area as they did so. Spreading out and advancing slowly at the half-crouch, their weapons at the ready, they cleared the whole flat area, found no one in it, then advanced even more carefully to the widely scattered columns of rock and another series of ridges. They wended their way between the high, potentially dangerous, rock formations, now almost in darkness though illuminated by pale moonlight, and again found them deserted.

The men who had fired upon them had disappeared like ghosts, leaving no trace behind.

'They could be anywhere,' Paddy Devlin whispered, 'and we've no way of finding them.'

'Let's go back down,' Scott said. He signalled the men to return to the camp, still in their original hiking order, though again with himself in the lead. Near the bottom of the track, they came to the body of Rudi Blackwood, now a hideous mess of blood and smashed bone. Two of them, big Arnie and Syd Loomis, picked Blackwood up by his ankles and wrists to carry him the few remaining yards back to the camp. When they lowered him gently to the ground, Big Arnie was sobbing.

'Fuck it, man,' he said between tears, shaking his head disbelievingly from side to side, 'I should never have made that stupid joke! Now Rudi's dead – just like I joked he would be – and I wish to hell I'd never opened my big mouth and put a curse on him. Oh, man, I feel bad!'

'You didn't curse him,' Pete Welsh said.

'It was a joke about a fucking leopard,' Syd said. 'Who the hell would have thought . . . ?'

'That's the whole point,' Arnie said. 'He was terrified of leopards. I scared him and then those bastards shot him. Then the sadistic shits deliberately drew it out by torturing the poor fuck to death. Like a leopard, man! Just like a big cat – tormenting its prey before killing it. Man, I just can't believe it.'

'You're talking bullshit,' Pete Welsh said. 'It was nothing to do with you, Arnie.'

'That's right,' Syd Loomis added. 'He went up that fuckin' hill to stand on guard and he was shot by a sniper. That's all there was to it.'

'No, it's not, man,' big Arnie insisted. 'I'm the one who's responsible. I put a curse on the poor fucker. I did! Oh, man, this is terrible!'

Killer Parker walked up to Arnie, grabbed him by the shoulders, shook him gently but firmly, and said, his voice a venomous whisper, 'Shut your mouth, Trooper. This is no time for hysterics. Your joke didn't kill Blackwood – those bastards up there did – and wherever they are now, they won't forget us, so let's bury your friend and then move on.' He turned to Scott, as if remembering his own place in the team, and said, 'We *are* moving on, boss?'

'Damned right,' Scott said. He glanced at each of the men in turn. 'The fault was all mine. Jokes don't even come into it. I should have had two men on watch before we made camp – so I'm the one who's responsible.'

'What now?' Paddy Devlin asked.

'Naturally we can't stay here, so as Parker says, let's bury Blackwood and then get the hell out of here.'

'I'll do it,' big Arnie said. 'I'll at least dig his grave.'

'Me, too,' Syd Loomis said.

'You two,' Paddy said to Killer Parker and Mad Mike Nicholson, 'take over the watch positions we were going to man before that bastard opened fire: one above, one below. When Blackwood's buried and when the rest of us have packed our kit, I'll send Loomis and Welsh to replace you, so you can pack up. Then we move out.'

Parker and Mad Mike nodded before loping off in opposite directions – Parker going back up the track, Mad Mike heading downhill – to take up the positions formerly assigned to Blackwood and Syd Loomis.

'Welsh,' Paddy said, 'it'll save a lot of time if you help these two dig a grave for Blackwood. We have to get out of here as soon as possible, so get to it, the three of you.'

Without a word, the three troopers removed their small

spades from their webbed belts and proceeded to dig a grave for Blackwood. While they were doing this, Scott and Paddy gathered their kit, rolled up their sleeping bags, packed their bergens and made ready to move out. However, while waiting for the grave to be dug, they had a private consultation, squatting side-by-side on the gravelled ground, their hands on their weapons, their eyes constantly scanning the areas not covered by the two men on watch. Night had fallen and a large moon shed its light from a sky filled with stars.

'Well, Paddy,' Scott said, 'I've just made my big career mistake and I don't feel good about it.'

'Fuck it,' Paddy responded. 'It wasn't even a mistake. We'd only been in that clearing a few minutes when that bastard on the ridge opened fire. My bet is that they knew exactly where we were – they must have seen our HALO drops – and they've been tracking us every inch of the way. They know these mountains; we don't. So we won't be the hunters any longer ... they'll be hunting us.'

'That's a very bad situation, Paddy. It means we're at a singular disadvantage. It makes us the victims.'

'Right. They know where we are, but we don't know where they are, and that means they can strike whenever they want to ... Something strange here, though.'

'I think I know what you mean.'

'Yeah, I think you noticed. I believe we're talking about the same thing.'

'They could have taken the whole lot of us out with one ambush, but they didn't. They only shot Blackwood, played their vicious game with him, making sure that we could see it, then when Parker and I advanced up the slope, they deliberately avoided hitting us ... they were just playing games again.'

'Exactly,' Paddy said. 'So what the hell's going on?'

'What, indeed?' Scott mused. 'And let us not forget that bastard calling out from the ridge and then having a good laugh at our expense. What was it he said? I didn't quite get it all – just the fact that he was addressing us in what seemed like pretty good English.'

'No, you're wrong,' Paddy said. 'He wasn't addressing all of us. He was only speaking to one of us. He said: "Come and find me, Englishman! Do your duty! I look forward to meeting you!"'

Recollecting that voice, Scott felt peculiar. He had felt that the voice was calling directly, personally, to him, though this was highly unlikely, a side effect of the man's effrontery in calling out at all; an auditory hallucination caused by his bold, mocking laughter. Probably Paddy, Killer Parker, all the others, had thought the same thing ...

'He was a foreigner speaking English,' Scott said, 'and he made a small grammatical mistake. That would explain it. Clearly, he was addressing the whole patrol – trying to wind us up.'

'Maybe,' Paddy said, 'but it didn't sound that way to me. For a start, he spoke perfect English, almost flawless, so I don't think he made a mistake. Then, again, we have to remind ourselves that his gang, almost certainly on his instructions, only killed one of us, deliberately letting the rest of us go – at least until the next time.'

'I'm finding this hard to grasp,' Scott said, feeling truly perplexed and oddly, unusually disorientated, perhaps even frightened. 'It doesn't make any sense.'

Paddy leaned forward to stare intently at Scott. '"English*man*," he said. "Do *your* duty. I look forward to meeting *you* . . ." No, boss, he knew just what he was saying. It was a straight-forward challenge to one of us. The question is: Which one?'

'He wouldn't know *any* of us,' Scott said, 'so it still doesn't make sense.'

'He may not know us personally,' Paddy continued relent-lessly, 'but he's challenging one of us to come and find him. I can't think why – and I'll admit it's bizarre – but that's almost certainly what that bastard is doing.'

'So he challenges one of us for his own reasons,' Scott concurred. 'How would he pick that man?'

'What kind of challenge would it be to him if he didn't pick out the one he thinks is either the best or the most important in our group? And that means, since he doesn't know any of us personally, that he picks out our leader.'

Scott felt even more disorientated and unreal, as if he was being haunted by a ghost that he could feel but not see. That eerie, mocking voice, albeit speaking perfect English, could only have belonged to Dmitry Petrov, the man he had come to find. Instead, Dmitry Petrov had found him and that was bad news.

'He would have checked our insignia through his binoculars,' Paddy continued doggedly, 'and seen that you had the highest rank. I think it's as simple as that.'

'But why play this extraordinary game? If he knows we're foreign soldiers, he must have guessed why we're here, so why not attempt to put an outright stop to us? Why challenge a man he's never met and doesn't even know?'

'Because that man represents something that he has to resolve. Who knows? Maybe he's a primitive bastard with primitive ways of thinking: he has to challenge our greatest warrior, our chief, to a duel – to prove his fucking manhood or something. Christ knows, but I think that's what it is and you're the man he's after. That's why he didn't kill all of us immediately and that's why he's inviting us to come and find him. He wants to measure his fighting men against our own, but in the end he has to know if he can beat *you*. Believe me, boss, it's something like that and I think we're in a bad fix here.'

'You mean *I'm* in a bad fix,' Scott said sardonically.

'I mean *us*. This isn't a proper fight, boss. These men can see us, but we can't see them; and I think they're going to watch us every step of the way and do just *what* they want *when* they want. We're not engaging them – they're engaging us – and that puts us on the defensive.'

'That isn't the role we've been trained for,' Scott said.

'No, it's not, which means this situation is dodgy. And you're going to have to be even more careful than the rest of us because, in the end, it's you he wants. This is like cowboys and fucking Indians, is what it is.'

'It would be. Except that we're up against a *Mafiya* drug baron and his gang of cut-throats and brigands.'

'Grave's ready, boss!' Trooper Loomis called out to them.

Climbing to their feet, they went over to where troopers Basham, Loomis and Welsh were standing by the six-foot hole they had skilfully managed to dig out of the ground. Scott and Paddy both gazed into the hole, hardly knowing what to say, then Paddy, perhaps wanting to get it over with, said brutally, 'Not much we can do except wrap him in his blanket and poncho, then roll him in. Put his bergen and other kit in with him, then fill the hole in again.'

'That's it?' Arnie Basham said.

'I'm afraid so,' Paddy replied.

'When he's buried, I'll say a prayer over the grave,' Scott told Arnie, hoping to make him feel better. 'I'm not a priest, so I can't do more than that. Okay, fill the grave in.'

Big Arnie kept shaking his head from side to side, expressing his shock and disbelief, as he and the other two troopers wrapped Blackwood in his blanket and poncho, then rolled him over the rim of the hole to fall brutally onto the soil at the bottom. After lowering his bergen and other kit in on top of him, they laboriously filled the hole in again, using the same small spades. When the job was done, they cleaned their spades, attached them to their bergen rucksacks, then picked up their rifles. Moonlight fell on the mound of earth between them and they studied it silently, before bowing their heads to let Scott recite a prayer.

'Well,' Paddy said, sighing, when Scott had finished his recitation, 'I guess that's it. Get your kit together, men. When you're ready, Welsh, get up that hill and relieve Corporal Parker. You, Loomis, relieve Corporal Nicholson.'

'What about me?' Arnie asked.

'You can have a rest, Trooper. Okay, get to it.'

The three troopers quickly and expertly packed up their kit, using every available inch of space in the bergens, then

Loomis and Welsh went off in opposite directions to relieve Parker and Nicholson. When the latter arrived back in the clearing, they, too, packed their kit, then Nicholson went back down the hill to call Loomis up. Once they were all gathered together in the clearing – with the exception of Trooper Welsh, still keeping watch above the point where Blackwood had been killed – they moved out again, hiking uphill until they had reached Welsh, who instantly fell into his original place in the single file formation.

With Killer Parker again out on point and Paddy bringing up the rear, they made their way up the dark track and crossed the strip of level ground that led to the bizarrely shaped rock formations. Fully aware that they could be ambushed at any moment and tense with expectation because of this knowledge, they wended their way carefully between the high rocks, moving repeatedly from swathes of moonlight to darkness, heading towards the snow-covered slopes that now soared eerily, majestically above them.

No one even glanced back to where Trooper Rudi Blackwood was buried. He had been killed (he had failed to beat the clock) and now he was history. His name would not be mentioned again because that was their code.

They advanced into the maze of high rocks to be swallowed by darkness.

CHAPTER SEVENTEEN

Lalya's home was her cave. She had nowhere else to go. The relentless, sweeping snow was like a curtain across the mouth of the cave, the wind howled like a demon, haunting her night and day, and although she had found one of the missing trapper's fur-lined leather jackets, she knew that she was too high up the mountain to ever make it back down. This thought was terrifying – she had her whole life to live and was completely trapped in this white hell – but the thought of returning to Dmitry Petrov's camp left her even more scared. So she stayed in the cave, refusing to die, regaining her strength, and gradually realised that even if she stayed alive, she might go insane.

Never mind the state of her mind – even physical survival was problematical. Though scarcely able to remember crawling into this cave, frozen almost to the point of hypothermia, she could certainly recall, as if receiving a vision from God, awakening on the missing fur trapper's primitive bed of straw, warmed by two blankets and the large open fire that she had built in the centre of the cave. Since that day, about five days ago, she had lived off the tinned food found in the cave, obviously left there by the trapper, and made herself hot tea with the tea leaves found in another tin. It was a life of a kind, but not much of a life, with the days drawn out interminably and the nights haunted by her fear that a wild animal would enter the cave – a brown bear or snow leopard. So far this had not happened but her fear of it remained, as did her growing fear over the thought of what would happen when the trapper's tinned food and tea ran out. To this end, she had even examined his rusty bear trap and contemplated cleaning it up and using it outside the cave, perhaps to catch small animals such as gophers, which she could skin, gut and cook. This, however, was not something she wanted to do unless she absolutely had to. Right now, she hadn't the stomach for it.

The five days had been like five years, each single day an eternity of loneliness and depression, each night a hell of restless sleep and nightmares and fear. Lying on the trapper's primitive bed of straw, under his two filthy, foul-smelling blankets, she would hear the wind howling outside and find herself straining fearfully for other, less familiar sounds – those representing danger. She often imagined such sounds – the distant growling of a brown bear, the soft padding of an approaching leopard – and when she looked at the shifting shadows on the cave wall, cast there by the flickering flames of the open fire, which she kept burning all night for comfort, she often imagined, for a brief, heart-stopping moment, that they were indeed the shadows cast by predatory beasts.

The sheer loneliness, she was convinced, would eventually destroy her sanity and she desperately tried to cling to that sanity by endlessly going over her past life and, in particular, by fondly recollecting those she had deeply loved. These memories, however, brought her grief as well as joy because all of those she had loved were now dead – killed, either directly or indirectly, by Dmitry Petrov.

When she thought of Petrov, the flame of her hatred was fierce enough to make her feel temporarily incandescent, more alive than normal. Yes, even now, in the middle of the day, as she lay back on her straw mattress, keeping warm beneath that unknown man's sordid blankets, she vividly recalled her childhood in the *kyshtak*, a Tajik village built during the time of the Soviets. The Kyrgyz and Tajik were Turkic peoples, former nomads whose history dated back to 200 B.C., but the Soviets had gradually resettled them under a collectivised agricultural system that included the building of the many *kyshtaks* located in Kyrgyzstan and Tajikistan. It was in just such a village, in Tajikistan, that Lalya had been born and raised.

Though an Ismaili Muslim, like her whole family, she was named after her mother's best friend, the wife of the Russian head of their collective farm. Life on the farm was modest yet decent and growing up there, with her loving parents and two brothers, had done her no harm. Then it changed for the worse, virtually overnight. The Soviet Union fell, the farmers of the *kyshtak* could no longer sell their grain, then Russian support for the village was withdrawn and starvation threatened. Desperate, the farmers, including Lalya's father, decided to leave the *kyshtak* and move with their families to Osh, the trade centre of Kyrgyzstan, where they hoped to find work in the silk, cotton or food-processing industries. In order to have money to sustain their families initially when they got there, they did what more and more people in the troubled region were doing: they bought opium from Afghanistan, hid it in the tyres of their trucks, armed themselves for protection against the murderous brigands in the Pamir mountains, and hoped that if they made it to Osh, they could sell the drugs there for a much higher price than they had paid for them and live off the proceeds long enough to settle their families and obtain decent jobs.

In this they had failed.

Now, when Lalya tried to keep herself sane by dwelling on the love she had known with her family, she was filled with the searing recollection of how they had died. Her mother and father had been the first to go, killed almost by accident when a hail of bullets from Dmitry Petrov's brigands tore through the canvas top and sides of the truck, striking them and some others. Lalya and her younger brother had been right beside them, but miraculously were not hit. Lalya would never forget, though, the horror of that moment when the noise of gunfire exploded, the canvas around them was ripped to shreds, and her mother and father convulsed violently as bullets peppered them and their blood poured forth. They collapsed against each other, both dead instantly, then fell at Lalya's feet.

Lalya sobbed just to recall it. Her sobbing reverberated around the cave. She closed her eyes and saw that even worse death: Dmitry Petrov's cold-blooded execution of her older brother, who had been an armed guard up front in their truck. He had faced his death with dignity, with great courage, though frightened, while the first of his friends was shot in the head, kneeling there right beside him. When his turn had come, though he was certainly frightened, he had denied that the convoy was carrying opium and been shot – as he had surely known he would be – for lying to Dmitry.

A witness to the execution, Lalya had wailed like the damned – just one of many who did so – but even the horror of that could not match the even worse murder: the merciless execution of her younger brother. A witness to that incident, also, the only emotion that had kept her sane was the burning force of her hatred for Dmitry Petrov. That hatred helped Lalya retain her sanity now.

Nevertheless, as she glanced around the darkening cave, the light of the flickering fire casting shadows on its walls, she felt lonely, frightened and perplexed, wondering if it would ever be possible to get back down the mountain or if she would have to stay here forever. If it were the latter case, she had a few serious problems to contend with: her diminishing food supply, the loneliness that could drive her mad, and the possibility that a predatory beast might decide to use the cave.

She was thinking this when she heard the sound of movement outside . . . and it was more than the howling wind.

Lalya listened again, wondering if she was hallucinating, but again she heard sounds, the crunching of snow as something heavier than a snow leopard approached the cave. Terrified, thinking that it might be a brown bear, she jerked upright on the straw mattress and looked to where the snow was being swept across the mouth of the cave by a fierce, howling wind. It was still daylight out there, though the light was gradually dimming, forming a pool of pale light on the ground. An elongated shadow fell across that patch of light and then a man – not a brown bear – came into view.

He looked very big and was made bulkier by his heavy, leather-skinned, fur-lined jacket, his knee-length boots and furred hat with ear-flaps. There was a sack and a leather bag slung over his left shoulder; a hunting rifle and the skins of brown bears dangled from the other. He was stepping into the cave in a confident manner, shaking the snow off his shoulders, when he saw the lit fire and then, just behind it, Lalya sitting upright on the primitive bed. That stopped him dead in his tracks.

He stared at her for some time, obviously taken by surprise, though Lalya could not see the expression on his face, which was hidden in shadow. She only knew that he was a very big man and that his presence here frightened her.

Eventually, he moved again, advancing into the cave, and stopped again when he reached the flickering fire. He stared steadily at her. His beard was thick around heavy, lascivious lips and the dirt on his unwashed face was like mud because of the melting snow. He studied Lalya at length.

Feeling naked, though she was wearing her cotton dress and a thick woollen pullover, Lalya rolled off the bed, stood up and slipped her feet into her fur-lined leather slippers. She then returned the man's steady, measuring gaze, realising by his clothing and other belongings that he was the fur trapper who had lived here before. Clearly, he had just gone off to hunt brown bear and had always intended returning. Now, when he stared intently at Lalya, she was too scared to speak.

'Who the hell are you?' he asked eventually, speaking in Kyrgyz, his voice rough and humourless.

'My name is . . .' But something about his look convinced her that he didn't give a damn who she was. That knowledge made her throat turn dry.

The man lowered everything he was carrying to the ground at his feet. When the sack fell to the floor, Lalya heard the unmistakeable rattling of more tinned food. 'I got lost,' she continued, almost stuttering with fear, 'and found this cave and came inside to . . .'

'You were a prisoner in that camp down there?' he interjected as his bloodshot eyes looked her up and down in a way that made her tremble.

'No,' she began, 'I . . .'

'You're a liar,' he said, withdrawing a bottle of vodka from one of the deep pockets of his jacket. The bottle was nearly empty, but he unscrewed the cap, finished it off, then threw it against the nearest wall were it smashed noisily to pieces. Wiping his lips with the back of his hairy hand, he stared contemptuously at her. 'You were a Kyrgyz prisoner in that camp down there, being used as one of their whores, and you tried to escape. Isn't that the truth of it?'

'Well, I . . .'

'Damned right, it's the truth,' he interjected, grinning to expose rotting teeth and reaching down to unbuckle his belt where his belly flopped over it. 'You're a whore on the run, you've nowhere to go, and I haven't had a woman in months, so let's see what you can do.'

Lalya tried to run past him, but he pushed her roughly back against the cave wall, then advanced upon her while still unbuckling his belt. Without thinking, Lalya bent over, picked up the rusty animal trap and threw it at him, aiming for his face. As he ducked, covering his head with his hands, she ran past him and bolted for the mouth of the cave.

'Come back, you whore!' he bawled behind her. 'You've got nowhere to go!'

But she took no notice of him and fled from the cave, too terrified to think of where she was going, oblivious to the freezing cold outside. She heard him swearing behind her, obviously still inside the cave, but the next time he swore, he was outside it and clearly coming to get her. She ran on, breathing heavily, her feet dragging through the snow, tripping on buried stones, bumping into rocky outcroppings, aware only of the vast sweep of the mountains and their ice-covered summits. He was coming up fast behind her, sometimes laughing, sometimes cursing, and she realised that he knew these mountains like the back of his hand. That hand fell upon her shoulder, gripping so hard it hurt, then he jerked her around and breathed warmly in her face and then brutally slapped her. She fell to the side, falling onto sloping rocks. He grabbed her throat with one hand and withdrew his sheathed knife with the other. Squeezing her throat until she could barely breathe, he touched the tip of the blade to her ear and said huskily, 'I'll shove this knife right through your damned head if you don't do what I say.'

Incongruously, even in the freezing cold, he was trying to manoeuvre his huge body over her to press down upon her, forcing her legs apart. She let her breath out and relaxed, sinking back against the rock, slightly opening her legs to let him wriggle between them; but then, when he relaxed slightly, also, sinking pleasurably into her, she grabbed the wrist of the hand holding the knife and sank her teeth into it.

He bellowed with pain and dropped the knife, flexing the fingers of his bloody hand, but he squeezed her throat with the other hand, practically lifted her off her feet, then threw her like a rag doll to the ground.

She lay there on her back, feeling hot though she was freezing, looking up at the brute as he grinned and spread his legs, then lowered himself upon her to trap her under his immense, heavy body. She saw his head and the stars swimming around it in the snow-swept, descending dusk. Just before he came down upon her, to pin her between his outspread thighs, she twisted sideways, grabbed the knife lying a short distance away, then twisted back and slashed left to right with it, barely knowing what she was doing.

The man gasped and his spine arched. One hand flew to his throat, but the blood spurted out between his fingers, then he clasped his free hand over the first as if this might stem the flow of blood. It did not. The blood geysered out between his fingers as he went into a dying spasm, quivering like a released bowstring, his legs still spread over her. Eventually, when the brute's eyes rolled upwards in their sockets, Lalya pushed him as hard as she could and he fell backwards, doubled over his bent legs, and crashed into the snow. His huge hands fell away from his throat and Lalya, as she sat upright, trembling with fear and revulsion, saw a deep, bloody gash that ran almost from ear to ear where she had slashed him. The blood was still gushing out of it.

Scarcely able to comprehend what she had done, she climbed to her feet, started sobbing hysterically and then, still crying, grabbed the man's hands and tried to drag him away, intending to hide him behind some shielding rocks. She had no idea why she wanted to do this as the snow would soon cover him up (and, besides, there was no likelihood of anyone else coming this far up the mountain) but she felt that she had to somehow bury him and that's what she was trying to do.

She failed, of course. He was too heavy for her. Nevertheless, she kept tugging at his two wrists – sobbing and tugging; tugging and sobbing – until, unable to move him even an inch, she dropped to her knees in the snow, sobbed even louder in frustration, then glanced at his bloody, slashed throat, jumped up and ran away.

She ran back to the cave.

Once inside the cave, she recovered her senses. Realising that she was shivering with cold, she placed more wood on the fire, then sat in front of it with her arms wrapped around her upraised knees. She sat there for a long time, rocking to and fro, until she had warmed up properly, then, still deeply shocked, though now able to think clearly, she slithered across the floor, checked the dead man's sack and was overjoyed to see that it was indeed filled with more tinned foods.

Lying beside the sack, the hunting rifle was well oiled and gleaming.

When Lalya, growing ever more excited, despite her fear, opened the shoulder bag, she found it packed with everything required for survival in the mountains, including needles and thread and scissors and razor blades.

Realising that the dead man had unintentionally brought her the key to life – food, a rifle to go hunting with, and the means of turning his bearskins into warm clothing now she could cut and sew, she picked up the rifle and lay down on the bed with the weapon beside her.

She watched the darkness descending outside. Seeing the swirling snow, listening to the moaning wind, she imagined predatory animals, or even predatory men, coming to get her. Though hardly heartened by the thought, she was not as frightened this time as she had been before.

She placed her hand on the loaded rifle and kept it there when she closed her eyes. Despite the moaning wind and the flickering shadows, she slept well that night, dreaming neither of Dmitry Petrov, as she often did, nor of the dead man. She slept the sleep of the innocent.

CHAPTER EIGHTEEN

As Scott hiked a good distance behind Corporal Parker, he found himself wrestling with the kind of self-doubt that he had not experienced since the death of his son. That this may have been caused by the very same man who had, in Scott's view, indirectly led to Johnny's tragically premature death in the streets of London, only made the dilemma worse and threatened to seriously damage his self-esteem.

'This is bad news,' he whispered to himself like someone going insane. 'You're going to have to deal with it.'

His men, in single file formation, were advancing with great care through the maze of rock-lined tracks that led up to the snow line where the cold would be bitter. They had not yet replaced their DPM tunics with Chairman Mao suits, but they would do so once the snow line was reached, as already that cold could be felt in this moonlit, starbright darkness.

Glancing back over his shoulder, Scott saw them strung out in a long line, each spaced well apart from the others to diminish the number of potential deaths in the event of an ambush. For this very reason, the column of six men (excluding Corporal Parker, still out front) was so long that Scott's best friend, Paddy Devlin, bringing up the rear as

Tailend Charlie, could not even be seen from this distance. The men formed a snake that coiled up the steep slope, winding this way and that around high columns of rock forming intricate, weaving pathways of darkness broken up with striations of pale moonlight.

This area was a gift to an assassin and that knowledge made Scott even more tense as he returned his gaze to the front. He saw Killer Parker far ahead and that gave him some comfort.

Not quite enough, though ... For the first time in his professional career, Scott was finding himself distracted by the anxieties of self-doubt and he knew that they were caused by Trooper Rudi Blackwood, who had died because he, Scott, had been careless.

Why had he been so? Maybe, just maybe, because he had come on this mission with only one thought in mind: vengeance against the Russian drug baron whose product had killed Scott's son.

And now that very same drug baron, this Dmitry Petrov, had systematically slaughtered Rudi Blackwood and then called out a mocking, personal challenge to Scott. Of course, Scott had no proof that it actually *had* been Petrov's voice, but his every instinct told him that this was the case and this conviction raised disturbing thoughts.

Already this Dmitry Petrov, whom he had never met and had only seen in a murky Green Slime intelligence photograph, was filling his thoughts as a haunting image of darkness. Now he wanted to see Petrov's real face, to look into his real eyes, to judge just what kind of man he was. The mission was becoming too personal and that was not a good thing.

There were other concerns as well, Scott realised, as he tried to control his harsh, erratic breathing while making the arduous climb up the steep slope to the approaching snow line.

His other concern – possibly his major concern – was with the effect that the sudden death of Rudi Blackwood, so early in the operation, would have on the morale of the other men. The SAS was a regiment trained to take the offensive, not the defensive, and this Dmitry Petrov, this Russian drug baron, this filth, had already managed to put his pursuers on the back foot and turn his hunters into the hunted. This knowledge, being unarguable, was soul-destroying to Scott and he knew that apart from his personal guilt over Blackwood's death, he would have to find a way of placing his men back on the offensive.

Still looking ahead, he saw that Corporal Parker had stopped advancing and was signalling for him to come up and join him. Scott did so, first indicating to the men behind him that they should remain where they were, then making his way up the gravel-strewn slope to where Parker was waiting for him, resting on one knee. When Scott reached him and also dropped to one knee, Parker silently pointed straight ahead.

Looking in that direction. Scott saw a narrow gorge formed by high, irregular walls of rock that disappeared eventually into darkness. Raising his gaze to survey the top of those rocky walls, he noted that they were about forty feet high and that beyond them were the snow-covered slopes of the mountain proper. In order to study the gorge in more detail, he surveyed it through the Orion 80 passive night sight fixed to his Heckler & Koch MP5 sub-machine gun, which gave him four times magnification. In this enhanced visibility he saw that the gorge, while being dangerously narrow and having high walls, also contained many areas of relatively level ground strewn with large boulders. Those areas would be ideal hiding places for enemy snipers.

'That gorge runs all the way to the snow line,' Parker said quietly, 'so we have to go through it.'

'Looks like it,' Scott responded, lowering his sub-machine gun to let it rest across his raised knee.

'Those men who shot at us,' Parker continued, carefully not mentioning the name of the dead Blackwood, 'would have had to come in this direction and that gorge looks like a perfect place for an ambush.'

'Perfect,' Scott said, 'but we *still* have to go through it.'

'I could go through first,' Parker said, 'and check it out as I go, but I wouldn't be able to see too much above ground level. That's where those bastards would be hiding, if they're there.'

'And,' Scott said, 'if they're there, they'd probably stay out of sight, letting us think the area is safe and only opening fire when we're all in the gorge.'

'That's it,' Parker said.

They both studied the gorge again, watching, listening, but nothing moved in that moonlit darkness and the only sound was the moaning wind. Scott raised his gaze to study the high areas of both sides and although he saw nothing up there, he knew that any snipers would be hidden behind the boulders on the level areas. Sighing, he lowered his gaze again.

'There's no way around it,' he said, 'so we'll just have to go through it. I might as well call the men up.' He signalled to them with his free hand and waited patiently for the last of them to arrive. When they were gathered around him, he pointed to the gorge and said, 'To reach the snow line, we have to advance through that gorge. Almost certainly, the enemy will be in position higher up, waiting for us, so we'll simply have to fight our way through.'

"'Scuse me for asking,' Trooper Pete Welsh asked in his deceptively dim manner, 'but isn't that particular enemy the one we've come to find?'

'Correct,' Scott said.

'So why are we trying to fight our way *through* them when we've actually come here to make contact? I mean, why not make this our last-ditch stand and fight it out to the finish? If we get through them, we'll end up with them on our tail.'

'Good question,' Syd Loomis added.

Realising once more that the lanky, pimply-faced Trooper Welsh was not as dim as he seemed, Scott said, 'I don't think the choice is really ours. The man we're after – this individual, Dmitry Petrov – is not going to be killed in a fire fight over a strip of gorge. For some mad reason of his own, he's practically invited us to come and find him, so almost certainly he's going to put us through the hoops while drawing us farther into his territory, which is higher up the mountain. My belief, therefore, is that he's going to try to whittle us down, one by one, until only a few of us are left.' He did not think it helpful to say at this stage that Dmitry Petrov had challenged him personally and almost certainly was intending to isolate him from the others, probably by eliminating his entire team, leaving only him. 'So they'll make us fight our way through that gorge, trying to kill as many of us as possible, and then they'll either force us to pursue them by moving on ahead, thus drawing us deeper into the territory they know so well, or they'll surround us and close in, in a pincer movement. So this is going to be a war of attrition and the first engagement will be in that gorge.'

'So how do we get through it?' Arnie Basham asked.

'The only way we can do it successfully, or with minimum casualties, is to advance in three separate two-man teams, with each man covering his own side of the gorge while giving covering fire to the other man in his team.'

'Sounds fucking suicidal,' Syd Loomis said boldly.

This being a Chinese Parliament, Scott ignored the obscenity whilst still addressing the question raised by the statement. 'We have the benefit of darkness—'

'So do they,' Nicholson interjected.

'—which means we can advance carefully,' Scott continued patiently, 'from one protected area to the next, in no fixed pattern, weaving at the half-crouch. We return enemy gunfire with the aid of our thermal imagers and PNGs. No hand grenades, as the explosions could bring the rocks down on our own heads.'

'Our gunfire could do that as well,' Mad Mike interjected.

'We'll just have to take that chance,' Paddy Devlin told him.

'So what order do we go in?' Arnie Basham asked.

'Since Corporal Parker's normally our lead scout and also our best marksman,' Scott said, 'he'll go first and attempt to either neutralise enemy snipers or keep them pinned down while the rest of us follow him through. I'll go next, accompanied by Trooper Welsh. Team 2 will consist of Corporal Nicholson and Trooper Basham. Team 3 will be Sergeant Devlin and Trooper Loomis. We move out at five-minute intervals and we start right now.' He turned to Killer Parker. 'I recommend you use the Barrett Light .50 rifle,' he said, 'to pick off those snipers.'

'Right, boss, I've got it.'

Nodding, not smiling, but somehow managing to convey his pleasure at the thought of some action, Parker covered his eyes with his passive night vision goggles, or PNGs, then checked the thermal-imaging sight on his Barrett Light .50 rifle by squinting through it with the aid of the PNGs. Satisfied, he turned away and loped at the half-crouch, weaving left and right, towards the dark mouth of the gorge. The rest of the men formed into the teams recommended by Scott and prepared to move out by doing just what Parker had done: lowering their PNGs over their eyes and checking their thermal imagers.

When Trooper Pete Welsh fell in beside him, Scott dropped to one knee and observed Parker as he carefully approached the gorge. In the moonlit darkness, he dropped to one knee, checked as much of the gorge as he could see through his PNGs and thermal imager, then indicated the all clear with his left hand. As Scott jumped back to his feet to advance at the half-crouch with Welsh beside him, though a safe distance from him, Parker disappeared into the gorge, swallowed by the darkness.

Scott and Welsh reached the mouth of the gorge at the same time, though the former was at the southern wall, the latter at the wall opposite. Hiding behind the high rock face and peering around it, Scott saw the shadowy form of Corporal Parker up ahead, moving from one rock outcropping to another, weaving at the half-crouch, then studying the gorge through the thermal imager on his supergun. When Parker was satisfied that he could see nothing either up ahead or high up the sides of the gorge, he gave the all clear with a hand signal, then immediately advanced again, darting from one protective area to another.

Scott and Welsh followed him, the former darting from one outcropping to another along the base of his side of the gorge, the latter doing the same at the other side, advancing roughly parallel to each other. When both were at the next position, Scott scanned the opposite side, moving his night-vision sight upwards from Welsh's position to search for movement directly above him while Welsh did exactly the same, covering the area directly above Scott. Having observed nothing unusual through the eerie glow of his night-vision sight, Scott glanced back over his shoulder and saw that Team 2 – Corporal Mad Mike Nicholson and Trooper Arnie Basham – had entered the mouth of the gorge. Scott gave them the all clear. When they rose from the kneeling position to commence their forward run, he stood up and bolted for the next protective outcropping, still at the half-crouch, still weaving. Pete Welsh did the same.

They continued advancing in this manner, inching painfully, dangerously, forward until all of them were well inside the gorge. Parker was still out front, repeatedly materialising in moonlight and disappearing back into darkness as he advanced, checking the area ahead and above, then giving Scott and those behind him the all clear, enabling them to do likewise.

They were deep inside the gorge, perhaps three-quarters of the way through, judging by the increased height and angle of the softly gleaming, snow-covered slopes beyond, when the first shots rang out.

Scott did not see the flashing of that first shot, but he saw those that followed, half-a-dozen aimed from high up on the opposite wall: minute, spitting, yellow-white flames, firing down upon Parker. Parker's Barrett Light .50 rifle roared almost instantly in response, a series of rapid single shots, and Scott certainly saw the flame created in the darkness by that fearsome weapon. The men high up stopped firing, there was the sound of tumbling stones and sliding gravel, then the body of a dead or wounded man, clearly visible in the moonlight, rolled down a rocky slope, and fell down a sheer drop of about thirty feet to crash to the floor of the gorge, creating a billowing cloud of dust.

Parker had just made his first kill.

The enemy weapons roared again, twice as many as before and clearly covering a much broader arc of fire, including not only Parker but also the rest of the SAS men. Luckily, the latter were in well-protected areas, sheltering behind high outcroppings, and they instantly returned the fire, some aiming at those yellow-white spurts of flame high above, hoping to hit the men behind them, others using their night-vision scopes for magnification and enhanced clarity. Another two men fell from ridges high above, rolling down in a minor avalanche of showering stones and gravel, one of them screaming in fear and pain as he bounced from one rock to another before finally smashing into the ground, creating more clouds of dust.

Opposite Scott, the normally quiet Pete Welsh released a spontaneous outcry of exultation.

We need this clean fight, Scott thought. These kills are working wonders. Maybe now we can reverse the situation and return to the offensive. Just do it, man. *Do it!*

Almost as exhilarated as Welsh, he jumped up and ran to the next safe point, another pile of high rocks, zigzagging all the way to avoid the bullets thudding into the dust about his feet. When he fell safely behind the rocks of his new firing position, he saw that Trooper Welsh had done the same and was firing at a high angle from a position almost directly opposite.

By now there was no need to signal to the men coming up behind as they were all working by instinct, waiting for a break in the enemy gunfire before launching themselves forward and zigzagging to the next position. So far there were no SAS casualties.

Pleased, Scott looked ahead and saw that Killer Parker had mounted his Barrett Light .50 rifle on its tripod and was using that fearsome weapon and its thermal imager to methodically pick off any man he saw located high up on the walls of the gorge. Parker had found himself a position right in the middle of the gorge, though with all-round rock protection, which enabled him to fire at both sides of the gorge and he was, with fearsome consistency, causing more bodies to fall, wriggling, kicking and sometimes screaming, into the gorge. Since he had mounted his weapon on a tripod, which aided its already awesome accuracy, he obviously intended holding that position for some good reason.

Wanting to know that reason, Scott checked that no enemy bullets were thudding into the ground between him and Parker, then, satisfied that they were not, he jumped up and ran like the wind, crouched low, zigzagging all the way, and threw himself down beside Parker just as bullets stitched a jagged line of dust in the ground behind him. Sitting up beside Parker, almost deafened by the regular roaring of the Barrett Light .50 rifle, he glanced to both sides, saw only the towering walls of rock, then looked ahead to the far end of the gorge, now only about a hundred feet away, and saw the snow-white slopes of the mountain, rising in the pale, eerie moonlight to ice-covered peaks. He lowered his gaze to Killer Parker when the rifle stopped firing.

'So what's up, Corporal?' he asked. 'Why aren't you advancing?'

Parker turned his lean, scarred face towards him to offer his steady, gelid gaze. 'You can see the end of the gorge from here,' he said.

'So?'

'It's not a long run, boss, but it's all open ground with practically no protection. My suggestion is that we set up the gimpy right here and have the team in charge of it rip the shit out of both sides of the gorge between here and the far end, keeping those bastards pinned down until the rest of us complete the short run. Once we've done that, we'll then use everything we've got to do the same until the gimpy team has made it as well. It's a high-risk run, but it's the only way to get there. So what do you say, boss?'

'I say we could be shot to hell, Corporal. Those men up on that ridge will have us clear and large in their sights. They'll see us clearly every inch of the way and that makes us sitting ducks.'

'We can solve that problem,' Parker responded as calmly as ever. 'Before we make the run, we shoot flares into the sky. You cover one side of the gorge, I cover the other. We aim the flares to ignite slightly behind the ridges on both sides of the gorge, instead of directly above them. The light of the flares will then illuminate those men up there, placing them in silhouette – which makes *them* sitting ducks – while keeping the bottom of the gorge in darkness and giving us pretty good protection. So what say you to that, boss?'

'I say you're right, Corporal.'

Glancing across the gorge, Scott saw that Trooper Welsh had come to a halt parallel with Parker's position, but directly under that wall of the gorge. Glancing backwards, he saw the other two teams making their way forward one at a time, each man moving at the half-crouch from one protective position to another, hugging the wall at his side while his partner gave him covering fire by raking the other side with repeated bursts of automatic gunfire.

Using hand signals, Scott indicated to the other men that they should try making their way to his and Parker's present position. The men did so, again advancing one at a time, crouched low and zigzagging while enemy bullets stitched lines of spitting sand that ran rapidly towards them and past them, with the bullets ricocheting noisily off rocks and stones, filling the air with flying splinters and billowing dust. The covering fire of the other men was effective, keeping most of the enemy snipers pinned down and, occasionally, causing another one of them to come tumbling, rolling down the side of the gorge or to make a clean fall down a sheer drop, striking the ground with a sickening thud.

Nevertheless, all of the SAS men managed to make the run safely and were soon gathered, each resting on one knee, around Scott and Parker. When the latter stopped firing his rifle, the enemy fire also tapered off, leaving an uneasy silence. Dust continued to drift across the gorge, settling on the dead, broken bodies in the dust-filled, moonlit darkness.

'What's up?' Mad Mike asked.

When Scott explained the situation, nobody put up an argument, so Arnie Basham and Syd Loomis began assembling the GPMG, first setting up the thirty-pound steel tripod, then placing the twenty-four-pound machine gun onto it, and finally closing the top cover on a belt of 200 7.62mm rounds. More 200-round belts were piled up beside the weapon, to be fed in by Syd as required while big Arnie did the actual shooting. As the GPMG, affectionately known as a gimpy, could fire 750–1000 rounds per minute, a lot of ammunition belts would be used up during the short run.

'All set,' Arnie said when he was kneeling behind the GPMG with the stock pressed against his right shoulder, with Syd kneeling on the ground beside him, preparing to feed in the belts of ammunition.

Scott nodded, then he and Parker took turns at firing the flares into the sky, each covering a separate side of the gorge and aiming the flares obliquely instead of vertically, to ignite beyond the top of the ridges and not directly above them. This the flares did, exploding just behind both ridges to illuminate them in their brilliant, flickering light, creating an eerie chiaroscuro, and placing the men up there in sharp silhouette. That light, being so bright above the ridges, helpfully made the gorge seem even darker.

'Give both sides of that gorge hell,' Scott instructed Arnie, 'and don't stop until we're all home and dry. Okay, commence firing.'

Big Arnie pressed the trigger and the GPMG roared into action, abruptly splitting the silence and filling the air with streams of smoke and the stench of cordite. Arnie swung the barrel left to right, spraying both sides of the gorge, turning the upper slopes, where Petrov's men were now clearly visible, silhouetted sharply in the weird, flickering light of the flares, into a hell of boiling dust, geysering gravel and flying rock splinters.

Parker jumped up and ran off at the half-crouch, zigzagging towards the far end of the gorge, his bulky form passing repeatedly from darkness to moonlight and then back to darkness again. Heavily burdened under his bergen and blankets, he looked like some bizarre, alien creature, but he moved with great speed.

Scott followed immediately, also low and zigzagging. Instantly, he heard the distant snap-and-crack of the weapons being fired by those attempting to defy Arnie Basham's ferocious, relentless fusillades from the GPMG. Still zigzagging, Scott saw a line of spitting dust shooting towards him as enemy bullets, obviously fired from a machine gun, thudded into the ground straight ahead. Turning to the left, he managed to avoid the hail of bullets, though many ricocheted off the rocks nearby, making a high-pitched, whistling sound, showering him in shards of stone and choking dust. He raced through enveloping darkness, caught a glimpse of the moon, saw moonlight illuminating the snowscapes of the middle slopes of the mountain, felt the hammering of his heart, heard his harsh breathing, and then hurled himself forward, practically sailing through the air, to crash into the ground at the far end of the gorge, less than a metre away from Killer Parker. He rolled over and was clambering back to his feet even as other men hit the ground on both sides of him.

Within seconds, all of the men, except Arnie Basham and Syd Loomis, had made the run safely and, forming into two teams, were taking up firing positions behind the high rocks at the end of the gorge.

Scott signalled to Basham and Loomis to prepare for their run. They stopped firing immediately, as did the enemy above, and the silence, when it descended, seemed unreal.

In that eerie silence, as the flares in the night sky fizzled out and died, plunging both ridges back into darkness, Basham and Loomis dismantled the GPMG, with the former clamping the steel tripod around his thick neck and the latter humping the heavy barrel on his shoulder. After dividing the remaining belts of ammunition between them, they signalled that they were ready to make the run.

Scott and Paddy fired more flares just beyond both ridges, illuminating them once more in that eerie, flickering light, placing Petrov's men back into sharp silhouette. Then Scott bawled 'Now!' and chopped the air with a downward movement of his right hand.

He and the others opened fire with their combined SA-80 assault rifles and MP5 sub-machine guns, turning both sides of the gorge into hellish infernos of ricocheting bullets, exploding rock and boiling dust. Instantly, given that blanket protection, Basham and Loomis began running as quickly as possible, bowed low under their heavy kit and zigzagging to avoid the few desultory shots that some foolhardy souls above insisted upon firing. Indeed, even before Basham and Loomis reached the end of their short run, another of Petrov's men was riddled by bullets, flopped shuddering over a low rock, fell rolling and bouncing down a sloping section of the wall, then plummeted the final twenty feet like a stone and crashed with a dull thud into the ground.

Reaching the end of the gorge, Basham and Loomis hurled themselves gratefully into the arms of their comrades.

'You two sure know how to run,' Pete Welsh said laconically, 'when you've got a good reason.'

'I float like a butterfly and sting like a bee,' Syd Loomis replied without malice. 'And that, my friend, is why I'm still alive, so go and suck your own dick.'

'We're *all* still alive,' Scott informed him, 'and that's a very good sign. At least we won this round.'

And it felt good to say it. It repaired a lot of damage. Feeling better, less humiliated than before, Scott watched the flares flickering out in the night sky, returning both ridges to darkness, then he led his men away from the gorge, towards the snow-covered slopes. They had not slept for twenty-four hours and now needed to basha down. They went in search of a place to hide.

CHAPTER NINETEEN

Crossing a steeply angled, open plain that led up to the snow line, Scott's men could find no place to hide and were forced to rest up where the ground did not allow defensive positions to be dug. For this reason – and because rocks of all shapes and sizes were scattered widely about the area – Scott picked a relatively level strip of ground for the construction of a sangar: an improvised wall of loose rocks arranged in a circle.

'Build the wall high enough,' he told the assembled group when they had placed their kit at their feet, 'to ensure good body protection from enemy gunfire, but low enough to enable us to set the GPMG on its tripod and fire personal weapons from the kneeling position.'

'Guards?' Paddy Devlin asked.

'Given the protection of the sangar, I don't think we need to place any guards outside it—'

'Hallelujah!' big Arnie Basham interjected with a white-toothed grin.

'—but I think we should line the perimeter with Claymore mines in case those bastards come after us.'

'Excuse me, boss,' Killer Parker said while staring steadily, fearlessly at Scott, 'but how come, since we came here to find those bastards, they've found *us* and placed *us* in the defensive situation?'

Trust Parker to hit the nail on the head and not be shy of letting him know it. Scott glanced at Paddy Devlin, saw him grinning and shrugging, then he turned back to face the rest of the men, meeting the gaze of each one in turn.

'I've already explained it,' Scott said, 'and at the risk of repeating myself, I can only say that the man we've come to find knows we're here and he's come down from the mountains to confront us. What's not so clear is why he hasn't launched an all-out attack instead of simply harassing us, as he's doing.'

'And doing pretty well,' Syd Loomis said.

'Not so well,' Paddy firmly corrected him. 'What he gained, he lost back in that gorge and he'll be smarting from that.'

'Quite so,' Scott said, relieved that Paddy had jumped so quickly to his defence. 'Nevertheless, for whatever reasons, it seems pretty obvious that he intends drawing us higher up the mountain, into the snow and bitter cold, before making his final move. In that way he'll place us in a situation where every move we make will be extremely difficult for us and where only his men know the terrain. We'll just have to live with this.'

'Some life!' Syd Loomis said sardonically.

'Anyway,' Scott continued hurriedly to prevent his disconcerted men from thinking too much about what was happening, 'they must know roughly where we are, so let's build the sangar immediately and give ourselves some protection.'

He put most of the men to work building the sangar: laying a five-metre circle of large, flat-bottomed stones, then piling one stone on top of the other until the wall was about two feet high. While the men were thus engaged, Pete Welsh, the demolitions specialist, placed Claymore mines equidistant around the sangar, about thirty metres out on all sides, to catch any advancing enemy troops. He angled the mines slightly upwards to ensure that the 350 metal balls contained in each of them would shred anyone in their path. After unscrewing the plastic fasteners used to secure the blasting caps, he inserted an end of detonator cord and screwed the fasteners back into place. The det cords were unrolled from each mine and the end of each cord was attached to a trigger slide. Some of these were fixed to rocks or tree stumps and would be activated if someone tramped upon, or tripped over, the appropriately named tripwires. The others were rolled all the way back to the sangar where they were attached to separate trigger slides, which were in turn fixed to electric batteries. When this job had been completed, Pete carefully covered up the Claymores and lengths of det cord with gravel, leaving the ground looking exactly as it had been before.

By now the rest of the men had completed the building of the sangar wall and were taking up their individual rest-and-firing positions behind it. Each of them was given one of the trigger slides to enable him to detonate his own Claymores if they had not already been activated by the tripwires.

'I just love these vicious little fuckers,' Arnie Basham said, holding his trigger slide in his right hand and pretending to kiss it. 'They make me feel well protected.'

'Keep your fingers off that fucking trigger,' Mad Mike snarled, 'until you're ready to use it. We don't want it going off by accident and telling the whole fucking world where we are.'

'Sorry, boss!' Arnie said, then placed the trigger carefully by his side. 'Just a moment of weakness there.'

'Fuckin' asshole!' Mad Mike retorted, laying the barrel of his SA-80 assault rifle on the rim of the sangar wall and squinting experimentally along his night-vision sight.

'Hey, boss!' Syd Loomis called out to Scott. 'Can we grab something to eat now?'

'Cold rations only,' Scott replied as he rolled out his sleeping bag and poncho beside those of Paddy Devlin. 'No hexamine stoves.'

'Why not?' Big Arnie asked, bold as brass as always. 'If those bastards know where we are, we might as well light our hexamine stoves and at least have a hot meal before they get here.'

'They don't know *exactly* where we are,' Paddy Devlin replied impatiently while glancing about him, at the snowscapes above and the dark valley below, at the clouds helpfully blotting out the large moon. 'They only know that we're somewhere between that gorge and the snow line, but they've no way of knowing just where – so no hexamine stoves.'

'They know which direction we took,' Arnie said stubbornly.

'They know *roughly* which direction we took,' Paddy responded, sounding even more impatient. 'They know we've left the gorge, but that's about all.'

'We'll have left our footprints in the snow,' Pete Welsh interjected.

Paddy held his right hand up to let the strong wind beat against it. The men studied his hand and saw the snow blowing around it. 'This wind will be blowing the snow across our tracks,' Paddy said, 'and that snow will soon cover them. So unless those bastards are really quick, they won't find our footprints.'

'I stand defeated,' Big Arnie said with a white-toothed grin. 'No hexamine stoves.'

With his own sleeping bag and poncho unrolled beside those of Paddy Devlin, Scott gave the others permission to do the same with the proviso that they only used them to keep warm and not for sleeping.

'Petrov and his men,' he explained, indicating the high ridge that ran from east to west, from the northern side of the gorge to the snow line of the mountain, 'are theoretically behind us, on the ridges of that gorge, but right now they could either be pursuing us or making their way along the northern ridge to ensure that they'll be in front of us by first light.'

'Or they'll be encircling us,' Killer Parker interjected flatly, 'to move in and crush us in a pincer movement.'

'That possibility exists as well,' Scott acknowledged, 'but I'm inclined to think that they haven't brought along enough men for that – so my bet is that either they intend following us or making their way around us, along that northern ridge, to place themselves between us and their base camp higher up the mountain. Either way, we have to stay awake until we can move on again, so by all means use your sleeping bags or ponchos for warmth, but make sure you don't fall asleep. No stoves. No ciggies.'

Moaning and groaning melodramatically at the lack of hot food and cigarettes, the men nevertheless went about creating their temporary bashas to suit themselves, some unrolling their sleeping bags as Scott and Paddy had done, others, less susceptible to the cold, simply wrapping their waterproof sheets, known as bivi-bags, around them and tucking into their scran.

'Wads and fuckin' biscuits,' Syd Loomis said despairingly, now leaning against the wall, his knees raised, his bivi-bag wrapped around him. He withdrew a packet of sandwiches from his rucksack. 'My fuckin' stomach will freeze over before I starve,' he added, 'if I don't get some soup or hot tea.'

'Well, you ain't gettin' neither,' Mad Mike snarled, still squinting into his night-vision sight, obviously hoping to see the enemy and be distracted from cold and hunger with some action, 'so shut your blubbering mouth.'

'My mouth's shut,' Syd replied, then he bit into his wad while Arnie, kneeling beside him, set the GPMG up on its tripod with the barrel aimed just over the low wall of the sangar. When he moved the barrel, it tapped lightly against one of the higher stones.

'Hey, watch that fuckin' gimpy,' Syd said, speaking while his mouth was still filled with masticated bread and processed meat paste. 'It's the only friend we've got, mate.'

'It's certainly the only friend *I've* got,' Big Arnie replied as he raised the tripod slightly to cover the lip of the wall, 'judging by the help I'm getting in setting it up.'

'You're the one who fires the bastard,' Syd said, 'so I'm letting you set it up.'

'Thanks a million,' Arnie retorted.

In fact, Scott had assigned Arnie and Pete Welsh to first watch, the former covering a north-east firing arc, the latter south-west. Thus, while the rest of the men were not allowed to sleep, they could at least eat, drink, check their weapons and kit, then relax for an hour. Those on watch would be replaced every hour throughout the rest of the morning.

Satisfied, Scott wriggled waist deep into his own sleeping bag, sitting upright against the sangar wall, and was pleased at how quickly his cold legs warmed up. Draping his bivi-bag around his shoulders for more warmth, he helped himself to a sandwich and some cold water, fully appreciating, when he drank the latter, just why Trooper Loomis was yearning for something hot to put into his stomach.

Nevertheless, even while eating the sandwich, he meticulously checked every item of equipment in his 80-litre Crusader square-frame bergen, including his own ammunition, extra GPMG ammunition (carried by every man on the patrol), spare radio batteries, a personal medical pack, explosives and two of his four Claymore mines, the other two having been laid out around the perimeter by Pete Welsh. As each man had been supplied with fourteen days' supply of food (and a man could get two days out of a one-day pack, if necessary) there was still enough food in the bergen to last for at least another fortnight.

Pleased, Scott repacked the bergen, finished off his high-calorie sandwich, then checked the survival kit worn on his belt. Though small and unobtrusive, this kit included enough emergency rations to last a man two days; vacuum-pressed plastic sheets, a small map of the area of operations, in this case Kyrgyzstan; a 'button' compass; a fishing line and weights; snares consisting of brass picture wire with eyelets and cord; lengths of nylon cord; flint and steel for making fires; a utility knife; a supply of potassium permanganate, which could be used as a marker in the snow; and, finally, a pencil and notebook. Satisfied that all was in order, he repacked the survival kit, attached it to his belt, then glanced sideways at Paddy Devlin who had been doing exactly the same as him.

'Okay over there, are you?' he asked.

'Aye,' Paddy replied. 'Sure I'm grand. I could do with a bit of a kip, but then couldn't we all?'

'We'll have a kip when we find a better protected area higher up the mountain.'

'He'll be waiting for us up there,' Paddy said.

'I hope so. I'd rather he was in front of us than behind us.'

'He won't be handing out welcoming cards, that's for damned sure.'

'No, he won't,' Scott replied. 'He'll just lure us higher up the mountain until he's ready to strike. Until . . .'

Paddy completed the sentence for him. 'Until he's eliminated all of us, except you. God knows what he's got planned for you, boss.'

Scott didn't reply because there was nothing to say. He was surprised, however, to note just how personalised this operation had already become, not only to him but to Paddy, who was also speaking of the enemy in the singular rather than the plural. Dmitry Petrov, with that single, mocking challenge to the patrol, had turned this into a personal fight between him and Scott. Petrov was playing some kind of game – a bizarre, perverse game – and Scott still didn't know what the rules were. He only knew that Petrov's intention was to lure him up into the mountains, well beyond the snow line, and once there isolate him from the others, most likely by killing them all, before playing his last card.

Understanding this, Scott was deeply distraught and gazed around the sangar, studying the faces of his men as they ate, drank, checked their kit and engaged in bantering bullshit. They talked more freely than regular soldiers, the greens, would have been allowed to do, and this made him feel even closer to them than usual. They were, he realised, the best friends he had ever had in his life and their words, even when they went against him, gave him some comfort.

'Christ!' Syd Loomis whined. 'What a fuckin' hike this is. It's worse than a fuckin' beat-up march and I'm startin' to feel it.'

'Dumb plan, if you ask me,' big Arnie responded. 'I mean, pursuing those bastards all the way to their base camp. Typical of the Green Slime Head Sheds, sitting back on their fat arses on their soft chairs in the Intelligence Corps in the Kremlin, Hereford. If it was up to me, I'd bin this bloody plan and beg for another.'

'Right,' Syd agreed. 'I mean, who's chasing who, anyway? I say we stay right here and wait for them to come and find us. We set up a box-type ambush – positions on both flanks and in front of the bastards – and turn them to shredded wheat when they pass through. I mean, bump the Russian bastards before they bump us and to hell with their bloody base camp higher up.'

'Right,' big Arnie said. 'Just get to Dmitry Petrov, and put his lights out with a good double tap, then burn out of here, leaving his drug-producing base camp to rot. That's the way to do it, boys.'

'I don't like it up here,' Pete Welsh said, speaking last as usual. 'We're completely isolated, with no comms – no *nothing*. We can't even get casevacked out if we cop a bad wound. We could be fucking doomed up here.'

'Look on the bright side,' big Arnie said. 'You fail to beat the clock here and you'll get your name on the base of the clock in Hereford. Then I'll write you up in *Mars and Minerva*,' he continued, referring to the regimental journal of the SAS, 'and you'll be remembered as the hero you ain't. So always look on the bright side.'

'To hell with that,' Pete replied, scratching at his long, pale, pimply face with restless fingers, then ruffling his dishevelled blond hair. 'I'd rather get back to my warm basha in the spider of the Sports and Social than get my name on the clock at Stirling Lines, or even in the regimental rag. I don't want to be buried in these fucking mountains. I don't know a soul.'

'I love it,' big Arnie said, grinning broadly, rolling his brown eyes. 'Pete wants to be buried where he knows a few souls. The man's religious at heart.'

'Hey, you lot!' Mad Mike Nicholson called out from where he was sitting beside Killer Parker, both ignoring the cold and wrapped only in their bivi-bags. 'Stop all that crap-hat talk. This isn't the fuckin' Parachute Regiment, where they give up as soon as their feet touch the ground. This is the SAS, you bunch of wankers, and don't you forget it. Any more of that whining bullshit and I'll personally castrate you.'

'Sorry, Corp!' Pete Welsh exclaimed.

'I stand corrected,' big Arnie said.

'I love the regiment and I love this job,' Syd Loomis drawled. 'You can count on me, Corp.'

'Dumb bastards,' Mad Mike muttered, glancing at Killer Parker while shaking his head from side to side in disgust. 'We should RTU the whole fuckin' lot of 'em when we get back to Hereford.'

'Not easy to do from here,' Parker replied with not the hint of a smile. 'We're a long way from Hereford.'

'Too true,' Mad Mike replied. 'What I'd give to be in the Paludrine Club,' he added, referring to the SAS bar at Stirling Lines, 'having a pint of best bitter and swopping some bullshit with my mates instead of these crap-hats.'

'They're not crap-hats and they *are* your mates,' Parker reminded him. 'You're just pissed off, that's all.'

'That's right, I'm pissed off.'

'Why?'

'We're supposed to be pursuing this Russian drug dealer and instead the bastard's coming after us. That's some turnaround, right?'

'Not the PC's fault,' Parker replied evenly, referring to Scott as Patrol Commander. 'He did what the Ruperts ordered him to do and he did it all correctly. He found the LZ and hiked us out of there and got us to the mountains in no time. Not his fault that the guy we came here to find saw us drop on that LZ and decided to come and find us instead. He wants to take us out before we reach his camp and that would certainly make sense.'

'So we hike up the mountains, trying to find their camp, with them knowing where we are all the time! It's a fucking sure-fire no-win situation and we're gonna get shat upon.'

'No, we're not,' Parker replied. 'They're gonna lead us up into the snow and then they'll start attacking for real. When they do, we can take the initiative and that'll make you feel better.'

'I doubt it,' Mad Mike said. 'I think we're wasting our fuckin' time. We should try to get that bastard before we reach his camp. We could get killed just trying to climb that mountain; we could get lost up there. Why the fuck do we have to take his whole camp when we could just take him out? Without a leader that camp would be useless and we could all go home feeling good.'

'No,' Parker said. 'The camp wouldn't be leaderless. Someone else, another *Mafiya* drug baron, would step in and take over. So we have to reduce the whole camp to dust, leaving nothing behind.'

'One good fucking Startrek to take the camp out,' Mad Mike insisted, using the SAS slang for an air strike. 'Leaving us to deal with only Mister Petrov. That's the way to do it, pal.'

'No can do,' Parker said calmly, remorselessly. 'The Russians can't be seen to be bombing their own people and our people can't get aircraft in there. That's why this is a covert op and why, officially speaking, we don't exist. If we lose, if Petrov wins, the Head Sheds in the Kremlin and those blistered-hand wankers in Whitehall will dream up a good reason for our disappearance . . . a fuckin' accident during a HALO exercise in Malaysia . . . or somethin' like that. So we're going all the way up that mountain, whether or not we cream Petrov beforehand. That mountain camp is our goal.'

'Train hard, fight easy,' Mad Mike said with a defeated sigh, referring to the motto of Training Wing, 22 SAS, where he had been a notoriously ruthless and efficient DS. 'If we're goin' up there, I'll go.'

'I knew you would,' Parker said.

Scott smiled. He had overheard the conversation. Turning to Paddy Devlin, he said, 'The usual bullshit's going back and forth, so I guess they're all right.'

'We got through the gorge,' Paddy replied, 'and that did them a lot of good. Despite the bullshit, I think they're feeling less victimised and more on the offensive. We have to keep it that way.'

'We will,' Scott said. 'If Petrov is going to move out ahead of us to make us pursue him up into the mountains, which I reckon he is, it will at least seem that we're pursuing him – and that, from a psychological standpoint, will be all to the good.'

'It may be good from a psychological standpoint,' Paddy responded, 'but tactically it doesn't leave us any better off. In fact, the higher up we go, particularly once beyond the snow line, the more difficult it'll be to defend ourselves. We don't know the terrain and the weather's going to be unpredictable and could represent a real threat to us. Speaking of which, what *is* the wet rep?'

He was referring sardonically to the weather report they could not receive because they were out of communication (they had no 'comms') and were only permitted to use their PRC 319 radio system for contact with the Russian air force base when the job was over and the survivors required lifting out. Understanding this, Scott could not help smiling as he twisted sideways to gaze up the soaring, snow-covered slopes ahead and observe that the stars above the ice-capped peaks were alternately appearing and disappearing behind dense, drifting clouds.

'More snow,' he said. 'Strong winds. It doesn't look good up there.'

'We get a white-out and we'll be fucked.'

'So will they, Paddy. At least, we'll have that to look forward to.'

'I wouldn't bet on it,' Paddy retorted. 'Those bastards live in these mountains, they eat snow and wind for breakfast, and they know every inch of the terrain – so a white-out won't make them as blind as us. Whichever way you look at it, boss, we're on a sticky wicket here.'

'We've been there before, Paddy. We'll be okay. Believe me, we'll make it.'

'Who dares wins,' Paddy said.

Scott glanced at him, smiled, then closed his eyes and leaned his head against the cold stone wall of the sangar. His experiences in the Falkland Islands and Iraq had taught him how to rest his eyes without actually falling asleep; now, with his eyes closed and resting, he let his thoughts wind back to the twenty-year-old, three-bedroom semi-detached house with its small, south-facing garden, located on the outskirts of Hereford, that he had shared for most of his married life with Vicki and Johnny. It had been a modest enough home, one dictated by his income, but his haven when he wasn't overseas; thus it still pained him to think of the good days he'd had there before the marriage broke up. Although his marriage had been, until the break-up, more stable than most, it had suffered from the enormous tensions common to SAS marriages, some due to the husband's frequent absences from home, others caused by the relentless strain induced in the woman by the tormenting awareness that her husband, particularly when overseas, was engaged in highly dangerous, potentially lethal tasks.

Thinking of this, Scott tried to remember just how many times Vicki had been compelled to watch SAS friends being buried in the regimental graveyard of St Martin's Church, Hereford, and realised that the fingers of both hands would not be enough to account for all of them. Few women, no matter how strong, could ignore the high body count amongst their husbands' friends; and Vicki, though admirably strong in many ways, had too often consoled bereaved, weeping girlfriends after their husbands had been killed in Northern Ireland, the Falklands, Iraq, or in anti-terrorist operations elsewhere, sometimes even in Britain.

What must have been even worse for her, he now realised, was that period, almost a decade ago, when the Regimental Security Officer had informed him that he, Scott, was on an IRA hit list because of his covert work in Northern Ireland and that his home and family would have to be placed under full-time protection. Scott would never forget the look of horror on Vicki's face when she learnt that the 'protection' included frequent visits by Home Office and local Special Branch security officers, the installation of a high-tech surveillance system and special bombproof mailbox in her home, the fixing of a UCBT (Under Car Booby Trap) alarm system to the family car, and, most frightening of all, the necessity for her personally to check the underside of the car with an extendable mirror and torch, looking for a bomb not detected by the UCBT, every single time she wanted to drive it. Far from making her feel secure, such measures had only made her more conscious of the fact that her whole family was in danger and this, in turn, was rendered even more frightening when it became clear that the alarms in both the house and the car could go off accidentally, which they did a lot, thus causing heavily armed QRF (Quick Reaction Force) army patrols to invade the whole area in general and her house in particular, looking for a bomb or an assassin. Before very long, Vicki was taking various sedatives and, as Scott later found out, drinking secretly.

Johnny had been ten years old at the time of that lengthy, nerve-wracking house security operation and how his mother's visibly growing tension had affected him would never be known. Nevertheless, Scott had secretly blamed that period, as well as his own frequent absences from home, for Johnny's childhood and adolescent insecurity. Certainly, it was no accident that Johnny, as a young man not yet turned twenty, had been unusually sensitive and nervous, which may have accounted for his growing need for drink and drugs. The latter need had led to that ultimate tragedy and the subsequent break-up of Scott's marriage – and for that, despite his own feelings of guilt, he blamed Dmitry Petrov.

Yes, there he was again ... Dmitry Petrov ... almost certainly the man who had called out that personal challenge after so brutally killing Rudi Blackwood. Now, reminded of Petrov, Scott recalled the identity photograph he had been shown by the Green Slime Head Shed in the Kremlin in Hereford. Dark and slightly out of focus, grainily enlarged from a long-distance surveillance shot, it had nevertheless shown the face of a man who could have been an old-fashioned Russian matinée idol had it not been for the scars that marred his otherwise perfect, albeit ascetic, good looks. One of the scars was the long, thin line of an old knife wound that ran down his left cheek; the other was a perfectly round area of badly wrinkled flesh, indicating a bullet wound to the right cheek. Normally a man with such wounds would have made most women wince, but Petrov, at least judging by the photo, remained oddly handsome and almost certainly would have been attractive to women. His face also revealed, however, an unusually cold-eyed intensity and, to Scott's possibly jaundiced eye, a brutality that transcended mere malice. Nevertheless, it was not the face of a mindless brute or a gutter-crawling drug dealer; not the kind of face Scott had seen when he went down to London to find the men who had sold drugs to his son. Certainly, it was not the face he had expected to find on Dmitry Petrov and now, for reasons both clear and unclear, he had to see it up close.

He was thinking of this when two Claymore mines exploded outside the sangar and Arnie Basham's GPMG roared into action.

Jerked violently from his reverie, Scott, still sitting upright, twisted around and stretched himself as much as possible to glance over the lip of the sangar wall.

Exploded gravel was still flying out in all directions as a man, screaming dreadfully, both arms shorn off from the shoulders, the stumps gushing blood, only a tattered hole of bloody bone splinters where one side of his face should have been, emerged from billowing smoke and took a few steps forward before falling to his knees. He stared wildly from one eye that flared unnaturally out of a blackened, blistered face, then flopped sideways onto the scorched ground as the man behind him, also emerging from the smoke, his shirt and belly in tatters, the latter pouring blood, his smashed ribcage exposed, was chopped almost in two by the fusillade of bullets from Arnie Basham's GPMG and danced wildly like a puppet on a string before also collapsing.

The GPMG continued roaring, then more Claymores exploded as Syd Loomis pressed the trigger slide given to him and Arnie. The explosions tore the darkness ahead with jagged sheets of silvery-white flame that were instantly obliterated by geysering gravel and more billowing smoke. What could not be seen from the sangar were the hundreds of metal balls that flew outward and upward at the speed of bullets to shred everything – flesh, bone, intestines and eyeballs – in their path. The screams coming from inside that billowing smoke were dreadful and only cut short when the murderous hail of bullets from Arnie's GPMG mercifully put an end to the enemy wounded.

Another man emerged from the darkness outside the billowing smoke, seemingly unharmed and firing a Kalashnikov rifle from the hip. Instantly, even before Arnie could swing the GPMG in that direction, all the men behind the sangar wall opened fire with their personal weapons and the advancing man was abruptly punched this way and that by bullets coming from different directions, then crashed backwards into the gravel and did not move again.

No more answering fire came from that direction, though men could be heard shouting to one another in Russian well beyond the still streaming smoke. Satisfied that no other advance was forthcoming, big Arnie removed his finger from the trigger of the GPMG and the other men stopped firing their weapons. Scott indicated no more firing and then listened intently, as did the others, to the voices speaking in Russian at the other side of the screen of smoke. The men shouting were obviously pulling back towards the gorge and eventually their voices faded out altogether.

The smoke drifting languidly above the kill zone gradually disappeared, letting the moonlight reveal the full extent of the devastation caused by the Claymore mines. There were five dead men out there, most badly mangled, and severed limbs were scattered here and there between them. Luckily, in that moonlit darkness, the blistered and peeling skin of those badly scorched could not be seen from the sangar.

'They're not coming back,' Paddy finally said to Scott. 'At least not right now.'

'I don't think they'll come back at all,' Scott said. 'Those men were sent here to find our location and now Petrov knows it. He'll have seen and heard the explosions from wherever he is. He wasn't one of those men. He sent them on a suicidal mission just to find out where we were.'

'A nice man,' Paddy said.

'Are we moving on, boss?' big Arnie asked from where he still sat behind the tripod-mounted GPMG with Syd Loomis kneeling beside him, preparing to feed in another belt of ammunition.

'No,' Scott said. 'We stay where we are. Petrov now knows where we are and he knows we're well defended, so he's going to move with his men along that ridge from the gorge to the snow line. We'll then be behind him, pursuing him, and that's just where we want to be. So we stay here and move out at first light as originally planned. If any of Petrov's men come back between now and then, which I doubt, they'll still have to pass through that perimeter of Claymore mines. So you men can basha down for the rest of the morning and get some shuteye. Sergeant Devlin and I will take turns on watch, with me going first. Okay, Sarge?'

'Right, boss.'

Paddy grinned, sighed histrionically with pleasure, then slid deeper into his sleeping bag and closed his eyes. The rest of the men gratefully followed suit while Scott wriggled out of his sleeping bag and knelt behind the sangar wall, resting the barrel of his MP5 upon it, aimed in the direction of the dead between him and the gorge. He remained there until first light, thinking about his former wife and late son, about the supposedly monstrous Dmitry Petrov, not bothering to waken Paddy Devlin, who needed the sleep more than he did, and he was still there when the sun rose above the mountains that he would soon have to climb.

His next goal was the snow line.

CHAPTER TWENTY

Dmitry had to smile when he saw the last of the SAS men, the two-man machine-gun team, make their final run along the gorge and hurl themselves to safety behind the high rocks where their comrades were hidden.

'By God, they're good,' he said to Misha who was lying belly-down beside him on the lip of the ridge, looking into the deepening darkness of the gorge, now that the last of the flares was dying, flickering out, overhead. 'Their leader is clever. Using those flares was a masterstroke.'

Misha could barely conceal his irritation. 'Don't let your admiration blind you to the fact that those men have been sent here to kill you. If they're that good – and they seem to be – you should fear them instead of admiring them. Admiration is blinding; fear makes a man think clearly. Please think clearly and stop treating this as a game. Let's put an end to it.'

'Not yet,' Dmitry said, determined to be deaf to reason, now driven by the need to push himself, as well as his SAS opponents, to the very limit. 'This is only the beginning. They've impressed me and now I need to see more. This is exciting, my friend.'

'Exciting?'

'Yes.' Dmitry glanced down and saw the dead men in the gorge, recalling how the SAS flares, fired deliberately behind the ridge, had brilliantly illuminated his own men in their flickering, brilliant light while leaving the bottom of the gorge in pitch darkness, thus protecting the SAS as they advanced to the far end. It had been an extremely clever strategy and he had to admire it, even though it had cost him half-a-dozen men. 'It's more than just another fight with a rival band of brigands. It's a different thing altogether. Those men are supposed to be the best in the world and now we're pitted against them. At last I have truly worthy opponents and this knowledge excites me.'

'You're jaded beyond measure,' Misha said, 'and now your boredom is driving you to extreme, suicidal limits. Look down there,' he added, pointing into the gorge where, in the flickering, dying light of the flares, they could still discern the many dead bodies of those killed by the SAS. 'Those are our men, Dmitry, and they all died in vain. We could have annihilated the SAS from that first ambush position, but instead you choose to play tricks with them, killing only one man and letting the rest make their escape. We could have annihilated them again when they entered this gorge, but again you deliberately gave them the time to organise themselves into teams to give themselves covering fire as they came through. You wanted most of them to get through, but *all* of them got through, and now seven of our men are dead. Those men didn't think this was a game and neither will their comrades.'

The final flare flickered out, plunging the gorge back into moonlit darkness. The dead men could no longer be seen and might never have been.

'To hell with them,' Dmitry said, gazing down into that moonlit darkness, then letting his gaze roam along the basin of the gorge to those high rocks where the SAS were hiding. He saw no movement there, other than the lazy spiralling of dust picked up by the wind. 'Their so-called comrades are *my* men and live or die by *my* will. They knew what they were in for when they joined up with me, so they can't complain if some of them are killed. That risk has always been present.'

'Your men will take that risk if they think it worth taking, but not if they think they're being sacrificed needlessly – and they're experienced enough to know when that's happening.'

'My men are the scum of the earth,' Dmitry replied, finally acknowledging something that had always secretly pained him, 'and so I'll use them as I see fit, whether they like it or not.'

'Am I included in that assessment?' Misha asked, turning his steady, pale grey gaze upon Dmitry as he waited for an answer.

Dmitry didn't hesitate. 'No, you're not – and you know it. I respect you above all the others and treat you as my own brother. Now stop being so negative, Misha, and let's prepare to move out and pursue those men.'

'They came here to pursue *us*,' Misha said, turning his gaze away from Dmitry and instead looking along the moonlit gorge to the high rocks at the far end. There was still no sign of movement down there.

'And they will,' Dmitry said, also studying the far end of the canyon, straining to hear sounds of movement. 'My bet is that they're moving out right now, heading for the snow line. My intention is to advance along this ridge, from here to the snow line, then turn south to cut across their path and place ourselves in front of them. Once there, we'll make our presence known and encourage them to pursue us up into the snow, towards the mountain's summit. The final engagement will take place there.'

'The engagement between you and their leader.'

'Yes, that's correct.'

Misha sighed, then rolled from one hip to the other, glancing left and right along the ridge where the rest of the men, well spread out, where still in their firing positions, weapons aimed at those tall rocks at the far end of the gorge, though not firing, not moving. Despite what Dmitry said, they were well trained and knew just what they were doing.

'They may head for the snow line,' he said, turning back to Dmitry, 'but we don't know which direction they'll take. They won't risk advancing into the snow until first light, so they'll make camp somewhere between here and the snow line. But as we don't know which direction they're going to take, we won't know where they are.'

'We can find out.' Dmitry raised his right wrist, checked the luminous dial of his wristwatch, then glanced again at the high rocks at the far end of the gorge, silhouetted in the moonlight like alien sentinels. 'They'll be gone already,' he said. 'They won't have hung around there. If we send some men down there immediately, they should find their footprints.'

'Not necessarily,' Misha said in his thoughtful manner. 'The wind's strong and will blow the dust across their tracks, covering them up fast.'

'No matter,' Dmitry said impatiently. 'Our men should still be able to find them. They're bound to leave tracks, no matter how good they are otherwise. Almost certainly they'll head initially along a straight route to the snow line and take a different direction before they reach it. However, they won't risk hiking too far in the darkness, so our men, if they fan out across a broad arc, will find their night camp.'

'That camp could be well protected,' Misha insisted. 'Maybe with Claymore mines.'

'If the Claymore mines are tripped,' Dmitry responded, showing callous disregard for the fate of his men, 'we'll certainly know where they are, since we'll see and hear the explosions. Indeed, that would be perfect.'

'What?' Misha asked rhetorically, disbelievingly.

'While our reconnaissance patrol is looking for the SAS,' Dmitry continued, unable to hide his enthusiasm for this dangerous, ruthless game, 'the rest of us will be making our way along the high ridge that leads from here to the snow line. We'll be overlooking the lower slopes all the way and will be able to see and hear the explosions. Thus the position of the SAS camp will be pinpointed and we'll know where they are.'

'True,' Misha said. 'But most of the men in that reconnaissance patrol will die if the Claymores are tripped.'

'Nothing in life is free,' Dmitry replied, 'and that's the price we must pay.'

'Correction,' Misha said softly, sardonically. 'It's the price *they* will pay.'

'So be it,' Dmitry said.

Rising from his belly to his knees, he used hand signals to indicate to eight men that they were to gather around him. When they had done so, each holding his Kalashinkov across his chest, all looking even bigger and broader than they actually were in their padded jackets and fur-lined caps, he instructed them to make their way down to the far end of the gorge and follow the SAS patrol from there. He elected one of them, Ivor Froklov, as leader and gave him an old British army A41 radio set, which Froklov carried on a backpack with shoulder straps. He had deliberately picked Froklov as leader because he wasn't too bright and was something of a crawler, always eager to make an impression. He wouldn't question his orders.

'When you make contact with the SAS,' Dmitry told Froklov, carefully not mentioning the possibility of a camp defended with Claymore mines, 'you will radio their position to us and then launch an immediate assault. If you fail to liquidate them, at least keep them engaged until we can get down from the ridge to lend support. Understood?'

'Yes, boss.'

Without another word, Froklov turned away and led his seven men along the top of the ridge, heading west. When they were overlooking the high rocks at the far end, they made their way to the bottom, one man at a time, inching along like shadows until they were all down. Dmitry watched them spreading out and advancing to the high rocks. They reached the rocks without incident and gradually disappeared behind them, then Froklov reappeared and, silhouetted in the moonlight, waved one hand to indicate that the SAS had already moved on. When Dmitry signalled an acknowledgement, Froklov disappeared around the rocks again to rejoin his men. They would, as instructed, head for the snow line in pursuit of the SAS.

'Right,' Dmitry said, 'let's go.'

Rising from his knees, he indicated that the rest of the men should prepare to move out and then, with Misha by his side, he hurried along to take up a position in front of them. Though the men behind them were falling automatically into single file formation, he and Misha, at the head of the column, marched side by side, not concerned with protecting their front and rear because they knew that they were in command of this territory and that the SAS were somewhere far below them, on the lower slopes of the mountain.

Glancing downwards to his left, Dmitry saw the high rocks behind which the SAS had briefly taken shelter while the last of them, the two-man machine-gun crew, made their way to the same place. Letting his gaze roam westward along the low hills to the snow line, seeing only the dark outlines of the hills and valleys, he tried imagining where his opponents might be and what their leader, that unknown man whom he had to face, was thinking right now. Ludicrous though it seemed to him in his less-impassioned moments, he still felt that he and the nameless man were spiritual brothers who had been brought together for some mysterious purpose. This conviction baffled and haunted him.

'I can't see a thing down there,' he said to Misha, 'but I'm convinced they've made camp.'

'Even if we find out where their camp is,' Misha replied, clearly still disapproving of Dmitry's personalisation of their mission to kill the SAS, 'we can't be sure of what direction they'll take when they break camp and head for the snow line.'

'This man, their leader, thinks like me,' Dmitry said. 'Of this I'm sure. And this being so, I believe he'll hike as far as he can in darkness, weaving this way and that, frequently changing direction, trying to cover his tracks, and eventually making camp close to the snow line. My belief, therefore, is that if we find out where his camp is – if our patrol reports his position or if we see it from the explosions of their mined perimeter – we can assume that come first light they'll take the most direct route from their night camp to the snow line – and that's where we'll wait for them.'

'More good men will die for this,' Misha responded, still hiking resolutely beside Dmitry, matching him step for step, ignoring the wind slapping at them. Every step was taking them closer to the snow line where the cold would be fierce.

'They're not good men,' Dmitry said, finally facing up to what he was and the kind of brutes he was leading. 'They're good fighters, but they're certainly not good men. They're the scum of the earth. Good men have intelligence and sensitivity and finer feelings; these men are good fighters because they lack those very qualities and are totally, even mindlessly, ruthless. Don't be confused between their value as fighters and their worth as human beings.'

'They do nothing that we haven't done ourselves,' Misha responded, 'and nothing that we won't do again if necessity calls. If they're scum, then we, too, are scum and cannot look down on them.'

'I can look down on anyone,' Dmitry retorted, 'and have spent most of my life doing so. Don't ask me to change now. These men of mine are scum and as such are dispensable, so I'll use them as I see fit.'

'You despise yourself,' Misha said, not frightened of speaking his mind. 'You pretend to be ruthless, to be beyond human feelings, yet now you talk of the lack of sensitivity and finer feelings in the killers you command. Your age is catching up with you. You were always old, but now you're feeling it. Like someone out of Dostoyesky, you seek redemption for your sins and hope to find it by opening yourself to self-loathing. You were weakened by that Lalya, by your love for her, and ever since her escape and probable death you've been seeing yourself in a different light. She weakened your defences, Dmitry, by reminding you that you're still human – and that side of you, the side you thought you had renounced, has come back to torment you. Now you wish to pay for your sins and make us pay as well.'

The very mention of Lalya's name made Dmitry's heart leap, but he still could not accept that he might have loved her, though his guilt was a sharp blade. 'Who's *us*?' he asked, determined to keep Lalya out of this.

'Me and your men,' Misha informed him.

'You think I'm making you all pay for my sins as well?'

'You acknowledge that you're trying to pay for your sins?'

'Stop trying to be clever with me, Misha. If I now wish to pay for my sins – and that's not an admission – I'll pay for them alone. No one else is included.'

'Those men who died in the gorge are included,' Misha insisted. 'And if those others down there . . .' he indicated the low hills below, still couched in moonlit darkness '. . . die from a mined perimeter just to indicate the SAS location, they'll be included as well. You *want* them to trip the wires, to lead you to the SAS, because you need that final confrontation to take you to the edge. That edge, where you live or you die, is what you hope will help you pay for your sins. We're all included in that, my friend.'

Glancing down into the darkly outlined, moonlit lower slopes of the mountain, then letting his gaze travel westward to where the snow line began and the snow-covered upper slopes soared to the gleaming ice on the jagged, star-drenched peaks, Dmitry knew that his friend was right and that his insistence on drawing this conflict out, on narrowing it down to a fight between himself and the unknown leader of the SAS team, was indeed a sign that he wished to go to the very edge and risk falling off. That fall, if it came, would take him into the abyss, into the cataracts of hell, where self-judgement was one's punishment, unrelenting, eternal, and where all of his inner conflicts would be resolved in the fires of damnation. He wanted those flames, the scorching of his very soul, the thawing of his chilled humanity, and was convinced that the man he sought – the very man who was hunting him – would either push him to, or draw him to, that edge where they would both meet their maker. This belief, in its opium-induced luminosity, was what drove him on.

Dmitry marched on, with Misha by his side, towards the eerily gleaming white hills above the snow line. He was about to respond to Misha, to explain his reasoning, when the man directly behind him, the radio operator, Alexander Kamenev, called out to say that a call was coming in. Dmitry and Misha both stopped marching, glanced at each other, then turned around to face Kamenev.

'Give me the phone,' Dmitry said, then, when he had the receiver in his hand, he switched it on and said simply, avoiding military jargon: 'Petrov. Come in.'

'Froklov, boss,' a static-smothered voice replied, as if speaking from the dark side of the moon.

'Yes, Froklov, continue.'

'We have the target in our sights. They've built a sangar not far from the snow line – about a hundred and fifty metres – and they're protecting it with a GPMG.'

Still not mentioning the possibility of a mined perimeter, Dmitry said, 'Do you think you can take them by surprise?'

'Yes, boss,' Froklov said, always eager to please. 'The ground slopes gently up to the sangar and clouds often blot out the moonlight. I think we could get pretty close to them before being seen. If we get as close as I believe we can, we could attack them before that machine gunner gets a chance to open up. If so, we could overrun the sangar with very few casualties.'

'Good,' Dmitry said, glancing at Misha, who was listening in, but seeing nothing in his pale grey, wintry gaze. 'We'll come down there and join you as soon as possible,' he lied, 'but we can't afford to lose the element of surprise, so you must attack immediately. When you've overrun the sangar, which I'm sure you will, contact me again.'

'Yes, boss,' Froklov said, as dumb as always and sounding excited. He gave Dmitry the grid-mark reading for his location and Dmitry thanked him for it, then said, 'Over and out.'

Dmitry handed the phone back to Alexander Kamenev, then indicated to the men strung out in a long line behind him, along the rim of the moonlit ridge, that they should take a break. Gratefully, they sank to the ground, most seeking protection from the cold wind by sheltering behind the largest rocks they could find. Dmitry and Misha remained out in the open, though kneeling side by side on the hard ground, the low hills stretched out below them, a dark pit, the snow-covered slopes of the mountain rising to the west.

'They're about to attack?' Misha asked.

'Yes,' Dmitry said, raising his binoculars to his eyes.

'Those poor, dumb bastards,' Misha said.

Smiling, Dmitry scanned the land below through his binoculars and saw only the outline of the undulating lower slopes of the mountain, black wave piled upon black wave. He knew they were down there somewhere, his enemies, his judge and jury, but it was impossible to see in the darkness and, also, they might well be hidden behind one of those rolling hills.

He was lowering the binoculars to his chest when he heard the first explosion.

Looking down again, this time without the binoculars, he saw a jagged sheet of silvery-white flame tearing the darkness below, about three or four kilometres out from the base of the ridge, about a hundred and fifty metres from the snow line. Even as he heard the distant roar of the explosion, a second sheet of flame tore through the first – one Claymore mine going off after the other. Almost immediately, the savage roar of a GPMG was added to the bedlam, then a third and forth Claymore exploded.

Raising his binoculars to his eyes, Dmitry scanned the area and soon focused on a cloud of billowing, swirling smoke in a rainfall of gravel and dust. About thirty metres to the west, but obscured by the smoke, he discerned what could have been the low, loose-stoned wall of a sangar, though he couldn't be sure of this until he moved the binoculars slightly and saw the minute, stabbing flame of what was unmistakably a firing machine gun. A few seconds later, the spitting flame of that machine gun was surrounded by the small, darting flames of rifles and sub-machine guns as, he surmised, the rest of the SAS lent their support with personal weapons. More Claymore mines exploded, the machine gun fell silent, then the firing of the other weapons also stopped, letting silence return.

Swinging the binoculars in the other direction, to where the Claymore mines had gone off, Dmitry saw the boiling smoke and raining gravel of the final explosions. As this settled down, a single shadowy figure, looking oddly misshapen, rose awkwardly from the ground and hurried away from the scene of devastation. Two more, equally shadowy, figures emerged from the settling smoke and followed the first.

Knowing that the oddly misshapen figure could only have been Ivor Froklov, burdened under his radio and followed by the only other survivors, Dmitry lowered his binoculars to his chest and signalled to Alexander Kamenev. The radio operator, gaunt-faced and unshaven, crawled up to Dmitry on his belly and handed him the phone. Dmitry waited patiently until the expected call came in, then he switched on the receiver.

'Yes,' he said. 'Petrov.'

'It's me, boss, Froklov.'

'What's the situation?'

'Negative. Those bastards had mined their perimeter, boss, and I lost five of my men. The remaining three of us can't attack them on our own – and the whole perimeter is still mined – so we're waiting for you to arrive and give us support.'

'You failed,' Dmitry said, not surprised, but trying to sound as outraged as possible. 'You not only failed, but you lost five of your men and now we've lost the element of surprise, so we can't attack either. I should shoot you for this.'

'*What?*'

'I said I should shoot you.'

'It wasn't my fault, boss! They had their perimeter lined with Claymore mines and they tore us to shreds! I can't be blamed for . . .'

'You stupid bastard,' Dmitry interjected. 'You advanced without checking for mines? Just how dumb can you be?'

'But, boss, you . . .'

'Don't bother rejoining us, Froklov. I'd only shoot you on sight. Make your way back to that watch team on the Osh–Fergana road and wait there with those other two cowards until we return. I'll attend to you when we get back. Over and out.'

Knowing that Froklov would now be too frightened to make his way back to the road watch team, convinced, as he was, that he would be executed on sight, Dmitry switched off the receiver before the fool could say anything else. He handed the receiver to Kamenev, waited until the radio operator had belly-crawled back to his position, then turned to the pale-eyed, watchful Misha.

'So,' Dmitry said, 'we now know where the SAS are and approximately where they'll enter the snow line.'

'Indeed, we do,' Misha said softly, sardonically. 'So what happens now?'

'Now we hike to the snow line and find a position from which we can observe the SAS advance. We strike when we're ready.'

'So be it,' Misha said.

They clambered back to their feet and their men, stretched out in a long, irregular line behind them, did exactly the same. At a hand signal from Dmitry, they moved off again, heading towards the vast, snow-covered slopes that soared, white and glistening and desolate, to jagged peaks illuminated by the moon and gleaming eerily in their mantles of ice. The howling wind grew colder with each mile of their advance and eventually, even before they reached the snow line, the snow started falling. When the snowflakes on the gravel turned to thick snow, they knew just where they were.

'When they move out to make their hike to the snow line,' Dmitry said, squinting into the white haze to the south, 'they'll move no more than two kilometres either side of their night camp and that gives us a four-kilometre front to cover. So we march south from here, patrolling along a four-kilometre front, and keep doing so until we see them.'

'And then?' Misha asked.

'Then we find a suitable site for an ambush and sit back and wait for them.'

'Let's move,' Misha said.

They made their way uphill, heading west, towards the summit of the mountain where the sun would soon rise, then turned southward to hike along that four-kilometre stretch of wind-whipped, snow-swept mountainside. Soon covered completely by the fresh, falling snow, they merged gradually into the vast, silent, night-enshrouded whiteness and eventually became at one with it, rendered almost invisible. In this state of grace, rendered almost invisible, they found what they were looking for.

CHAPTER TWENTY-ONE

Before crossing the snow line and advancing up the mountain proper, just after first light, the SAS men prepared themselves for the dramatic change in climate by putting on Arctic clothing, starting with dark green long johns that were tight up to the knee but baggy above the knee to trap air for heat insulation. The upper sleeve was long-sleeved but had elasticated wrists to prevent heat from escaping.

'Not as sexy as my normal jockstrap,' Arnie said, 'but at least there's no women around to see me.'

'You wear a jockstrap?' Syd Loomis enquired.

'Sure,' big Arnie said. 'Why?'

'I just thought that with that equipment of yours you'd have needed a jib and crane.'

'Tut, tut, the boy's jealous!'

'Just put your fucking trousers on,' Mad Mike snarled, 'and cut the bullshit.'

'Yes, Corp!' Arnie and Syd sang simultaneously.

To combat the bitter cold of the mountain they had brought along Royal Marine cotton DPM trousers with a velcro slash from the ankle to the knee to allow a quick change to be made if necessary, with velcro pockets and large buttons that could be manipulated by hands covered in gloves. In fact, each man had two sets of gloves: an inner pair of thin cotton and an outer pair of white nylon, both covered with mittens taped to the torso to enable the trooper to yank them off in a second if he had to fire his weapon. Normal shirts were replaced with Goretex smocks with hoods that covered the woolly hats favoured over balaclavas because they did not inhibit hearing. The standard British army quilted, insulated jacket, known as a Chairman Mao suit, was put on over the smock. To prevent frostbite to the face, they wore masks consisting of a thin silk lining that went next to the skin and an outer lining of cotton. A light, white nylon cover was then worn over the trousers, smock, Chairman Mao suit *and* bergen, covering each man from the ankles to the neck and making him look like a veritable snowman.

'Just give me one of them stick-on red noses,' Big Arnie said, 'and you can keep me in your garden for Christmas.'

'I didn't know you big black Sambos celebrated Christmas,' Syd Loomis said. 'It must be hard to do when up there in the trees munching on your bananas.'

'Come, come,' Arnie replied, tying the strings on his white nylon covering and putting on his white hood. 'No need to sneer at me, Syd. At least I'm a white man at last. God works in mysterious ways.'

'He sure fucking does. He torments me with the likes of you, for a start. God knows what else He's planned for me.'

'New neighbours back home,' big Arnie helpfully informed him. 'They're probably moving in right now. An enormous family from the West Indies and they all play in steel bands. Being black, they don't keep to English hours, so they rehearse through the night. You'll soon be in for a good time.'

'I told you,' Mad Mike snarled, 'cut the bullshit and hurry up getting dressed.'

'I'm dressed,' big Arnie said.

'So am I,' Syd added.

'You haven't changed your fucking footwear,' Mad Mike sneered. 'So get to it, you fuck-ups.'

'Yes, boss!'

Footwear consisted of two pairs of good mountaineering socks over the feet – a wool pair next to the skin and a nylon pair on top – with Goretex seals worn over the socks to allow perspiration vapour to exit while preventing water from entering. The boots were Berghaus mountain boots, which had a cleat enabling the wearer to put on Goretex gaiters and clips for skis or snow shoes.

'Did you ever think,' big Arnie asked of Syd, 'when you were a child in the slums of Newcastle-on-Tyne, unloved, uneducated and with holes in your pockets, that one day you'd actually be able to ski? Did that ever enter your head, Syd?'

'No, it fucking didn't,' Syd replied. 'But at least I had a head with *something* in it, which is more than can be said for you and your ebony brothers.'

'Ebony and ivory go together hand in hand,' Arnie replied. 'Paul McCartney said that.'

'He sang it,' Syd corrected him.

'He also wrote it,' Pete Welsh added.

'Paul McCartney writes shit,' Syd replied, 'and Arnie's just proved it. Of course Arnie writes himself – he seems to think he's a fucking poet – and that explains why he likes the lyrics of Paul McCartney. Those two are on the same level.'

'When I get published in *Mars and Minerva*,' Arnie replied with a big grin, 'you're gonna have to eat those words, my friend, and I hope you choke on 'em.'

'I'll choke the fucking pair of you,' Mad Mike said, 'if you don't shut your mouths.'

'Yes, boss!'

Once fully dressed, each trooper attached a set of goggles to his waist-belt. These would be used when it snowed heavily or when the sun became too bright and could blind a man with its ultraviolet rays reflecting dangerously off a snow-covered surface. The goggles were the same as those worn in the desert but in this case were camouflaged with white tape. Finally, since it was possible to get sunburnt in cold climates when the rays of the sun reflected upwards from snow or ice, all the soldiers applied sunburn cream to the exposed areas of their face and chapstick to the eyelids, around the nose and to the lips. After doing this, big Arnie pursed his lips and blew a kiss to Syd. 'Love ya, baby!' he cooed.

'Don't make me throw up,' Syd said.

Pete Welsh was about to pitch in when Scott called the men to a Chinese Parliament. When they had all gathered around him, most resting with one knee on the ground, he said, 'Here's the sit rep, for what it's worth.' With a nod of his head, he indicated the mountain beyond the snow line, about 150 metres away. 'We're going to go up there,' he said, deliberately leaving a pause to emphasise his point. 'Almost certainly, Petrov and his men will be somewhere up there, waiting for us, hoping to lay an ambush. However, it's now time for us to take the initiative and we'll do it by becoming invisible and finding them before they see us. This is, however, a volatile, unpredictable situation, so from this point on each man here will have to use his brains.'

'What does that mean?' Killer Parker asked.

'It means that you could, for instance, find yourself in a shoot-and-scoot situation, in which case you just get up and go, not waiting for orders. In other words, though we're obviously going to try to stick together, from this point on we're in a potential shake-out situation and have to be prepared at all times.'

'What does *that* mean?' Mad Mike Nicholson asked.

'Keep low. Keep your eyes peeled. Keep your ears open. Shoot at anything that moves and shoot to kill.'

'Just like Northern Ireland,' Syd Loomis said.

'I categorically deny that,' Paddy Devlin said, bland-faced. 'That was just a piece of filthy propaganda put out by Sinn Fein.'

'Yeah, sure,' Killer Parker said.

'Parker,' Scott said, turning his head to look into those flat grey eyes, 'you're the best scout we've got so I'd like you to go out front – not on point, a lot farther – to check what's out there and clear the way for us. Take Trooper Loomis's 319 and keep in touch with it. Is that okay with you?'

'My pleasure,' Parker said, clearly keen to be out there on his own, while Syd, relieved to get rid of his cumbersome radio system, started removing its straps from his shoulders.

'I'll go out on point as the lead scout,' Scott continued, 'and you can report directly back to me.' He turned to Pete Welsh, who was kneeling beside him. 'You stick with me, Welsh, and be ready for any calls coming in from Corporal Parker.'

'Right, boss. Will do.'

Scott caught Mad Mike's darkly intense gaze. 'I want you, Nicholson, to stay behind me and Welsh, to give us covering fire and protect the radio system.' What he meant by this, in fact, was that if Welsh was shot, Mad Mike was to take charge of the all-important radio system, but he didn't state the case that baldly out of a superstitious, regimental fear that it might come true. 'You, Basham, and you, Loomis, will fall in behind Nicholson, still sharing the GPMG between you, and you, Paddy, will bring up the rear as usual. Any questions before we move out?' All the men shook their heads from side to side, indicating that they had no questions. 'Right, let's move out. Off you go, Parker.'

Parker had taken the second PRC 319 off Syd Loomis and now, with the radio system strapped to his backpack, his SA-80 assault rifle in his right hand, and the Barrett Light .50 strapped across the top of the bergen, he turned away and hurried off to get a good distance ahead of the main group. Scott waited until Parker had crossed the snow line, about a hundred and fifty metres away, before indicating to his men that they should fall into column behind him, then he, too, moved out, indicating that the men should follow him.

He led them straight to the snow line. This was not an abrupt transition from uncovered earth to deep snow, but, rather, a broad expanse of ground, about three kilometres long, where the dry, steeply sloping ground gradually gave way to patches of frost and snow, with the latter becoming progressively more widespread and deeper, until eventually it covered everything in sight. To cross the snow line, therefore, and reach the snow-covered upper slopes of the mountain, they had to hike about three kilometres, mostly up an ever steeper gradient that was strewn with patches of loose gravel and rocks, and filled with potentially dangerous potholes.

Another danger, Scott recalled from his Kremlin briefings as he led his men across the snow line, was the fact that these mountains were still used by fur trappers, which meant that potentially damaging animal traps could be buried in the snow. As such traps could chop through a man's ankle, almost amputating the foot, Scott advanced with extreme care, looking into the deepening snow for the glint of steel teeth with as much care as he would normally have looked for land mines. Thus progress was necessarily slow.

As the sun rose, bright, beautiful and potentially blinding, already reflecting off the glistening, virgin snow covering the slopes on all sides, Scott saw that Killer Parker was already far ahead and, wrapped in his white nylon covering and hood, merging with the brightening white landscape, practically disappearing. In fact, he disappeared shortly after, cut off from view when he crossed over the summit of this gradient, the far end of the snow line, and started down the other side into the valley between one hill and the next.

Scott knew what he would be doing. He would be advancing at the half-crouch, moving from one piece of cover to another whilst eyeballing the terrain and also using his military binoculars in the hope of catching sight of the enemy. He would also be checking every inch of his chosen route for the slightest sign of human movement: footprints in the snow, overturned pebbles or small rocks; even broken twigs or the bent branches of the few trees scattered indiscriminately on the upper slopes. Last but not least, he would be looking for the smoke of camp fires, which would be indicative either of the enemy or of local fur trappers.

Scott was able to advance more quickly now because he was following Parker's footprints in the deep snow and therefore less concerned with hidden animal traps. As he continued marching, scanning the sweeping snowscapes on either side and glancing frequently back over his shoulder to ensure that his men were still strung out behind him, he felt increasingly that he was on an alien planet, a frozen world at the far side of the cosmos, where nothing lived except him and his men. This was, of course, an illusion created by the vast silence, the awesome, all-white desolation, but he knew that the mountains were the home of predatory beasts, notably the brown bear and the snow leopard, and that Petrov and his men, even more dangerous than the wild animals, were somewhere out there.

Wherever you are, you cunt, Scott thought with a vehemence that he had never known before, I'll find you and finish you. Take that as read, Petrov.

Eventually, after a couple of hours, when the sun was rising over the mountain peaks to reflect off the dazzling snow, Parker called in on his PRC 319. Scott took the receiver from Pete Welsh while the men behind him, having been given a hand signal, rested by squatting in the snow, though still strung out in a long, well-spaced, watchful line.

'Scott here. What is it?'

'Petrov's men are ahead of us,' Parker said. 'They're not even trying to cover their tracks. Right now, they're somewhere above us, but it's one hell of a climb, boss.'

'Anything they can climb, we can climb.'

Parker didn't even chuckle, but he was as precise as always. 'If we want to follow their tracks, we're going to have to climb an almost sheer cliff face. By that I mean we'll have to go up by rope.'

'We can do that,' Scott said. 'Is that where you are now?'

'Yes, boss. I'm at the base of the cliff face. But I have the idea that they might have come this way deliberately, forcing us to climb, in order to shoot us to hell while we're doing it.'

'That's a distinct possibility, Parker, but we don't have a choice.'

'I know. Naturally, I'll go up first and check out the situation, but I can't do it until you get here.'

'We're on our way, Parker. What's your grid reading?' When Parker had given him the reading for his local map, Scott said, 'Over and out.' He handed the phone back to Pete Welsh, indicated that the rest of the men should follow him, then started off again, still following Parker's footprints in the snow but also double-checking the grid readings against his map. Judging from the map, Parker was approximately half a kilometre away. Scott figured he could make the journey in about fifteen or twenty minutes, assuming the weather did not suddenly turn against him. Right now, it was a sunny late morning, approaching noon, with the sun rising high in the sky, almost directly overhead, spreading its light through a brilliant azure sky and turning the untouched snowscapes into a pure, dazzling whiteness tinged with pale blue shadows.

Indeed, the whole mountainside looked unnaturally perfect, too clean to be real, but Scott knew that those soaring hills, as smooth as cream on a birthday cake, were filled with dangerous fissures and crevasses, some hundreds of metres deep, into which a man could fall to his death. Even here, where Scott was marching, had it not been for Parker's footprints in the otherwise untouched snow, he would have had to advance at a snail's pace in order to check for loose rocks and potholes, both of which could trip a man and break his ankle, as well as for animal traps and hidden fissures. Parker, however, was the best scout and tracker in the regiment and, as such, could move across terrain like this far quicker than any man Scott had ever met. He had clearly done so in this instance, scanning the terrain with eyes that saw more than most, which is why, though he had only left their night camp a couple of minutes before the main patrol, he had managed, in four hours' marching, to place himself a good ten or fifteen minutes ahead of the others.

Still marching out ahead of the main patrol, though

with Pete Welsh right behind him, carrying the second PRC 319, Scott saw the sheer cliff face before he actually saw Parker. The last ten minutes' hiking had been mostly uphill, up an increasingly steep, icy gradient where Scott and the others had frequently slid backwards or been forced to drag their feet out of patches of particularly deep, thick snow. However, even as the gradient had started levelling out, thus making the climb much easier, Scott had seen the top of the cliff beyond it, long and narrow at first, running from north to south, with most of the cliff face hidden from view by the gradient. That cliff rose and seemed to expand dramatically as Scott approached the almost level ground that ran out to its base where Parker, a mere speck in the distance, was waiting for them.

When Scott saw the cliff face in all its splendour, his heart sank, because it was, indeed, imposingly high and too sheer to be ascended by natural means.

They surely would, as Parker had stated confidently, have to go up by rope.

The cliff face, now a towering wall of granite and brown earth that showed in numerous patches through the wind-blown, drifting snow, rather like a vast jigsaw, loomed ever larger and seemed more intimidating with each step that Scott took towards it. As he approached, he saw Killer Parker more clearly, not resting up as most men would have done, but already uncoiling his rope in preparation for the climb.

Determined to be the first to climb, for what he thought were good reasons, Scott quickened his pace, though he still found it hard going to lift his feet out of the deep snow, and finally reached the base of the cliff where Parker, balanced on one knee, had unwound his rope. He looked up when Scott and Welsh stopped in front of him, then jerked his head upwards a couple of times, indicating the soaring face of the cliff.

'A real motherfucker, isn't it?' he said. 'If Petrov lured us this way deliberately, he made a good choice. This climb won't be easy.'

'We'll find out just how hard it is when I've climbed it,' Scott replied evenly, 'because I'm going first.'

Parker looked surprised, even offended, but before he could say anything, Troopers Basham and Loomis arrived on the scene. They both gazed up the sheer face of the cliff, then Loomis gave a low whistle of appreciation.

'Wow! Now ain't that somethin'?' big Arnie said, imitating a Yank.

'It sure is,' Syd agreed.

Mad Mike Nicholson arrived a minute later and also looked upwards with widening eyes, before lowering his gaze to his friend, Killer Parker, while shaking his head from side to side and grinning lopsidedly. 'Shit,' he said, 'this is showtime.'

Paddy Devlin, having brought up the rear, came in last of all. Like the others, he automatically glanced upwards, then, lowering his gaze, he turned to Scott. 'Don't tell me. We're going to climb.'

'That's right,' Scott said.

'If those bastards are up there,' Paddy said, referring to Petrov and his men, 'they'll be waiting for the first man up and they'll surely blow him to hell.'

'That's exactly why I'm going up first,' Scott replied, glancing down at the still kneeling Corporal Parker who was, he knew, feeling offended. 'Sergeant Devlin and I believe,' he continued, speaking directly to Parker though he wanted the rest to hear, 'that for reasons we can't as yet comprehend our target, Dmitry Petrov, wants a personal confrontation with the leader of this patrol, namely myself, and to that end he's going to try to isolate me from the rest of you. Logically speaking, given the circumstances, the best way for him to do that is to dispense with everyone in the group, leaving me to the last. Given this, it's my belief that if Petrov or his men are up there . . .' with a nod of his head, he indicated the top of the cliff face '. . . they won't fire on me if I'm the first one up – and that's exactly why I'm going up there first.'

'So what if they *are* up there,' Mad Mike asked, 'and they *don't* fire at you? They'll just wait till the next man appears and then blow *him* to hell. Either that or they'll wait until we're all up there and *then* cut us to pieces.'

'That's probably what they intend to do,' Scott replied, 'but willy-nilly we still have to get up there ... and me going first gives us the only chance we've got.'

'How come?' Paddy Devlin asked.

'If they don't fire at me, if they want to leave me to the last, I can act as a human shield for Corporal Parker long enough for him to find some kind of cover. I can then do the same for the others and each man, as he gets up there and takes cover, will add to our aggressive capability should Petrov's men lose interest in keeping me to the last and open fire anyway.'

'I'll buy that,' Parker said, flat-voiced.

Paddy Devlin sighed. 'It's a high-risk plan,' he said, 'but I agree that it's the only one we've got.'

'Why not wait until last light,' Syd Loomis asked, 'and then go up under cover of darkness?'

'Because we can't climb up that cliff face in darkness,' Paddy Devlin informed him. 'Any more dumb questions?'

'Not from me,' Syd said with a cocky grin.

'Right,' Scott said, looking at each man in turn. 'Uncoil your ropes and prepare to climb. I go first as the be-layer, with Parker as the first climber after me, starting his climb at my signal, and the rest of you coming up in the same order as you were in the file formation. Okay? Let's do it.'

As the men started uncoiling their ropes, Scott glanced up the cliff face and carefully checked all available platforms and ledges. After satisfying himself as to which could be used as stopping stages, or resting-up areas, he studied the lowest one he had picked and saw a vertical spike of rock that could be used as an anchor. Instantly, he uncoiled his own rope, placed the two ends together, then swung the whole rope above his head and released it to let the curved middle part sail upwards and, hopefully, loop over that spike of rock. As he had expected, he missed the first few throws, but eventually the rope fell over its target and he was able to tug on it to ensure that it would hold. After tugging as hard as possible, he leaned back as far as he could, checking that the rope could take the full weight of his body. Satisfied that it could, he passed both ends of the rope between his legs from the front, brought them around the left side of his body, across his chest, then over his right shoulder and down across his back. He held the rope at the front with his left hand and at the back with his right. He was now ready to climb.

'Hail Mary and Hallelujah,' he joked. 'Here we go, boys.'

'Enjoy the trip,' Paddy Devlin said.

Taking a deep breath, Scott planted his feet about forty-five centimetres apart, pressed them firmly against the face of the cliff, leaned backwards, then started pulling himself upwards, using both hands except when he had to briefly let go with one hand in order to grab intermediate holds. He moved upwards with great care, concentrating on keeping his weight evenly balanced on the rope, trying to avoid sharp edges that could cut either him or the rope, and eventually made it up to the first narrow ledge that he had chosen for a stopping point. Scrambling onto the ledge, which was about fifteen feet above the ground, he took enough time to catch his breath, then he signalled to Parker to throw up his rope. When Parker did so, Scott caught the rope and tied it around the spike of stone being used as an anchor. When Parker started hauling himself up, as Scott had done, Scott threw his rope up over another preselected anchor, another fifteen feet or so above him, and started to haul himself up even higher. By the time he reached the second anchor, Parker had reached the first ledge; both men then did the same as before, with Scott ascending to the third staging post, Parker to the second, and the third man, Pete Welsh, ascending to the first. Thus they went up, one by one, in painful, dangerous stages.

By the time Scott was nearing the top of the cliff face, he was sweating despite the bitter cold, breathing harshly from the sheer physical exertion, and experiencing slight panic and a sensation of dizziness when he glanced downwards, which he had to do at least every time he reached the next platform. Glancing down from the last platform before the top, he saw Parker ascending towards him and the rest of the men doing the same below him, like black flies on a white wall. Glancing down beyond the last man, Paddy Devlin, to the flat, snow-covered plain, Scott felt dizzy again. Taking a deep breath, he glanced to the east and saw the snow-covered slopes falling away to the snow line – that mile or so of whiteness giving way to bare rock – then the lower slopes falling away to the vast sweep of the Fergana Valley, which was verdant, abundant with trees, and with rivers and streams. There was no snow down there and the sky was a vast bright blue sheet above the green of the earth.

Turning away from that sight, trying to control his slight but taunting feeling of vertigo, Scott planted his feet firmly against the rocky face of the cliff, pushed himself out again, then hauled himself up the final few metres to the summit. His last anchor was a spike of rock jutting out about five feet below where the cliff face levelled out in a series of natural steps and, when he reached the spike, he was able to rest on the narrow ledge, or platform, slip the rope off the rock, then coil it up again and hook it over his shoulder. Freed from this encumbrance, he found it easier this time to catch Parker's upflung rope and loop it over the rock. Then, as Parker began his ascent from the second-to-last ledge, Scott took his MP5 from his other shoulder and held it in his right hand.

Feeling unprotected, almost naked, he made his way up those last few metres by alternately grabbing rock holds with either his right hand or his left whilst transferring the weapon from one to the other. Reaching the last ledge, he was grateful to see that the top of the cliff was not shaped as a sharp, right-angled turn, but sloped gradually up to level ground. That ground, as expected, was covered in a deep layer of snow.

Now able to stand upright, though aware of the strength of the howling wind, which hammered at him relentlessly, Scott advanced carefully up to level ground, automatically dropping lower as his body became exposed, and saw a flat stretch of snow-covered ground running away to higher ground that was littered with immense, densely packed boulders and rock outcroppings, some of which formed narrow passageways. Up here, the snow was deep and windblown, the sky dark and ominous.

Fully aware that Petrov's men could be hiding behind those massive rocks, about eighty metres away, but forced to assume that they would not fire at him because he was to be saved until last, Scott turned around, facing that magnificent view over the Fergana Valley, and waited for Parker to reach the final ledge, directly below. When he had done so, Scott signalled the all clear, indicating that Parker should come on up, then he turned to the front again, facing the rocky higher ground where Petrov's men might be located, and held his MP5 at the ready, preparing to give Parker covering fire, no matter how inadequate. He waited for the sound of gunfire, for the sight of movement over there, but heard only the howling of the wind and saw only the sweeping, spiralling snow.

I need my goggles, he thought.

But he didn't put them on. Instead, he just stood there, his weapon at the ready, until Parker had reached the final ledge and then come up behind him.

'Stay directly behind me,' Scott said, 'close to me, then make a run for those rocks to the right. If you manage to get there in one piece, prepare to give covering fire to the others.'

'Right, boss, will do.'

After coming up behind Scott, mere inches behind him, Parker launched himself to the side and raced to the snow-covered rocks located about six metres to the right. He crashed into the snow behind the rocks, then instantly righted himself and took up a firing position, preparing to give covering fire to the others.

No shots had been fired.

Heaving a sigh of relief, Scott told Pete Welsh, who had reached the final ledge and called out for instructions, to do exactly the same as Parker, but to take up a position to Scott's left, rather than his right. Welsh did so, coming up directly behind Scott, stopping close behind him, then launching himself to the left and taking up a firing position behind another bunch of snow-covered, high rocks.

Again, no shots had been fired.

The rest of the men reached the final ledge, one by one, and, one by one, did exactly as Parker and Welsh had done, with each man taking a direction opposite to the man before him, until all of them were safely behind high rocks, three to one side of Scott, another three to the other side.

Still no shots had been fired.

Sighing with relief, studying the rocky high ground directly ahead, squinting against the sweeping snow and aware that the sun was sinking again, but hearing nothing and seeing no sign of movement, Scott indicated with a hand signal that he was going to advance and that the rest of the men should follow him at safe intervals.

Scott advanced. He did so slowly and carefully, holding his weapon at the ready, never taking his eyes off that rocky high ground and listening intently. Seeing nothing, hearing nothing, he kept advancing and his men stood up and followed him, one by one, until all of them were coming up behind them, well spread out and with their weapons at the ready.

A gunshot split the silence.

CHAPTER TWENTY-TWO

Syd Loomis jerking violently and almost doubling up as if punched in the midriff, then being thrown onto his back as his weapon fell to the snow. 'Shoot and scoot!' Scott bawling, 'Shoot and scoot!' Seeing Syd on the ground, writhing and groaning in pain, deliberately shot – yes, Scott knew it had been a deliberate, sadistic shot to the stomach, the very worst place to be wounded, the slow, agonizing death – as he felt the rage scorching him, the contempt, the disgust, and dropped to his belly and rolled away behind the nearest rock, preparing to open fire. Bawling again, 'Shoot and scoot! Shoot and scoot!' which the men were doing anyway, scattering in all directions, firing their weapons on the run, from the hip, the SA-80s rifles and MP5 sub-machine guns making a shocking, deafening din, the men shouting to each other, words that only they understood, weaving left and right, darting from cover to cover as they kept up sustained bursts of fire to cover Killer Parker who had jumped out into the open to reach down while still firing his SA-80 from the hip and grab Syd by one of his wrists and drag him to safety.

'Fuck, no!' Syd screamed. 'You're tearing me in half! Fuck, no, Parker! Leave me here!'

Scott opened fire with his MP5, adding to the general

bedlam, aiming at the rocky high ground ahead where the enemy fire was coming from, but seeing no one, nothing, just firing blind, hoping to keep them pinned down long enough for Parker to drag Syd to safety, which would still mean a lingering death.

'Fuck, no, Parker! Fuck, you're killing me! Jesus Christ, let me go!' Syd screaming and writhing as Parker tried to pull him to safety, bullets stitching the ground around them, snow spitting and steaming in long jagged lines. Then those spitting lines found Syd, cut across him, finished the job, and he screamed again, a long, drawn-out sibilance, inhuman, that stopped abruptly as he shuddered and convulsed and collapsed like a punctured balloon on a carpet of blood, shockingly red against the pure white of the snow, dribbling out all around him.

'Bastards!' big Arnie bawled.

Parker released Syd's wrist and spun to the front, firing his rifle, as Mad Mike hurled himself forth, out there in the open, firing his MP5 wildly from the hip, then stopped long enough to swing his right arm and send a fragmentation grenade sailing through the air before throwing himself behind another pile of rocks located nearer the high ground. The frag exploded with a deafening roar, a sheet of dazzling light ripping a hole in the sky, throwing stones and gravel and steaming snow upwards on a billowing cloud of black smoke above the rocks. A scream emanated from the smoke, men bawled at one another, then a shadowy form fell sideways, falling out from behind a rock, and dropped through the smoke to the ground as another fusillade of gunfire from that direction added to the bedlam.

Up and running at the half-crouch, weaving left and right, Scott heard bullets whistling past on either side and saw lines of spitting snow, a hail of bullets from a machine gun, darting around him and passing on, making soft thudding sounds. Pete Welsh was to his left, on one knee behind a high rock, misshapen under his bulky radio system, but still firing his MP5 in short, precise bursts. Beyond him Arnie

Basham, looking stricken because of Syd, tears in his eyes as he swung his right arm to let another frag sail through the air and come down on the high ground. Beyond Arnie, glancing keenly around him with his SA-80 at the ready, Paddy Devlin was still covering their rear. Mad Mike was well ahead, darting from one rock to another, firing his weapon on the move, but he threw himself to the ground as the frag exploded, tearing the blue sky again, creating jagged holes of white light, throwing up more gravel and stones, covering the enemy positions in billowing black smoke as someone else hidden from view screamed. Mad Mike, covered by sustained bursts from Parker's SA-80, ran forward again, firing on the move.

'Yallup!' he bawled – or something like that.

Scott hurled himself forward, crouched low, weaving constantly, avoiding those spitting lines of snow that indicated advancing bullets, hearing other bullets whistling past on both sides, waiting for one to impact. He felt incandescent, all his senses razor sharp, his perception acute – saw the sheer blue of the sky, the glittering ice on the mountain peaks, the vast vistas of sloping snowscapes and, nearer to hand, indeed very close now, the tall rocks of the high ground, bizarrely shaped, white with snow – saw it all, including his men, in unnatural, startling clarity, heightened reality, and was moved to the point of transcendence by his hatred for Petrov.

Syd had been shot deliberately in the stomach to cause maximum pain.

Oh, you bastard! Scott thought.

He was on the ground again, having thrown himself down on his belly in the snow, soaked in snow, eating snow, now close to the high ground, though not as close as Killer Parker and Mad Mike, both moving in on the enemy positions from opposite sides, coming in on their blind sides, firing their rifles and hurling frags to cause bedlam and confusion, the fiercely flaring light of the explosions, the flying gravel and stones, the geysering, steaming snow, the boiling black smoke that now billowed across the rocks to form a protective curtain that Scott strained to see through, wanting a clear glimpse of Petrov's men, just a *glimpse*, for Christ's sake.

He thought he saw someone moving in the murk and so fired a short burst from his MP5, then saw Pete Welsh, burdened under his radio system, jumping up to advance, doing it for Syd Loomis, wanting to make them pay for that, and he raced forward weaving, firing his weapon from the hip, letting out a strangled, incoherent cry, and was still firing when a line of machine-gun bullets, clearly marked by the spitting snow, raced towards him to cut him down and then, when another frag from Mad Mike exploded, clearly close to the machine gunner, the jagged line of spitting snow went off course, passing Welsh by mere inches, and he did a kind of hop, skip and jump, glancing down, then threw himself behind another rock and commenced firing again.

Killer Parker was advancing on the enemy position, coming up on their blind side. Mad Mike was coming up on the other side, both of them obscured in the swirling black smoke which thickened each time they threw another frag. The noise of the grenades was deafening, the smoke swirled like dark curtains, but Scott advanced with the others, crouched low and zigzagging, darting from one rock to the next, confident that his men were performing as they should, as a team, each giving covering fire to the other, and aware that big Arnie was right behind him, receiving confirmation of this when his MP5 roared.

Parker and Mad Mike both threw frags simultaneously, working in tandem, and when they exploded, creating more noise and smoke, they raced in on the enemy position from both sides, advancing up the high ground, to vaporise like ghosts in the smoke and then disappear around the back of the first rocks, firing their personal weapons on the move in sustained, savage bursts.

Scott raced up behind them, glancing left and right, not firing, but holding his MP5 at the ready, and realised that the enemy gunfire had suddenly stopped. He ran around the back of the first rocks to find Parker and Mad Mike standing there, frustrated. There was no sign of the enemy.

'Damn!' Scott exploded.

'They're not far away,' Parker said, his gaze flicking left and right, missing nothing, taking in the two dead men lying at his feet, both bulky in heavy coats and furred hats, both drenched in blood, then the maze of snow-covered pathways and ledges formed by the many high rocks on the steep slopes. 'They're drawing us in there and we've no choice but to go after them.'

'Let's do it,' Scott said.

Frustrated almost unendurably by being so close to Petrov yet still not able to confront him, more than willing to engage in close-quarter battle with him, he was about to follow Parker and Mad Mike, stepping over the two dead bodies and advancing up the nearest winding path, between the oddly shaped high rocks, when big Arnie and Pete Welsh came up behind him, the latter still humping his radio system. Paddy Devlin came after them.

'What's up?' Paddy asked.

'We've lost them,' Scott said. 'They've retreated farther back into the rocks and we'll have to pursue them.'

'Then let's get on with it,' Paddy said pragmatically.

Scott turned to Pete Welsh. 'You stick behind me,' he told him. Turning to Arnie, he said, 'You stay behind Welsh to protect the radio. And you, Paddy,' he continued looking at Devlin, 'keep protecting our rear.'

'Will do,' Paddy said.

'Okay, let's go.'

Parker and Mad Mike had already disappeared around bends in their separate paths when Scott advanced again, taking a different path from them, his visibility dangerously reduced by the still swirling black smoke from the many frags thrown by the first two, his nostrils filled with the smell of the same smoke as well as with cordite. He advanced in silence, hearing only his own harsh breathing, moving his gaze constantly from the narrow path directly ahead to the ledges on either side and above him, his finger on the trigger of his MP5, preparing to fire at the slightest sign of movement, though aware that he had to be extremely careful lest he score an own goal by mistaking one of his own men, probably Parker or Mad Mike, for one of the enemy.

As he made his way along the path, he realised that he was bitterly cold even in his Arctic clothing and that the sun, which had passed overhead, was going down again, dimming the daylight. He saw this when he moved out of the smoke, approaching another bend in the narrow, winding path formed by opposing high walls of rock.

He was just about to round the bend when he heard the staccato roaring of a sub-machine gun up ahead, which he assumed was Mad Mike's MP5. Hearing that sound, he stopped when he reached the bend, listened intently for sounds of movement, but heard none. Satisfied, he started advancing again.

Rounding the bend, he saw Mad Mike up ahead, framed by high rocks that had formed another path, jumping over the dead body of one of Petrov's brigands, obviously just shot by him, and hurrying on, his MP5 at the ready, to disappear around another outcropping. Parallel to Mad Mike, Killer Parker was also advancing carefully along his chosen path, repeatedly disappearing behind high rocks and then appearing again, his head moving left and right as he searched for the enemy.

Glancing back over his shoulder, Scott saw Arnie and Pete Welsh, the former carrying his heavy GPMG like a rifle, the latter holding an MP5 and still humping his radio system, both weaving between the rocks and advancing crouched low, followed carefully by Paddy Devlin. Relieved, Scott looked to the front again.

Suddenly, more shots rang out ahead – single rifle shots followed by the roaring of Mad Mike's MP5 and Killer Parker's SA-80. Scott was just about to break into a run, to lend his support, when he saw movement to his right and above him, then heard the sound of loose stones rolling down rocks, obviously dislodged by a booted foot, then the snapping of a rifle firing single shots. He swung his MP5 upwards as a bullet ricocheted off the rocks behind him with a sharp, ringing sound, and fired a sustained burst, swinging the weapon from left to right, even before he had fully seen the sniper. Caught by the wide arc of the fusillade of bullets, chopped across the middle, the sniper shuddered violently, dropped his rifle, leaned forward as if taking a bow, then flopped forward and rolled down the sloping rock, falling off it to crash into the deep snow.

Up ahead, Killer Parker and Mad Mike, both out of sight, were letting off occasional bursts from their weapons, indicating that they, too, were firing at snipers. Even as Scott heard them firing once more, he saw another of Petrov's men jumping up from behind a rock to fire a fusillade from a PPsh-41 Soviet sub-machine gun. Once more, the burst was not aimed at him but at the men spread out behind him and he was reminded by this fact, even as he raised his own weapon and fired, that Petrov was keeping him till the last and had obviously told his brigands not to fire at him. The man he had shot at took most of the rounds and went into convulsions, dropping his weapon as he was punched this way and that by the bullets, his feet slipping in the snow, then crashed onto his back and slid out of sight down the far side of the rocks.

Glancing back over his shoulder, Scott saw that Arnie, Pete and Paddy were still advancing unharmed, so he turned back to the front and kept going.

He wanted to see Petrov, whom he knew he would recognise (that scarred face), but that bastard was keeping out of sight and letting his men do all the damage. So far the damage was minimal, almost as if they were playing games, some of them dying in order to do so, to satisfy Petrov. But even as Scott thought this, wondering at the perversity of it, he heard bawling behind him, Arnie shouting out a warning, and he spun around as a sub-machine gun roared and he saw Pete Welsh staggering forward, his eyes wide with shock, his body twitching and turning this way and that, being punched by a hail of bullets from the gun of the brigand standing right behind him, between him and Paddy. The latter had fired instantly, as soon as he saw the Russian, who had obviously stepped out behind Pete from the shelter of some rocks, and was still firing, riddling the Russian, who became epileptic and dropped his weapon, as Pete staggered forward, as ungainly as a cripple trying desperately to walk, saying, 'No! Oh, Jesus Christ!' He fell to his knees, swayed like a reed in a storm, reaching up distractedly to his chest, as if attempting to release the harness of the radio system on his back, now shot all to hell, its wires and cables hanging out, then coughed blood and flopped face down into the snow, exposing his savaged, bloody back. The Russian collapsed to the snow behind Pete as Scott and Arnie rushed up to him.

'Oh, fuck!' Arnie said, grabbing Pete and rolling him onto his back, then checking the pulse in his throat and wrist. Pete's eyes were wide open but blind and there was no pulse to feel. 'Oh, fuck, man, he's dead!'

'So's this bastard,' Paddy said flatly from where he was kneeling over the Russian shot by him.

'Let's go,' Scott said, turning away from Pete's dead body and rising to his feet, moving on because there was nothing else to do under the circumstances and this was no time for sentiment. Parker and Nicholson were still ahead, the 'Killer' and 'Mad Mike', and they were both living up to their fearsome reputations by fighting their way through the maze of pathways formed by the rocks, darting at strategic moments from one outcropping to another, each taking turns at giving covering fire, both shooting quickly enough – and accurately enough – to pick off those brigands exposing themselves when firing their own weapons. The snowy maze was now littered with dead enemy bodies, but Scott, coming up behind Killer Parker and Mad Mike, was concerned only with seeing Dmitry Petrov and repaying him for the deaths of Syd, Pete and Rudi, as well as young Johnny.

Fuck him and his filthy games, he thought. Let's face each other and end this.

But it wasn't to end just yet. He realised this when the enemy gunfire tapered off, enabling him to catch up with Parker and Nicholson. When he reached them, he saw that they had reached the end of the rock-littered slope and come to a narrow path that curved up another sheer cliff face and had obviously been used in the past by local traders. Footprints left blatantly in the snow indicated that Petrov's men had retreated up that track and were somewhere above.

'Waiting for us,' Parker said calmly, his flat grey gaze taking in the track, the sheer cliff face on one side of it, the dizzying drop to a deep gorge on the other. 'They'll be sitting at the top of that track with big grins on their faces.'

'Maybe not,' Scott said.

'There's only one way to find out,' Paddy said.

'Who dares wins,' Mad Mike said.

Killer Parker nodded, as if agreeing with Mad Mike, then started up the winding track, but Scott quickly jumped in front of him, saying firmly, 'Me first.'

'You're the PC,' Parker protested. 'You shouldn't go first.'

'It's the same story, Corporal. They're less likely to open fire on me, so I'll go first and you can use me as a shield.'

Parker shrugged. 'It's your choice, boss.'

'Who gives a fuck who goes first?' Arnie said, sounding unusually agitated, clearly distraught over the deaths of Syd and Pete. 'Just let's get up there and have a go at those murderous bastards.'

'You calm down, Trooper,' Paddy Devlin said. 'Don't let your heart rule your head. Don't let those bastards turn you into a hothead who doesn't think straight. That's just what they want – to make you lose your cool – but that's the one thing we can't afford to give them in this kind of fight. Those who failed to beat the clock are ancient history and you can't even consider them. You're here to do a job that needs a cool head and without that you're fucked – and if you're fucked, we're *all* fucked. Have you got that?'

'Yes, Paddy.'

'Good. Glad to hear it.' Paddy turned to Scott. 'Okay, boss, we're behind you.'

Scott nodded. 'Move out.'

He had tried to sound as cool as possible, agreeing with what Paddy had said, but as he led them up the narrow track, sticking close to the cliff face, away from that dizzying drop into the deep, shadowed gorge, feeling the cold more than ever and dragging his feet through the thick snow, he could not help feeling as outraged as big Arnie had sounded – outraged and grief-stricken – over the deaths of Syd and Pete and, before them, Rudi Blackwood. He had, of course, seen other friends die – in the Falkland Islands and in Iraq, in Northern Ireland and in Europe – but they had died as soldiers should, in the heat of battle, by accident, not killed slowly, sadistically, as fodder for some kind of perverse game, as Blackwood and Loomis had done. Scott loathed Petrov for that – loathed him even more, if it were at all possible, than he had loathed him for indirectly causing the death of young Johnny – and now, as he made his way up the winding track, he desperately wanted to face him.

Let me look at you, he thought. Let me see the face of evil. Let your face explain to me what it is that I can't understand . . . the needless loss of a child. Fuck you, Petrov, you owe me this.

It was an extraordinary thought, a desire to bridge vast chasms, to comprehend the unknowable, to accept the unacceptable, but it had little to do with what he had been sent here for, which was, beyond any shadow of doubt, to fight a battle and win it. In this, he realised, he was no better than big Arnie, no less emotional, no more cool-headed, and if Paddy had known what he was thinking, Paddy would have been angry.

And damned right, Scott thought.

Thus resolved, having chastised himself, he concentrated

on leading his men up the narrow, winding track, a track winding around the cliff face, the towering cliff on one side of it, a dizzying drop on the other side, snow-white splendour spread out beyond the gorge to the lower slopes of the mountain where, beyond the snow line, the Fergana Valley ran out to the horizon, free of snow and verdant – another world altogether. Scott felt divorced from that world, remote, not quite human, and realised that his only reality was the path he was treading ... Hiking uphill, breathing harshly, senses heightened, nerves on edge, desperate to see, even as he dreaded seeing, what waited for him at the end of the track, high above where they had been.

The track wound around the sheer face of the cliff and led to a short stretch of open ground surrounded by more bizarrely-shaped rocks – a perfect site for an ambush.

Scott froze where he stood.

CHAPTER TWENTY-THREE

There was his man again. Dmitry smiled to himself as he placed his binoculars to his eyes and studied the leader of the SAS, the captain, where he stood at the far end of the stretch of open, snow-covered ground, slightly over a hundred metres away, silhouetted by the sinking sun. Again, Dmitry was taken aback to see just how normal the captain looked, how decent, how refined, his face not remotely the kind that one expected to see on a professional soldier. One thing, however, was certain: this SAS captain, no matter how civilised he looked, was certainly a professional, as he had proved only too well over the past couple of days, sticking resolutely to his task despite what he and his men had been put through, with three dead already. Dmitry was particularly impressed with the bold and clever manner in which the captain had led his men through that gorge, killing a lot more of Dmitry's men that he had anticipated, and, just an hour ago, his superbly coordinated assault on the high ground when, despite losing two men, he (and they, Dmitry was only too willing to acknowledge) had displayed real skill and enormous courage. Now, as he studied the captain, who was standing there boldly, making no attempt to hide himself, he realised that the man was smart as well as courageous.

'Obviously, he's realised that he's being left until the last and that we're not going to deal with him until we've dealt with his friends. That's what he's counting on.'

'Precisely,' Misha said, lying belly-down in the snow beside Dmitry, their men spread out behind them, and also studying the captain, though without the aid of binoculars. 'And so he's going to do what he did during that last engagement: use himself as a human shield.'

'Yes, he will.'

'Courageous,' Misha said.

'Yes.'

'And dumb,' Misha concluded. 'So let's surprise him by doing what he *doesn't* expect.'

'And what would that be?' Dmitry asked.

'We put a hole in his belly. Then we kill all the others as they come up the track and put an end to this craziness.'

Dmitry smiled, lowering the binoculars until they were resting on the snow in front of his chin. 'You're so impatient, Misha. We're playing this wonderful game and you wish to spoil my fun. All the years, all the things we've done together, I thought you were my friend.'

'I *am* your friend, Dmitry.'

'So be my friend and humour me in this. Let me have my perverse little game.'

'Perverse it is,' Misha said with conviction.

'We were never straight, you or I,' Dmitry said soothingly, recalling what they had been through together, the blood and the ruin, the torture and the blackmail, the robbery and what could only be called rape – Lalya, for instance, and all those who had come before her – yes, those perverse little games that had taken them both right to the edge, to that awesome abyss where man could practically taste his own soul, sweet or rancid or hopelessly poisoned, and, in so doing, know that he had reached the point of no return and could only go on into the darkest depths where the very concept of right and wrong did not exist and only experience of the most extreme kind was all that was left to him. He and Misha had been there and back again, which is why they remained friends. 'So why try to straighten me out now, my friend. Why not let me take this to the limit and see where it leads us both?'

'Because even I have my limits,' Misha said, 'but I don't think you have. Or, at least, you've forgotten the limits you once might have set yourself. What is this, Dmitry, this madness? This game that costs the lives of our men in order to gratify a demented dream of yours? This Englishman is just like any other – a good soldier, maybe, worthy of our respect, but not someone you need to confront personally as you insist that you must do. You're as crazy over this Englishman, this SAS Captain, as you were over Lalya – and that's the truth of it.'

Thus brutally reminded of Lalya, Dmitry found himself haunted by the image of her face, the brown eyes that had made him feel the full weight of his sins, and he tried to imagine just where she was now. He was, in fact, convinced that she died somewhere on the mountain, almost certainly frozen to death, and now lay buried under a mound of snow, perhaps preserved by the freezing cold. It was this image that haunted him – the image of a dead Lalya with her beauty preserved by the snow – and so he wanted to find her and bury her properly, in a hole in the ground.

Just what was it with Lalya that had made her different from all the others, at least in the turmoil of his thoughts? Had she, in truth, been any different from the others? Hardly. Born and raised in lowly circumstances in Tajikistan, her greatest gift from God, according to her, had been the love of her family, her mother and father and brothers. They had, of course, all been killed by Dmitry, the first two indirectly during the assault on the convoy of Tajik trucks, the second two deliberately as part of Dmitry's perverse test of the limits of Lalya's will to live. But what had she really lost when she became his prisoner and mistress? Her father, like many local farmers, had lost everything with the collapse of the Soviet Union and was turning to drug-smuggling as so many of them had been forced to do. Sooner or later, he would have been caught and imprisoned; then Lalya, in a world controlled by the drug barons, would almost certainly have come to a bad end anyway, either drug-addicted herself or as the whore of one of the drug peddlers. Few of them were known for their high regard for women; most of them would, in fact, sell their women in the streets to finance their next fix. No, Dmitry had possibly saved Lalya from a fate worse than death – the slow death of a living hell in a drug-peddling community or incarceration in some hellish brothel in a border town near Afghanistan – and he now refused to accept the condemnation that he had seen so often in her eyes ... At least, so he told himself each time her face floated accusingly before him, as it too often did, in his opium-ravaged, self-loathing thoughts.

'Damn it,' he said to Misha. 'Why bring Lalya into this? I simply pushed her as far as I could, as I had pushed all the others, to see how much she would accept, how low she would sink in self-abasement, and in her case she proved me wrong for once. It was just one of those things.'

'Admit it,' Misha responded. 'You *wanted* Lalya to prove you wrong, to show you that she had more self-respect than you could imagine, and she did so by choosing to die alone in the mountains rather than live as your mistress and slave. Now you want this Englishman, this man you've never met, to do the same. You're a masochist, Dmitry, you wish to pay for your sins, and you think that this Englishman will help you to do that – and I do sincerely believe that this is what you want – by defeating you instead of being defeated by you. But why do you think this, Dmitry? That's what *I'd* like to know. You don't know this man personally, you've never met him in your life, and he's been sent here simply because he's a good soldier, not because of any imagined, spiritual relationship with you. So why do you feel that you know him and that he's your equal or soul brother?'

'I don't know,' Dmitry confessed. 'I only know that I feel it and that alone makes me need to find out if it's true or not. Curiosity is stronger than commonsense and I'm a curious man.'

'You're possibly a madman,' Misha said.

Dmitry nodded. 'Who knows?'

Raising his binoculars to his eyes, he studied the English officer, who was still standing boldly in the open, his shadow stretching out beside him as the sun sank. The stretch of open ground on which he stood was white with deep snow and that snow also covered the rock outcroppings on both sides of the track he had just come up. The rocks formed a rough semi-circle that advanced on both sides to join up with this second maze of rocks and pathways where Dmitry and his men were hiding. Directly behind Dmitry was another narrow track that led to an old trader's road over which the occasional vehicle still travelled from Osh to Fergana. Dmitry had radioed for a small van to be brought up there and parked at the side of the road. In the back of the van was another surprise for the SAS men, but Dmitry didn't want the captain to be the one to receive it. He did, however, want him and his men to advance across that clearing and hike up the second track.

'The van's in place,' he said to Misha, 'so let's send them another invitation.'

'Fuck the van,' Misha said. 'Let's get this over and done with. Our men are becoming restless over your antics and concerned that so many are being killed. If any more are shot by those Englishmen, they're not going to like it. I say, let our men finish this right now and risk no more lives. Put a bullet through that English captain's head and then slaughter the others. The time for games is now over.'

'One more game,' Dmitry insisted, then, ignoring Misha's sigh of despair, he turned onto his side and indicated with a hand signal that the men spread out behind him should quietly make their way up the second track to the main road. They did so, rising silently, brushing the snow off their *telogreikas* and *shinyels*, heading away in single file, holding their personal weapons across their chests. The last of them were still making their way uphill when Dmitry rolled back onto his belly and gazed once more at the English captain.

He was still standing out in the clearing, holding his MP5 at an angle across his chest, while the first of his men came up the track behind him, using him as a shield, and then, at a signal from him, darted across to the rocks located either to his left or to his right, with each successive man taking the side opposite to the other until all of them were safely behind the rocks, with an equal number on either side of the track. The captain stood on, fully exposed, gazing steadily in the direction of Dmitry and his men, having worked out that he would not be shot, confident in his reasoning.

'Kill that bastard!' Misha said, practically hissing.

Smiling, Dmitry raised his AK-47 Kalashnikov rifle to the firing position and squinted carefully along the sight. He saw the English captain's ordinary, decent, refined features in the crosshairs of his sight, squeezed gently on the trigger, then changed his mind and lowered the barrel until the crosshairs of the sight were centred over the captain's heart. He took a deep breath, shifted slightly again, then squeezed the trigger all the way, firing a precisely aimed, single shot.

CHAPTER TWENTY-FOUR

Scott was staring intently across the clearing, trying to see where Petrov's men where, knowing they were there, watching him, when that single shot rang out and the bullet thudded into the snow between his booted feet, causing the snow to spit up and soak him. He did not move a muscle. He knew that Petrov didn't want him dead just yet, that he was only toying with him, and that this single shot, so precisely placed, had been designed to humiliate him rather than harm him. He had been expecting it, or certainly something like it, so when the shot was fired he was ready, determined not to be humiliated and showing his defiance.

For a long time after the shot there was silence, then that familiar voice rang out again, coming from behind the snow-covered rocks at the far side of the clearing.

'Very good, Englishman! Very courageous! Now come and find me, my friend!'

Scott replied by aiming his MP5 in the general direction of the voice and firing a short burst from it, spraying the area indiscriminately from left to right. He stopped firing and the silence was total . . . until that voice interrupted it.

'You missed me, my friend. You didn't even come near. Now I'm going to leave and if you want me, you'll have to come after me. I invite you to do so. Goodbye, English-man!'

Scott fired another burst in the general direction of that mocking voice, but he didn't really expect to hit anyone and did it purely to express his contempt. When there was no further response, he took it as read that Petrov and his men had left their ambush position and headed even higher up the mountain, which was the only way they could have gone, probably up that narrow track that he, Scott, could see from where he stood. Nevertheless, he was taking no chances and signalled for his men to advance one at a time, from his left and from his right alternatively, using the cover of the rocks strung along both sides of the clearing and running all the way up to where Petrov and his men had clearly been hiding.

Killer Parker went first, advancing at the half-crouch and zigzagging, darting from one rock outcropping to the next to the left of Scott. Mad Mike went next, in the same manner as Parker, but on the opposite side. The rest followed suit as Scott, deciding to take no more chances, mindful of the fact that one of Petrov's hotheads could lose patience and shoot at him despite Petrov's instructions, also slipped into the shadows behind the rocks and followed big Arnie up to the area just vacated by Petrov's men. The rest of the men were already there when he arrived, waiting for him, with only Paddy Devlin left to come up behind him. When they were back together again as a group, including Paddy, they all gazed up that narrow track, to where it disappeared around the curving face of the cliff.

The sun was going down, casting shadows across the mountain peaks, across the snow-whitened slopes, but Scott knew that it wouldn't set for another hour and right now, although the light was dimming, visibility was good. Up this high in the mountain, whipped by wind and soaked by wind-driven snow flakes, he knew that his local map would be useless to him and he could only judge by the direction the path was taking that it led even higher while twisting in a south-westerly direction.

'That direction,' Scott said, 'leads towards the general area that the Russian authorities have assessed, according to intelligence reports, as being the location of Petrov's camp. They couldn't tell the Green Slime *exactly* where the camp is located, but they were adamant that it was in that general direction.'

'Which means,' Paddy Devlin said, 'that Petrov is still deliberately luring us in that direction and, of course, we have no choice but to follow him.'

'True enough,' Scott said.

'Follow him *to where*?' Parker asked. 'I mean, what the fuck's up that track, boss? We can only go up one man at a time and that leaves us defenceless.'

'Their very idea,' Mad Mike said.

'What the fuck?' big Arnie said, still hurting over the deaths of his fellow troopers, Syd and Pete. 'We either go up there or we turn back and we're obviously not taking the second option. So let's get the fuck up there and be prepared for anything those cunts throw at us. They're playing with us, making fools of us, and they've already killed three of us for sport. Are you gonna fuckin' stand for that, boss, or do we go up there and do something to make amends for what's been done to us?'

'We're going up,' Scott said. 'Single file obviously. I'll go first, then the rest of you fall in behind me in the same order. Okay?' They all nodded assent. 'Then let's do it.'

Scott led them up the track which, like the previous one, snaked around the side of the cliff face soaring vertically to his right, and to his left, formed the lip of a dizzying drop to a valley of deeply shadowed snow drifts. It was an extremely dangerous track, littered with loose stones and snow-covered, ice-filmed gravel plus the occasional, potentially ankle-breaking, pothole, so he went up with extreme care. He was mindful, also, of the animal traps left in the wrong places by isolation-crazed fur trappers, and with each bend he turned he braced himself for some fresh, potentially dreadful, surprise from Dmitry Petrov. In the event, nothing happened. The climb to the top of the track took just under thirty minutes and brought him out to what looked like, beneath its thick mantle of wind-blown, constantly drifting snow, something resembling a road.

He knew it was a proper road when he saw the recent tyre tracks that were still imprinted in the middle of it, then curved off it to the opposite side, where they ended up at the rear of a small, snow-covered van. The vehicle was parked well back from the side of the road, about five metres back, in a natural shelter formed by the high, snow-covered rocks on both sides. That rock-enclosed five metres formed a natural, closed-in pathway up to the rear of the van.

'I don't believe what I'm seeing,' Killer Parker said.

'If you're seeing what I'm seeing,' Mad Mike told him, 'you *can* believe what you're seeing.'

'A van parked halfway up the mountain,' Paddy Devlin said. 'It has to be there for a reason.'

'Related to . . .'

'Dmitry Petrov,' Scott said, responding to the unfinished remark of Arnie Basham.

'Right,' Paddy Devlin said. 'So just what have they planned for us over there? They're over there somewhere, right? And that van's there for a purpose.'

'Booby-trapped,' Killer Parker said, having spent a lot of time working undercover in Northern Ireland, both before and after the so-called 'peace'.

'Right,' Paddy said, wiping snow from his bushy eyebrows with a snow-covered hand. 'Why else would they leave it there? To move on, we have to move around it, so either the van's ready to explode or the ground around it has been mined or booby-trapped. Either way, it's a pretty blatant set-up and those fuckers must know that we know that. They're probably watching us right now and having a good fucking laugh at our predicament.'

'No predicament,' big Arnie said, his brown eyes bright

with newly gained passionate conviction. 'There ain't nothing about bombs, booby-traps or explosives that we don't know, so I say we go over there, check that van out, dismantle the fucker or neutralise the ground around it, then move on to confront those murderous bastards.'

'You're making this sound personal, Trooper,' Paddy said, 'and that's not how we operate.'

'Fuck how we normally operate,' big Arnie retorted. 'These aren't normal circumstances, those fuckers aren't a normal kind of enemy – they're picking us off one by one and making us look like bloody fools – and, yes, I've got a couple of personal scores to settle. So let's go over there and let me check that van out while you guys give me cover. What *else* can we do?'

'Not much else,' Mad Mike said.

'So let's do it,' Paddy said.

'Okay,' Scott said, accepting the majority vote, 'but I still think that I should go first. *I'll* check out the van.'

'Why?' big Arnie asked, rank having no special privileges during a Chinese Parliament.

'Because, as I've explained before, Petrov intends keeping me to the last in order to have some kind of personal confrontation. Don't ask me why – I haven't a clue – but that's what he's doing. So I'm less likely than anyone else to be picked off while checking out the van.'

'I don't buy that,' Parker said. 'That lunatic may be *hoping* to keep you to the last, but he's also toying with the rest of us – that, too, is pretty obvious – and that van's been placed there for that very reason. He may be *hoping* to keep you to the last, but he's testing us all to the fucking limit and that van's a part of it.'

'Oh, how?' Mad Mike asked.

'We know – and he knows that we know – that either the van is booby-trapped or the ground around it is mined and that either way one of us – not necessarily you, boss – has to deal with it. Petrov knows that and he's waiting to see what we do and that means he doesn't necessarily assume that you're the one who'll do it. So I say you *don't* do it, boss. Let's not give him that pleasure.'

'So who does it?' Scott asked.

'Me,' Arnie said.

'Me,' Killer Parker said.

'Me,' Mad Mike said.

'Me,' Paddy Devlin said.

'So what do we do here?' Scott asked. 'Draw straws or what?'

'Let me do it, boss,' Arnie said. 'I know explosives and bombs and booby traps like I know my own dick.'

'We're not interested in your big dick,' Mad Mike said, 'and there's nothing you know that I don't know. Shit, we're *all* experts, man.'

'I've got the right,' big Arnie said, looking pleadingly at Scott. 'Those were my friends, my best buddies, that they did back there,' he added, referring to Syd Loomis and Pete Welsh without actually mentioning their names, 'and that *gives* me the right. So you let me do this one, boss.'

'Okay, Arnie, you do it. But be very careful.'

'There ain't a booby trap ever been fuckin' made that'd get past *my* eyes, boss. You just leave this to me.'

'I will.'

'Right. Let's get to it.'

They crossed the road one by one, each one covered by the others, each expecting to hear the chilling crack of a firing enemy rifle before he reached the far side, though this did not happen. Eventually, when they had all crossed, they took up positions behind the outcroppings along the road, some covering the road, the rest with weapons aimed at the parked van.

At a nod from Scott, big Arnie approached the van, treading carefully through the deep snow, his broad shoulders covered in snow, keeping his gaze on the snow-covered ground and frequently kneeling down to grope around in the snow to check for tripwires and detonators. Advancing in this manner, it took him a long time to reach the rear of the van and, once there, it took him just as long to check the ground all around it out to a couple of metres on every side. Eventually satisfied that the ground was clear, he approached the van and stopped mere inches away from it, listening carefully. Hearing no sound, he slung his MP5 over his shoulder, then dropped onto his belly and crawled as far under the van as he could get to check for an Under Car Booby Trap. Finding no UCBT, he slithered back out again and moved slowly up one side of the van, checking the driver's cabin for booby traps and finding none, then trying the side door and finding it closed. He moved on again, going around the front of the van and checking the bonnet, which he failed to raise. Turning around the far side of the car, he checked the other door and found that it, too, was locked, which left only the rear door to be checked. Removing his MP5 from his shoulder and tucking it between his right elbow and hip, ready to fire it from that position, he reached out to check the door handle with his free hand. If the door was locked, he would blow it open with a simple delayed explosive charge, but clearly it was not locked because he managed to turn the handle – the click was audible in the silence, even from where Scott and the others were watching – and very carefully pulled the door open and peered into the gloom.

Suddenly, the doors burst fully open and a snow leopard flew out to hurl itself, talons curved, jaws agape, upon the screaming Arnie.

CHAPTER TWENTY-FIVE

Thrown backward to the ground by the weight of the leopard, Arnie was trapped under it, screaming, kicking frantically, trying to push its head away, as the beast pinned him down with its claws, ripping his shoulders to shreds in seconds, exposing bone and blood, while opening its jaws to sink its fangs into his throat, mauling the lower half of his face. Looking on, horrified, Scott and the others could not fire at the leopard because it and Arnie were too closely intertwined. Mad Mike, however, before anyone else could do anything, jumped up and ran straight towards the struggling pair, man and beast, withdrawing his Five-seveN pistol from its holster while still on the move and raising it to take aim and fire from close range.

Instantly, a fusillade of shots rang out from the high, snow-covered rocks beyond the van and Mad Mike screamed, his smashed legs buckling under him, and fell mere feet away from the wildly thrashing, screaming Arnie and the fiercely growling leopard that was still astride him and mauling him to a shredded, bloody mess. Even more horrified, realising that Petrov's men had deliberately fired low to keep Mad Mike alive as another victim to the leopard, Scott opened fire with his MP5 and the others did the same, covering a broad arc beyond the van in the hope of at least pinning down those unseen men, though it did little to help Arnie or Mad Mike.

Obviously half-crazed with fear and hunger, its attention drawn by the agonized screaming of Mad Mike, whose legs were bent under him at an unnatural angle, blood-streaked white bones thrusting out from torn skin, the leopard left one victim to pounce upon the other, its already bloodied jaws clamping over Mad Mike's groin, making him scream even louder as Arnie, a mess of blood and torn flesh, his formerly handsome face unrecognizable, convulsively kicked his legs and made a feeble attempt to wriggle backwards to safety. Hearing that noise, the leopard, now blood-crazed and indecisive, turned away from Mad Mike, whose groin was now blood-soaked, and leaped again on Arnie, grabbing him by the throat and then, with a terrifying display of strength, dragging him away, still kicking feebly, between the nearest rocks, leaving a trail of his blood in the snow behind them.

Miraculously, Mad Mike managed to raise himself high enough to aim and fire his pistol at the disappearing beast, but the shot went wild, ricocheting off the rocks, and then the pistol dropped from Mad Mike's trembling fingers and he fell onto his back again as the leopard and its bloody, weakening victim disappeared altogether.

'Check Mike!' Scott bawled as he jumped up and ran at the half-crouch, zigzagging, to the narrow passageway formed by opposing rock formations along which the leopard had taken Arnie, doubtless hoping to drag him into a cave. In fact, Arnie, now unconscious, was too heavy for it and Scott, as he approached a small clearing at the far side of the rocks, saw that the animal had stopped its flight and was trying to bite through Arnie's badly-shredded, bloody neck. When it heard Scott approaching, it turned its head to stare at him and he fired his MP5 at close range before it could charge him. The sustained fusillade made a mess of the leopard's head and punched through to its body, picking it up and flinging it back to the ground, about a metre away from Arnie, where it kicked and thrashed about convulsively, then coughed blood and died. Rushing up to the dead beast, Scott fired another burst into its body, making sure that it *was* dead, then he turned and knelt beside Arnie, whose blood was pumping out of him at a prodigious rate – from his mauled face, his torn throat, his shredded shoulders and chest – to turn the white snow around him bright red. Scott checked Arnie's pulse and confirmed that he was dead.

Thank God, he thought, hearing the gunfire from behind him where Killer Parker and Paddy Devlin were still fighting Petrov's men. If he'd survived, he'd have looked like a walking nightmare. He wouldn't have been able to stand that . . . Jesus, those bastards!

Galvanised back into action by his rapidly growing hatred for that sick swine, Dmitry Petrov, Scott turned away from Arnie and hurried back through the narrow passageway to find Paddy Devlin giving covering fire to Killer Parker from behind the protection of the parked van as the latter made his way towards the rocks where Petrov's men were hiding, firing his SA-80 rifle while on the move and darting boldly from one outcropping to another. Mad Mike lay a few feet behind Paddy, his groin practically torn away, and it was clear from the blood around him and from his stillness that he had bled to death. Now virtually consumed with rage, forgetting the manual of engagement or any SOPs he might normally have considered carefully, thinking only of how many of his men had been killed and, worse, how they had died, Scott knelt beside Paddy and said, 'Fuck it, Paddy, I've had enough of those bastards. Now let's put an end to them.'

'Killer Parker thinks the same way,' Paddy replied, stopping firing only long enough to speak and looking as distraught as Killer Parker obviously felt, 'and you won't stop him now. He's so angry I can hardly believe it, so we'd better get up there.'

'Right,' Scott said, 'let's go.'

Yet before he could jump to his feet, Paddy was already

up and advancing at the half-crouch, zigzagging, firing on the move, hoping to keep Petrov's men pinned down while he darted from cover to cover, catching up with Parker. Scott followed him on the instant, filled with grief and rage and hatred, wanting only to annihilate all those bastards and then personally take out Dmitry Petrov. He was beyond cool reason now, lost to objectivity, and moved in a trance, gliding on air, aware only of the need to put an end to this and let his head clear again. Yet his instincts were sure, his years of training not deserting him, and he darted forward and took cover, fired his weapon, advanced again, and then saw Killer Parker swinging his right arm, releasing a frag, and watched it curving over and down, falling accurately behind the rocks, then was temporarily deafened by the explosion. Automatically closing his eyes, he opened them again to see boiling smoke and spiralling streams of dust and flying gravel, then he heard screams of pain and saw two men materialise, rising up from behind the rocks and turning away to retreat; but, cut down by a fusillade of bullets from both Parker and Paddy, they dropped their weapons, shuddered spasmodically and collapsed, sinking into snow softened by their gushing blood.

Scott followed Parker and Paddy, clambering over the sloping sides of the high rocks, trying to catch up with them, but they had already moved on by the time he reached the two men shot by them. They had sunk into the blood-soaked snow and nearby were another two men, not shot but badly shredded and scorched by the fragmentation grenade thrown by Parker. Feeling only an unsavoury pleasure at the sight of them, not respecting himself for it but unable to help it, Scott stepped around the dead men nearest to them and continued to clamber on over the rocks, which rose and fell like grey waves and were dangerously slippery with snow. Beyond this sea of rocks were more soaring, snow-covered slopes leading up to the ice-limned, gleaming peaks.

The sharp crack of single rifle shots and the sustained roaring of sub-machine guns came from up ahead, where

Parker and Paddy were obviously pursuing Petrov's men. Occasionally another frag went off, erupting with a deafening roar and filling the air with boiling smoke, spiralling clouds of dust, rapidly melting, steaming snow and debris consisting mainly of flying stones and gravel. As Scott continued advancing, clambering up the steep sides of the great rocks, sliding down through the snow on the other sides, then commencing the next ascent, he passed more dead men, either shot by Parker and Paddy or caught in the blast of one of their frags, and he was taken by a growing frustration that he was still merely bringing up the rear and was still not in close contact with Dmitry Petrov. His frustration was only increased by the fact that most times, when he reached the summit of a high rock, he could see over that rocky sea, the rise and fall of other rocks, Petrov's men doing the same thing, beating a deliberate, tactical retreat by clambering up and down the great waves of rocks and boulders, all the time firing back at Parker and Paddy, who were now about fifteen metres ahead.

The sea of rocks ended, however, about forty metres ahead where the mountainside levelled out for a good distance, in a broad, natural amphiteatre, before soaring again to those ice-covered, glittering peaks. From where he stood, on the top of one of the highest rocks, Scott could see Petrov's men retreating across that field of snow, dragging their feet, leaving the clear marks of their bootprints, and he wondered if one of the two out front was Dmitry Petrov.

He stood there, watching, as the first two men made it to the far side and ascended up the next snow-whitened rise by taking what looked like another narrow track with a cliff face on one side of it, a steep drop to the other. Those first two men stopped a good way up the track and, though Scott could not see them in detail, they had clearly turned around to see what was happening below. What they would have seen was just what Scott was observing: two SAS men, Killer Parker and Paddy Devlin, kneeling behind rocks at one side of that broad expanse of flat ground, its crystalline whiteness now pockmarked with many footprints, and systematically picking off the retreating men with their personal weapons. That broad expanse of snow was littered with bodies and even more were falling.

He doesn't care how many men he loses, Scott thought as he moved on again, determined to catch up. He's paying a high price to get me.

It took him only another minute to catch up with Parker and Paddy, both of whom were still kneeling at the near edge of that broad, open expanse of flat, snow-covered earth. The last of Petrov's men had made it across and even now were making their way up the next track, hugging the cliff face, eventually disappearing around a bend about twenty metres up. By the time Scott knelt beside his own two men, Petrov's remaining men, about fifteen, with approximately the same number killed, had vanished entirely.

'Christ,' Scott said, studying the dead littering that exposed stretch of ground, 'you two certainly copped yourselves a high score.'

'About the best thing that's happened to us so far,' Paddy said, 'but it doesn't make up for the rest of it. Christ, what a mess! What a fucking, awful tragedy. And the way those last two poor sods died . . . Christ, that Petrov is something!'

'A piece of shit,' Parker said.

'Still,' Scott said, 'those dead out there are some compensation.'

'Not much,' Parker said, pragmatic as always. 'We got that many because they were sitting ducks when crossing that stretch of dead ground. Now, we have to cross it as well, which makes *us* sitting ducks.'

'Not until we get most of the way over there,' Paddy pointed out. 'We were shooting at them from right here, but they'll be firing at us, if they do, from that bend and it's high enough up the mountainside to keep us out of firing range until we've practically reached the bottom of the same track.'

'I don't think that's even relevant,' Scott said.

'Oh?' Parker said. 'How come, boss?'

'They disappeared around that bend in the track and as the track's so narrow, only allowing for single file, they must have climbed in the same formation even higher, to a point where they can regroup and take up another ambush position.'

'An ambush or something worse,' Paddy said sourly.

'Quite,' Scott said. 'Either way, it seems to me that they're going to let us cross that exposed area and deal whatever filth they have to deal as we're making our way up the track. This is strictly between me and Petrov now, so if either of you wants to stay here, I'll understand perfectly.'

'I'm going after those bastards all the way,' Killer Parker said emphatically.

'Me, too,' Paddy said. 'Let's get going, boss.'

They moved off together, automatically spreading out in a well-spaced horizontal line and virtually following in the footprints of those who had gone before, which took them past those killed by Parker and Paddy. In fact, a couple of the 'dead' were actually only wounded, though the wounds in both cases were bad enough to be mortal and the pain had rendered them unconscious. Stopping by these men, as they came to them in turn, they discussed the possibility of putting them out of their misery with a quick bullet through the head, which might have been a blessing to them, but in both instances they could not bring themselves to do it and instead just left them lying there, justifying this decision with the shared belief that the wounded men would almost certainly freeze to death while still unconscious, which was a relatively painless way of going compared to what they might have suffered otherwise.

As they progressed across the exposed area, advancing into the deep shadows caused by the sinking sun, now almost touching the horizon, Scott studied the mountain face intently, looking for signs of movement, but he saw nothing but the shadows of birds streaking across the still glittering snowscapes. Ten minutes later, they had reached the end of the open stretch and were at the beginning of the steep, curving track. There they stopped for another brief discussion.

'That sun will set completely in about thirty minutes,' Parker said, 'which means we could find ourselves in darkness halfway up that track. If that happens, we won't be able to move a fucking inch, so I think we'll have to basha down here for the night and move out again at first light.'

'The track may not go that high,' Scott said.

'What makes you think that?' Paddy asked.

'Petrov's men went up that track in well-spaced single file and if the track was longer than half-an-hour's march, at least a third of his men wouldn't make it to the top before last light. I don't think he'd allow that, so the track must be relatively short and lead to another open area. He probably expects us to stay down here until first light, not knowing how long the track is, so if we go up it now we can rest up just below the top of the track until the sun sets, then advance on Petrov's position under cover of darkness, taking him and his hooligans by surprise. What say you, men?'

Paddy and Parker glanced thoughtfully at each other, as if each was reading the other's mind, then they nodded and turned back to Scott.

'I agree,' Paddy said.

'Me, too,' Parker said, 'but it means we haven't a second to waste.'

'Then let's go,' Scott said and immediately started moving up the track, leaving the other two to fall in behind him in single file, first Parker, still humping the all-important radio, then Paddy behind him.

They had only gone about ten metres, well short of the bend in the track, when Scott realised just how high up the mountain they now were and just how deep was the gorge to his right. The curving wall of the cliff face was practically at his left elbow and rose as high as he could see, but the other side of the track was less than thirty centimetres away from his right foot and ended abruptly at a sheer drop of well over a hundred metres. Though not normally suffering from vertigo, Scott could not help but feel nervous at the sight of that dizzying drop and, beyond it, even lower down, the great white snowscapes running all the way back to the Fergana Valley in the deepening twilight. Wondering if the two behind him were suffering the same way, but unable to turn back and check with them, he kept marching uphill, still sticking as close to possible to the soaring cliff face, and motivating himself by thinking of how close he was to Dmitry Petrov and of how this dreadful business, in which most of his men had died, could soon be over, one way or the other.

Soon enough, pushed onward by that last, positive thought, he reached the bend in the track, stopped advancing, indicated with a hand signal that those behind him were to stop also, then inched forward until he was far enough around the bend to see farther uphill. In fact, contrary to his expectations, the track curved sharply here to a narrow, wooden bridge that led across some kind of drop – a gap of about ten metres – to where the path began again, continuing up another fifteen metres or so until it gradually levelled out, disappearing over what had to be another flat stretch. Studying that area carefully, Scott saw no sign of movement and could only pray that Petrov's men could not see him from there. Moving forward carefully to study the bridge in detail, he saw that it was more of an aerial walkway than a proper bridge and that it spanned a gorge that dropped, like the side of the path, well over a hundred metres to the snow-covered rocks below. Constructed of four planks laid side by side, joined together with wooden cross pieces, supported by angle bars cemented into the stone sides of the gorge and with only two fragile handrails to prevent those crossing from falling off the walkway, it was visibly shaking in the high wind and looked very precarious indeed. Nevertheless, it had to be crossed before darkness fell.

Glancing along the gorge, Scott saw its sides framing the vast sweep of the lower mountain slopes and the Fergana Valley, the light dimming swiftly towards darkness. With no time to waste, he used another hand signal to indicate that Parker and Paddy should follow him up. They did so, still moving with extreme care, and eventually were grouped tightly around him, one on each side of him. They studied the fragile bridge in total silence, then looked at Scott.

'It probably looks worse than it is,' Scott said hopefully. 'I mean, Petrov's men would have had to cross it and if they could, we can.'

'They could have weakened it deliberately,' Paddy said.

'Or booby-trapped it,' Parker added.

'I can't see any signs of weakening,' Scott informed them, 'and there's nowhere to hide a booby trap, except under the walkway.'

'Then one of us has to cross the walkway belly-down,' Parker said, 'and check by hand and by eyeballing for a booby trap as he crawls along the whole length of it. That means shifting constantly from one side to the next and practically hanging off the walkway to look underneath it. I think I'd better do it.'

'Not this time,' Paddy said. 'You're too valuable as a scout and you're also in charge of the radio system, so I'll go first this time.'

'I agree,' Scott said.

'Suit yourselves,' Parker said, then turned away to drop to one knee and aim his SA-80 at the track on the other side of the bridge, preparing to give Paddy covering fire.

'Once Paddy's over, I'll go next,' Scott said to Parker, 'then you bring up the rear.'

'Right,' Parker said.

Paddy was already down on his knees at the near end of the bridge and, after slinging his MP5 over his right shoulder, he dropped to his belly and crawled forward onto the walkway. Like Parker, Scott prepared to give his friend covering fire as he made the dangerous crossing, but he was constantly distracted by the sight of him on the walkway. What Paddy was doing was hair-raising. The walkway was hardly wider than his body and he was inching forward on his belly, staying as straight as possible, then, every few feet, twisting sideways until his head was beyond the edge, out over that awesome drop to the bottom of the wind-swept gorge; then lowering his head, practically hanging off the edge, until he could see under the walkway and check that no booby trap was there. He had to do this frequently because the wooden supports, crossing the underside of the planks about every two metres, prevented him from checking the whole length of the walkway at once. His crossing of the bridge therefore seemed interminable and was made even more dangerous – indeed, almost terrifying – by the wind that howled like a banshee along the gorge, kept hammering at the bridge, making it shake, rattle and squeak, and threatened to sweep Paddy away. Nevertheless, after what seemed like an eternity, he made it to the other side, rose to his feet again, then turned around to wave Scott and Parker across.

The instant Scott stepped onto the bridge, he realised just how brave Paddy had been. Scott's first movement on the bridge, his first step on it, made it shake even more than the wind was doing and he was inordinately conscious of its constant swaying, creaking and rattling. Halfway across, when he was sweating despite the fierce cold, he made the mistake of glancing down and felt instantly that he was being sucked into those rapidly darkening, vertiginous depths. Jerking his head up, he saw Paddy waiting for him, though with his back turned to him and his MP5 aimed up the track that led, hopefully, to level ground. The sight of his friend gave Scott both comfort and courage, letting him cover the last couple of metres without incident and step gratefully back onto solid earth.

Breathing deeply, he glanced back over his shoulder and saw that Killer Parker had already stepped onto the bridge and was crossing it like a trained tightrope-walker. Realising why Parker was considered the best scout in the regiment, envious and admiring of him at the same time, Scott turned away to give covering fire should someone materialise at the top of the track. There was no movement up there, but Paddy, obviously aware that the sun had nearly set and that darkness would fall about them within minutes, started up the track without a parting word. As keen to get up there as Paddy, Scott kept his friend covered until the resourceful, seemingly fearless Parker stepped off the bridge and took up a firing position beside him.

'Let me get about halfway up,' Scott said, since Paddy was already up that far, 'before you follow me.'

'Will do,' Parker said, spreading his legs and raising his SA-80 to the firing position.

Scott had just started up the track when he thought he saw movement up there and heard distant laughter.

He and Paddy stopped advancing at the same time.

Looking up more intently, Scott saw that Paddy was about three-quarters of the way up the track, standing as still as a rock, and that something was definitely moving in the near darkness of the level ground above him, at the top of the track. Then Scott heard that distant laughter again – the muffled laughter of three or four men at once, coming from where that large dark shape was moving, rolling, across the top of the track until it had blocked out the sky.

'Go back!' Paddy bawled like a wild man, then he fired his MP5 up the hill.

He was too late.

The dark shape blocking the top of the track was a large, ball-shaped boulder, its diameter only slightly less than the width of the track. Levered forward by those laughing behind it, it started rolling down the track just as Paddy's fusillade of bullets ricocheted noisily, uselessly, off it. As the boulder rolled down the track, picking up snow as it gathered momentum, becoming not only bigger but more visible every second, first a mere dark shape, then a huge white snowball, Paddy turned away from it and tried running downhill. Realising that he wouldn't make it, he had to choose between pressing himself against the face of the cliff, in which case the boulder would have smashed him to pieces, or throwing himself over the open side and hoping he might land on snow-covered ground not too far below. He threw himself over the side.

Scott saw Paddy disappearing from view before he turned away and ran the few steps back down the track to the small clearing at the end of the bridge, where Parker, quick to see what was happening, was already throwing himself to the side, out of the path of the immense, noisily-rolling boulder – growing bigger with every second as it collected more snow on its downward path. Scott managed to reach the bottom of the track and throw himself to the side, as Parker had done, landing right beside him, just before the boulder reached the bottom of the track, rolling past him at high speed, churning up and collecting snow, making a rhythmic rumbling sound, like the end of the world. Then it rolled onto the bridge, the snow flying off it in a glittering, unreal fountain, and crashed through the handrails, then the walkway itself, before its weight tore the supports from the sides of the gorge and everything – walkway, handrails, supports and the snow-spewing boulder – fell to the bottom of the gorge and struck it with the impact of an earthquake.

Though shocked by that spectacle, scarcely able to comprehend it, Scott jumped back out onto the track and looked along its open end to see Paddy lying on his back on a platform of frozen snow, above a drop of over a hundred metres. Paddy was trying to move, but he seemed to be having trouble, and Scott assumed, from the ungainly movements of his body, that his spine had been broken. Even worse, the platform of snow was breaking up and the more Paddy moved, the quicker the snow beneath him gave way.

Filled once more with outrage and grief, Scott started up the track, intending to save Paddy in some miraculous way, but he was pulled back and hurled to the ground by Killer Parker.

'It's too late!' Parker shouted, standing over him. 'That platform's going to fall and take him with it. We can't do a damned thing.'

And indeed, even as Scott twisted around to look along the open end of the track, he saw the snow platform breaking up, falling to pieces beneath the frantically waving Paddy –

waving his hands as if trying to cling to the darkening sky, to the ascending moon, to the stars or to God – and then the platform gave way completely and Paddy went down with it, first falling backwards, then spinning rapidly, arms and legs kicking, making no sound at all, perhaps too terrified or shocked to scream, and then he vanished, along with the falling snow, into the darkening depths.

That death made Scott weep like a child, then his rage took command.

'We stay here,' he said through his tears, 'and then we go up in darkness. Fuck it, fuck him, fuck them all, we'll make them pay for this, Parker.'

'Damned right,' Parker said.

CHAPTER TWENTY-SIX

Lalya had not forgotten Dmitry Petrov and only kept herself sane through dark dreams of vengeance. She endured in the dead fur trapper's cave on a day-by-day basis, by being as practical as most peasants had to be in order to survive poverty and oppression, but she knew that her continued survival was contingent upon retaining her sanity and for that she needed her memories of Dmitry, who had destroyed her life. She thought about him night and day, silently cursing him, not loving him as he had imagined (in his outrageous vanity, his opium-induced perversity) and kept her strength up by keeping the flame of her burning hatred alive.

Nevertheless, even when feeling strong, she often wondered how much longer she could endure this living nightmare, this incarceration in a dark cave on a freezing, snow-swept mountain, and yearned for the spring to come and the snow to melt, when she might, though even this was not guaranteed, make her way back down the mountain. Having lost all track of time, she had no idea of how long she had been here, but it seemed like forever.

She had survived physically by being able to stay warm and eat regularly. The warmth had come from the open fire that she had managed to keep going with the aid of sticks and twigs gathered from the otherwise barren mountainside and, more importantly, from the clothing she had been able to make by cutting and stitching together the bearskins of the trapper she had killed and left to rot in the snow outside the cave, having found in his shoulder bag needles, thread, scissors and razor blades. Eating had been, and remained, more problematical. So far, she had eaten regularly by alternating between the dead man's plentiful supply of tinned foods and the mountain gophers she had managed to shoot occasionally with his hunting rifle. Now, however, the tinned foods were running out and, being neither an expert hunter nor good shot, she wasn't too sure that in the deepening, now dangerous cold of the mountain she could hunt and kill animals regularly enough to ensure her survival.

While the thought of imminent starvation terrified her, it was far from being her only potential nightmare. The return of the fur trapper and his instant attempt to rape her had merely served to remind her of just how precarious her position was. She was not only under constant threat, she realised, from predatory animals – the snow leopard or brown bear – but also from predatory males: the hunters who roamed these desolate, harsh mountains and were often crazed from loneliness and sexual deprivation; and, also, the many drug traffickers who traversed the mountains either to smuggle drugs in from Afghanistan or to hijack the drugs being smuggled in by others or even grown and transported along the mountain road by local, increasingly desperate farmers.

Naturally, of all the local drug traffickers, the most powerful and dangerous was Dmitry Petrov, whose ruthlessness was legendary. When Lalya thought of him, which was often, she trembled with fear and invariably, reminded of what he had done to her parents and brothers, was reduced to the tears of inconsolable grief.

Indeed, she had wept often in the endless darkness of her nights, in that bitter cold only eased by her open fire and clothes of bear skin, thinking not only of her mother and father, of her two murdered brothers, of the monstrous Dmitry Petrov who had murdered them, of her helpless whoredom to Dmitry, but also of the man who had originally owned the bear skins and had been killed by her, stabbed with a knife in a frenzy of fear, then left to rot in the snow not far from the cave.

She still could not believe that she had actually done such a thing – and though that dead man was still lying there, mere yards from the cave, she had never found the courage to go back and bury him properly. As a consequence (she assumed) she had been subjected to many nightmares in which he rose from the dead, his flesh peeling from the bone, and made his way back to the cave where, with an evil, victorious leer, he threw his foul-smelling, putrescent remains upon her, raping her, as it were, from the grave and then ... she never knew what he did after that, because she always woke up.

To make her nights even more dreadful, her nightmares of the dead man's return had often dissolved into dark dreams of mountain bandits bursting into the cave to gang-rape her, cut her throat, then throw her defiled, lifeless body on top of the rotting corpse of the man she had killed. Those dreams, in turn, invariably faded into dreams of Dmitry entering the cave alone, finding her on the bed, smiling that cool, mocking, deadly smile of his and then raising his pistol to fire at her. Invariably she awakened just before the pistol fired, being jerked back to consciousness by her own screaming.

She was returning, she sensed, to a primitive condition, to what her ancestors might have been when they actually inhabited these caves, frightened of the darkness, of predatory animals, of unknown invaders who would rape and pillage and pass on like the wind, creating a nightmare and then leaving devastation behind. That devastation would be the last of her sanity, the shreds of her self-respect, the solitary life she had led (if she could even call it 'life') in this cold, dark cave far removed from the slightest touch of humanity.

It was the isolation that was destroying her, making her lose her mind, turning her into a primal being haunted by the slow glide of the moon and the staring, accusing eyes of the stars. She was certain that the moaning wind was speaking to her and that she knew what it said.

Stay alive, it was telling her. Because if you give up, if you let yourself die, you will be letting Petrov get away with everything. Stay alive at least until the snow melts and offers some options. Stay alive for what you desperately need: a day of reckoning ... Judgement Day.

She thought of this every day, but mostly at night, when she had to stretch out beside that open fire, the shadows flickering on the wall, and somehow try to sleep when she knew that the dead man was still rotting just outside, hopefully buried in snow, and that Dmitry Petrov's men were crawling all over the mountains and might eventually find her. She knew what Dmitry would do if he came across her again: he had his pride to consider, the humiliation that her escape would have caused him, and to make up for that he would have to put her through hell in full view of his men. In that way, by her public torture and, ultimately, more importantly, her public death, he would regain their respect. Right now he ruled them with fear, but he had lost the important thing. This, in its luminous simplicity, was her singular victory – her gain and his loss.

Nevertheless, it was not enough to keep the hounds of hell at bay. Yes, she felt that she was in hell, eternally damned, suffering endlessly. Every flickering shadow cast on the dark cave wall by the open, otherwise warming, fire was the moving image of an evil, frightening spirit. The moaning of the wind outside the cave, while at least reminding her of the real world, seemed to her, in her fearful, exaggerated, hallucinating loneliness, to be the crying of the dead and the damned, returning to haunt her. Thus, she lay on her bed of straw, the dead man's bed, still haunted by him, and she looked at the mouth of the cave with wide, fearful, expectant eyes.

She heard the wind howling, saw the snow swirling outside, and expected, with every second of every minute of every hour – for so did she now judge time – that something, a wild beast, or someone, a brutal brigand, would come eventually to make her nightmares real and take her beyond the merely imaginable.

When, finally, she heard something other than the moaning wind ... an unfamiliar sound of movement ... something definitely crawling through the snow just outside the cave ... she collapsed into hysteria, choked back a sob, then, regaining her senses, picked up the dead man's shotgun, rolled off the straw mattress, cocked the weapon and advanced on her slippered feet to the mouth of the cave.

It was dark out there, the wind howling, snow swirling. It was hell on earth and she saw in its fearful depths something slithering along on its belly, hump-backed, breathing heavily, inching implacably towards her.

Her heart was racing and she let out a silent scream as she raised the shotgun and took aim.

CHAPTER TWENTY-SEVEN

Scott and Parker spent a hellish night on the mountain, at the bottom of the track, in that small cleared area above the deep gorge. They were resting up, letting themselves calm down, but they were also waiting long enough to let Petrov think that they were actually lying up until first light. Scott was hoping that by doing this, by letting a couple of hours pass, he would encourage Petrov to let his men bed down for the night. He was hoping that when he went back up that track he would find most of them sleeping.

Neither he nor Parker slept. Instead they took turns at either watching the track or resting up while cleaning and oiling their personal weapons. While doing this, Scott tried not to think of Paddy, but as he was seated with his back to the cliff face, looking at the remains of the bridge over the gorge, he couldn't help thinking of his friend far below, smashed to pieces and probably buried in snow already. The thought of it filled him with grief and rage, but the latter gave him more energy.

Nevertheless, the next couple of hours were truly hellish, with the wind howling and hammering at him, the cold fierce and numbing. To make matters worse, snow started falling and soon it was covering him where he sat. He had not felt so cold since taking part in the ill-fated assault on the Fortuna Glacier in South Georgia during the Falklands War and that, he realised, had been a long time ago. Wrapped in his poncho but still shivering, he gazed out over the moonlit gorge at the mountain peaks beyond, and was convinced that he would never escape from here and return to his own world. When he thought of that world, which now seemed so far away, he released a flood of memories about his wife and son, saw them clearly in his mind, and was reminded that they had once known happy days. The pain of those recollections was intense, almost bringing tears to his eyes again, but it was made bearable by the rage that came hot on its tail when he thought of the connection between young Johnny's tragic death and the man that he, Scott, had come here to find.

Dmitry Petrov.

It seemed extraordinary to Scott that the man almost certainly resting at the top of that narrow track, mere minutes away from him, the man he had yet to meet, had so profoundly influenced his life. Johnny had died in the streets of London from an overdose of drugs that had originated right here in Kyrgyzstan – originated, in point of fact, with Dmitry Petrov – and Scott's marriage, formerly a sound one, had been destroyed in the wake of that singular tragedy. Were that not enough, the same Dmitry Petrov had slaughtered all but one of Scott's men, including Paddy, his best friend, thus causing him even more grief and pain, as well as excruciating humiliation. Eight highly trained men had come here to eliminate Dmitry Petrov and only two were left. Scott could not bear the thought of it.

'Fuck it,' he said, speaking against the howling wind and sweeping snow. 'Let's put an end to it.'

'Fucking A,' Parker said.

They both clambered to their feet, checked their weapons once more, than looked up the narrow, dark track. There was nothing to see up there but the sheer wall of the cliff on one side, the black void on the other – that dreadful drop that had taken Paddy's life – and, at the very top, a night sky filled with clouds, with few stars, though dimly lit by a pale moon. The snow was still falling, constant and dense, adding fresh layers to the frozen snow on the track.

'That track's going to be as slippery as hell,' Parker said, 'and it's not wide enough to leave room for mistakes.'

'Agreed,' Scott said. 'So let's go up on our bellies. It's the only safe way.'

'Right,' Parker replied.

Scott went down on his knees, then stretched flat-out on his belly, facing the steeply climbing track, holding his MP5 out in front of him, elbows resting on the ground. He felt the cold instantly, even through his Arctic clothing, as the mattress of impacted snow sank under his weight. The wind was still howling, sweeping the falling snow into waving, spiralling curtains, and he felt it hammering relentlessly at his body as he started inching painfully up the track with Parker close behind him. The crawl seemed to take forever (he could have walked it in two minutes) but eventually he reached the point, about three-quarters of the way up, where Paddy, faced with that huge, rolling boulder, had been compelled to throw himself over the side. Scott stopped there for a moment, silently paying his respects, glancing down into that fearful abyss, then he glanced up the track, saw nothing and started crawling again. The ground levelled out gradually, leading to another open space surrounded by high rocks. A lot of men were lying there, wrapped up in sleeping bags, but one of them was guarding the track, looking straight at Scott.

Scott froze where he lay.

The man did not move and after a while Scott realised that he was practically asleep, facing the track, supposedly guarding it, but with heavy-lidded eyes that were turned down to distractedly study his own booted feet. He had an AK-47 assault rifle resting across his lap and he looked unnaturally large, certainly larger than he was, in his snow-covered greatcoat and high furred cap.

Scott could hear himself breathing. He could hear his own heartbeat.

Raising his right hand, he signalled silently for Killer Parker to come up beside him. Parker did so, wriggling up through the deep snow until he was hip-to-hip with Scott, their twinned bodies virtually covering the whole width of the track, with Scott right on the edge of the dreadful drop that had taken Paddy. Parker studied the scene before him – the somnolent guard right in front of them, the men sleeping behind him – then nodded to Scott and withdrew an L2A2 hand grenade from his webbed belt. Scott switched his MP5 sub-machine gun to three-round bursts and aimed for the chest of the somnolent guard. Ready to fire, he nodded at Parker who did a hand-press that lifted him to his knees and enabled him to swing his arm and hurl the frag. He was, of course, seen instantly by the somnolent guard who, jerked awake by that rapid movement, frantically raised his AK-47 to fire. Scott fired first – a single, three-round burst that punched the guard backwards off his perch, a small rock, just as the frag exploded in the midst of the men sleeping behind him.

The explosion broke the silence with a thunderous clap, briefly illuminated the night with a jagged sheet of flame, filled the air with billowing smoke and flying debris, led to screams of pain and galvanised those not wounded or killed into action. Scott and Parker used that period of noisy confusion to get up off the track and then advance into the clearing and move around it, each taking a different direction while raking the scattering, bawling, shadowy men with bursts of automatic fire. Some of them screamed when hit and fell spinning to the ground; others were grabbing their weapons, fleeing behind the rocks for shelter, or desperately looking about them, trying to ascertain where the gunfire was coming from. This was not easy, as Scott and Parker were moving swiftly here, there and everywhere, under cover of darkness, firing from many different positions, while gradually making their way around opposite sides of the clearing to join up at the far side. Two of the scattering men fired sub-machine guns wildly while on the move and hit some of their own men.

As he fought his way around the clearing, which took less than a minute, Scott searched in the moonlit darkness for the scarred, handsome features of Dmitry Petrov, but failed to see anyone resembling him. He *did* catch a glimpse of a tall, slim young man, rather poetic-looking in the fractured moonlight, who seemed to be in charge and was shouting orders with an air of authority while taking cover behind nearby rocks. Scott fired a short burst at him but failed to hit him and by the time he had joined up with Parker at the far end of the clearing, Petrov's men, possibly marshalled by that slim young man, seemed more organised and were starting to fire their weapons from sheltered positions.

When the first of those enemy bullets whipped past his head, Scott fired a burst in a broad arc, heard the bullets ricocheting noisily off the rock formation shielding Petrov's men, then dropped behind the rocks nearest to him. Parker hurled another frag, then threw himself down beside Scott as it exploded, creating more billowing smoke, swirling dust and steaming, flying lumps of impacted snow.

'Fuck it,' Parker said when the explosion had died away. 'They've all taken cover again and we can't charge them. They'd just cut us to pieces.'

'There's a rise behind that rock formation,' Scott replied, seeing it in the moonlight, 'and I think we could circle around and get to it, then come down behind them from above them.'

'Sounds good, boss,' Parker said.

Scott turned left and led them between the rock formations that lay between them and the clearing. Though confident that he and Parker would not be seen in the darkness, he had to be careful not to trip over small boulders or kick loose stones as he made his way slightly uphill, then circled around the back of the rise that overlooked the enemy position. The firing of Petrov's men tapered off, since they were receiving no response, and Scott knew from this that they would soon deduce what was happening. Reaching the back of the rise, which ascended in a series of irregular ridges to a height of about ten metres, he went up crouched low, treading as lightly as possible, with Parker close behind him, then dropped onto his belly and crawled up the last few metres until he could look down the other side. Parker did the same.

Looking down the moonlit slope, Scott saw about a dozen men at the bottom, most in firing positions behind protective rock formations, aiming their weapons at the area where Scott and Parker had been previously, their backs turned to the downward slope. Two of them, however, were talking intently to each other and one of them was the tall, slim, poetic-looking young man that Scott had previously seen and heard giving orders. As those two were clearly the leaders of the gang, the other man, Scott realised with a sudden rush of exhilaration and hatred combined, had to be his tormentor, Dmitry Petrov.

Scott automatically raised his MP5 to fire, then hesitated, not wanting to shoot either man in the back and, he was stunned to discover, feeling the need to personally confront Petrov. Parker, however, had no such inhibitions and before Scott could say a word, he was standing up to swing his right hand and release a fragmentation grenade. That swift movement was enough to draw the attention of the two men down the hill and they glanced up, startled, even as the frag left Parker's hand and sailed down towards them.

In that instant, which seemed to be frozen in time, the moonlight showed clearly the handsome, but badly scarred face that Scott had seen in the Green Slime intelligence photo: the long, thin scar of an old knife wound on one cheek; the round-shaped scar of an old bullet wound in the other. That man was certainly the notorious Dmitry Petrov.

'*Vperyod!*' Petrov snapped at the younger man as the hand grenade sailed down towards him; then, with startling speed, he and his friend hurled themselves out into the clearing and rolled across the ground to disappear behind some rocks just as the frag exploded. Scott and Parker commenced firing downhill, into the receding flash and billowing smoke of the explosion, spraying in wide arcs to cut down anyone not already killed by the blast. The jagged silvery flash of the explosion had briefly silhouetted some of those men as they were picked up and flung back down, or simply shuddered and collapsed, but that searing, momentary light had already died and the remaining men were obscured by the screen of smoke and raining dust and gravel.

Frustrated beyond measure that Petrov and his friend had seen the frag in time to make their escape, Scott continued firing on automatic for a few more seconds, then, scarcely able to control himself, but also knowing that he and Parker had surely decimated the men directly below, he moved down the slope, firing at anything moving down there. Parker, advancing parallel to him, though well away from him, was doing the same and between them, though occasional bullets whipped past their heads and ricocheted noisily off the rocks nearby, they put paid to all those still down there, leaving only Dmitry Petrov and his friend, both somewhere out there beyond the clearing, though now out of sight.

Not saying a word to each other, communicating with nods and hand signals, Scott and Parker stepped gingerly over the frag-shredded, scorched and bullet-riddled bodies scattered haphazardly, bloodily on the rocks at the edge of the clearing. As he reached the clearing, Scott started lowering himself to take advantage of the cover of the low rocks, but before he sank down behind them, he saw the tall, slim young man disappearing between the rocks at the far side of the clearing.

Dmitry Petrov was also there, but standing upright, as bold as brass, looking directly at Scott and offering a distinct, mocking smile. Before Scott could recover from the shock of this, Petrov, who was holding an AK-47 in his left hand, hanging loosely by his side, perhaps as a deliberate gesture of contempt, raised his right hand and waved in ironic farewell. Then he spun on the ball of one foot and, before Scott could fire at him, followed his friend and disappeared between the same rocks.

'It's a challenge,' Parker said. 'No doubt about it. He wants us to follow him.'

'I'll follow him to hell if necessary. Come on, Killer, let's go.'

Scott advanced at the half-crouch, practically running, determined that this time Petrov would not escape and prepared to follow him as far as necessary. Parker followed hot on his heels and soon they were both making their way between the same high rocks that Petrov and his friend had gone through. The rocks led them up over a low rise and back down to a broad swathe of smooth, snow-covered ground with high banks of rock on one side, more rock formations at the far end, about thirty metres away and, surprisingly, to the right, a hill that actually contained a few trees, their gnarled, bare branches white with snow, and fell down to a series of gently rolling, lightly wooded hills. There was no sign of Petrov or his friend, but two sets of footprints were clearly visible in the formerly virgin snow and they led directly along that swathe of level ground to the rocks at the far end.

'We'll be exposed all the way,' Killer Parker said, standing beside Scott and studying the swathe of dead ground. 'And almost certainly they'll be watching us from those rock formations at the far end. They'll just sit there, waiting.'

Scott glanced at the rock formations to their left, but could see little protection there. He then looked down the steep hill to his right and studied the trees. 'We can go a short distance down that hill, then advance by making our way from one tree to the next. That should get us practically all the way to the far end of that dead ground. Once there, *if* we get that far, we'll simply have to take a chance and get into those rocks as quickly as possible.'

Parker glanced left and right with his hard, grey eyes, then nodded agreement. 'Doesn't look like we have a choice,' he said.

'Right, Killer, let's do it.'

They were able to make their way to the edge of the dead ground, the top of the hill, while protected by the rock formations, but once there, they were completely exposed except for the thinly dispersed trees. Scott glanced at the far end of the dead ground, saw no movement in the rocks, so took a deep breath and stepped out to make his way gingerly down the steep, snow-covered, slippery hill to the nearest tree, which was approximately half-a-dozen metres away. He made it without incident, then indicated to Parker that he was to remain where he was until he, Scott, had made it to the next tree. When Parker nodded that he understood, Scott loped on at the half-crouch, zigzagging as best he could, though he was slowed down considerably by the thickness of the snow, which clung to his boots, as well as by the steep angle of the hill. Nevertheless, he made it to the second tree without incident and, once there, indicated that Parker was to make his run to the first tree while he kept him covered. Parker immediately moved out from behind the rocks and started making his way down the hillside towards the first tree.

A single rifle shot rang out and a bullet thudded into the snow, making it spit angrily, mere centimetres from Parker's left foot. The shot had clearly come from behind the rock formations at the far end of the field and Scott instantly fired a burst from his MP5 in that direction, hoping to keep Petrov and his friend pinned down long enough for Parker to make it to the tree, which he did within seconds. Now covered by Parker, Scott advanced to the next tree, again without incident. Yet when Parker made his run to the second tree, another shot was fired at him and this bullet whistled past his head to ricochet off the tree behind him, sending pieces of bark flying off in all directions. Scott fired another burst from his MP5, again giving covering fire and enabling Parker to complete his second run in safety. Then their roles were reversed and they started off all over again, gradually making it most of the way along the hill, to the very last tree, with shots only being fired, quite deliberately, at Killer Parker.

They're toying with us again, Scott thought grimly. But they'll have to stop playing their games when we come face to face, which we will very soon now. When that happens, either they kill us or we'll kill them. That's when this game will turn serious.

He was behind the last tree, waiting for Parker to come and join him. At a wave from Parker, he opened fire with his MP5, swinging it from left to right to cover a broad arc of fire, covering about five metres on either side of the space in the rocks through which Petrov and his young friend had disappeared. The instant his sub-machine gun roared into action, Parker launched himself forward and made it all the way, this time without being shot at even once, perhaps because of Scott's unrelenting fusillade of fire. When Parker was safely beside Scott, the latter stopped firing and the only sound that could be heard was the breeze's soft whispering.

Looking uphill from behind the safety of the last tree, both men studied that gap between the rocks carefully, then Scott said, 'We don't have a choice. We'll just have to get up there as quickly as possible and then charge that position under cover of constant automatic fire.'

'A couple of frags first,' Parker said, 'to keep them distracted. We advance the instant the frags explode.'

'Good thinking.'

'Here goes, boss.' Parker was quick, his right hand swinging over once, then twice, to release two fragmentation grenades in long, gliding arcs that covered the rest of the hill and looped languidly down towards the rocks. He had his SA-80, set to automatic, back in his hands even before the frags had exploded and was running uphill, as fast as he could make it in the deep snow, even before Scott had realised he was doing so. The exploding frags, which sounded unnaturally loud, impelled Scott forward and he followed Parker up the hill, his feet dragging in the deep snow, as the smoke, dust and gravel from the explosions was forming a natural curtain across the rock formation.

Nevertheless, rifle shots rang out from beyond that pall of smoke, making snow spit up around Parker's feet as he advanced up to level ground. He was heading straight for the thinning curtain of smoke, through which the gap in the rocks was again visible, when the ground gave way beneath him, the snow sinking down around his feet, and with a cry of surprise, he dropped vertically down into a hidden, narrow fissure and was stopped from dropping farther only by the bulk of his bergen and radio system.

Trapped up to his waist, holding his rifle above his head, he made no attempt to wriggle free in case his body movement broke up more snow and allowed him to drop all the way down the unknown depths beneath him, either to freeze to death or to be buried alive.

The opening of that hidden fissure had caused snow to roll down the top few yards of the hill and this in turn had made Scott lose his balance, slip and fall backwards. He had just clambered back to his feet and was starting uphill again, trying to cover the last couple of metres to the level ground, when he saw Dmitry Petrov stepping out from the gap in the rock formation and walking deliberately up to the trapped Parker. After nodding and smiling directly, mockingly at the still struggling Scott, Petrov went down on one knee in front of Parker while withdrawing a Browning 9mm High Power handgun from his holster. Still smiling, he aimed the pistol right between Parker's eyes, mere inches from him, forcing him to look right into the barrel.

'No!' Scott screamed, desperately trying to swing his MP5 up into a firing position while still struggling against the falling snow and, instead, falling to his knees again.

Petrov pressed the trigger of the handgun, putting a bullet right between Parker's eyes and practically blowing his head apart.

'You bastard!' Scott screamed, then managed to bring his MP5 up to a firing position.

At that moment, Petrov's friend stepped out from the gap in the rocks behind him, walked resolutely forward, his features distorted with rage, his pale grey eyes gleaming. He was raising an AK-47 to the firing position and aiming it straight at Scott.

'Enough is enough,' he said as he advanced. 'It ends right now, Dmitry.'

'No, Misha!' Dmitry called out, moving as if to try to prevent the other man from firing.

Scott saw no more. In that brief second before Misha fired his sub-machine gun, Scott hurled himself to the side and let himself roll down the snow-covered slope, gaining momentum until he could not stop himself, crashing into tree trunks, spinning around them and rolling on again, feeling pain lancing through him, then receiving a blow to the head, rendering him unconscious.

Recovering his senses almost instantly, he found himself lying on level ground at the bottom of the hill, still clinging to his MP5, the packed bergen still strapped to his back, dull aches and sharp pains all over his body, his head ringing and spinning. After letting his head clear, he glanced back up the hill and saw that he had fallen a long way and that Dmitry and Misha had not followed him, though almost certainly they would come down some other way and check to see if he was dead or alive.

Feeling nauseous, haunted by the image of Parker staring into the barrel of Petrov's handgun, Scott forced himself back to his knees, then his feet, and hiked unsteadily over the level ground to where the trees he had seen from above were at their most dense, forming what was virtually a small forest. He entered the shelter of those trees and kept going, not knowing where he was going, intent only on putting as much distance as possible between himself and the two who would be pursuing him. The marching caused him great pain, but he managed to keep going, gritting his teeth to prevent himself from crying out, and frequently falling to his knees, sometimes onto his belly, but always forcing himself upright again and marching on. Eventually, however, he lost the strength to stand upright and found himself crawling along on his belly, passing in and out of consciousness. The snow was still falling, making the forest look beautiful, and when finally he came out of the trees, he found himself back once more on one of the many broad, sloping sides of the mountain, being whipped by a fierce wind that made the snow swirl about him.

He was still crawling on his belly, losing strength every minute, feeling the pain of his broken ribs, pulling himself along by his hands, breathing harshly, sometimes retching, and by the time he came to another soaring cliff face, he was almost drained of strength and dangerously close to hypothermia. Accepting that this might indeed be the end of the road for him, he was about to rest his forehead on his folded arms, to close his eyes and let himself freeze to death, when he saw, beyond the curtain of falling snow, the mouth of a cave.

He took hope from that sight and started crawling forward again, but stopped when someone stepped tentatively out of the cave. To his amazement and disbelief, he saw an attractive young woman wearing a bizarre outfit of stitched bear hides, with her long black hair hanging down almost to the bottom of her spine. There was something wild about her, something primitive, perhaps mad, and she raised a shotgun to her shoulder and aimed it right at him, preparing to fire.

Scott closed his eyes.

CHAPTER TWENTY-EIGHT

Dmitry was distraught at the loss of the English captain and furious with Misha for attempting to kill him. 'If you hadn't fired at him,' he said to his friend as they looked down the hill at the trail of churned-up snow left by the captain's rolling body, 'he wouldn't have thrown himself down the hill and could have been my prisoner right now.'

'I doubt it,' Misha replied calmly, though his pale grey eyes were afire with suppressed anger. 'The Englishman had no intention of surrendering. In fact, he was preparing to fire at you when I took aim at him. He was outraged by the way you killed his friend, by your so-called bit of sport, and was preparing to fire at you when I took aim at him. So if he hadn't thrown himself down that hill, you would have been shot before I could have fired at him.'

'Damn you, Misha, I don't care what you think. I told you not to fire and you ignored me. Now the man I wanted alive is somewhere down there, possibly dead, certainly hurt, and I have to find out either way before we leave here.'

'Why?' Misha asked, sounding strained, his patience clearly running out. 'All of those sent to destroy us are dead except for that one man – and if he's not dead, he's certainly badly wounded and will freeze to death down there. He has nowhere to go and no one to help him. He'll have been hurt by that long roll down the hill, bones broken for sure, and in that condition, in this weather, on this mountainside, he's bound to die. So why bother trying to find out if he's alive or dead? It makes no difference anymore, Dmitry.'

'It makes a difference to *me*.'

'*Why?*' Misha asked, losing his normal detachment for the first time and ready to explode. 'We've already lost all of our men – nearly thirty for their seven – and now you want to risk our lives again – yours and mine – for this single officer who's doomed anyway. This is madness, Dmitry – the ultimate insanity – and I refuse to condone it.'

'You refuse to *condone* it? Do I hear correctly, Misha?' Dmitry felt a fury with his friend that he had never known before, a rage boiling up out of the knowledge that for the first time in his experience, Misha, who had waded through pools of blood for him, was rebelling against him. He knew what it was due to – Misha's cold-blooded pragmatism; his extraordinary gift for detachment from anything human that was not in itself extraordinary; his basic contempt for normal or, as it were, *everyday* human life – but this was not enough to make him accept that he could be wrong in his thinking. Dmitry *knew* the English captain – his opium dreams had *created* him – not necessarily a real person, but an image suggesting the ultimate challenge of his life: to destroy someone who was possibly the personification of what Petrov had always wanted to be and now never could be: an honest, courageous man. He was convinced, either by instinct or through his seductive, self-deceiving, opium-induced dreams, that the only man they could have sent here to find him would have had to be remarkably gifted at his work – soldiering – and, also, be a man of unusual, even unorthodox, motivation. In other words, a man just like himself ... and he had to meet that man face-face, either dead or alive. 'Are you telling me,' he continued in his own fury, 'that I now have to ask your permission to do what I want? Don't tell me this, Misha. Don't even suggest it. Because if you do – and make no mistake about this – I will slit your throat.'

'Try to slit my throat,' Misha replied without a second's hesitation, 'and I'll slit yours first.'

'Wonderful,' Petrov replied. 'Please help yourself.'

'Fuck you,' Misha said. 'You picked me out of a gutter in Moscow and gave me self-esteem. I loved you for that and still do but I won't play this crazy game. My respect for you only goes so far – beyond that, there is nothing. You've killed off all our men on this trip for no good reason – and while those men leave no deep impression upon me, I still won't sacrifice myself for your self-destroying fantasy. We finish it now, Petrov, and go home . . . or I go back alone.'

Petrov hardly knew what to say, since no words could explain it, but his dream, whether opium-induced or not, was that his life, seemingly meaningless, perhaps blighted by his low boredom threshold, where nothing was enough and everything was reduced to dust, would have some meaning if he could simply confront the man who had been sent to kill him. That man, who had risked his life to come here, would know what the real world was – Dmitry's world: the world of absolute risk – so he would also surely know that what Dmitry had done was not completely inexcusable. He would know, and recognise, that Dmitry's monstrous acts were not those of some beast from hell, but those of a lost soul. He would know (because he had come so far to find out) that Dmitry was just like he was: a sinner seeking redemption.

He, that SAS officer, knew it, just as Dmitry knew it, and so they had to meet in life or in death and this would now come about.

'Okay,' Petrov said. 'We'll return to the camp. But first – please bear with me, Misha – we must go down there and find that English officer to check if he's alive or dead and enable me to put my mind at rest. Will you bear with me, Misha?'

'For the last time,' Misha replied bluntly,

'That's all I ask,' Dmitry said.

Together they stared down the thinly wooded hill, through the thickly falling snow, to the more densely forested area far below. They could see clearly from the track left by his rolling body where the SAS captain had rolled over sharp rocks and bounced off tree trunks, almost certainly damaging himself physically. It wasn't possible to judge just where his body had come to rest, though they knew that it had to be somewhere in that forested area.

'Let's go down there,' Dmitry said.

'We'll have to go the long way around,' Misha replied, indicating with a sweep of his hand the edge of the slope running east to west a few hundred metres to the south. 'The hill's too steep and the snow's deep and covers ice, so if we try to go straight down we'll probably end up doing just what your English captain did – falling and rolling helplessly all the way. So we'll have to go around the hill instead of straight down.'

'That'll take a lot longer,' Dmitry insisted, fully aware that his passion to find the Englishman was affecting his normally sound judgement, but unable to check himself. 'This is a heavy snowfall and it's liable to cover up his tracks before we get down there.'

'At least we'll get there,' Misha responded firmly, though with visibly growing impatience, 'which we won't do if we try to go straight down. Now every second we stand here discussing it increases the chances of his tracks being covered up by the snow, so let's stop talking about it and just do it.'

'Yes, you're right. Let's go.'

As Dmitry turned away from the hill to hike to its southern rim, he glanced to the side and saw the top half of the body of the SAS corporal, still sunk waist-deep in the fissure, but with his head turned into a dreadful mess of bone splinters and blood, hardly recognisable as a human head. His shoulders and arms and the snow around him were soaked in the blood that had geysered out of his blown-apart temples. He might as well have been guillotined.

A bad way to die, Dmitry thought dispassionately. To be forced to look directly into the barrel of the pistol pointed right between your eyes, knowing exactly what's going to happen to you. His final thoughts must have been extraordinary and he has me to thank for them.

He couldn't help smiling as he made his way to the southern rim of the hill, with Misha, silent and grim, just behind him. They turned east at the end of the hill and started down, making their way over snow that was a lot less deep than it had been on the hill and which lay on solid rock that would contain no hidden fissures. When they reached the bottom, they turned north and advanced to the forested area where the falling Englishman would have come to rest, either dead or alive.

Entering the forested area, they did indeed come to the deep, broad single track running down from the hill, over loose branches and rocks, and terminating at a thick tree trunk. Dmitry was initially elated when he saw a similar track which showed that the Englishman had moved on, once stopped by the tree, probably crawling on his belly, doubtless trying to find some form of shelter. Unfortunately, as Dmitry had feared, the falling snow had gradually covered up the Englishman's tracks and the last signs of his painful journey petered out a couple of hundred metres farther on.

'He was alive,' Dmitry said, 'and he crawled on, heading west. He might still be alive not too far ahead.'

Misha did not respond immediately. Instead, he glanced at the sky, at the falling snow, then held his hand up to the wind which was rapidly becoming more violent and noisy, whipping the falling snow into a frenzy. 'This feels like the start of a *myatel*,' he said, 'and if it is, your English captain will die for certain and you and I, if we're foolish enough to continue this fruitless search, will possibly die as well. We have to get out of here, Dmitry, before the *myatel* comes in. We have to get back to our road-watch team and have the snow ploughs lead us back to the camp. If we don't, we're finished.'

'Damn!' Dmitry exploded, now frustrated beyond measure, feeling cheated, but realising that Misha was right. He had lost his Englishman ... he would now have to accept it ... and although he found it difficult to do so, he let commonsense prevail at last. 'You're right, Misha. I can't argue the point. Yes, we have to get out of here immediately, whether or not the Englishman is still alive. He's doomed anyway – that much is certain – and if we don't get out of here, we'll be doomed as well. But damn it, this hurts!'

'It'll hurt less,' Misha replied, smiling once more, 'when we get back to the camp and can enjoy a good *zakuski* and vodka in front of an open fire. Come, my brother, let's go.'

Dmitry shrugged. 'Why not?'

Nevertheless, he could not resist glancing about him once more before they left, still hoping desperately to catch a glimpse of the man that he had felt he was destined to meet. He saw no sign of that man and knew that now, with the *myatel* starting to rage, he would certainly die and all traces of his existence would be covered up. Dmitry had lost his Englishman, the man he sensed was his mirror-image, just as he had lost the one woman, Lalya, who might have made him feel human. Now, feeling much less than that, he turned away and, with Misha gladly following him, hurried back the way they had come.

He was tempted more than once to look back over his shoulder – still desperately hoping to see what in truth he would not see – but he managed to resist the temptation and soon he and Misha were marching towards their road-watch station, which they had left only a few days before, though it seemed like months.

They were lucky to make it back. The fierce white-out blizzard of the *myatel* swept across them just as they were approaching the seven-kilometre stretch of forest that ran parallel to the Osh–Fergana highway, where the SAS had crossed the road to enter the mountains. From there, they had to climb higher, to the ancient traders' road where Dmitry's watch patrol was located. They were just approaching the road when the already dense snowfall was whipped up by the fierce winds of the incoming *myatal*. The original three men and the man added to their number after Misha's execution of their leader were still in their makeshift encampment hidden from the road by a high rocky outcropping on the edge of that terrible drop into the snow-covered gorge. With the blizzard now roaring around them, they were practically invisible from mere metres away and, since their fire had been blown out, pressing themselves back against the rocks for as much shelter from the wind as they could find, obviously feeling the biting cold even through their thick greatcoats, leather boots and furred caps.

Again, Dmitry had the odd feeling that he had not been here for years, but he knew that it had only been a couple of days when he saw the three troop trucks parked by the side of the road. The knowledge that those trucks, which had originally been filled with thirty of his best troops, would be going back empty was a bitter reminder to him that although he had managed to terminate the eight SAS men, the price had been uncommonly high. In this sense, then, although the SAS men had all been killed, they were in fact the victors.

This knowledge made Dmitry feel even more the frustration of not having met the SAS captain face to face for a personal confrontation. Like Lalya, the SAS captain had foiled him, albeit dying in order to do so. To Dmitry, the awareness of this felt like chains falling over him.

As Dmitry shivered in the clearing, looking around distractedly, noticing that all the men had covered their personal weapons in plastic sheeting and were carefully resting them on their laps rather than on the ground (Misha's summary execution of their former leader had obviously done them some good), Misha was shouting against the howling wind at the other men in the clearing – the drivers of the trucks and snow ploughs – telling them to return to their vehicles and prepare to move out. Obviously pleased to be so informed, the men jumped to their feet and hurried back to their vehicles.

'You men come as well,' Dmitry said to the men of the watch guard, understanding that they had been here long enough and would likely be driven mad by the *myatel* if not replaced soon. 'No one will be coming up the road in this blizzard, so we'll take you back now and send other men to replace you when the *myatel*'s over. So move! *Quickly!*'

Not believing their good luck, the men jumped to their feet and followed the drivers across to the trucks. Dmitry and Misha again shared the driver's cabin of the first truck, but the snow ploughs, like gigantic, bright-yellow insects, moved out ahead, lumbering slowly, carefully through the wind-driven snow and clearing the road of fallen snow as they advanced. A journey that would normally have taken thirty minutes took them two hours in the white-out, but eventually they turned in between the two high watchtowers that guarded the entrance to the camp.

Stepping down from the truck, into the howling wind, Dmitry saw that the chimneys of the opium-processing huts were still pouring black smoke, defying the storm, and that everything else seemed to be in order. He had to admit, however, that given the black smoke, the grim barracks-style buildings, the execution posts in the clearing and the machine-gun teams in the watchtowers, all swept by thick snow and hammered by the raging wind, the place did indeed look like hell on earth.

Which is just what it is, he thought despairingly. *My* hell on earth. I'm back where I belong.

That evening, while the *myatel* roared and howled, covering the whole camp in a flawless new layer of snow, making it merge with the eerily beautiful white mountainside, Dmitry and Misha shared a warming *zakuski* – pickled herring and mushrooms, caviar, slices of tongue, hard sausage, cheese, onions, dark Borodinskii bread, and vodka with lemon rinds – in front of the open fire in Dmitry's renovated log cabin. Moving on from vodka to Georgian brandy, they became drunkenly philosophical, studied the many art reproductions on the walls – recently imported to replace the ones burnt in the fire started by Lalya – and discussed art, literature, political history, the impossibility of moral laws in an ever-changing world, the corruption of the New Russians, and the fact that they had, at least, terminated all the men sent to find them. Warmed by this knowledge, as well as by the food and drink, they parted just after midnight, feeling closer than they had done in a long time.

In the early hours of the morning, however, after indulging himself outrageously with a terrified young female prisoner, making the unfortunate creature pay for Lalya's sins against him, Dmitry was jerked out of his sleep by a dreadful nightmare in which the English captain, risen from the dead, returned like a dark avenger to destroy the whole camp, turning it into a fiery hell, and execute Dmitry.

Dmitry jerked out of his nightmare, screaming himself awake, just as the captain was aiming a pistol between his eyes and about to squeeze the trigger.

That shot was never fired – certainly not in the dream – and Dmitry awakened to the dreadful howling of the *myatel*, which now ruled the mountain. The howling went on all night, keeping Dmitry awake, driving him back to his Georgian brandy, but when dawn broke and the wind died away, the ensuing silence was even worse.

It seemed like eternity.

CHAPTER TWENTY-NINE

When he recovered consciousness, Scott thought he was either dreaming or experiencing the afterworld. At first he couldn't even remember what had happened to him and was only aware of the woman's face floating above him, a young woman with darkly luminous brown eyes and black hair that hung all the way to her waist. There was something wild about her, though he didn't quite know why he thought that except, perhaps, for the fact that she was living in a cave and was wearing a very odd outfit sewn together crudely from bear hides.

Even as she leaned over him to place her hand on his forehead and, presumably, check his temperature, he recalled what had happened just before he lost consciousness – this same young woman pointing a hunter's shotgun at him – and then, as if viewing an unwinding ribbon of film, he recalled everything that had gone on before that.

Clearly, instead of shooting him, as he had thought she was going to do, this strange young woman had dragged him into this cave and, judging by the crude bandages wrapped around him, looked after him while he was unconscious. Scott had no idea of how long he had been out, but when he looked at the mouth of the cave, he saw that no snow was falling and suspected that it might have been a long time. He was aching all over – he hurt badly in some places – but otherwise, he seemed to be in one piece. When the young woman removed her hand from his forehead, he felt an extraordinary rush of emotion that helped to revive him.

'Who . . . ?' he began, but didn't know how to continue, so took a deep breath and started again. 'Where . . . ?'

'You're not Russian or Kyrgyz,' she responded, speaking in Russian, which Scott had learned at the Hereford School of Languages. 'What are you doing here?'

'What are *you* doing here?' he responded, glancing around the cave and wondering if this was really happening, though the pain in his ribs told him that it was. Glancing down at his own body, he saw that she had stripped his Arctic clothing off him, including his long johns, to bandage him crudely but effectively by wrapping strips of bear skin tightly around his ribcage. When he tried to breathe deeply, he found that he could do so without too much pain, which suggested that his ribs had not been broken. There were other bandages wrapped around his arms, but again, not much pain, though dull aches persisted, and he noticed that where his arms were free of bandages, his skin was badly bruised.

'You live in this cave?' he asked, when she did not answer immediately. He was wondering if perhaps she might be mad, though he suspected not, since the cave was well organised and had obviously been used at one stage by a local fur trapper. The snow had stopped falling outside and although the cave was deathly cold, there was a large fire burning in the middle of the floor. The shotgun that had formerly been pointed at him was lying on the ground near the girl's right hand and he suspected that if he made a sudden move, she would pick it up and use it.

She shook her head from side to side, answering his question. 'No. I got lost and found this place by accident. Then the falling snow kept me trapped here.'

The explanation didn't sound right and the girl was speaking as if in a trance, so Scott decided to approach her more obliquely. He sensed a certain buried hysteria in her and did not wish to arouse it.

'Are you alone?'

'Yes.' But she glanced at the shotgun beside her, as if she thought she might need it. Then, brushing the black hair from her large brown eyes, she returned her solemn gaze to him. She was well formed, he realised, but too thin by far. He saw emptied cans of food lying a short distance away and surmised that she had been here a long time on subsistence rations, practically starving to death. Once more, he felt unreal.

'How long have you been here?' he asked.

She shrugged and bit at a fingernail. All of her fingernails, he noticed, were filthy and badly broken. That fact, combined with the dirt on her face and arms, made her look like a savage.

'I'm not sure,' she said. 'I've lost track of time. I think a long time, many weeks, since before the bad snowfall.'

'But why did you stay when you found yourself lost? Was there someone else in this cave?'

Her dark eyes flared with the light of panic, with fearful recollection, then she vigorously shook her head from side to side, indicating, 'No.'

Scott indicated the food and hunter's equipment with a wave of his hand. 'You found all this here?'

The girl nodded, this time indicating, 'Yes.'

'That was lucky,' Scott said.

'Yes . . . lucky.'

'And no one else has been here since you found the cave?'

The girl shook her head from side to side, indicating, 'No.' But Scott sensed that she was lying and may, perhaps, have had a bad experience during her stay here. Indeed, no sooner had he thought this than she burst into tears and cried, 'Yes! Yes! There was a man, a hunter, and he tried to rape me. I defended myself with a knife and . . .' But she couldn't say any more and merely shuddered and turned her head aside, still sobbing profoundly.

Scott waited until her tears had ceased, then asked gently, 'Where is he?'

The girl pointed to the mouth of the cave. 'Out there. Not far from the cave. Buried under the snow.' She shuddered again, started sobbing, then bit her lower lip and controlled herself.

'When did this happen?' Scott asked, still speaking gently, cajolingly.

'Long time ... A long time ago. Many weeks ago.'

Well, at least he's dead, Scott thought, and can't come back to complicate matters. Shocked to have had such a thought, he added in his mind: Now I'm as heartless, or as ruthless, as Petrov. Maybe now I can beat him.

'So why did you stay on here?' Scott asked of the girl, 'instead of trying to make it back down the mountain?'

'Mainly because of the snow,' the girl responded. 'I can't get back down the mountain until the spring comes and the snow starts to melt. But even then, I might not succeed.'

'Why not?'

Looking nervous again, she glanced again at her shotgun. She made no move to pick it up, however, and instead simply returned her gaze to him and, abruptly changing the subject, asked, 'Who *are* you? Where do you come from?'

'I'm a British army officer,' Scott informed her, omitting to mention the SAS and knowing that if this strange girl later told the local authorities about his presence here, they would not believe that the man she had encountered in the Pamir Mountains could possibly belong to the British army. Indeed, even in the unlikely event that they *did* believe her, the British army, not knowing about the operation, would be able to honestly deny all knowledge of it.

Also, apart from his failure to mention the SAS, which would mean nothing to her anyway, Scott wanted her to know the truth because she had to be a local, she was obviously hiding out in this cave for some serious reason, and she could, if handled properly, be useful to him.

For a start, he was almost certain she would know the

location of Dmitry Petrov's camp and that was the subject he wanted to raise as soon, and as carefully, as possible.

'My name's Captain Neil Scott.'

'So what are you doing here?' she asked him immediately, still scarcely able to comprehend that an Englishman, let alone a British soldier, would be found in this condition in these remote, hostile mountains.

'I came here with seven other men, on behalf of the British army, to put an end to the activities of the drug barons in these mountains, particularly one known as Dmitry Petrov.'

Instantly, at the very mention of Petrov's name, he saw what seemed like a flash of fear and hatred in the girl's eyes.

'Unfortunately,' he continued with quiet deliberation, 'all of my men were killed. I'm the only survivor. That's why you found me crawling towards your cave. I was trying to escape from Petrov and one of his men. Do you know who I'm talking about?'

She didn't answer the question, but the fear and hatred in her lovely brown eyes were replaced with wonder and disbelief.

'You're an ... *English* soldier?' she asked.

'Yes,' Scott confirmed.

'And you came here to find Dmitry Petrov?'

'That's right,' Scott said. He looked down the length of his own body and spread his hands to indicate the many bandages. 'I got this in a fire fight with him and his friend,' he explained, but she only looked even more confused.

'A ... *fire fight*?' she queried.

Scott pointed at her shotgun, then at his own weapons, which were piled up with his bergen and Arctic clothing at the far side of the fire, in the shadow of the cave wall. 'A fight with weapons,' he said. 'We call it a fire fight. Do you *know* Dmitry Petrov?'

The girl visibly shuddered and again her eyes filled up with that combination of hatred and fear. 'Yes, I know him,' she said, then turned away, suddenly looking frail, clearly reluctant to even think about him.

'So what's your name?' Scott asked after a considered pause, not wanting to push too quickly with regard to Petrov.

'Lalya.'

'That sounds like a Russian name; not a Kyrgyz name.'

'I was raised on a Soviet settlement in Kyrgyzstan and named after one of my parents' Russian friends.'

'So what kind of accident brought you to this cave?' Scott asked, easing her back onto the subject dearest to his heart. 'And why do you think you may not make it back down the mountain, even in the spring? Is it because of Petrov?'

She nodded affirmatively, then turned back to face him. Her face, with its dark, distracted beauty, was rendered even more lovely in the flickering light of the open fire. 'Yes,' she said. 'I was one of his prisoners . . . one of his slaves.'

'*Slaves?*'

Lalya nodded. 'Yes. Petrov is a monster, a man beyond the pale. When he makes his raids on the Opium Road – the Osh–Fergana Highway – he kills most of the men and takes the male children and women as prisoners. He takes them back to his camp, that white hell in the mountains, and there he separates them as he sees fit, without thought for the feelings of the mothers for their sons and daughters. The sons are separated from their mothers and sisters, raised in the male barracks, and trained to be brigands as ruthless as those Dmitry already has. The daughters are also separated from their mothers, but divided up between the brigands to be used as their housemaids and whores. The mothers, who are forced to observe daily the humiliation of their children, are turned into housemaids and general labourers, working in the kitchens, the laundries, the latrines and, most of all, in the opium-processing plants. They're worked to the bone and fed little and, if they complain, Petrov has their children punished, so few ever complain. If they have no children, he has them personally punished and his punishments are dreadful. The man is a monster, a sadist, a mad dog to be put down.'

'He's also intelligent, so I'm told,' Scott said. 'Some even say, cultivated.'

Lalya shook her head from side to side, as if in despair, but then she nodded agreement, looking almost perplexed by her recollections of the man who had clearly tormented her. 'Yes, captain, he is that as well. That's what makes the other – his dark side – so hard to accept, but I know just what he's like.'

'Which is?'

'A demon from hell. A charming devil. A man who takes his pleasures from the torments of others.'

Hearing this description, Scott imagined yet again, as he had done so often, the shadow of Dmitry Petrov spreading like a pestilence all the way from Kyrgyzstan to England to descend upon Johnny and destroy him. His hatred for Petrov instantly welled up again, but he was also intrigued. This was not a common criminal he was dealing with and, of course, it was this fact that rendered him fascinating. Again, Scott had the feeling that he knew the man – or would, at least, recognise something in him if or when they finally met.

'Just how well do you know him?' he asked.

'Too well,' Lalya said. 'I was one of the daughters, but I was luckier than most, since Petrov took me as his personal housemaid and mistress. He was better than most of his men, but that isn't saying much. As you say, he's cultivated. He reads books and collects paintings. He can even talk like a gentleman. But he killed all of my family – *all* of them – and in the case of my brothers, he did it in front of my very eyes, just to spite me or punish me. He did that and I still had to share his bed, which made me feel less than human. And that, Captain Scott, was what he wanted: to make me feel less than human.'

'He sounds less than human himself.'

'In my eyes, he is.'

'But you managed to escape.'

'Yes.'

'How?'

'By burning his house down and using the fire as a diversion while I got out of the camp. I managed to get this far before the snow set in, but then I was forced to stay here. Now I cannot get back down because of the snow and even then, maybe even before the spring, I'll be recaptured by that barbarian's men. In which case, I will surely die.'

'So you know where his camp is?' Scott asked, suddenly feeling excited and automatically straightening up on what he had just realised was a makeshift bed of straw with rolled up bear skins for a pillow.

'Of course.'

'You know how to get back there from here? I mean, you said you were lost, so you may not be able to find your way back there.'

'I know how I came here and I know how to get back.'

'Will you take me back there when I'm ready?'

'No!' she said, almost shouting in her panic. 'I don't want to ever see that place again. *I cannot go back there!*' She turned away from him, her body shaking, and stared distractedly at the steel pot hanging over the fire with steam coming out of it.

'Take me back there,' Scott said quietly, insistently, knowing just what he was doing, a small hearts-and-minds campaign, 'and I'll destroy the camp and hopefully kill Petrov. That's all I ask of you, Lalya ... Just take me back. You won't have to go near the camp itself. Just point it out to me.'

'No!' she cried out again, almost sobbing, but this time clenching her fists and pressing them against her cheeks as if about to beat herself unconscious. 'I can't do it. *I won't!*'

Scott deliberately did not respond, wanting her to settle down again, and after a while, perhaps compelled by his silence to do something, distract herself, she shuffled over to the fire, her delicate feet in furred slippers, saying, 'You have to eat. You haven't eaten since you got here. I've made you some gruel.'

She filled a small wooden bowl with the steaming gruel, or stew, a concoction of beef and beans, obviously made up from a mixture of tinned foods, and came back to hold the plate up in front of him. It smelt delicious and he realised that he was starving, but his bandaged arms rendered him helpless. Seeing this, Lalya smiled for the first time, then scooped some of the stew up onto the spoon and held it out to his lips. When he swallowed the first mouthful, it tasted like the most wonderful food in the world, though he knew it couldn't be that good. He was starving and this told him that he was alive and that, in turn, was what made the food taste wonderful.

He said nothing as Lalya continued to spoon-feed him. He let her speak first, which she did when she lowered the spoon back to the bowl to look steadily, more thoughtfully at him.

'You want to go there in order to kill Petrov?'

'Yes,' Scott replied. '*And* to destroy his camp.'

'And the prisoners there. You'll set them all free?'

Scott nodded. 'Yes. They'll be free to go where they choose. But you must take me there. Will you do that, Lalya?'

Her haunted brown gaze wandered around the dark walls of the cave – dark except for the flickering illumination from the flames of the fire – and then, with a sigh of despair or reluctant acceptance, she turned back to him, nodding, and said, 'You can't destroy the camp on your own.'

'I think I can, Lalya.' He nodded towards the bergen and weapons piled up in the corner. 'I've been specially trained for this and I've everything I need over there. I can do it. Believe me.'

Now she was looking more boldly at him, as if the fear she had felt before his arrival was already falling away, to be replaced with the healthy need for vengeance. 'But *how* will you do it? How can one man destroy his whole camp?'

Scott nodded again towards his bergen and weapons. 'With

explosives placed in the right places – and the explosives are over there. Those explosives will not only destroy the camp, but distract Petrov's men while I go in and get him. Just take me there, Lalya.'

She smiled at him, but her brown eyes were now bright and hard with the hope of a desperately desired revenge.

'So will you take me there, Lalya?' he repeated.

She nodded. 'Yes . . . But I can do more than that. I can draw you a map of the whole camp, show you where everything is and, if necessary, guide you through the camp when you enter it.'

'I thought you didn't want to do that.'

'I was frightened, but I suspect you're a man possessed and I think you can do this successfully. I'll go in with you if it helps to get Petrov. For that, I'd risk anything.'

'Good,' Scott said, though he felt slightly ashamed of himself, being aware that he was risking this girl's life for his own selfish interests and was, as she had cleverly recognised, obsessed with getting Petrov. Of course, he had his good reasons – the killing of all his men and, before that, the indirect killing of his son and the ruination of two lives, his own and that of his wife – but even so, he was starting to feel that he was becoming as inhuman as Petrov and this was not a good feeling. Nevertheless, he wanted Petrov more than ever and so had to go on with it. 'We'll leave as soon as I'm fit.'

'That may not be so long,' Lalya said, raising the bowl of soup once more and spooning him mouthfuls of gruel. They didn't speak until the meal was nearly finished.

'How long was I unconscious?' Scott asked, having studied his bandaged ribs and arms again.

'Two days.'

'Is much broken? My ribs? My arms?'

'Nothing,' she said. 'I thought perhaps your ribs were broken, but like your arms they were only badly bruised – *very* badly bruised and swollen – so I wrapped them in skins soaked in boiling water to make the swelling go down.'

He glanced at his bandaged arms, then held them upright. 'These are the same? No broken bones?'

She shook her head from side to side. 'No broken bones. Just very bad bruising. If you keep applying the hot skins to them – as hot as you can bear – the swelling should go down in a few days.'

Scott glanced across the cave to where his Arctic clothing had been piled up against the wall and was now support- ing his bergen and weapons. He could only assume that the thickness of his Arctic clothing, their padding and air-cushioning, combined with the packed bergen and its rolled blankets, had prevented him from breaking his ribs or bones. He also realised, however, when he looked at the bergen, that the last PRC-319 radio system had been lost with Killer Parker. Even if he succeeded in doing what he now intended doing, he would have no way to contact the Russian air force and arrange to be lifted out. He would have to think about that.

'Right,' Scott said. 'A few days. That sounds fine by me.'

Suddenly feeling weak, he let his head fall back onto the pillow of rolled-up bear skins, his aching bones sinking grate- fully onto the bed of straw, under the warming blanket.

'Tell me about Petrov,' he said. 'Tell me everything, Lalya.'

She told him a lot.

CHAPTER THIRTY

Five days later, just before first light, Scott, with his bruises almost healed, prepared to move against Petrov's camp. As he intended making his assault under cover of darkness and, also, because he would have to be able to move quickly, he discarded his snow-white Arctic clothing in favour of a Chairman Mao suit with a loose standard-issue combat smock and Helly-Hansen cold-weather pullover. There were no identifying insignia on the clothing; and nor was there an SAS badge on the peaked camouflaged combat cap he had chosen over the woolly hat and face mask worn previously.

Once dressed, he camouflaged his face to help it blend in with the forthcoming night, using a cosmetic 'cam' cream to make the eyes, nose and mouth more difficult to identify, even at very close ranges. He put the camouflage on in three stages: first he applied a thin base coating diluted with his own saliva and covering all the exposed areas of skin; next he broke up the outline of his features by drawing diagonal patterns across his face with stick camouflage; finally, he darkened the normally high-lighted areas – forehead and chin, nose and cheekbones – while leaving the areas normally in shadow a lighter shade.

When he finished with his own face, he turned his attention to Lalya, who had been watching with fascination as he prepared himself. After searching through his seemingly bottomless bergen, he gave her warm clothing to put on under the bizarre jacket of bear skin that she had made for herself. When she was dressed, he made her bind up her long black hair, then he camouflaged her face in exactly the same way as he had done his own. Lalya smiled with helpless amusement as he did this.

He had already checked his weapons, including the MP5, and found them to be in working order. Now, however, he completed the job by comouflaging the sub-machine gun with masking tape that would blur its outline and prevent it from reflecting the moonlight and giving away his position. Lalya had insisted on bringing along her shotgun, which she claimed to have learned to use when hunting gophers and other small animals for extra food, so Scott camouflaged that with masking tape as well.

Finally, when he and Lalya were both ready, he humped his bulky bergen onto his back and said simply, 'Let's go.' Lalya nodded and led him out of the cave, into the fading light of the sunset, into more falling snow.

Scott had been both frustrated and elated to learn from Lalya that Petrov's camp was not very far away – hardly more than an hour's hike down the mountainside. His frustration sprang from the knowledge that his men, before being brutally annihilated, had managed to get so close without knowing it; his elation came from the awareness that he would be there very soon and that this grim affair would finally be resolved, one way or the other.

Thus, as he hiked down the snow-swept mountainside, a few metres behind Lalya, who was carrying her shotgun like a trooper, determined to do her bit and have her revenge, he thought of all she had told him about Dmitry Petrov and automatically boiled up with a rage that gave him added strength. Nevertheless, as he made his way over the snow-covered terrain, carefully avoiding loose rocks and hidden crevasses, being careful not to slip on ice or frozen gravel, sticking close behind Lalya who was moving forward with confidence, he was forced to accept that while Petrov's behaviour, as related by Lalya, was even worse than he had imagined, there was a side to the man that now baffled him and, therefore, intrigued him. Judged by his actions, Petrov would seem to be an immoral criminal, a brutal monster, a sadist, almost the devil incarnate; but the same man, according to Lalya, read literature, collected paintings, loved classical music, was an authority on Russian history, and conducted lengthy, philosophical discussions about these subjects and others with his friend and second-in-command, Misha Tolkachov. Clearly, Petrov, despite his dark side, was educated, sophisticated and possessed of certain, possibly suppressed finer feelings. He was certainly no simple-minded brute like most of his brigands.

As for Petrov's friend, Misha Tolkachov, if the description given by Lalya was anything to go by, he was almost certainly the same tall, slim, oddly poetic-looking young man that Scott had seen giving orders to Petrov's men during some of their fire fights with the SAS. More importantly, he was the same young man who had attempted to fire his weapon at Scott shortly after Dmitry's deliberately sadistic killing of Corporal Parker. Scott could never recall that murder without a deep feeling of revulsion, but he was also reminded by the recollection that Misha had attempted to put an end to Petrov's brutal game – the game he was playing with Scott – by attempting to kill Scott when Petrov hesitated to do so. Before hurling himself down that snow-covered slope, Scott had seen the anger in Misha's eyes and sensed the conflict between him and Petrov. That knowledge could possibly come in useful.

Glancing east, he saw once more the vast sweep of the Fergana Valley, covered in grey-black clouds, eerie in the fading light, great swathes of shadow sweeping across its lush greenery, located far below the snow line which he and his men had crossed in what now seemed like another age:

many years ago instead of mere days ago. Thinking of that crossing, and of the men he had led into the snow, Scott filled up with grief, with a feeling of dreadful loss, and with the knowledge that he was, in a real sense, despite Lalya's presence here, all alone now and much farther from his own world than he could ever have imagined. This could, of course, have contributed to the illusion he now had that he somehow knew Dmitry Petrov, had something in common with him, and perhaps would learn a great deal about himself when they had their final, potentially fatal, confrontation.

This illusion, which surely is all it could be, had grown stronger during the past five days when Lalya's revelations about Petrov, her vivid descriptions of him, drawn from a dreadful intimacy, had helped him to see Dmitry in his mind, as a distinctive face as well as a personality. Now that face, which was oddly attractive despite its scars, which tended to brutalise its basic fine features, was starting to dominate his every thought. For this reason, as Misha had said when preparing to kill him, it had to end now.

'There!' Lalya said suddenly, stopping briefly to point to a high ridge not far ahead. 'That's the smoke from the opium-processing plants. We'll be at the camp in ten minutes.'

Looking beyond the summit of the ridge, Scott saw what at first he had thought were low, black rainclouds but which were, he now realised, clouds of smoke. They had looked like rainclouds because the sun had nearly set and the sky was becoming darker each second, letting the clouds of smoke blend with the real clouds.

'Good,' he said, trying to hide his excitement. 'Keep going, Lalya. We have to get there before the sun sets and that doesn't leave us too much time.'

'Yes, I know,' Lalya said.

She started forward again, leading him up the white, snowy slope that merged into the steeper climb of the high ridge. Following her, Scott was keeping his eyes and ears peeled for any unusual sights or sounds, swinging his MP5 repeatedly from left to right, to the front and to the rear, while at the same time carefully checking the ground on either side for signs of recent activity or hidden land mines. He neither saw nor heard anything unusual until about five minutes later, when, as they were making their way up the last few metres to the summit of the ridge, he noticed a fluctuating yellow glow in the sky, indicating the lights and fires of the camp below. Just before reaching the rim of the ridge, where the ground levelled out briefly before sloping down the other side, Scott hurried up beside Lalya and forced her to the ground by tugging her shoulder as he, too, lowered himself to his belly. In this position, he crawled forward, now taking the lead, and glanced down the other side of the ridge.

The camp was spread out before him in a natural amphitheatre of high ridges, with the mountains soaring up around it in an immense horseshoe shape. The eerie, yellow flicker in the sky was indeed being caused by the camp's many electric lights, powered by large generators, and by the open fires that burned in the rubbish tip and in the grounds between log cabins and the long, barracks-style wooden huts. The black smoke that Scott had at first mistaken for rainclouds was belching out of the chimneys of the brightly lit opium-processing workshops. The whole place, framed on each corner by high watchtowers and lined on all four sides by the wooden buildings, all surrounded and dominated by the soaring, snow-covered slopes of the mountains, looked like a concentration camp located on a forbidding, alien planet. That was a white hell down there.

Still on his belly, propped up on his elbows, Scott opened the map drawn for him by Lalya, spread it out on the hard snow in front of him and checked it with the aid of a small torchlight carefully turned downwards, its beam concealed with his left hand, while asking Lalya, lying close beside him, to point out each of the buildings in the camp and relate them to their positions on the drawing. Eventually, satisfied that she had drawn the map correctly and that he knew where everything was, he refolded it, tucked it into the side pocket of his Chairman Mao suit, then stood upright, knowing that he could not be seen from here even by the men in the watchtowers. The sun was now sinking rapidly and he wanted to get down there and reach the camp before darkness fell.

Without a word to Lalya, merely indicating with his finger the direction in which he wished to go, he led her down the other side of the ridge, holding on to the rocks for support, slipping and sliding occasionally, but gradually making it all the way down to the level ground that ran out a distance of approximately fifty metres to the rear of the long wooden barracks used as accommodations for the prisoners. With another hand signal, he indicated that Lalya was to remain here, hidden behind the rocks, until he returned for her, then he slithered on his belly, all the way to the rear wall of the barracks directly in front of him.

Knowing that most of the prisoners would now be in the barracks for the night, and having promised Lalya that he would try to avoid hurting them in the necessary violence to come, he turned sideways and inched his way along the wooden rear walls until he came to the buildings housing the armoury and ammunition depot. Lying there, he checked left and right, looking up at the tall watchtowers which were manned with machine-gun crews and spotters with high-power military binoculars and infrared thermal imagers for night viewing. When he saw that none of the guards were looking in his direction, he crawled under the raised floor of the buildings, found enough space to just about sit upright, then removed his bergen from his shoulders, withdrew his explosives from it and proceeded to make the first of the many bombs he intended using to demolish the camp. These would all be the same: simple DIY bombs consisting of C3/C4 slab explosive, a blasting cap with bridge wire, an electrical initiator, and a small timing device that would, at a preset time, pass a current through the wires in the blasting cap and detonate the main explosive charge.

Putting it together was relatively simple. Once Scott had judged the amount of slab explosive required for the particular job at hand, he had only to insert the blasting cap and initiator into it, attach the initiator's bridge wire to the cap's two electrical wires, fix these in turn to the preset timer, set the timer, then tape the completed bomb – still small in size but powerful enough to do the job – to the underside of the floor of the building. Having already judged just what buildings he intended blowing up and approximately how long it would take him to crawl around the perimeter of the camp and place each bomb, he was able to reduce the timing of each bomb in direct relationship to the timing of the one set before it, thus ensuring that the last bomb set was detonated at the same time as the first – in other words, to ensure that all the bombs went off at once, causing maximum damage both physically and psychologically.

If it worked, he reasoned, it would seem that the whole camp was exploding.

Once the first two bombs had been placed under the armoury and ammunition depot, he crawled back out from under the building, checked that the watchtower searchlights were not moving in his direction, then made his way under cover of darkness to his next target, which was the first of the watchtowers. Once directly under the tower itself, where he intended placing a bomb, he would be out of sight of the machine-gun crew and spotter high above, but another guard was standing at the base of the tower, facing the guard standing at the gable end of the building opposite which, with the tower itself, formed a vehicle entrance and exit without a gate.

Realising that the two guards could see each other, although they were obviously distracted with their own thoughts more often than not, Scott quietly raised himself to one knee, lowered his MP5 to the ground, removed his fighting knife from its sheath and waited patiently for the nearest guard to move around the back of the watchtower to urinate. As soon as the man did so, leaning his rifle against one of the struts of the watchtower and spreading his legs to open his pants, Scott moved swiftly up behind him, slapped one hand over his mouth to silence him, jerked his head back, slashed his throat in one clean sweep, then clamped his arm around the cut throat, letting the man's gushing blood soak his sleeve, while pulling him backwards into his own body to ensure that he did not immediately, noisily, fall to the ground. Held firmly in Scott's embrace, the man shuddered violently for a moment, but went still soon enough. When he had sagged, lifeless, in Scott's embrace, Scott lowered him gently to the ground, cleaned the blade of his knife in the snow, slipped it back into its sheath, then slung his MP5 over his shoulder and advanced into the shadows under the watchtower, out of sight of the guard at the opposite building, to place his next bomb.

All silent killing techniques were detestable to Scott, making him feel like a barbarian, but as he moved on around the perimeter of the camp, from watchtower to building, from one guard to the other, he had no choice but to despatch each of the guards by the same bloody, albeit highly effective, method and in each case managed to do so without drawing attention to himself. Thus, by the time he had made his way around the whole perimeter, he had planted bombs under the armoury and ammunition depot, on the struts of all four watchtowers, on the petrol drums stacked near the motor pool (he had left the vehicles in the motor pool untouched for a very good reason) and on the rear walls of the supply huts. This had taken nearly a dozen bombs in all, but as the biggest part of them, the preset timers, were themselves quite small, he had been able to carry everything required in the bergen and in separate pouches fixed to his belts. Nevertheless, he felt considerably lighter when he had rid himself of most of the explosives and demolition equipment and knew that he would be able to move a lot quicker without them.

Having promised Lalya that he would try to keep the prisoners from harm, he did not place bombs either on the barracks used by Petrov's brigands, who would have prisoners as housemaids and mistresses, or on the opium-processing workshops where prisoners also worked. The former he would leave standing, having reasoned that once the camp was destroyed and Petrov despatched, most of the brigands would flee. The latter he would clear himself, despatching any guards with his personal weapons, ordering the prisoners out and then destroying the processing units with hand grenades and the last of his explosives.

Now having come full circle and being back at the rear of the barracks for the prisoners, he remained on his belly, hiding under the raised building, until the beams of the nearest watchtower's searchlights had passed over his location. Darkness had now fallen completely and the beams of light were dazzling. Taking advantage of the darkness before the searchlights turned back in his direction, he crawled out from under the building and ran back at the half-crouch to where Lalya was impatiently waiting for him, still protected by the same high rocks. Resting on one knee beside her, Scott checked the luminous dial of his wristwatch, then looked up again.

Lalya's eyes were very big and very brown, with a radiant intensity. She looked wildly beautiful.

'I timed it to the last five minutes,' he informed her. 'The bombs should all go off at once, just under five minutes from now. When they do, we'll run through the gaps between the prisoners' two main barracks, which won't be ablaze. I won't have time to look at the map after that, so you'll have to guide me. I want to get rid of Petrov while his men are still in a state of complete confusion, so make that our first stop after the prisoners' barracks.'

'What about the prisoners?'

'When they see the scale of the destruction, the brigands will think they're being attacked from all sides by a major assault force. Most of them will swarm up into the surrounding hills, either fleeing or attempting to find what they think is an enemy force. Either way, they won't be too concerned with the prisoners and the latter can make their escape by simply leaving the camp and going back down the mountain.'

'How?'

'A lot of the prisoners will be able to drive,' Scott said. 'And certainly their sons will be able to do so. I've deliberately not planted bombs in the motor pool in order to let the prisoners have access to the vehicles. So tell them they're being rescued, that the camp is being destroyed, that a lot of jeeps in the motor pool have been deliberately left undamaged, and that they're to reunite with their sons and daughters and take a vehicle from the motor pool and drive out of here. The jeeps have snow-chains on their tyres and the brigands will be too busy to bother with escaping prisoners, so they should all make it down the mountainside. Now do you think you can manage this?'

'Yes,' Lalya said firmly.

Scott studied her for a moment, not sure if she could do it, wondering if she would let him down, then, seeing the radiant intensity of her gaze and the grim set to her normally full lips, he decided that he would have to take that chance.

Looking down at his wristwatch again, he counted off the minutes as the main hand moved around the dial; then, with one minute to go, he counted off the seconds . . . thirty seconds, twenty seconds, fifteen seconds, ten . . . and finally, with only that ten seconds to go, he pressed himself and Lalya to the ground and waited for the explosions.

The bombs went off on time.

CHAPTER THIRTY-ONE

The noise was catastrophic, a series of explosions that came at slightly different times, but in such quick succession that they sounded like the one mighty, lengthy roar. Even protected by high, thick rocks, a good fifty metres from the nearest explosions, Scott felt the force and heat from the blasts and waited for them to recede before daring to raise his eyes and look out. When he did, he saw an extraordinary spectacle. Many of the buildings were still spewing debris or collapsing in upon themselves; the fuel dump had turned into a veritable sea of coiling, spitting yellow flames; the armoury and ammunition depot were still erupting in a series of explosions as the ammunition went up; and all four watchtowers were in varying degrees of trouble. One was collapsing in a spiralling pillar of boiling dust, smoke and steam while the men, falling with it, screamed dementedly; another two were badly damaged, with the base of one in flames and the other snapping and screeching as it began to break up; and the fourth had already collapsed with crushed men yelling in agony from the rubble.

'Go!' Scott bawled at Lalya.

He jumped up and ran with Lalya beside him, heading straight for that gap between the untouched prisoners' barracks, though glancing over the fiery, still exploding remains of the armoury and ammunition depot, to the compound beyond, where he could see men and women pouring out of buildings to form a rapidly growing, panic-stricken mass. Smoke from the many fires and dust from the ruins was boiling over all, giving the place a hellish, infernal appearance as Scott and Lalya ran to the untouched barracks and made their way through to the other side. Now in the lead, Lalya turned right and ran along the front of the prisoners' barracks, heading in the general direction of the blazing fuel dump. In fact, she was heading for Petrov's log cabin which was located well inside the main clearing, between the fuel dump and the buildings of the camp perimeter, which is why Scott had not been able to bomb it when he did the others.

As they continued running towards Petrov's house, neither Scott nor Lalya were bothered by the many brigands who were now crowding the compound, as most of them were making their way out through the demolished, blazing buildings, through the billowing, choking clouds of smoke, either intent on fleeing altogether or on making contact with the enemy whom they imagined were swarming all over the surrounding hills. Terrified, not too sure of what was happening and always fearful of doing the wrong thing, most of the prisoners had remained in their barracks, but a few of the bolder women had come out onto the steps and were glancing about them at the spectacular destruction with hope in their eyes. Scott stopped in front of these prisoners and then turned to Lalya.

'Do what I told you,' he said, speaking Russian, 'while I go on to Petrov's house. You can join me there.'

'I will,' Lalya said, her brown eyes also bright with hope as well as the hard light of anticipated revenge.

She was already turning to speak to the female prisoners – to tell them to find their sons and daughters, then take vehicles from the untouched motor pool and drive out of the camp and down the mountain road while the brigands were otherwise engaged – when Scott continued on his way.

Ignored in the screaming, bawling, pushing, pulling mass of brigands and prisoners, he raced past more burning buildings just as another watchtower collapsed, screeching and banging and tearing, sending an immense fountain of sparks into the sky on more boiling clouds of dust and smoke. More explosions could be heard from the fuel dump, where great ribbons of yellow flames were tearing through the night sky, fluttering sheets of incandescence, and these were followed by more explosions from behind, where the ammunition in the armoury and depot was still exploding and, in turn, making even more explosions to create a frightening, deafening cacophony.

As Scott approached Petrov's house, he saw that three armed brigands were standing guard outside, all of them glancing this way and that in disbelief at the sheer extent of the devastation. Though they held their rifles at the ready, they were too engrossed in what was going on around them to notice that Scott wasn't one of their own. Scott was only a few metres from them, well within the firing range of his MP5, when one of them saw his raised weapon and shouted a frantic warning to the others. Scott fired instantly, a single, sustained burst on a wide arc of fire that cut across all three guards at once, punching them backwards, making them jerk convulsively, like epileptics, then throwing them backwards into the snow, which instantly turned red with their spreading blood.

At that moment, perhaps hearing the sound of gunfire, though more likely because he had been preparing to come out anyway, Dmitry Petrov stepped onto his porch. Bare-headed and wearing an unzipped quilted jacket, he was holding an AK-47 automatic rifle across his chest and looking at the devastation all around him with what seemed like remarkably detached, almost inhuman, curiosity.

'Petrov!' Scott bawled, initially not knowing why he would want to give that warning, but then, when Petrov looked down and saw him, understanding completely.

He had wanted to meet Petrov face-to-face and see how

he would react in the presence of the man who had come to kill him.

Petrov merely smiled at him.

Scott stopped his advance, taken by surprise, hardly knowing what he was doing, looking into the face of the man who had caused him so much grief, both indirectly and directly, yet finding himself unable to move. Petrov, though badly scarred, had the face of a cast-out angel, a tormented saint, a pure soul who had lost his way; yet his bright gaze held the darkness of eternity and showed the doorways to hell. He was a man like no other that Scott had seen and he would not give an inch.

Instead of raising his weapon to fire at Scott, he held it above his head with his right hand and jabbed at his own chest with the forefinger of his other hand.

'You want to kill me, Englishman?' He was speaking in perfect English. 'You've come all this way to do that? Then do it while I stand here undefended. Put the bullets right here.' He indicated the area above his heart with a jabbing forefinger. 'Right here. I invite you.'

Scott raised his weapon to fire but his trigger-finger refused to move, which made Petrov smile all the more . . . until he saw Lalya.

Having done as Scott had asked, directing the prisoners to the motor pool, she had now come up beside him and was staring at Petrov as if gazing into the very fires of hell. Petrov, in his turn, looked at her as if seeing a ghost . . . Then, as he lowered his weapon to his side, he seemed to shrink where he stood.

'No!' he exclaimed in dread and yearning, not believing his own eyes.

'Yes!' Lalya snapped back, then she raised her shotgun to take aim and fire . . . though she, too, could not do it. He had taken all of her life but let her live; now what little she had left was due to him and that made him her Maker. She could not defy God. 'Do it!' she screamed, turning instead to Scott. 'Damn you, kill him! *You promised!*'

Scott raised his MP5 to fire just as Petrov looked beyond him with widening eyes and then bawled, 'Misha, *no!*'

Spinning on the ball of one foot, Scott saw Petrov's friend, Misha, the tall, slim, handsome one, now silhouetted dramatically by the spiralling yellow flames and billowing black smoke from the blazing petrol dump, marching resolutely towards him and Lalya, his poet's face taut, almost demoniac, with fury as he raised his pistol and took aim. Scott would never know who Misha intended killing first because before he could find out, he heard the short, savage roaring of the AK-47 and saw Misha convulsing, staggering backwards like a drunken man, dropping his pistol into the snow, and then looking up at Petrov with pale grey, poetic, questioning eyes.

'What . . . ?' he managed to say as his face drained of the blood that was bubbling with strands of grey slime from his trembling lips.

'Fuck you, Misha, they're mine!' Petrov shouted like a wild man. Then, as Misha fell, sinking face first into the snow, staining it with his spreading blood, Scott spun back to face Petrov, determined to finish him, and saw him raising his rifle once more, this time aiming at Lalya.

'Damn you, Lalya,' Petrov said, having recovered from his shock and now taking this as far as he could push it. 'You almost defeated me and I think I loved you for it, but now you've spoiled it all by returning and showing me just how weak you are. Certainly too weak to kill me, too debased by your own acceptance of my sundry humiliations, too deprived of self-volition, of will, to do what has to be done.' He nodded in Scott's direction. 'Just like the Englishman here . . .' and he turned to give Scott a mocking smile '. . . who hides his principles behind decency and cruelly disappoints me by so doing. Goodbye, Lalya. I loved you.'

'Fuck you!' Scott said, jolted out of his trance by rage and raising his MP5 to fire at Petrov.

'No!' Lalya screamed.

Scott heard her shotgun firing, an explosion that filled his whole world, then he felt himself picked up and flung back down though a whirlpool of darkness and light. He felt no pain at all, just the numbing of his senses, then the pain started making its presence felt and forced his eyes open. He looked up and saw the blazing fuel dump, the burning, crumbling watchtowers, the smouldering wooden buildings collapsing into clouds of billowing dust, the armed brigands swarming out of the smoke-obscured compound and heading up into the hills, either to flee or fight; and, finally, most heart-lifting of all, the prisoners cheering jubilantly and raising their hands to the sky, thanking God perhaps, as they roared out of the motor pool in jeeps that had tyres covered in snow-chains. When Scott heard the first of the jeeps heading down the mountain road, he could not resist smiling.

'God, you fool!' Petrov said.

Lowering his gaze, Scott saw Lalya's shotgun – the one she had shot him with – lying in the snow and then, when he raised his gaze a little, he saw her making her escape from the camp by going out the same way they had come in: through the gap between the untouched prisoners' barracks, obviously heading back to her cold, dark cave and probably preparing to die there. Groaning, Scott rolled onto his back and looked up at Petrov.

'*God*, you fool,' Petrov repeated, this time placing the emphasis on the word 'God'. 'You could have had me and you just couldn't do it until I goaded you into it. Why did you come all this way to find me and then behave so stupidly, like a normal man? Come on, my friend, let's find out. It's all finished here anyway.' He nodded in the direction of the four cardinal points of the compass, indicating the blazing, crumbling buildings of the compound, already almost deserted, then he slung his rifle across his shoulder and leaned over Scott. 'This is going to hurt a hell of a lot,' he said. 'But it's the least you deserve. Grit your teeth. Be a Georgian.'

So saying, he took hold of Scott's wrists and started dragging him backwards to his log cabin, which was one of the few buildings still left standing. Scott's pain was excruciating, but he refused to let Petrov know that, instead forcing himself to lie as limp as possible, distracting himself by gazing around him at the flames, smoke and boiling dust of the havoc he had wreaked in this place. He had not, in the end, managed to destroy the opium-processing workshops, but given that both the workers and their masters had fled, they weren't likely to be producing any opium for a long time to come. He was taking pleasure from this thought when Petrov dragged him, with little regard for his suffering, up the steps of his cabin.

Scott screamed in pain before he could stop himself.

'Come, come, my friend,' Petrov said, dragging him off the top step, where the pain eased a little, then backwards across the porch to the front door. 'We are only truly alive when we suffer pain, so you mustn't complain too much. Here we are at my humble home.'

'Fuck your humble home,' Scott said.

Petrov kicked his front door open with the heel of one booted foot then, perhaps to punish Scott for his impertinence, jerked him deliberately hard, causing him even more pain. Scott cried out again, not trying to hide it this time, preferring to cry out than to pass out, wanting to gaze into Petrov's eyes and not miss a thing. He was dragged backwards across the floor and then propped upright against the far wall, under an impressive reproduction of Surikov's *The Boyarinya Morozova*. Lowering his gaze, he saw where he had been wounded by Lalya ... a bad wound ... a jagged, bloody hole in his left thigh ... Looking around him, he saw a large room, flawless in its good taste, with reproductions so good that they looked like the real thing (so good, in fact, that had Lalya not told him they were reproductions, he would not have known) and shelves filled with what looked like antique books and rare first editions of classic Russian literature. There was also a state-of-the-art multimedia system and a large collection of albums and CDs, though Scott couldn't see what they were. Clearly, however, judging from what he *could* see, including the furniture, he was in the home of a man of considerable sophistication and good taste.

He was trying to wriggle into a position that afforded him more comfort when the man of sophistication and good taste kicked him deliberately on his wounded thigh and made him scream out again.

'That's it,' Petrov said with a pleasant smile. 'That's what I like to hear. So what's your name, my dear friend?'

'Captain Neil Scott, British army. Serial number . . .'

But Petrov interjected by kicking him again and then saying, when Scott's brief, helpless scream had tapered off, 'Don't bother with that Geneva Convention shit because it means nothing to me. Besides, we're not in a real war, Captain, so the Geneva Convention has no place here at all. I'm a trained killer, Captain Scott, and that's what you are as well—'

'*What?*'

'—because you're not just in the plain old British army. You are, in fact, in the famous SAS. Which means that we share something, at least. We're both professional killers.'

'That's horseshit,' Scott said.

It was his gesture of defiance because the blood was seeping out of him, slowly but steadily, draining him of energy, and though it seemed that he'd been defeated by Petrov, he had his pride to consider. There was that and all the pain that Petrov had caused him from afar and that, of course, had to be repaid in kind. Though weakening, though slipping away steadily, he still wanted to do that.

'Horseshit?' Petrov said, turning Scott's statement into a question as he walked across the large room to gaze out at the blazing, smoking ruination of his compound and shake his head from side to side as if merely bemused. Eventually, he closed the front door, then walked back to kneel in front of Scott and gaze steadily, unblinkingly at him. 'No, I don't think so, Captain Scott. You kill for a living and so do I. That makes us roughly the same. What makes you think you're so different?'

'I kill for a purpose.'

'So do I,' Petrov said.

'I kill as a professional soldier,' Scott said.

'And I kill as a professional gangster. What's the difference, my friend? To slit the throat of a fellow human being is a terrible thing and no motive can hope to justify it or make it any less terrible.'

'I don't kill for profit,' Scott insisted.

'You kill for wages, Captain Scott. Your country pays you to kill. I, too, am paid to kill. Though our motivations may be different, we both profit from death and that, I fear, makes you the same as me. Whether or not you like it, my friend, you and I share some common ground.'

'You killed my son,' Scott said, having come all this way to say it and wanting to get it off his chest while he still had the strength to speak. He was growing weaker by the second, slowly but surely, his draining blood like a dripping tap, seeping out of his thigh and spreading gradually over the floorboards near the edge of the carpet.

Petrov glanced with concern at his endangered carpet, then returned his penetrating gaze to Scott and raised his fine, almost feminine, eyebrows in a questioning manner. '*I* killed your son? And how, pray, did I manage to do that?'

'You produced the drugs that killed him.'

'*I* produced them?'

'Yes. You produced them and arranged for their shipment to England and some bastards there hooked my son on them and he died from an overdose. He was a lovely boy, my son. His mother and I both loved him. When he died, our world ended overnight and so did our marriage. Now my wife's on drugs as well – not your kind: tranquillisers – and she'll never be the woman she was and that's your fault as well. I detest you, you scumbag.'

Smiling, Petrov walked away, entered a room nearby, then returned holding a towel in his hands. Kneeling beside Scott, he jerked his leg off the floor, not being careful about it, letting Scott suffer again, then wrapped the towel around the wound, tightened it like a tourniquet – Scott screamed like a stuck pig – then tied a knot in it. He let Scott's leg fall back to the floor, then he carefully checked the towel to see if the blood had stopped seeping out.

'The carpet,' he explained. 'I can always wash the floor-boards, but I'd never get the blood out of the carpet. Thankfully, the towel's stopped the bleeding, so we've no need to worry.'

'I'm not worried,' Scott said.

'You're not worried about my carpet,' Petrov said, 'yet you expect me to worry about your son. Sorry, Scott, I can't help you. People die every day. They die for a multitude of reasons and mostly by accident. You despise the Opium Road? Well, you've no right, my friend. It brings life as well as death. It brings tranquillisers to your wife and saves others from dreadful pain, so my activities do good as well as bad and I refuse to feel guilty about your son. Your son was in the West, therefore he was one of the world's few privileged, and probably had more good times in his few years that many of my kind have had in a whole lifetime. Good and bad lurks in the heart of every man and is present in everything, including opium. But for everything bad produced by opium, there's also something good. Dwell on this, my friend, while you sit there and I seek the truth elsewhere – over there at that table.'

So saying, he turned away from Scott and went to the low table by the cushion-packed sofa to go down on his knees behind it, as if at an altar. There were bowls and opium pipes of various kinds on the table and Petrov, from what Scott could see, was using them to mix some kind of opium-based substance with tobacco, which he then packed into a pipe and proceeded to smoke. He did so like a man on his knees in worship, head thrown back, eyes opening and closing repeatedly, his breathing escaping in ever longer, ecstatic sighs. Eventually, after what seemed like an eternity, during which Scott felt himself slipping in and out of consciousness, only kept awake by pain, Petrov rose from the low table and returned to kneel beside Scott. He leaned forward, offering a dreamy smile, and said, 'Look into my eyes.'

Scott, who could barely turn his head, had no choice but to do so. As Petrov's eyes were mere centimetres from Scott's face, the latter found himself looking into exceptionally big, unnaturally shining, coal-black pupils, obviously enlarged by the opium and now focused elsewhere – inward – to some place deep in his blighted soul where infinity lurked.

'I'm looking,' Scott said.

'So what do you see?'

'The drugged eyes of an opium addict,' Scott replied, refusing to indulge him.

Petrov, being high, was not offended. 'And why is that so bad? Is your soldiering not an addiction? And has not opium, throughout the ages, done more good than all of history's great armies? More good than the SAS?'

'I don't know what you're talking about,' Scott said, weakening more slowly now that the towel was causing less seepage, but losing blood all the same ... and losing his senses with it. Yet he was listening. He had nothing else to do and not much else to look forward to. He had failed and now Petrov would surely kill him and that would be the end of it. But despite this, defying his pessimism, his instinct for survival was telling him that talk could buy time. What for, he still didn't know.

'Think about it,' Petrov said, staring steadily, intensely, at him with a smile like ice and fire combined. 'Think of the history of warring nations, of the blood and the ruination, then think of the history of what I produce and smuggle – the opium that incidentally killed your son – and clearly there can be no comparison. Opium has its destructive side? Yes, of course it has – just like soldiering. But unlike soldiering, it also has its good side, which is what you're ignoring. Without opium, the dreams of man would be sadly reduced, as would his great achievements, which is exactly why man has been addicted to the substance from as far back as prehistoric times, when it was used as a painkiller and also in religious ceremonies. And since then? Where would civilisation have been without its opium? It was used by the Sumerians, by the Assyrians, by the ancient Egyptians and ancient Greeks as a medicine, for spiritual and occult enlightenment, and as an aid to the discovery of dreams. The Arabs then developed and organised the production of it, initiated trading in it, and did so when Arab culture was at its most glorious. The Venetians used it. Columbus was instructed to bring it back from the New World. In Europe, in the sixteenth century, the emerging medical sciences were dependent upon it and Paracelsus called it "the stone of immortality". Then the English took it up in the form of laudanum – taken, please note, from the Latin verb, *laudare*, meaning to praise – and by the twentieth century its use in medicine, particularly in the shape of morphine, was worldwide and invaluable.'

'So was its use in drug addiction and crime,' Scott interjected sardonically.

Still smiling, Petrov reached down to place his hand over Scott's wound and give it a hard, brutal squeeze. The pain made Scott jerk forward, gasping, but he managed not to scream this time. Nevertheless, when he sank back against the wall, he was breathing heavily and sweating.

'What a bad boy you are,' Petrov said, removing his hand. He put his head back, closed his eyes, breathed deeply, then opened his eyes again and lowered his intense, possibly deranged gaze to Scott. 'Because of your son,' he continued, 'you insist upon looking on the dark side, but please look on the bright side instead. Do not despise me, Scott. Please stop being so superior. You deal in death, my friend, excusing yourself with good intentions – service to your country, right or wrong – while I, whom you accusing of dealing in death for mere profit, at least deal in a product, opium, that has done as much good as bad – and possibly *more* good than bad. Never mind De Quincey, Scott – a good writer, a weak man, a bad example to us all. You being English, think instead of Coleridge, of Elizabeth Barrett Browning, of John Keats and Sir Walter Scott and Bramwell Brontë, of Byron and Shelley – why, even my personal favourite, your great Grahame Greene! – all users, to a greater or lesser degree, of the drug you despise. Think, also, of the great musicians and painters whose work, without the help of opium, would not be with us now. In other words, my friend, my fine hypocrite, opium has been, and remains to this day, an invaluable aid to the betterment of mankind, be it in medicine, in the arts or in religion. I should get an award!'

'That's a neat, one-sided summary,' Scott said, 'but it's only the half of it. When I think of opium, I think of warlords, drug barons, mobsters, murderous laundrymen, people enslaved by addiction, and innocent kids, like my own son, you shit, who die at too young an age. So go fuck yourself, Petrov.'

Petrov slapped Scott's face, though the blow was light, almost playful, then he shook his head from side to side, smiling sadly, as if wearied by hearing so much stupidity. 'My poor friend,' he said, 'you know nothing at all. You're going to quote me junkies and the living dead – all that ghoulish, melodramatic nonsense served up by Hollywood. But it isn't that way at all. Even the dark side has its good side. Your average warlord, Scott, which includes we so-called drug barons, invariably exists where the poppy seed is the only thing available to trade. True enough, he sells it to your mobsters and laundrymen, but think of the hypocrisy expressed by so-called honest men, the politicians and lawmakers – including those in the very government you fight and kill for – who publicly condemn the opium trade while covertly supporting it. Is it not true that the first Anglo-Chinese war – the so-called Opium War of 1840 – was actually fought to decide who should control the opium trade, the Chinese or the British? That the Japanese actively encouraged, and profited by, the opium trade in all territories held by them during the Second World War? That during the same war, US Naval Intelligence supported Mafia drug dealers in return for help with the invasion of Sicily. That in 1947 the CIA funded drug-dealing Corsican gangsters, notably in Marseilles, merely to disrupt Communist-led unions in that area, thus enabling the Corsicans to cement their relationship with the Mafia? Is it not true, also, that the most notorious opium-producing area of modern times – the so-called Golden Triangle straddling the frontiers of Laos, Thailand and Burma, just south of the Chinese border – could not have become what it is today without the support of the CIA, who felt that opium was less dangerous than Communism. And, finally, is it not true that your presence here in Kyrgyzstan, representing your government, which has its own interests, which are not those of this country, is a threat not only to my personal livelihood, but to the already meagre living standards of the local farmers who can no longer survive without the profits from their pitiful opium trade? The Opium Road, my stupid friend, is the lifeline of this area and if you destroy it, in the process of destroying me, then you destroy the whole country.'

'I wanted to destroy you because you killed my son,' Scott reminded him, being too weak to give considered thought to whatever else Petrov was implying.

'Your son could have died of alcoholism,' Petrov replied brutally, 'or been run down by a London bus. Would this give you grounds for assassinating the men in charge of the English breweries or the people in charge of London Transport? No, I don't think so.'

'You're a ruthless, immoral bastard,' Scott said, 'and that's all there is to it.'

'I'm a bastard, true enough,' Petrov replied, 'but that's all I'll concede to you.' He opened the palm of his right hand to reveal a couple of tablets, then he put his head back, closed his eyes and popped the tablets into his mouth. He swallowed, kept his head back for a while, then sighed like a man having an orgasm and opened his eyes again to look directly at Scott. Now the pupils of his eyes were even bigger and they glittered like blue ice. 'You know what I am, Captain? Oh, yes, I'm a bastard. I was born a bastard in the wildest, most impoverished part of Chechnya – where, incidentally, most of the Russian *Mafiya* come from – and I was brought up by my mother, a ~~peasant idiot fucked frequently~~ by passing strangers, one of whom, I must assume, was my father, here and gone like the wind. I had brothers and sisters – all bastards like me; all the product of passing strangers – and my mother brought us up like wild animals, feeding us only when absolutely necessary and thinking that by hiring us out to work for local farmers, she was doing us a favour. In fact, more often than not the local farmers, who lived a life of extreme isolation, hired us, boys and girls both, not for work but for sex, straight *and* perverted. So I was buggered and tortured for many years and learnt only one thing as I grew up – that life was purely a matter of survival and the surviving was all that mattered in the end.'

'You had a hard childhood,' Scott said sarcastically, though he didn't feel as cynical as he sounded. 'My heart goes out to you.'

Petrov smiled at that, his eyes glittering, then he reached down with his right hand to brutally squeeze Scott's wound and make him scream helplessly again. When Scott had finished screaming and was trying to get his breath back, Petrov nodded approvingly, smiling again, and continued as if talking to an old friend: 'I respect a man who can inflict pain on others without batting an eyelid. You've just done that to me, my English friend, but I know you'll never believe that fact.'

'No,' Scott said, 'I won't.'

'Never mind,' Petrov responded brightly, glancing at the blood-soaked towel on Scott's thigh, perhaps thinking of giving it another squeeze, but deciding, for whatever reason, not to do so. 'By the time I was fifteen, I'd been buggered so many times, forced to suck cock so many times, received torture so many times, that my only real interest in human beings was in knowing just how much they could take before they broke. Thus, when still fifteen and just about to be buggered and tortured yet again by another local moron, I knocked him unconscious with a hammer, tied him to a chair, tortured him until he told where he kept his money hidden, then slit his throat with the breadknife he'd often used on me and walked out of there to find a new life. I didn't even say goodbye to my mother. I simply walked away from it all – and I never went back.'

He paused in his monologue, waiting for Scott to say something, but this time Scott had no sarcastic remarks to offer and so kept his mouth shut. He was starting to think more highly of Dmitry Petrov while thinking less of himself. This was not a good feeling.

'I travelled around,' Petrov continued, 'begging here, stealing there, using violence when necessary, and eventually ended up in a travelling circus, first doing manual labour, then becoming partner to a man who staged fake wrestling matches on which bets were laid.' Petrov grinned and raised his eyebrows in an amused, questioning manner. 'You know? Enormous and muscle-bound, he'd invite members of the public to wrestle with him for money and naturally most were frightened to take him on. So then I, much smaller and certainly not muscle-bound, would step out of the crowd and challenge him to a match, placing a big bet on it, and he'd let me beat the hell out of him and then, with a great show of frustration, hand me a fistful of his money. Then others, thus encouraged, would step out of the crowd, thinking they could do the same, and of course he'd beat them and we'd pocket their money. It was a nice, easy earner ... I speak good English, yes?'

'Very good,' Scott said.

'So!' Petrov said, pleased. 'After a few years of this, I struck out on my own, doing a similar act, and eventually made my way to Moscow where I deliberately searched out, and fell in with, the local *Mafiya* who were profiting handsomely from drugs and organised prostitution in the new, more liberated, Russia. I had already killed men, of course, but usually on my own and always with lingering moral reservations, but with the *Mafiya*, even more ruthless than the original Mafia, I learnt that killing was merely part of the business, an economic necessity – like your soldiering or like drug-trafficking or whoring – and after that, what you insist is my ruthlessness or immorality, what I insist is merely my work, became something that I could take my pride from. I was respected in my profession – and it *is* a profession – and that gave me the confidence to climb higher up the ladder, eventually meeting Boris Yeltsin and becoming his personal bodyguard when the country had become a hotbed of political corruption. That corruption taught me the rest of what I needed to know about the bottomless pit of mankind, the cesspool of life ... I think you know all the rest.'

'Yes,' Scott said, 'I do.'

'You still think I'm a barbarian? Well, you're wrong, my English friend. I'm no more a barbarian than you are. Nor was my friend, Misha – the one I killed in defence of you and the lovely Lalya. Now Misha ... he had the face of an angel, the sensitivity of a poet, the mind of a philosopher ... yet he could kill without blinking, torture without remorse, wallow in blood, and he could do so because that's all he knew as he grew up – as it was all that I knew. So if Misha was a barbarian – and if I am – then so, too, are you. Because you, my English captain, do the same, though you might pretend otherwise. Your good reasons do not exonerate you; it's the deeds that finally matter. So what say you to that?'

Scott had to think about it, but he didn't find it easy because the blood was still seeping out of him and he was slipping away. He kept thinking about his dead son, about the destruction of his marriage, about the deaths of all his men at the hands of Petrov, and he tried to cling to the hatred that had sustained him, but he could no longer do it. Yet he could not, in all truth, accept what Petrov was saying, could not exonerate him just because he had been abused, because a man, in the end, was given a choice and the choice made the man. Therefore Scott, though no longer sustained by hatred, spoke the first words that came to him – the only words that made sense to him.

'I say that a soldier can have honour and that a gangster cannot. I say that no soldier worth his salt would sell drugs for profit. I say that your philosophy is designed to hide the fact that you sold your soul to the devil and don't want to acknowledge it. I say you're condemned, Dmitry Petrov. There the case rests.'

Petrov's face hardened on the instant and lost all of its humour. His eyes, which had been wide and intense, illuminated with opium, now narrowed to become those of a reptile. There was a very long silence.

'Are you still in pain?' Petrov asked eventually, his voice a deathly, unnatural whisper, almost a hissing.

'Yes,' Scott confessed.

'How much more pain do you think you could stand?'

'I don't know,' Scott admitted, feeling the fear creeping up his spine and deeply ashamed of it.

'Let's find out,' Petrov said.

CHAPTER THIRTY-TWO

Scott was now too weak to move, so Petrov tugged him sideways, making him fall over, then stepped behind him again, grabbed him under the shoulders and started dragging him backwards across the room, towards the front door. As Scott was being dragged along, trying to fight his growing fear over what Petrov had in store for him, he tried to distract himself by glancing around at the reproductions on the four walls, at the books and CDs, and understood at last why a man like Petrov, instinctively artistic and clearly self-educated, therefore obviously highly intelligent, would be driven mad by the immense gap between what he could have become and what he actually was. Petrov was not a psychopath, though his cruelty was pronounced; rather, he was a man whose rich imagination and creative urges had been perverted by his chronic inability to find an outlet for them. Now his only outlet, based on his nightmarish experiences in early life, was to test others to the absolute limit and see if they could endure as much as he had. If they could not, he would despise them and cast them into oblivion (which might, by that point, be a blessing to them); if they could, thus proving themselves his equal (which had not happened so far but had almost happened with Lalya) he would find himself without the will to live, but almost certainly take his victim down with him: a death and a suicide. Either way, those tested were doomed to die and now it was Scott's turn.

For Scott, it was not the thought of dying that made him fearful, but the thought of how long it would take and just how much pain he would have to bear. With Petrov, who wanted to test him to the limit, it could take a long time ... and that would certainly, given Petrov's skill in torture, be an eternity in hell.

Scott closed his eyes, but his own thoughts terrified him, so he opened them again and took one last look at the room before Petrov kicked the front door open and dragged him out onto the porch. He knew when the pain would start. He knew it even as Petrov was dragging him across the porch and actually felt it when Petrov, sophisticated and educated, a philosopher like his best friend Misha, hauled him backwards down the steps, letting his hips and spine bounce from one step to the other, filling his body with shooting pains that made him practically convulse and groan childishly, helplessly, then commenced to drag him across the compound like a sack of potatoes towards what, Scott realised with ever deepening dread, was the location of Lalya's so-called 'torture-and-execution posts'.

Many prisoners had been tied to those posts and shot; others prisoners, according to Lalya, had been tied to them and skinned alive.

Scott, still being dragged across the compound, through virgin snow that had been desecrated with dust, ash, the shells of spent bullets, blood and the debris from exploding buildings and watchtowers, past the blood-stained body of that other poetic soul, Misha, tried to struggle against his fate by kicking and wriggling, but his strength was too far gone to help him much and he finally gave in. Instead, he let himself sag, becoming as heavy as he could be, but Petrov had the unnatural strength of the obsessed and dragged him on without bother. When they reached the three posts in the middle of the compound, he abruptly released Scott, letting him fall backwards to the snow-covered ground.

Looking straight up, Scott saw the snow falling over him, the white flakes drifting down in slow motion, heartbreakingly beautiful. Lowering his gaze and moving his eyes to take in a broad field of vision, as much of the compound as possible, he saw the awesome devastation he had wrought, with only the prisoners' barracks and the opium-processing plants still standing. The rest of the buildings, including the four watchtowers, were smouldering ruins and the fuel dump was still blazing, illuminating the night with an eerie glow. Beyond those flames, clearly there for eternity, were the majestically soaring, ice-covered mountain peaks.

When Scott looked up again, he saw Petrov staring down at him, unsmiling, his handsome, scarred face now as white as the snow, his gaze otherworldly. Despite himself, Scott was terrified.

'Are you pleased with your handiwork?' Petrov asked, nodding left and right to take in the destruction on all sides. 'Are you pleased that you've done at least half of what you came here to do?'

'Yes,' Scott said, 'I am.'

'And did it with Lalya's help,' Petrov said, 'though alas, in the end, she betrayed you as she once betrayed me. I could have loved her, you know. I really could have. But then, of course, if I'd sensed that I *did* love her, I'd have viewed such love as a potentially dangerous weakness and would then have plugged the leak by putting her down; so perhaps it's best this way. On the other hand, dear Scott, I'm now faced with the ruination of my compound – and you and Lalya caused that. I hope you're proud of yourself.'

'Yes, I am,' Scott repeated, trying to hide his growing fear with defiance.

'You damned fool,' Petrov said. 'Eventually my men will come back down from the mountains and those opium-processing workshops will be back in operation just as soon as we raid the Opium Road again and pick up some more prisoners. You've set me back a little, I'll admit, but it won't be for long.'

'You're wrong,' Scott said, still fighting his fear by being defiant. 'When those escaped prisoners make their way down to Osh, the authorities won't be able to ignore them or what they're told by them. They'll come looking for you, Petrov – they'll have to – and then you'll be finished.'

'You're finished already, my friend. And I have to say that just as it was with Lalya, so it is with you. You *almost* defeated me and for that I respect you. Unfortunately for you, it's the very fact that I respect you that makes me determined to find out just how far you'll go to earn it.' Though standing upright, he bent over a little to let Scott see more clearly his unnaturally bright, accusing, tormented eyes. 'You're suffering pain, Scott? It brings tears to your eyes already? Well, my friend, it's nothing to what you're going to suffer when I string you up to that pole. You'll know what eternity's like before you get there and it's not something you'll want to experience. So let's start right now.'

He was just about to bend down farther and tug Scott to his feet when a distant, ghostly voice rang out, calling his name.

'Dmitry! I'm here!'

Petrov had been holding Scott by the collar of his Chairman Mao suit, but that eerie voice acted upon him like a whip across his back and he instantly released Scott, letting him fall back into the snow, then straightened up and spun around on the ball of one foot to look in the opposite direction. Scott, rolling painfully onto his side, stared that way, also.

Lalya was standing at the far end of the smoke-filled compound, looking bizarre in her hand-made bearskin outfit, but with her face cleaned of Scott's camouflage make-up and her long black hair hanging down her spine again. Despite the bearskin coat, she was ethereally beautiful and the smoke, still drifting across the compound, made her look like a ghost.

'Lalya!' Petrov cried out automatically, though it didn't sound like him, his voice drained of its arrogance and mockery, offering instead what he had always denied himself: the joy and pain of pure love.

Scott knew, in that instant, that Petrov loved her and would have to hate himself for it.

'Dmitry!' Lalya repeated, just standing there, about thirty metres away, obscured by the drifting smoke but illuminated by the flickering flames, by the moonlight, by the stars, and offering nothing other than that one word, which meant everything to him. 'I couldn't kill you and I can't stay away,' she continued, 'so I had to come back. Do what you will with me, Dmitry, because I can't live without you.'

Petrov's gaze revealed the love that he would always deny himself, then he withdrew his handgun from its holster and started walking towards her through the wind-driven snow.

'Fuck you,' he said, raising the handgun to the firing position and aiming it at her, 'I could have loved you and that's damage enough. Now you'll pay the price, Lalya.'

'That's why I'm here,' Lalya said.

Scott was outstretched on the ground, observing the ground from eye-level, and from there he could see a line of footprints in the snow, leading up to a small, snow-covered mound. That mound was directly in Petrov's path and it wasn't a landmine.

'Oh, my God!' Scott whispered.

Petrov didn't even see it. He was blinded by love and hatred. He only knew that it was there when he stepped in it and it snapped closed, its steel teeth, as sharp as they were hard, slicing through the skin of his ankle and then brutally smashing the bone to take hold and trap him.

Petrov screamed, sounding like a wounded animal. He was caught in a bear trap deliberately laid there by Lalya and the pain was beyond what even he could stand. He dropped his handgun and jerked upright, quivering like a bowstring, twisting this way and that, hardly aware of himself, but each movement caused him even more pain and further mangled his ankle bones. He looked like a man being jolted by electricity, one bolt after another, but despite that, and despite the insane pain, he could not fall down for fear of tearing his trapped foot off altogether.

Obviously knowing that, and just as obviously having planned it, Lalya advanced steadily upon him, her long black hair, covered with snowflakes, blowing out in the wind.

Scott called out her name.

Lalya ignored him. She ignored Petrov's screaming. Like a ghost in a dream, she emerged from the smoke and advanced through the slowly falling snow until she was standing right in front of the still screaming Petrov. When he saw her, he proved what he was made of by abruptly falling silent and gradually controlling his body movements. He just stood there in front of her, held by the steel claws of the bear trap, enduring unimaginable hell and refusing to show it.

Lalya knelt at his feet, picked up his fallen handgun, then straightened up again and aimed the weapon at him, forcing him to stare right into the barrel. Quite deliberately, as if she had all the time in the world, she released the safety catch.

'What's it like,' she asked him, 'to have another human being in absolute control of your life? Tell me that, you bastard.'

Though the night was freezing and the snow was falling over him, Petrov was sweating with pain. Nevertheless, showing extraordinary, almost superhuman will, he managed to offer Lalya an icy smile.

'I'm not like you,' he said contemptuously. 'Nor like any of the others. I'd rather die like a man than live like an animal, so put that fucking bullet in my head and see how you feel afterwards. You won't feel satisfied.'

'That would be too easy,' Lalya said. 'So let's try it another way.'

Lowering herself to the ground and slipping the handgun back into her belt, she withdrew a small spade from her bear-skin jacket – obviously the same spade that she had used when digging a hole for the bear trap – and proceeded to dig up the soil around it. She did it quietly, calmly, no longer in fear of Petrov, knowing full well that as soon as the trap was loosened, his smashed ankle would not be able to sustain him and he would fall to the ground. Which he did. When the steel stakes of the bear trap were released from the hard-packed soil, the trap itself came out sideways, enabling Petrov to fall over without tearing his foot off. After striking the ground, he rolled onto his back and Lalya dropped the small spade and stood over him, looking down upon him, smiling, her brown eyes bright with victory and the fires of her hatred.

'You're not frightened of death,' Lalya said, 'because you're frightened of life . . . So that's what I'm giving you – life – but on my terms, Dmitry. If you truly can only love the things you hate, then you'll love me forever. What woman could ask for more?'

'No, Lalya!' Scott screamed.

But he was too late. Lalya had already removed the handgun from her belt and she fired all thirteen of the fourteen chambers into Petrov without damaging anything that might kill him. The bear trap had already mangled his right foot and ankle beyond repair, so she did the same to his left with two bullets: one through the bones of the foot, the other through the ankle bone at a point where it could never be repaired. After that, despite Scott's desperate, increasingly hoarse pleadings, she demolished all of Petrov's other joints – kneecaps, hipbones, elbows, shoulderblades – reserving the last three bullets for the base of his spine, thus leaving him paralysed for life.

Petrov screamed each time she shot him, his fear greater than his pain, and when she finally put the bullets into his spine, he knew just what she was doing.

'Christ, no!' he screamed. '*No!*'

He passed out, of course – even Petrov had his limits – then Lalya threw the pistol down, not one bullet left in it, and slipped her hands under his shoulders, just as he had done with Scott, and dragged him, albeit with great difficulty, to the same 'torture-and-execution' pole that he had picked out for Scott. She couldn't haul him upright – he was too heavy for that and Scott, still lying helpless on the ground, was in no position to help her – but she managed to drag him into a sitting position with his mangled legs stretched out in front of him. She tied his wrists together around the back of the pole, then tied his body to the pole with the rope that was always left there for the prisoners. When he was tied firmly to the pole, sitting upright, she turned her attentions on Scott.

'You can't leave him there,' Scott said, still stretched out on his side. 'Predators will know that this place has been deserted and they'll soon coming in looking for food. If they get here before Petrov's brigands, they'll make a meal of him. They'll eat him alive as he's tied to that pole.'

'*If's* a big word,' Lalya replied, 'and the brigands might get here first.'

'In which case, when they see the state of him, they'll put a bullet through his head and take what they can find here in the camp and light out again.'

'According to Petrov,' Lalya said, 'he doesn't fear death, but only hates life, so a bullet in the head would be a blessing. Personally, I'd rather that the animals got some benefit out of him, but I think the authorities will be up here before that, which means that Petrov will live.'

'Paralysed,' Scott reminded her.

'Yes, paralysed,' Lalya replied without remorse. 'Which means that even suicide will be difficult and he's faced with a long life. Since he hates life, that's what I hope he gets, but I leave that to the fates. So what about you?'

'Whether it's the authorities or the brigands who get here first, I can't be found here. I have to get out of here, get my leg fixed up and then find a friendly member of the border patrols to quietly get in touch with certain people I know in Moscow. Can you help me with that?'

When Lalya smiled, her lovely brown eyes caught the moonlight and became even lovelier. 'All we drug smugglers,' she said, 'have friends among the border patrols – so, yes, I can help you. Wait here, Captain Scott.'

He watched her walking off, heading towards the motor pool, where some vehicles were still available, and as he lay there, waiting for her to come back, Petrov's eyes fluttered open. He glanced blearily left and right, at the devastation of his world, looked down at his own bloody, smashed body, then caught Scott's gaze at last.

'I'm not frightened,' he said.

'You will be,' Scott replied.

'Where is she?'

Scott, still stretched out on his side, could only nod in the general direction of the motor pool. 'Over there,' he said.

Petrov passed out again.

Scott heard the healthy roaring of a jeep starting up, then Lalya drove back to where he lay and climbed down to help him into the vehicle. She had to haul him into a sitting position, then she placed her bent arms under his shoulders and forced him to kick himself upright despite the dreadful pain in his wounded thigh. Eventually, however, after a great deal of wrestling between them, he fell into the rear seat of the jeep and just lay there, exhausted, letting the snow fall lightly over him. Through the falling flakes of snow, he saw the moon, gliding in and out from behind the low clouds, which appeared to be painted there in the sky by God's invisible hand. Scott closed his eyes, hoping to sleep, but then he heard Petrov screaming.

'Don't leave me here!' he screamed like a man knowing terror for the first time; a man going berserk. 'Don't leave me to live on in this condition! Damn you, kill me, at least! Let me die like a man!'

'Learn to live, Dmitry,' Lalya replied evenly. 'It's a whole new experience. You might even enjoy it.'

'*No!*' Petrov screamed and that sound reverberated and seemed to rise to the very heavens, the lament of the damned, as Lalya gunned the jeep's engine and took off, driving away from the still smouldering, ruined camp and turning onto the snow-covered mountain road without looking back.

Scott looked back. He was as helpless as a child. He had

come here to do a job and in one sense he had done it, but in another, he had merely been a victim of life's inexorable currents. He had already lost his wife and son before coming here, one through separation, the other through death, and since then he had lost seven good men; and all of them were, in a very real sense, Dmitry Petrov's victims. Yet he knew that in the end, despite all, he had come to secretly respect Petrov, to see in him some of the virtues that he had lost in himself and some of the vices that he feared in himself or, perhaps, even worse, already possessed. He had merely managed to cover them up because his world, far removed from Petrov's hell, was one in which more choices were on offer to the average man.

And I am, he thought, an average man, which Dmitry Petrov certainly was not. I'll grant him that much, at least.

He heard the growling of the jeep, felt it vibrating beneath him, saw the mountain road unwinding behind him and looked out to where the snow line disappeared into the barren lower slopes that swept out to the verdant green of the vast, forested valley far below. For all he knew, it could have been the Garden of Eden down there; and when he drifted out of himself, rendered unconscious by loss of blood, that's what he saw it as in his confusing dreams.

Scott was unconscious a long time, through dreams good and bad, and he never saw Lalya again. Only later, during his SAS debriefings, did he learn that she had driven him to a Kyrgyz border patrol where, with a calm acceptance of the corruption she was forced to live by, not ashamed or embarrassed by it as Scott might have been, she bribed them to take Scott off her hands and transfer him to a military hospital in Osh. Only later did he learn that once there, the hospital administrator, having deduced that Scott was a British soldier, contacted the military authorities in Moscow, had his call transferred to the commander of a Russian air force base located just outside Moscow, and was told to hold his English patient there until an air force helicopter was sent for him. Only later did he learn, since he was still unconscious at the time, that a Russian air force helicopter had been sent for him within the hour, that it immediately transferred him to the air force base just outside Moscow, and that from there, a mere fifteen hours later, he was airlifted home.

Scott regained consciousness in a hospital bed. Not recalling one moment of the journey back from Russia – neither the Hercules transport that had flown him to RAF Brize Norton, Oxfordshire, nor the British army ambulance that had transferred from there to the SAS base at Stirling Lines – he saw, through the window directly opposite, the lush green hills of Hereford.

He was still in the Garden of Eden and would stay there a long time, letting old wounds heal, wondering what good and evil meant, and, as he gradually came to realise, feeling out of his time. His SAS days were over.